JAMES FENIMORE COOPER was born in Burlington, New Jersey, in 1789; his family moved to Cooperstown, New York, while he was still an infant. He attended Yale College but was expelled. Sailing before the mast, he saw Europe for the first time on a merchant vessel. In 1808 he became a midshipman in the U. S. Navy. He resigned in 1811 and married. Cooper lived, at various periods, in Westchester and New York City, but spent his later years in Cooperstown. From 1826 to 1833 he traveled extensively in Europe. The Leatherstocking Tales were published during the period from 1823 to 1841. Arranged according to the chronology of their hero, Natty Bumppo, who appears under various sobriquets in all five romances, the sequence is *The Deerslayer* (age 22-24?), *The Last of the Mohicans* (age 35-37?), *The Pathfinder* (age 37-39), *The Pioneers* (age 71-72?), *The Prairie* (age 80-83). With his story *The Pilot* (1823) Cooper set the style for a new genre of sea fiction. A caustic social critic, he wrote *The American Democrat* (1838) as a critique of American civilization at that time. His works have been translated into numerous languages and have been enthusiastically received because of their vigor and robust narration. Never able to ignore a challenge, Cooper spent much of his later life in disputes with and suits against various journals. He died in 1851 at his home in Cooperstown.

JAMES FENIMORE COOPER

The
Pioneers

or

The Sources of the Susquehanna

A DESCRIPTIVE TALE

With an Afterword by
ROBERT E. SPILLER

Revised and Updated Bibliography

A SIGNET CLASSIC

NEW AMERICAN LIBRARY

Author's Introduction

As this work professes, in its title page, to be a descriptive tale, they who will take the trouble to read it may be glad to know how much of its contents is literal fact and how much is intended to represent a general picture. The author is very sensible that had he confined himself to the latter, always the most effective as it is the most valuable, mode of conveying knowledge of this nature, he would have made a far better book. But in commencing to describe scenes, and perhaps he may add characters, that were so familiar to his own youth, there was a constant temptation to delineate that which he had known, rather than that which he might have imagined. This rigid adhesion to truth, an indispensable requisite in history and travels, destroys the charm of fiction; for all that is necessary to be conveyed to the mind by the latter had better be done by delineations of principles, and of characters in their classes, than by a too fastidious attention to originals.

New York having but one county of Otsego, and the Susquehanna but one proper source, there can be no mistake as to the site of the tale. The history of this district of country, so far as it is connected with civilized men, is soon told.

Otsego, in common with most of the interior of the province of New York, was included in the county of Albany, previously to the war of the separation. It then became, in a subsequent division of territory, a part of Montgomery; and, finally, having obtained a sufficient population of its own, it was set apart as a county by itself, shortly after the peace of 1783. It lies among those low spurs of the Alleghanies which cover the midland counties of New York; and it is a little east of a meridional line drawn through the center of the state. As the waters of New York either flow southerly into the Atlantic or northerly into Ontario, and its outlet, Otsego Lake, being the source of the Susquehanna, is, of necessity, among its highest lands. The face of the country, the climate as it was found by the whites, and the manners of the settlers are described with a minuteness for which the author has no other apology than the force of his own recollections.

Otsego is said to be a word compounded of Ot, a place of meeting, and Sego, or Sago, the ordinary term of salutation used by the Indians of this region. There is a tradition which says that the neighboring tribes were accustomed to meet on the banks of the lake to make their treaties, and otherwise to strengthen their alliances, and which refers the name to this practice. As the Indian agent of New York had a log dwelling at the foot of the lake, however, it is not impossible that the appellation grew out of the meetings that were held at his council fires; the war drove off the agent, in common with the other officers of the crown; and his rude dwelling was soon abandoned. The author remembers it a few years later, reduced to the humble office of a smokehouse.

In 1779 an expedition was sent against the hostile Indians who dwelt about a hundred miles west of Otsego on the banks of the Cayuga. The whole country was then a wilderness, and it was necessary to transport the baggage of the troops by means of the rivers—a devious but practicable route. One brigade ascended the Mohawk until it reached the point nearest to the sources of the Susquehanna; whence it cut a lane through the forest to the head of the Otsego. The boats and baggage were carried over this "portage," and the troops proceeded to the other extremity of the lake, where they disembarked and encamped. The Susquehanna, a narrow though rapid stream at its source, was much filled with "floodwood," or fallen trees; and the troops adopted a novel expedient to facilitate their passage. The Otsego is about nine miles in length, varying in breadth from half a mile to a mile and a half. The water is of great depth, limpid, and supplied from a thousand springs. At its foot, the banks are rather less than thirty feet high; the remainder of its margin being in mountains, intervals, and points. The outlet, or the Susquehanna, flows through a gorge in the low banks just mentioned, which may have a width of two hundred feet. This gorge was dammed, and the waters of the lake collected: the Susquehanna was converted into a rill. When all was ready, the troops embarked, the dam was knocked away, the Otsego poured out its torrent, and the boats went merrily down with the current.

General James Clinton, the brother of George Clinton, then

governor of New York, and the father of De Witt Clinton, who died governor of the same state in 1827, commanded the brigade employed on this duty. During the stay of the troops at the foot of the Otsego a soldier was shot for desertion. The grave of this unfortunate man was the first place of human interment that the author ever beheld, as the smokehouse was the first ruin! The swivel alluded to in this work was buried and abandoned by the troops on this occasion; and it was subsequently found in digging the cellars of the author's paternal residence.

Soon after the close of the war, Washington, accompanied by many distinguished men, visited the scene of this tale, it is said, with a view to examine the facilities for opening a communication by water with other points of the country. He stayed but a few hours.

In 1785 the author's father, who had an interest in extensive tracts of land in this wilderness, arrived with a party of surveyors. The manner in which the scene met his eye is described by Judge Temple. At the commencement of the following year the settlement began; and from that time to this the country has continued to flourish. It is a singular feature in American life that, at the beginning of this century, when the proprietor of the estate had occasion for settlers on a new settlement, and in a remote county, he was enabled to draw them from among the increase of the former colony.

Although the settlement of this part of Otsego a little preceded the birth of the author, it was not sufficiently advanced to render it desirable that an event, so important to himself, should take place in the wilderness. Perhaps his mother had a reasonable distrust of the practice of Dr. Todd, who must then have been in the novitiate of his experimental acquirements. Be that as it may, the author was brought an infant into this valley, and all his first impressions were here obtained. He has inhabited it ever since, at intervals; and he thinks he can answer for the faithfulness of the picture he has drawn.

Otsego has now become one of the most populous districts of New York. It sends forth its emigrants like any other old region; and it is pregnant with industry and enterprise. Its manufacturers are prosperous; and it is worthy of remark that one of the most ingenious machines known in European art is derived from the keen ingenuity which is exercised in this remote region.

In order to prevent mistake, it may be well to say that the incidents of this tale are purely a fiction. The literal facts are chiefly connected with the natural and artificial objects and the customs of the inhabitants. Thus, the academy and courthouse and jail and inn, and most similar things, are tolerably exact. They have all, long since, given place to other buildings of a more pretending character. There is also some liberty taken with the truth in the description of the principal dwelling: the real building had no "firstly" and "lastly." It was of bricks, and not of stone; and its roof exhibited none of the peculiar beauties of the "composite order." It was erected in an age too primitive for that ambitious school of architecture. But the author indulged his recollections freely when he had fairly entered the door. Here all is literal, even to the severed arm of Wolfe and the urn which held the ashes of Queen Dido.*

The author has elsewhere said that the character of Leatherstocking is a creation, rendered probable by such auxiliaries as were necessary to produce that effect. Had he drawn still more upon fancy, the lovers of fiction would not have so much cause for their objections to his work. Still the picture would not have been in the least true, without some substitutes for most of the other personages. The great proprietor resident on his lands, and giving his name to, instead of receiving it from his estates, as in Europe, is common over the whole of New York. The physician, with his theory, rather obtained than corrected by experiments on the human constitution; the pious, self-denying, laborious, and ill-paid missionary; the half-educated, litigious, envious, and disreputable lawyer, with his counterpoise, a brother of the profession, of better origin and of better character; the shiftless, bargaining, discontented seller of his "betterments"; the plausible carpenter, and most of the others, are more familiar to all who have ever dwelt in a new country.

It may be well to say here, a little more explicitly, that there was no intention to describe with particular accuracy any real characters in this book. It has been often said, and in pub-

---

* Though forests still crown the mountains of Otsego, the bear, the wolf, and the panther are nearly strangers to them. Even the innocent deer is rarely seen bounding beneath their arches; for the rifle and the activity of the settlers have driven them to other haunts. To this change (which, in some particulars, is melancholy to one who knew the country in its infancy) it may be added that the Otsego is beginning to be a niggard of its treasures.

lished statements, that the heroine of this book was drawn after a sister of the writer, who was killed by a fall from a horse now near half a century since. So ingenious is conjecture that a personal resemblance has been discovered between the fictitious character and the deceased relative! It is scarcely possible to describe two females of the same class in life, who would be less alike, personally, than Elizabeth Temple and the sister of the author who met with the deplorable fate mentioned. In a word, they were as unlike in this respect as in history, character, and fortunes.

Circumstances rendered this sister singularly dear to the author. After a lapse of half a century, he is writing this paragraph with a pain that would induce him to cancel it, were it not still more painful to have it believed that one whom he regarded with a reverence that surpassed the love of a brother was converted by him into the heroine of a work of fiction.

From circumstances which after this introduction will be obvious to all, the author has had more pleasure in writing *The Pioneers* than the book will, probably, ever give any of its readers. He is quite aware of its numerous faults, some of which he has endeavored to repair in this edition; but as he has—in intention, at least—done his full share in amusing the world, he trusts to its good nature for overlooking this attempt to please himself.

The

Pioneers

CHAPTER I

See, Winter comes, to rule the varied year,
Sullen and sad, with all his rising train;
Vapors, and clouds, and storms.—

THOMSON

NEAR the center of the State of New York lies an extensive district of country whose surface is a succession of hills and dales or, to speak with greater deference to geographical definitions, of mountains and valleys. It is among these hills that the Delaware takes its rise, and flowing from the limpid lakes and thousand springs of this region, the numerous sources of the Susquehanna meander through the valleys until, uniting their streams, they form one of the proudest rivers of the United States. The mountains are generally arable to the tops, although instances are not wanting where the sides are jutted with rocks that aid greatly in giving to the country that romantic and picturesque character which it so eminently possesses. The vales are narrow, rich, and cultivated, with a stream uniformly winding through each. Beautiful and thriving villages are found interspersed along the margins of the small lakes, or situated at those points of the streams which are favorable to manufacturing; and neat and comfortable farms, with every indication of wealth about them, are scattered profusely through the vales and even to the mountaintops. Roads diverge in every direction, from the even and graceful bottoms of the valleys to the most rugged and intricate passes of the hills. Academies and minor edifices of learning meet the eye of the stranger at every few miles, as he winds his way through this uneven territory; and places for the worship of God abound with that frequency which characterizes a moral and reflecting people, and with that variety of exterior and canonical government which flows from unfettered liberty of conscience. In short, the whole district is hourly exhibiting how much can be done, in even a rugged

13

country, and with a severe climate, under the dominion of mild laws, and where every man feels a direct interest in the prosperity of a commonwealth of which he knows himself to form a part. The expedients of the pioneers who first broke ground in the settlement of this country are succeeded by the permanent improvements of the yeoman, who intends to leave his remains to molder under the sod which he tills, or, perhaps, of the son, who, born in the land, piously wishes to linger around the grave of his father. Only forty years * have passed since this territory was a wilderness.

Very soon after the establishment of the independence of the States, by the peace of 1783, the enterprise of their citizens was directed to a development of the natural advantages of their widely extended dominions. Before the war of the revolution the inhabited parts of the colony of New York were limited to less than a tenth of its possessions. A narrow belt of country, extending for a short distance on either side of the Hudson, with a similar occupation of fifty miles on the banks of the Mohawk, together with the islands of Nassau and Staten and a few insulated settlements on chosen land along the margins of streams, composed the country, which was then inhabited by less than two hundred thousand souls. Within the short period we have mentioned, the population has spread itself over five degrees of latitude and seven of longitude and has swelled to a million and a half of inhabitants, † who are maintained in abundance and can look forward to ages before the evil day must arrive when their possessions shall become unequal to their wants.

Our tale begins in 1793, about seven years after the commencement of one of the earliest of those settlements which have conduced to effect that magical change in the power and condition of the state to which we have alluded.

It was near the setting of the sun on a clear, cold day in December, when a sleigh was moving slowly up one of the mountains in the district we have described. The day had been fine for the season, and but two or three large clouds, whose color seemed brightened by the light reflected from the mass of snow that covered the earth, floated in a

* The book was written in 1823.
† The population of New York is now (1831) quite 2,000,000.

sky of the purest blue. The road wound along the brow of
a precipice, and on one side was upheld by a foundation of
logs, piled one upon the other, while a narrow excavation in
the mountain, in the opposite direction, had made a passage
of sufficient width for the ordinary traveling of that day.
But logs, excavation, and everything that did not reach
several feet above the earth lay alike buried beneath the
snow. A single track, barely wide enough to receive the
sleigh,* denoted the route of the highway, and this was sunk
nearly two feet below the surrounding surface. In the vale,
which lay at a distance of several hundred feet lower, there
was what in the language of the country was called a
clearing, and all the usual improvements of a new settlement;
these even extended up the hill to the point where the road
turned short and ran across the level land, which lay on the
summit of the mountain; but the summit itself remained
in forest. There was a glittering in the atmosphere as if it
were filled with innumerable shining particles, and the noble
bay horses that drew the sleigh were covered, in many parts,
with a coat of hoar frost. The vapor from their nostrils
was seen to issue like smoke, and every object in the view, as
well as every arrangement of the travelers, denoted the depth
of a winter in the mountains. The harness, which was of a
deep dull black, differing from the glossy varnishing of the
present day, was ornamented with enormous plates and
buckles of brass, that shone like gold in those transient
beams of the sun which found their way obliquely through
the tops of the trees. Huge saddles, studded with nails and
fitted with cloth that served as blankets to the shoulders of
the cattle, supported four high, square-topped turrets,
through which the stout reins led from the mouths of the
horses to the hands of the driver, who was a Negro of ap-

* Sleigh is the word used in every part of the United States to
denote a traineau. It is of local use in the west of England, whence
it is most probably derived by the Americans. The latter draw a
distinction between a sled, or sledge, and a sleigh; the sleigh being
shod with metal. Sleighs are also subdivided into two-horse and one-
horse sleighs. Of the latter, there are the cutter, with thills so arranged as to permit the horse to travel in the side track; the
"pung," or "tow-pung," which is driven with a pole; and the
"gumper," a rude construction used for temporary purposes, in the
new countries.
    Many of the American sleighs are elegant, though the use of this
mode of conveyance is much lessened with the melioration of the
climate, consequent on the clearing of the forests.

parently twenty years of age. His face, which nature had
colored with a glistening black, was now mottled with the
cold, and his large shining eyes filled with tears; a tribute to
its power, that the keen frosts of those regions always extracted from one of his African origin. Still there was a
smiling expression of good humor in his happy countenance
that was created by the thoughts of home and a Christmas
fireside, with its Christmas frolics. The sleigh was one of
those large, comfortable, old-fashioned conveyances which
would admit a whole family within its bosom, but which
now contained only two passengers besides the driver. The
color of its outside was a modest green, and that of its
inside a fiery red. The latter was intended to convey the
idea of heat in that cold climate. Large buffalo skins,
trimmed around the edges with red cloth cut into festoons,
covered the back of the sleigh and were spread over its
bottom and drawn up around the feet of the travelers—one
of whom was a man of middle age and the other a female,
just entering upon womanhood. The former was of a large
stature, but the precautions he had taken to guard against
the cold left but little of his person exposed to view. A
greatcoat that was abundantly ornamented by a profusion of
furs enveloped the whole of his figure, excepting the head,
which was covered with a cap of marten skins lined with
morocco, the sides of which were made to fall, if necessary,
and were now drawn close over the ears and fastened beneath his chin with a black riband. The top of the cap was
surmounted with the tail of the animal whose skin had
furnished the rest of the materials, which fell back, not un-
gracefully, a few inches behind the head. From beneath
this mask were to be seen part of a fine manly face, and
particularly a pair of expressive, large blue eyes that promised extraordinary intellect, covert humor, and great
benevolence. The form of his companion was literally hid
beneath the garments she wore. There were furs and silks
peeping from under a large camlet cloak with a thick flannel
lining that, by its cut and size, was evidently intended for a
masculine wearer. A huge hood of black silk that was
quilted with down concealed the whole of her head, except at a small opening in front for breath, through which
occasionally sparkled a pair of animated jet-black eyes.

Both the father and daughter (for such was the connection

between the two travelers) were too much occupied with their reflections to break a stillness that received little or no interruption from the easy gliding of the sleigh by the sound of their voices. The former was thinking of the wife that had held this their only child to her bosom, when, four years before, she had reluctantly consented to relinquish the society of her daughter in order that the latter might enjoy the advantages of an education, which the city of New York could only offer at that period. A few months afterwards death had deprived him of the remaining companion of his solitude, but still he had enough of real regard for his child not to bring her into the comparative wilderness in which he dwelt until the full period had expired to which he had limited her juvenile labors. The reflections of the daughter were less melancholy and mingled with a pleased astonishment at the novel scenery she met at every turn in the road.

The mountain on which they were journeying was covered with pines that rose without a branch some seventy or eighty feet and which frequently doubled that height by the addition of the tops. Through the innumerable vistas that opened beneath the lofty trees, the eye could penetrate until it was met by a distant inequality in the ground or was stopped by a view of the summit of the mountain which lay on the opposite side of the valley to which they were hastening. The dark trunks of the trees rose from the pure white of the snow in regularly formed shafts until, at a great height, their branches shot forth horizontal limbs that were covered with the meager foliage of an evergreen, affording a melancholy contrast to the torpor of nature below. To the travelers there seemed to be no wind, but these pines waved majestically at their topmost boughs, sending forth a dull, plaintive sound that was quite in consonance with the rest of the melancholy scene.

The sleigh had glided for some distance along the even surface, and the gaze of the female was bent in inquisitive and, perhaps, timid glances into the recesses of the forest, when a loud and continued howling was heard, pealing under the long arches of the woods like the cry of a numerous pack of hounds. The instant the sound reached the ears of the gentleman, he cried aloud to the black:

"Hold up, Aggy; there is old Hector; I should know his

bay among ten thousand! The Leatherstocking has put his hounds into the hills this clear day, and they have started their game. There is a deer track a few rods ahead, and now, Bess, if thou canst muster courage enough to stand fire, I will give thee a saddle for thy Christmas dinner."

The black drew up with a cheerful grin upon his chilled features and began thrashing his arms together in order to restore the circulation to his fingers, while the speaker stood erect, and, throwing aside his outer covering, stepped from the sleigh upon a bank of snow, which sustained his weight without yielding.

In a few moments the speaker succeeded in extricating a double-barreled fowling piece from among a multitude of trunks and bandboxes. After throwing aside the thick mittens which had encased his hands, that now appeared in a pair of leather gloves tipped with fur, he examined his priming and was about to move forward when the light, bounding noise of an animal plunging through the woods was heard, and a fine buck darted into the path a short distance ahead of him. The appearance of the animal was sudden, and his flight inconceivably rapid, but the traveler appeared to be too keen a sportsman to be disconcerted by either. As it came first into view he raised the fowling piece to his shoulder, and, with a practiced eye and steady hand, drew a trigger. The deer dashed forward undaunted and apparently unhurt. Without lowering his piece, the traveler turned its muzzle towards his victim and fired again. Neither discharge, however, seemed to have taken effect.

The whole scene had passed with a rapidity that confused the female, who was unconsciously rejoicing in the escape of the buck, as he rather darted like a meteor than ran across the road, when a sharp, quick sound struck her ear, quite different from the full, round reports of her father's gun, but still sufficiently distinct to be known as the concussion produced by firearms. At the same instant that she heard this unexpected report, the buck sprang from the snow to a great height in the air, and directly a second discharge, similar in sound to the first, followed, when the animal came to the earth, falling headlong and rolling over on the crust with its own velocity. A loud shout was given by the unseen marksman, and a couple of men instantly appeared from behind the trunks of two of the pines, where they had evidently placed themselves in expectation of the passage of the deer.

"Ha! Natty, had I known you were in ambush, I should not have fired," cried the traveler, moving towards the spot where the deer lay—near to which he was followed by the delighted black with his sleigh. "But the sound of old Hector was too exhilarating to be quiet, though I hardly think I struck him, either."

"No—no—Judge," returned the hunter, with an inward chuckle and with that look of exultation that indicates a consciousness of superior skill. "You burnt your powder only to warm your nose this cold evening. Did ye think to stop a full-grown buck, with Hector and the slut open upon him within sound, with that popgun in your hand? There's plenty of pheasants among the swamps; and the snowbirds are flying round your own door, where you may feed them with crumbs and shoot them at pleasure any day; but if you're for a buck, or a little bear's meat, Judge, you'll have to take the long rifle, with a greased wadding, or you'll waste more powder than you'll fill stomachs, I'm thinking."

As the speaker concluded, he drew his bare hand across the bottom of his nose and again opened his enormous mouth with a kind of inward laugh.

"The gun scatters well, Natty, and it has killed a deer before now," said the traveler, smiling good-humoredly. "One barrel was charged with buckshot, but the other was loaded for birds only. Here are two hurts; one through the neck and the other directly through the heart. It is by no means certain, Natty, but I gave him one of the two."

"Let who will kill him," said the hunter, rather surlily, "I suppose the creature is to be eaten." So saying, he drew a large knife from a leathern sheath which was stuck through his girdle or sash and cut the throat of the animal. "If there are two balls through the deer, I would ask if there weren't two rifles fired—besides, who ever saw such a ragged hole from a smoothbore, as this through the neck?—and you will own yourself, Judge, that the buck fell at the last shot, which was sent from a truer and a younger hand than your'n or mine either; but for my part, although I am a poor man, I can live without the venison, but I don't love to give up my lawful dues in a free country. Though, for the matter of that, might often makes right here, as well as in the old country, for what I can see."

An air of sullen dissatisfaction pervaded the manner of the hunter during the whole of this speech; yet he thought it prudent to utter the close of the sentence in such an undertone as to leave nothing audible but the grumbling sounds of his voice.

"Nay, Natty," rejoined the traveler with undisturbed good humor, "it is for the honor that I contend. A few dollars will pay for the venison, but what will requite me for the lost honor of a buck's tail in my cap? Think, Natty, how I should triumph over that quizzing dog, Dick Jones, who has failed seven times already this season and has only brought in one woodchuck and a few gray squirrels."

"Ah! The game is becoming hard to find indeed, Judge, with your clearings and betterments," said the old hunter with a kind of compelled resignation. "The time has been when I have shot thirteen deer, without counting the fa'ns, standing in the door of my own hut!—and for bear's meat, if one wanted a ham or so, he had only to watch anights, and he could shoot one by moonlight, through the cracks of the logs; no fear of his oversleeping himself neither, for the howling of the wolves was sartin to keep his eyes open. There's old Hector"—patting with affection a tall hound, of black and yellow spots, with white belly and legs, that just then came in on the scent, accompanied by the slut he had mentioned. "See where the wolves bit his throat, the night I druv them from the venison that was smoking on the chimbly top. That dog is more to be trusted than many a Christian man, for he never forgets a friend and loves the hand that gives him bread."

There was a peculiarity in the manner of the hunter that attracted the notice of the young female, who had been a close and interested observer of his appearance and equipments from the moment he came into view. He was tall, and so meager as to make him seem above even the six feet that he actually stood in his stockings. On his head, which was thinly covered with lank, sandy hair, he wore a cap made of foxskin, resembling in shape the one we have already described, although much inferior in finish and ornaments. His face was skinny and thin almost to emaciation; but yet it bore no signs of disease—on the contrary, it had every indication of the most robust and enduring health. The cold and the exposure had, together, given it a color of uniform red. His gray eyes were glancing under a pair of shaggy brows that overhung them in long hairs of gray mingled with their natural hue; his scraggy neck was bare and burnt to the same tint with his face, though a small part of a shirt collar, made of the country check, was to be seen above the overdress he wore. A kind of coat, made of dressed deerskin with the hair on, was belted close to his lank body by a girdle of colored worsted. On his feet were deerskin moccasins, ornamented with porcupines' quills after the manner of the Indians, and his limbs were guarded with long leggings of the same material as the moccasins, which, gartering over the knees of his tarnished buckskin breeches, had obtained for him, among the settlers, the nickname of Leatherstocking. Over his left shoulder was slung a belt of deerskin, from which depended an enormous ox-horn, so thinly scraped as to discover the powder it contained. The larger end was fitted ingeniously and securely with a wooden bottom, and the other was stopped tight by a little plug. A leathern pouch hung before him, from which, as he concluded his last speech, he took a small measure, and, filling it accurately with powder, he commenced reloading the rifle, which, as its butt rested on the snow before him, reached nearly to the top of his foxskin cap.

The traveler had been closely examining the wounds during these movements, and now, without heeding the ill-humor of the hunter's manner, he exclaimed:

"I would fain establish a right, Natty, to the honor of this death, and surely if the hit in the neck be mine, it is enough; for the shot in the heart was unnecessary—what we call an act of supererogation, Leatherstocking."

"You may call it by what larned name you please, Judge," said the hunter, throwing his rifle across his left arm, and knocking up a brass lid in the breech, from which he took a small piece of greased leather, and wrapping a ball in it, forced them down by main strength on the powder, where he continued to pound them while speaking. "It's far easier to call names than to shoot a buck on the spring, but the cretur came by his end from a younger hand than either your'n or mine, as I said before."

"What say you, my friend," cried the traveler, turning

pleasantly to Natty's companion; "shall we toss up this dollar for the honor, and you keep the silver if you lose; what say you, friend?"

"That I killed the deer," answered the young man with a little haughtiness, as he leaned on another long rifle, similar to that of Natty.

"Here are two to one, indeed," replied the Judge, with a smile. "I am outvoted—overruled, as we say on the bench. There is Aggy; he can't vote, being a slave; and Bess is a minor—so I must even make the best of it. But you'll sell me the venison; and the deuce is in it, but I make a good story about its death."

"The meat is none of mine to sell," said Leatherstocking, adopting a little of his companion's hauteur. "For my part I have known animals travel days with shots in the neck, and I'm none of them who'll rob a man of his rightful dues."

"You are tenacious of your rights this cold evening, Natty," returned the Judge, with unconquerable good nature. "But what say you, young man; will three dollars pay you for the buck?"

"First let us determine the question of right to the satisfaction of us both," said the youth, firmly but respectfully, and with a pronunciation and language vastly superior to his appearance. "With how many shot did you load your gun?"

"With five, sir," said the Judge, a little struck with the other's manner. "Are they not enough to slay a buck like this?"

"One would do it; but"—moving to the tree from behind which he had appeared—"you know, sir, you fired in this direction—here are four of the bullets in the tree."

The Judge examined the fresh marks in the bark of the pine, and shaking his head, said, with a laugh:

"You are making out the case against yourself, my young advocate—where is the fifth?"

"Here," said the youth, throwing aside the rough overcoat that he wore and exhibiting a hole in his undergarment, through which large drops of blood were oozing.

"Good God!" exclaimed the Judge with horror. "Have I been trifling here about an empty distinction, and a fellow creature suffering from my hands without a murmur? But hasten—quick—get into my sleigh—it is but a mile to the village, where surgical aid can be obtained; all shall be done at my expense, and thou shalt live with me until thy wound is healed, aye, and forever afterward."

"I thank you for your good intention, but I must decline your offer. I have a friend who would be uneasy were he to hear that I am hurt and away from him. The injury is but slight, and the bullet has missed the bones; but I believe, sir, you will now admit my title to the venison."

"Admit it!" repeated the agitated Judge. "I here give thee a right to shoot deer, or bears, or anything thou pleasest in my woods, forever. Leatherstocking is the only other man that I have granted the same privilege to, and the time is coming when it will be of value. But I buy your deer—here, this bill will pay thee, both for thy shot and my own."

The old hunter gathered his tall person up into an air of pride during this dialogue, but he waited until the other had done speaking.

"There's them living who say that Nathaniel Bumppo's right to shoot on these hills is of older date than Marmaduke Temple's right to forbid him," he said. "But if there's a law about it at all, though who ever heard of a law that a man shouldn't kill deer where he pleased!—but if there is a law at all, it should be to keep people from the use of smooth-bores. A body never knows where his lead will fly when he pulls the trigger of one of them uncertain firearms."

Without attending to the soliloquy of Natty, the youth bowed his head silently to the offer of the bank note and replied:

"Excuse me; I have need of the venison."

"But this will buy you many deer," said the Judge. "Take it, I entreat you," and lowering his voice to a whisper, he added; "it is for a hundred dollars."

For an instant only, the youth seemed to hesitate, and then, blushing even through the high color that the cold had given to his cheeks, as if with inward shame at his own weakness, he again declined the offer.

During this scene the female arose, and, regardless of the cold air, she threw back the hood which concealed her features and now spoke with great earnestness.

"Surely, surely—young man—sir—you would not pain my father so much as to have him think that he leaves a fellow creature in this wilderness whom his own hand has injured. I entreat you will go with us and receive medical aid."

Whether his wound became more painful, or there was something irresistible in the voice and manner of the fair pleader for her father's feelings, we know not; but the distance of the young man's manner was sensibly softened by this appeal, and he stood in apparent doubt, as if reluctant to comply with and yet unwilling to refuse her request. The Judge, for such being his office must in future be his title, watched, with no little interest, the display of this singular contention in the feelings of the youth; and advancing, kindly took his hand, and as he pulled him gently towards the sleigh, urged him to enter it.

"There is no human aid nearer than Templeton," he said, "and the hut of Natty is full three miles from this; come—come, my young friend, go with us, and let the new doctor look to this shoulder of thine. Here is Natty will take the tidings of thy welfare to thy friend, and shouldst thou require it, thou shalt return home in the morning."

The young man succeeded in extricating his hand from the warm grasp of the Judge, but he continued to gaze on the face of the female, who, regardless of the cold, was still standing with her fine features exposed, which expressed feelings that eloquently seconded the request of her father. Leatherstocking stood, in the meantime, leaning upon his long rifle with his head turned a little to one side, as if engaged in sagacious musing; when, having apparently satisfied his doubts by revolving the subject in his mind, he broke silence.

"It may be best to go, lad, after all; for if the shot hangs under the skin, my hand is getting too old to be cutting into human flesh as I once used to. Though some thirty years agone, in the old war, when I was out under Sir William, I traveled seventy miles alone in the howling wilderness with a rifle bullet in my thigh and then cut it out with my own jackknife. Old Indian John knows the time well. I met him with a party of the Delawares, on the trail of the Iroquois, who had been down and taken five scalps on the Schoharie. But I made a mark on the redskin that I'll warrant he carried to his grave! I took him on his posteerum, saving the lady's presence, as he got up from the ambushment, and rattled three buckshot into his naked hide, so close that you might have laid a broad joe upon them all." Here Natty stretched out his long neck and straightened his body as he opened his

mouth, which exposed a single tusk of yellow bone, while his
eyes, his face, even his whole frame seemed to laugh, although no sound was emitted except a kind of thick hissing
as he inhaled his breath in quavers. "I had lost my bullet
mold in crossing the Oneida outlet, and had to make shift
with the buckshot; but the rifle was true and didn't scatter
like your two-legged thing there, Judge, which don't do, I
find, to hunt in company with."

Natty's apology to the delicacy of the young lady was unnecessary, for, while he was speaking, she was too much employed in helping her father to remove certain articles of
baggage to hear him. Unable to resist the kind urgency of
the travelers any longer, the youth, though still with an un-
accountable reluctance, suffered himself to be persuaded to
enter the sleigh. The black, with the aid of his master, threw
the buck across the baggage, and entering the vehicle themselves, the Judge invited the hunter to do so likewise.

"No, no," said the old man, shaking his head; "I have
work to do at home this Christmas Eve—drive on with the
boy, and let your doctor look to the shoulder; though if he
will only cut out the shot, I have yarbs that will heal the
wound quicker than all his foreign 'intments." He turned and
was about to move off when, suddenly recollecting himself,
he again faced the party and added—"If you see anything
of Indian John, about the foot of the lake, you had better
take him with you and let him lend the doctor a hand; for
old as he is, he is curious at cuts and bruises, and it's
likelier than not he'll be in with brooms to sweep your Christmas ha'arths."

"Stop, stop," cried the youth, catching the arm of the black
as he prepared to urge his horses forward. "Natty—you need
say nothing of the shot, nor of where I am going—remember,
Natty, as you love me."

"Trust old Leatherstocking," returned the hunter significantly; "he hasn't lived fifty years in the wilderness and not
larnt from the savages how to hold his tongue—trust to me,
lad, and remember old Indian John."

"And, Natty," said the youth eagerly, still holding the
black by the arm, "I will just get the shot extracted and
bring you up tonight a quarter of the buck for the Christmas
dinner."

He was interrupted by the hunter, who held up his finger

with an expressive gesture for silence. He then moved softly
along the margin of the road, keeping his eyes steadfastly
fixed on the branches of a pine. When he had obtained such a
position as he wished, he stopped, and cocking his rifle,
threw one leg far behind him, and stretching his left arm to
its utmost extent along the barrel of his piece, he began
slowly to raise its muzzle in a line with the straight trunk of
the tree. The eyes of the group in the sleigh naturally preceded the movement of the rifle, and they soon discovered the
object of Natty's aim. On a small dead branch of the pine,
which, at the distance of seventy feet from the ground, shot
out horizontally immediately beneath the living members of
the tree, sat a bird that in the vulgar language of the country
was indiscriminately called a pheasant or a partridge. In size
it was but little smaller than a common barnyard fowl. The
baying of the dogs and the conversation that had passed near
the root of the tree on which it was perched had alarmed the
bird, which was now drawn up near the body of the pine
with a head and neck so erect as to form nearly a straight
line with its legs. As soon as the rifle bore on the victim, Natty
drew his trigger, and the partridge fell from its height with a
force that buried it in the snow.

"Lie down, you old villain," exclaimed Leatherstocking,
shaking his ramrod at Hector as he bounded towards the
foot of the tree, "lie down, I say." The dog obeyed, and
Natty proceeded with great rapidity, though with the nicest
accuracy, to reload his piece. When this was ended, he took
up his game, and showing it to the party without a head, he
cried, "Here is a titbit for an old man's Christmas—never
mind the venison, boy, and remember Indian John; his yarbs
are better than all the foreign 'intments. Here, Judge," holding up the bird again, "do you think a smoothbore would
pick game off their roost and not ruffle a feather?" The old
man gave another of his remarkable laughs, which partook
so largely of exultation, mirth, and irony, and shaking his
head, he turned, with his rifle at a trail, and moved into the
forest with steps that were between a walk and a trot. At
each movement he made, his body lowered several inches,
his knees yielding with an inclination inwards; but as the
sleigh turned at a bend in the road, the youth cast his eyes
in quest of his old companion, and he saw that he was already nearly concealed by the trunks of the trees, while his

dogs were following quietly in his footsteps, occasionally scenting the deer track that they seemed to know instinctively was now of no further use to them. Another jerk was given to the sleigh, and Leatherstocking was hid from view.

CHAPTER II

All places that the eye of Heaven visits
Are to a wise man ports and happy havens:—
Think not the king did banish thee.
But thou the king.

RICHARD II

AN ancestor of Marmaduke Temple had, about one hundred and twenty years before the commencement of our tale, come to the colony of Pennsylvania, a friend and co-religionist of its great patron. Old Marmaduke, for this formidable praenomen was a kind of appellative to the race, brought with him to that asylum of the persecuted an abundance of the good things of this life. He became the master of many thousands of acres of uninhabited territory and the supporter of many a score of dependents. He lived greatly respected for his piety, and not a little distinguished as a sectary; was intrusted by his associates with many important political stations; and died just in time to escape the knowledge of his own poverty. It was his lot to share the fortune of most of those who brought wealth with them into the new settlements of the middle colonies.

The consequence of an emigrant into these provinces was generally to be ascertained by the number of his white servants or dependents and the nature of the public situations that he held. Taking this rule as a guide, the ancestor of our Judge must have been a man of no little note.

It is, however, a subject of curious inquiry at the present day to look into the brief records of that early period and observe how regular, and with few exceptions how inevitable, were the gradations, on the one hand, of the masters to poverty, and on the other, of their servants to wealth. Accustomed to ease and unequal to the struggles incident to an infant society, the affluent emigrant was barely enabled to maintain his own rank by the weight of his personal superiority and acquirements; but the moment that his head was laid in the grave, his indolent and comparatively uneducated offspring were compelled to yield precedency to the more active energies of a class whose exertions had been stimulated by necessity. This is a very common course of things, even in the present state of the Union; but it was peculiarly the fortunes of the two extremes of society in the peaceful and unenterprising colonies of Pennsylvania and New Jersey.

The posterity of Marmaduke did not escape the common lot of those who depend rather on their hereditary possessions than on their own powers, and in the third generation they had descended to a point below which, in this happy country, it is barely possible for honesty, intellect, and sobriety to fall. The same pride of family that had, by its self-satisfied indolence, conduced to aid their fall now became a principle to stimulate them to endeavor to rise again. The feeling, from being morbid, was changed to a healthful and active desire to emulate the character, the condition, and, peradventure, the wealth of their ancestors also. It was the father of our new acquaintance, the Judge, who first began to reascend in the scale of society; and in this undertaking he was not a little assisted by a marriage which aided in furnishing the means of educating his only son in a rather better manner than the low state of the common schools in Pennsylvania could promise, or than had been the practice in the family for the two or three preceding generations.

At the school where the reviving prosperity of his father was enabled to maintain him, young Marmaduke formed an intimacy with a youth whose years were about equal to his own. This was a fortunate connection for our Judge and paved the way to most of his future elevation in life.

There was not only great wealth, but high court interest, among the connections of Edward Effingham. They were one of the few families then resident in the colonies who thought it a degradation to its members to descend to the pursuits of commerce and who never emerged from the privacy of domestic life, unless to preside in the councils of the colony or to bear arms in her defense. The latter had, from youth, been the only employment of Edward's father. Military rank under the crown of Great Britain was attained with much longer probation, and by much more toilsome services, sixty years ago, than at the present time. Years were passed without murmuring in the subordinate grades of the service; and those soldiers who were stationed in the colonies felt when they obtained the command of a company that they were entitled to receive the greatest deference from the peaceful occupants of the soil. Any one of our readers who has occasion to cross the Niagara may easily observe not only the self-importance, but the real estimation enjoyed by the humblest representative of the crown, even in that polar region of royal sunshine. Such, and at no very distant period, was the respect paid to the military in these states, where now, happily, no symbol of war is ever seen, unless at the free and fearless voice of their people. When, therefore, the father of Marmaduke's friend, after forty years' service, retired with the rank of Major, maintaining in his domestic establishment a comparative splendor, he became a man of the first consideration in his native colony—which was that of New York. He had served with fidelity and courage, and having been, according to the custom of the provinces, intrusted with commands much superior to those to which he was entitled by rank, with reputation also. When Major Effingham yielded to the claims of age, he retired with dignity, refusing his half pay or any other compensation for services that he felt he could no longer perform.

The ministry proffered various civil offices, which yielded not only honor but profit; but he declined them all, with the chivalrous independence and loyalty that had marked his character through life. The veteran soon caused this act of patriotic disinterestedness to be followed by another of private munificence that, however little it accorded with prudence, was in perfect conformity with the simple integrity of his own views.

The friend of Marmaduke was his only child; and to this son, on his marriage with a lady to whom the father was particularly partial, the Major gave a complete conveyance of his whole estate, consisting of moneys in the funds, a town and country residence, sundry valuable farms in the old parts of the colony, and large tracts of wild land in the new—in this manner throwing himself upon the filial piety of his child for his own future maintenance. Major Effingham, in declining the liberal offers of the British ministry, had subjected himself to the suspicion of having attained his dotage,

by all those who throng the avenues to court patronage,
even in the remotest corners of that vast empire; but, when
he thus voluntarily stripped himself of his great personal
wealth, the remainder of the community seemed instinctively
to adopt the conclusion also, that he had reached a second
childhood. This may explain the fact of his importance
rapidly declining; and, if privacy was his object, the veteran
had soon a free indulgence of his wishes. Whatever views the
world might entertain of this act of the Major, to himself
and to his child it seemed no more than a natural gift by
a father, of those immunities which he could no longer
enjoy or improve, to a son, who was formed, both by nature
and education, to do both. The younger Effingham did not
object to the amount of the donation; for he felt that while
his parent reserved a moral control over his actions, he was
relieving himself from a fatiguing burden: such, indeed, was
the confidence existing between them, that to neither did it
seem anything more than removing money from one pocket
to another.

One of the first acts of the young man on coming into
possession of his wealth was to seek his early friend, with a
view to offer any assistance that it was now in his power to
bestow.

The death of Marmaduke's father and the consequent division of his small estate rendered such an offer extremely ac-
ceptable to the young Pennsylvanian: he felt his own powers
and saw, not only the excellences, but the foibles, in the
character of his friend. Effingham was by nature indolent,
confiding, and at times impetuous and indiscreet; but
Marmaduke was uniformly equable, penetrating, and full of
activity and enterprise. To the latter, therefore, the assistance,
or rather connection, that was proffered to him seemed to
produce a mutual advantage. It was cheerfully accepted, and
the arrangement of its conditions was easily completed. A
mercantile house was established in the metropolis of Pennsylvania with the avails of Mr. Effingham's personal property; all, or nearly all, of which was put into the possession
of Temple, who was the only ostensible proprietor in the
concern, while, in secret, the other was entitled to an equal
participation in the profits. This connection was thus kept
private for two reasons; one of which, in the freedom of
their intercourse, was frankly avowed to Marmaduke, while

the other continued profoundly hid in the bosom of his friend. The last was nothing more than pride. To the descendant of a line of soldiers, commerce, even in that indirect manner, seemed a degrading pursuit; but an insuperable obstacle to the disclosure existed in the prejudices of his father.

We have already said that Major Effingham had served as a soldier with reputation. On one occasion, while in command on the western frontier of Pennsylvania against a league of the French and Indians, not only his glory, but the safety of himself and his troops were jeoparded by the peaceful policy of that colony. To the soldier, this was an unpardonable offense. He was fighting in their defense—he knew that the mild principles of this little nation of practical Christians would be disregarded by their subtle and malignant enemies; and he felt the injury the more deeply because he saw that the avowed object of the colonists, in withholding their succors, would only have a tendency to expose his command without preserving the peace. The soldier succeeded, after a desperate conflict, in extricating himself, with a handful of his men, from their murderous enemy; but he never forgave the people who had exposed him to a danger which they left him to combat alone. It was in vain to tell him that they had no agency in his being placed on their frontier at all; it was evidently for their benefit that he had been so placed, and it was their "religious duty," so the Major always expressed it, "it was their religious duty to have supported him."

At no time was the old soldier an admirer of the peaceful disciples of Fox. Their disciplined habits, both of mind and body, had endowed them with great physical perfection; and the eye of the veteran was apt to scan the fair proportions and athletic frames of the colonists with a look that seemed to utter volumes of contempt for their moral imbecility. He was also a little addicted to the expression of a belief that where there was so great an observance of the externals of religion, there could not be much of the substance. It is not our task to explain what is, or what ought to be, the substance of Christianity, but merely to record in this place the opinions of Major Effingham.

Knowing the sentiments of the father in relation to this people, it was no wonder that the son hesitated to avow his connection with, nay, even his dependence on the integrity of, a Quaker.

It has been said that Marmaduke deduced his origin from the contemporaries and friends of Penn. His father had married without the pale of the church to which he belonged and had, in this manner, forfeited some of the privileges of his offspring. Still, as young Marmaduke was educated in a colony and society where even the ordinary intercourse between friends was tinctured with the aspect of this mild religion, his habits and language were somewhat marked by its peculiarities. His own marriage at a future day with a lady without, not only the pale, but the influence of this sect of religionists, had a tendency, it is true, to weaken his early impressions; still he retained them in some degree to the hour of his death and was observed uniformly, when much interested or agitated, to speak in the language of his youth. But this is anticipating our tale.

When Marmaduke first became the partner of young Effingham, he was quite the Quaker in externals; and it was too dangerous an experiment for the son to think of encountering the prejudices of the father on this subject. The connection, therefore, remained a profound secret to all but those who were interested in it.

For a few years, Marmaduke directed the commercial operations of his house with a prudence and sagacity that afforded rich returns. He married the lady we have mentioned, who was the mother of Elizabeth, and the visits of his friend were becoming more frequent. There was a speedy prospect of removing the veil from their intercourse, as its advantages became each hour more apparent to Mr. Effingham, when the troubles that preceded the war of the revolution extended themselves to an alarming degree.

Educated in the most dependent loyalty, Mr. Effingham had, from the commencement of the disputes between the colonists and the crown, warmly maintained what he believed to be the just prerogatives of his prince; while, on the other hand, the clear head and independent mind of Temple had induced him to espouse the cause of the people. Both might have been influenced by early impressions; for, if the son of the loyal and gallant soldier bowed in implicit obedience to the will of his sovereign, the descendant of the persecuted follower of Penn looked back, with a little bitterness, to the unmerited wrongs that had been heaped upon his ancestors.

This difference in opinion had long been a subject of amicable dispute between them; but, latterly, the contest was getting to be too important to admit of trivial discussions on the part of Marmaduke, whose acute discernment was already catching faint glimmerings of the important events that were in embryo. The sparks of dissension soon kindled into a blaze; and the colonies, or rather, as they quickly declared themselves, THE STATES, became a scene of strife and bloodshed for years.

A short time before the battle of Lexington, Mr. Effingham, already a widower, transmitted to Marmaduke, for safekeeping, all his valuable effects and papers and left the colony without his father. The war had, however, scarcely commenced in earnest, when he reappeared in New York, wearing the livery of his king; and, in a short time, he took the field at the head of a provincial corps. In the meantime, Marmaduke had completely committed himself in the cause, as it was then called, of the rebellion. Of course, all intercourse between the friends ceased—on the part of Colonel Effingham it was unsought, and on that of Marmaduke there was a cautious reserve. It soon became necessary for the latter to abandon the capital of Philadelphia; but he had taken the precaution to remove the whole of his effects beyond the reach of the royal forces, including the papers of his friend also. There he continued serving his country during the struggle, in various civil capacities, and always with dignity and usefulness. While, however, he discharged his functions with credit and fidelity, Marmaduke never seemed to lose sight of his own interests; for, when the estates of the adherents of the crown fell under the hammer by the acts of confiscation, he appeared in New York and became the purchaser of extensive possessions at comparatively low prices.

It is true that Marmaduke, by thus purchasing estates that had been wrested by violence from others, rendered himself obnoxious to the censures of that sect which, at the same time that it discards its children from a full participation in the family union, seems ever unwilling to abandon them entirely to the world. But either his success or the frequency of the transgression in others soon wiped off this slight stain from his character; and, although there were a few who, dissatisfied with their own fortunes or conscious of their own demerits, would make dark hints concerning the sudden prosperity of the unportioned Quaker, yet his services, and possibly his wealth, soon drove the recollection of these vague conjectures from men's minds.

When the war ended and the independence of the States was acknowledged, Mr. Temple turned his attention from the pursuit of commerce, which was then fluctuating and uncertain, to the settlement of those tracts of land which he had purchased. Aided by a good deal of money and directed by the suggestions of a strong and practical reason, his enterprise throve to a degree that the climate and rugged face of the country which he selected would seem to forbid. His property increased in a tenfold ratio, and he was already ranked among the most wealthy and important of his countrymen. To inherit this wealth he had but one child—the daughter whom we have introduced to the reader, and whom he was now conveying from school to preside over a household that had too long wanted a mistress.

When the district in which his estates lay had become sufficiently populous to be set off as a county, Mr. Temple had, according to the custom of the new settlements, been selected to fill its highest judicial station. This might make a Templar smile; but, in addition to the apology of necessity, there is ever a dignity in talents and experience that is commonly sufficient, in any station, for the protection of its possessor; and Marmaduke, more fortunate in his native clearness of mind than the judge of King Charles, not only decided right, but was generally able to give a very good reason for it. At all events, such was the universal practice of the country and the times; and Judge Temple, so far from ranking among the lowest of his judicial contemporaries in the courts of the new counties, felt himself, and was unanimously acknowledged to be, among the first.

We shall here close this brief explanation of the history and character of some of our personages, leaving them in future to speak and act for themselves.

Chapter III

All that thou see'st, is nature's handiwork;
Those rocks that upward throw their mossy brows
Like castled pinnacles of elder times!
These venerable stems, that slowly rock
Their towering branches in the wintry gale!
That field of frost, which glitters in the sun,
Mocking the whiteness of a marble breast!—
Yet man can mar such works with his rude taste,
Like some sad spoiler of a virgin's fame.

Duo

Some little while elapsed ere Marmaduke Temple was sufficiently recovered from his agitation to scan the person of his new companion. He now observed that he was a youth of some two or three and twenty years of age and rather above the middle height. Further observation was prevented by the rough overcoat which was belted close to his form by a worsted sash, much like the one worn by the old hunter. The eyes of the Judge, after resting a moment on the figure of the stranger, were raised to a scrutiny of his countenance. There had been a look of care, visible in the features of the youth, when he first entered the sleigh, that had not only attracted the notice of Elizabeth, but which she had been much puzzled to interpret. His anxiety seemed the strongest when he was enjoining his old companion to secrecy; and even when he had decided and was rather passively suffering himself to be conveyed to the village, the expression of his eyes by no means indicated any great degree of self-satisfaction at the step. But the lines of an uncommonly prepossessing countenance were gradually becoming composed; and he now sat silent, and apparently musing. The Judge gazed at him for some time with earnestness, and then smiling, as if at his own forgetfulness, he said:

"I believe, my young friend, that terror has driven you from my recollection; your face is very familiar, and yet for the honor of a score of bucks' tails in my cap, I could not tell your name."

35

"I came into the country but three weeks since," returned the youth coldly, "and I understand you have been absent twice that time."

"It will be five tomorrow. Yet your face is one that I have seen; though it would not be strange, such has been my affright, should I see thee in thy winding sheet walking by my bedside tonight. What sayst thou, Bess? Am I compos mentis or not?—Fit to charge a grand jury or, what is just now of more pressing necessity, able to do the honors of a Christmas Eve in the hall of Templeton?"

"More able to do either, my dear Father," said a playful voice from under the ample enclosures of the hood, "than to kill deer with a smoothbore." A short pause followed, and the same voice, but in a different accent, continued—"We shall have good reasons for our thanksgiving tonight, on more accounts than one."

The horses soon reached a point where they seemed to know by instinct that the journey was nearly ended, and bearing on the bits as they tossed their heads, they rapidly drew the sleigh over the level land which lay on the top of the mountain and soon came to the point where the road descended suddenly, but circuitously, into the valley.

The Judge was roused from his reflections when he saw the four columns of smoke which floated above his own chimneys. As house, village, and valley burst on his sight, he exclaimed cheerfully to his daughter:

"See, Bess, there is thy resting place for life!—And thine, too, young man, if thou wilt consent to dwell with us."

The eyes of his auditors involuntarily met; and if the color that gathered over the face of Elizabeth was contradicted by the cold expression of her eye, the ambiguous smile that again played about the lips of the stranger seemed equally to deny the probability of his consenting to form one of this family group. The scene was one, however, which might easily warm a heart less given to philanthropy than that of Marmaduke Temple.

The side of the mountain on which our travelers were journeying, though not absolutely perpendicular, was so steep as to render great care necessary in descending the rude and narrow path which, in that early day, wound along the precipices. The Negro reined in his impatient steeds, and time was given Elizabeth to dwell on a scene which was so rapidly altering under the hands of man that it only resembled, in its outlines, the picture she had so often studied with delight in childhood. Immediately beneath them lay a seeming plain, glittering without inequality and buried in mountains. The latter were precipitous, especially on the side of the plain, and chiefly in forest. Here and there the hills fell away in long, low points and broke the sameness of the outline, or setting, to the long and wide field of snow, which, without house, tree, fence, or any other fixture, resembled so much spotless cloud settled to the earth. A few dark and moving spots were, however, visible on the even surface, which the eye of Elizabeth knew to be so many sleighs going their several ways, to or from the village. On the western border of the plain, the mountains, though equally high, were less precipitous and, as they receded, opened into irregular valleys and glens or were formed into terraces and hollows that admitted of cultivation. Although the evergreens still held dominion over many of the hills that rose on this side of the valley, yet the undulating outlines of the distant mountains, covered with forests of beech and maple, gave a relief to the eye and the promise of a kinder soil. Occasionally spots of white were discoverable amidst the forests of the opposite hills, which announced by the smoke that curled over the tops of the trees the habitations of man and the commencement of agriculture. These spots were sometimes, by the aid of united labor, enlarged into what were called settlements, but more frequently were small and insulated; though so rapid were the changes, and so persevering the labors of those who had cast their fortunes on the success of the enterprise, that it was not difficult for the imagination of Elizabeth to conceive they were enlarging under her eye, while she was gazing, in mute wonder, at the alterations that a few short years had made in the aspect of the country. The points on the western side of this remarkable plain, on which no plant had taken root, were both larger and more numerous than those on its eastern, and one in particular thrust itself forward in such a manner as to form beautifully curved bays of snow on either side. On its extreme end an oak stretched forward, as if to overshadow with its branches a spot which its roots were forbidden to enter. It had released itself from the thralldom that a growth of centuries had imposed on the branches of the surrounding forest trees, and threw its gnarled and fantastic arms abroad, in the wildness of liberty. A dark spot of a few acres in extent at the southern extremity of this beautiful flat, and immediately under the feet of our travelers, alone showed by its rippling surface and the vapors which exhaled from it, that what at first might seem a plain, was one of the mountain lakes, locked in the frosts of winter. A narrow current rushed impetuously from its bosom at the open place we have mentioned, and was to be traced for miles as it wound its way towards the south through the real valley, by its borders of hemlock and pine, and by the vapor which arose from its warmer surface into the chill atmosphere of the hills. The banks of this lovely basin, at its outlet or southern end, were steep but not high; and in that direction the land continued, far as the eye could reach, a narrow but graceful valley, along which the settlers had scattered their humble habitations, with a profusion that bespoke the quality of the soil and the comparative facilities of intercourse.

Immediately on the bank of the lake and at its foot stood the village of Templeton. It consisted of some fifty buildings, including those of every description, chiefly built of wood, and which, in their architecture, bore no great marks of taste, but which also, by the unfinished appearance of most of the dwellings, indicated the hasty manner of their construction. To the eye, they presented a variety of colors. A few were white in both front and rear, but more bore that expensive color on their fronts only, while their economical but ambitious owners had covered the remaining sides of the edifices with a dingy red. One or two were slowly assuming the russet of age; while the uncovered beams that were to be seen through the broken windows of their second stories showed that either the taste or the vanity of their proprietors had led them to undertake a task which they were unable to accomplish. The whole were grouped in a manner that aped the streets of a city, and were evidently so arranged by the directions of one who looked to the wants of posterity rather than to the convenience of the present incumbents. Some three or four of the better sort of buildings, in addition to the uniformity of their color, were fitted with green blinds, which, at that season at least, were rather strangely contrasted to the chill aspect of the lake, the mountains, the forests, and the wide fields of snow. Before the doors of these pretending dwellings were placed a few saplings, either without branches, or possessing only the feeble shoots of one or two summers' growth, that looked not unlike tall grenadiers on post near the threshold of princes. In truth, the occupants of these favored habitations were the nobles of Templeton, as Marmaduke was its king. They were the dwellings of two young men who were cunning in the law; an equal number of that class who chaffered to the wants of the community under the title of storekeepers; and a disciple of Aesculapius, who, for a novelty, brought more subjects into the world than he sent out of it. In the midst of this incongruous group of dwellings rose the mansion of the Judge, towering above all its neighbors. It stood in the center of an enclosure of several acres, which were covered with fruit trees. Some of the latter had been left by the Indians and began already to assume the moss and inclination of age, therein forming a very marked contrast to the infant plantations that peered over most of the picketed fences of the village. In addition to this show of cultivation were two rows of young Lombardy poplars, a tree but lately introduced into America, formally lining either side of a pathway, which led from a gate that opened on the principal street to the front door of the building. The house itself had been built entirely under the superintendence of a certain Mr. Richard Jones, whom we have already mentioned, and who from his cleverness in small matters, and an entire willingness to exert his talents, added to the circumstance of their being sisters' children, ordinarily superintended all the minor concerns of Marmaduke Temple. Richard was fond of saying that this child of his invention consisted of nothing more nor less than what should form the groundwork of every clergyman's discourse; viz. a firstly, and a lastly. He had commenced his labors, in the first year of their residence, by erecting a tall, gaunt edifice of wood, with its gable towards the highway. In this shelter, for it was little more, the family resided three years. By the end of that period, Richard had completed his design. He had availed himself, in this heavy undertaking, of the experience of a certain wandering eastern mechanic, who, by exhibiting a few soiled plates of English architecture, and talking learnedly of friezes, entablatures, and particularly of the composite order, had obtained a very undue influence over Richard's taste, in everything that pertained to that branch of the fine arts. Not that Mr. Jones did not affect to consider Hiram Doolittle a perfect empiric in his profession, being in the constant habit of listening to his treatises on architecture with a kind of indulgent smile; yet, either from an inability to oppose them by anything plausible from his own stores of learning, or from secret admiration, Richard generally submitted to the arguments of his coadjutor. Together, they had not only erected a dwelling for Marmaduke, but they had given a fashion to the architecture of the whole county. The composite order, Mr. Doolittle would contend, was an order composed of many others, and was intended to be the most useful of all, for it admitted into its construction such alterations as convenience or circumstances might require. To this proposition Richard usually assented; and when rival geniuses, who monopolize not only all the reputation, but most of the money of a neighborhood, are of a mind, it is not uncommon to see them lead the fashion, even in graver matters. In the present instance, as we have already hinted, the castle, as Judge Templeton's dwelling was termed in common parlance, came to be the model, in some one or other of its numerous excellences, for every aspiring edifice within twenty miles of it.

The house itself, or the "lastly," was of stone; large, square, and far from uncomfortable. These were four requisites on which Marmaduke had insisted with a little more than his ordinary pertinacity. But everything else was peaceably assigned to Richard and his associate. These worthies found the material a little too solid for the tools of their workmen, which, in general, were employed on a substance no harder than the white pine of the adjacent mountains, a wood so proverbially soft, that it is commonly chosen by the hunters for pillows. But for this awkward dilemma, it is probable that the ambitious tastes of our two architects would have left as much more to do in the way of description. Driven from the faces of the house by the obduracy of the material, they took refuge in the porch and on the roof. The former, it was decided, should be severely classical, and the latter a rare specimen of the merits of the composite order.

A roof, Richard contended, was a part of the edifice that the ancients always endeavored to conceal, it being an excrescence in architecture that was only to be tolerated on

THE PIONEERS 41

account of its usefulness. Besides, as he wittily added, a chief
merit in a dwelling was to present a front, on whichever side
it might happen to be seen; for as it was exposed to all eyes
in all weathers, there should be no weak flank for envy or
unneighborly criticism to assail. It was therefore decided
that the roof should be flat, and with four faces. To this
arrangement, Marmaduke objected the heavy snows that lay
for months, frequently covering the earth to a depth of three
or four feet. Happily, the facilities of the composite order
presented themselves to effect a compromise, and the rafters
were lengthened, so as to give a descent that should carry
off the frozen element. But unluckily, some mistake was
made in the admeasurement of these material parts of the
fabric: and as one of the greatest recommendations of Hiram
was his ability to work by the "square rule," no opportunity
was found of discovering the effect until the massive timbers
were raised on the four walls of the building. Then, indeed,
it was soon seen, that, in defiance of all rule, the roof was
by far the most conspicuous part of the whole edifice. Richard and his associate consoled themselves with the belief
that the covering would aid in concealing this unnatural elevation, but every shingle that was laid only multiplied objects to look at. Richard essayed to remedy the evil with
paint, and four different colors were laid on by his own
hands. The first was a sky blue, in the vain expectation that
the eye might be cheated into the belief it was the heavens
themselves that hung so imposingly over Marmaduke's
dwelling; the second was what he called a "cloud color,"
being nothing more nor less than an imitation of smoke; the
third was what Richard termed an invisible green, an experiment that did not succeed against a background of sky.
Abandoning the attempt to conceal, our architects drew upon
their invention for means to ornament the offensive shingles.
After much deliberation and two or three essays by moonlight, Richard ended the affair by boldly covering the whole
beneath a color that he christened "sunshine," a cheap way,
as he assured his cousin, the Judge, of always keeping fair
weather over his head. The platform, as well as the eaves of
the house, were surmounted by gaudily painted railings, and
the genius of Hiram was exerted in the fabrication of divers
urns and moldings that were scattered profusely around this
part of their labors. Richard had originally a cunning ex-

pedient, by which the chimneys were intended to be so low, and so situated, as to resemble ornaments on the balustrades; but comfort required that the chimneys should rise with the roof in order that the smoke might be carried off, and they thus became four extremely conspicuous objects in the view.

As this roof was much the most important architectural undertaking in which Mr. Jones was ever engaged, his failure produced a correspondent degree of mortification. At first, he whispered among his acquaintances that it proceeded from ignorance of the square rule on the part of Hiram; but as his eye became gradually accustomed to the object, he grew better satisfied with his labors, and instead of apologizing for the defects, he commenced praising the beauties of the mansion house. He soon found hearers; and, as wealth and comfort are at all times attractive, it was, as has been said, made a model for imitation on a small scale. In less than two years from its erection, he had the pleasure of standing on the elevated platform and of looking down on three humble imitators of its beauty. Thus it is ever with fashion, which even renders the faults of the great subjects of admiration.

Marmaduke bore this deformity in his dwelling with great good nature and soon contrived, by his own improvements, to give an air of respectability and comfort to his place of residence. Still there was much of incongruity, even immediately about the mansion house. Although poplars had been brought from Europe to ornament the grounds, and willows and other trees were gradually springing up nigh the dwelling, yet many a pile of snow betrayed the presence of the stump of a pine; and even in one or two instances, unsightly remnants of trees that had been partly destroyed by fire were seen rearing their black, glistening columns twenty or thirty feet above the pure white of the snow. These, which in the language of the country are termed stubs, abounded in the open fields adjacent to the village, and were accompanied, occasionally, by the ruin of a pine or a hemlock that had been stripped of its bark, and which waved in melancholy grandeur its naked limbs to the blast, a skeleton of its former glory. But these and many other unpleasant additions to the view were unseen by the delighted Elizabeth, who, as the horses moved down the side of the mountain, saw only in gross the cluster of houses that lay like a map at her feet;

the fifty smokes that were curling from the valley to the clouds; the frozen lake as it lay imbedded in mountains of evergreen, with the long shadows of the pines on its white surface, lengthening in the setting sun; the dark riband of water that gushed from the outlet, and was winding its way towards the distant Chesapeake—the altered, though still remembered, scenes of her childhood.

Five years had wrought greater changes than a century would produce in countries where time and labor have given permanency to the works of man. To the young hunter and the Judge the scene had less novelty, though none ever emerge from the dark forests of that mountain and witness the glorious scenery of that beauteous valley as it bursts unexpectedly upon them without a feeling of delight. The former cast one admiring glance from north to south and sank his face again beneath the folds of his coat; while the latter contemplated, with philanthropic pleasure, the prospect of affluence and comfort that was expanding around him, the result of his own enterprise and much of it the fruits of his own industry.

The cheerful sound of sleigh bells, however, attracted the attention of the whole party, as they came jingling up the sides of the mountain at a rate that announced a powerful team and a hard driver. The bushes which lined the highway interrupted the view, and the two sleighs were close upon each other before either was seen.

Chapter IV

How now? whose mare's dead? what's the matter?—Falstaff

A LARGE lumber sleigh, drawn by four horses, was soon seen dashing through the leafless bushes which fringed the road. The leaders were of gray, and the pole horses of a jet black. Bells innumerable were suspended from every part of the harness where one of the tinkling balls could be placed; while the rapid movement of the equipage, in defiance of the steep ascent, announced the desire of the driver to ring them to the utmost. The first glance at this singular arrangement acquainted the Judge with the character of those in the sleigh. It contained four male figures. On one of those stools that are used at writing desks, lashed firmly to the sides of the vehicle, was seated a little man, enveloped in a greatcoat fringed with fur, in such a manner that no part of him was visible excepting a face of an unvarying red color. There was a habitual upward look about the head of this gentleman, as if dissatisfied with its natural proximity to the earth; and the expression of his countenance was that of busy care. He was the charioteer, and he guided the mettled animals along the precipice with a fearless eye and a steady hand. Immediately behind him, with his face towards the other two, was a tall figure, to whose appearance not even the duplicate overcoats which he wore, aided by the corner of a horse blanket, could give the appearance of strength. His face was protruding from beneath a woolen nightcap; and when he turned to the vehicle of Marmaduke as the sleighs approached each other, it seemed formed by nature to cut the atmosphere with the least possible resistance. The eyes alone appeared to create any obstacle, for from either side of his forehead their light, blue, glassy balls projected. The sallow of his countenance was too permanent to be affected even by the intense cold of the evening. Opposite to this personage sat a solid, short, and square figure. No part of his form was to be discovered through his overdress but a face that was illuminated by a pair of black eyes that gave the lie to every demure feature in his countenance. A fair, jolly wig furnished a neat and rounded outline to his visage, and he, as well as the other two, wore marten-skin caps. The fourth was a meek-looking, long-visaged man, without any other protection from the cold than that which was furnished by a black surtout, made with some little formality, but which was rather threadbare and rusty. He wore a hat of extremely decent proportions, though frequent brushing had quite destroyed its nap. His face was pale, and withal a little melancholy, or what might be termed of a studious complexion. The air had given it, just now, a slight and somewhat feverish flush. The character of his whole appearance, especially contrasted to the air of humor in his next companion, was that of habitual mental care. No sooner had the two sleighs approached within speaking distance, than the driver of this fantastic equipage shouted aloud:

"Draw up in the quarry—draw up, thou king of the Greeks; draw into the quarry, Agamemnon, or I shall never be able to pass you. Welcome home, cousin 'duke—welcome, welcome, black-eyed Bess. Thou seest, Marmaduke, that I have taken the field with an assorted cargo to do thee honor. Monsieur Le Quoi has come out with only one cap; Old Fritz would not stay to finish the bottle; and Mr. Grant has got to put the 'lastly' to his sermon, yet. Even all the horses would come—by the by, Judge, I must sell the blacks for you immediately; they interfere, and the nigh one is a bad goer in double harness. I can get rid of them to——"

"Sell what thou wilt, Dickon," interrupted the cheerful voice of the Judge, "so that thou leavest me my daughter and my lands. Ah! Fritz, my old friend, this is a kind compliment, indeed, for seventy to pay to five-and-forty. Monsieur Le Quoi, I am your servant. Mr. Grant," lifting his cap, "I feel indebted to your attention. Gentlemen, I make you acquainted with my child. Yours are names with which she is very familiar."

"Velcome, velcome, Tchooge," said the elder of the party, with a strong German accent. "Miss Petsy vill owe me a kiss."

"And cheerfully will I pay it, my good sir," cried the soft voice of Elizabeth; which sounded, in the clear air of the hills, like tones of silver, amid the loud cries of Richard. "I have always a kiss for my old friend, Major Hartmann."

By this time the gentleman in the front seat, who had been addressed as Monsieur Le Quoi, had arisen with some difficulty, owing to the impediment of his overcoats, and steadying himself by placing one hand on the stool of the charioteer, with the other he removed his cap, and bowing politely to the Judge, and profoundly to Elizabeth, he paid his compliments.

"Cover thy poll, Gaul, cover thy poll," cried the driver, who was Mr. Richard Jones; "cover thy poll, or the frost will pluck out the remnant of thy locks. Had the hairs on the head of Absalom been as scarce as thine, he might have been living to this day." The jokes of Richard never failed of exciting risibility, for he uniformly did honor to his own wit; and he enjoyed a hearty laugh on the present occasion, while Mr. Le Quoi resumed his seat with a polite reciprocation in his mirth. The clergyman, for such was the office of Mr. Grant, modestly, though quite affectionately, exchanged his greetings with the travelers also, when Richard prepared to turn the heads of his horses homeward.

It was in the quarry alone that he could effect this object, without ascending to the summit of the mountain. A very considerable excavation had been made in the side of the hill, at the point where Richard had succeeded in stopping the sleighs, from which the stones used for building in the village were ordinarily quarried, and in which he now attempted to turn his team. Passing itself was a task of difficulty, and frequently of danger, in that narrow road; but Richard had to meet the additional risk of turning his four-in-hand. The black civilly volunteered his services to take off the leaders, and the Judge very earnestly seconded the measure with his advice. Richard treated both proposals with great disdain:

"Why, and wherefore, cousin 'duke?" he exclaimed, a little angrily. "The horses are gentle as lambs. You know that I broke the leaders myself, and the pole horses are too near my whip to be restive. Here is Mr. Le Quoi, now, who must know something about driving, because he has rode out so often with me; I will leave it to Mr. Le Quoi whether there is any danger."

It was not in the nature of the Frenchman to disappoint expectations so confidently formed; although he sat looking down the precipice which fronted him, as Richard turned his leaders into the quarry, with a pair of eyes that stood out like those of lobsters. The German's muscles were unmoved, but his quick sight scanned each movement. Mr. Grant placed his hands on the side of the sleigh, in preparation for a spring, but moral timidity deterred him from taking the leap that bodily apprehension strongly urged him to attempt.

Richard, by a sudden application of the whip, succeeded in forcing the leaders into the snowbank that covered the quarry; but the instant that the impatient animals suffered by the crust, through which they broke at each step, they positively refused to move an inch further in that direction. On the contrary, finding that the cries and blows of their driver were redoubled at this juncture, the leaders backed upon the pole horses, who, in their turn, backed the sleigh. Only a single log lay above the pile which upheld the road, on the side towards the valley, and this was now buried in the snow.

The sleigh was easily forced across so slight an impediment; and before Richard became conscious of his danger, one half of the vehicle was projected over a precipice, which fell, perpendicularly, more than a hundred feet. The Frenchman, who, by his position, had a full view of their threatened flight, instinctively threw his body as far forward as possible and cried, "Ah! Mon cher monsieur Deeck! Mon Dieu! Que faites vous!"

"Donner and blitzen, Richart," exclaimed the veteran German, looking over the side of the sleigh with unusual emotion. "Put you will preak ter sleigh and kilt ter horses."

"Good Mr. Jones," said the clergyman, "be prudent, good sir—be careful."

"Get up, obstinate devils!" cried Richard, catching a bird's-eye view of his situation, and, in his eagerness to move forward, kicking the stool on which he sat—"Get up, I say—Cousin 'duke, I shall have to sell the grays too; they are the worst broken horses—Mr. Le Quaw!" Richard was too much agitated to regard his pronunciation, of which he was commonly a little vain; "Monsieur Le Quaw, pray get off my leg; you hold my leg so tight that it's no wonder the horses back."

"Merciful Providence!" exclaimed the Judge. "They will be all killed!"

Elizabeth gave a piercing shriek, and the black of Agamemnon's face changed to a muddy white.

At this critical moment, the young hunter, who during the salutations of the parties had sat in rather sullen silence, sprang from the sleigh of Marmaduke to the heads of the refractory leaders. The horses, who were yet suffering under the injudicious and somewhat random blows of Richard, were dancing up and down with that ominous movement that threatens a sudden and uncontrollable start, still pressing backwards. The youth gave the leaders a powerful jerk, and they plunged aside and re-entered the road in the position in which they were first halted. The sleigh was whirled from its dangerous position, and upset with the runners outwards. The German and the divine were thrown, rather unceremoniously, into the highway, but without danger to their bones. Richard appeared in the air, describing the segment of a circle of which the reins were the radii, and landed at the distance of some fifteen feet, in that snowbank which the horses had dreaded, right end uppermost. Here, as he instinctively grasped the reins, as drowning men seize at straws, he admirably served the purpose of an anchor. The Frenchman, who was on his legs in the act of springing from the sleigh, took an aerial flight also, much in the attitude which boys assume when they play leapfrog, and flying off in a tangent to the curvature of his course, came into the snowbank head foremost, where he remained, exhibiting two lathy legs on high, like scarecrows waving in a cornfield. Major Hartmann, whose self-possession had been admirably preserved during the whole evolution, was the first of the party that gained his feet and his voice.

"Ter deyvel, Richart!" he exclaimed, in a voice half serious, half comical. "Put you unloat your sleigh very hantily."

It may be doubtful whether the attitude in which Mr. Grant continued for an instant after his overthrow was the one into which he had been thrown, or was assumed, in humbling himself before the power that he reverenced, in thanksgiving at his escape. When he rose from his knees, he began to gaze about him, with anxious looks, after the welfare of his companions, while every joint in his body trembled with nervous agitation. There was some confusion in the faculties of Mr. Jones also; but as the mist gradually cleared from before his eyes, he saw that all was safe, and, with an air of great self-satisfaction, he cried, "Well—that was neatly saved, anyhow!—It was a lucky thought in me to hold on the reins, or the fiery devils would have been over the mountain by this time. How well I recovered myself, 'duke! Another moment would have been too late; but I knew just the spot where to touch the off-leader; that blow under his right flank and the sudden jerk I gave the rein brought them round quite in rule, I must own myself." *

"Thou jerk! Thou recover thyself, Dickon!" he said. "But for that brave lad yonder, thou and thy horses, or rather mine, would have been dashed to pieces—but where is Monsieur Le Quoi?"

"Oh! Mon cher Juge! Mon ami!" cried a smothered voice. "Praise be God, I live; vill you, Mister Agamemnon, be pleas come down ici, and help me on my leg?"

---

* The spectators, from immemorial usage, have a right to laugh at the casualties of a sleigh ride; and the Judge was no sooner certain that no harm was done, than he made full use of the privilege.

The divine and the Negro seized the incarcerated Gaul by his legs and extricated him from a snowbank of three feet in depth, whence his voice had sounded as from the tombs. The thoughts of Mr. Le Quoi, immediately on his liberation, were not extremely collected; and when he reached the light, he threw his eyes upwards, in order to examine the distance he had fallen. His good humor returned, however, with a knowledge of his safety, though it was some little time before he clearly comprehended the case.

"What, monsieur," said Richard, who was busily assisting the black in taking off the leaders; "are you there? I thought I saw you flying towards the top of the mountain just now."

"Praise be God, I no fly down into the lake," returned the Frenchman, with a visage that was divided between pain, occasioned by a few large scratches that he had received in forcing his head through the crust, and the look of complaisance that seemed natural to his pliable features. "Ah! Mon cher Mister Deeck, vat you do next? Dere be noting you no try."

"The next thing, I trust, will be to learn to drive," said the Judge, who had busied himself in throwing the buck, together with several other articles of baggage, from his own sleigh into the snow. "Here are seats for you all, gentlemen; the evening grows piercingly cold, and the hour approaches for the service of Mr. Grant: we will leave friend Jones to repair the damages, with the assistance of Agamemnon, and hasten to a warm fire. Here, Dickon, are a few articles of Bess's trumpery that you can throw into your sleigh when ready; and there is also a deer of my taking that I will thank you to bring. Aggy! remember that there will be a visit from Santa Claus * tonight."

The black grinned, conscious of the bribe that was offered him for silence on the subject of the deer, while Richard, without in the least waiting for the termination of his cousin's speech, began his reply:

"Learn to drive, sayest thou, cousin 'duke? Is there a man in the county who knows more of horseflesh than myself? Who broke in the filly that no one else dare mount; though

* The periodical visits of St. Nicholas, or Santa Claus as he is termed, were never forgotten among the inhabitants of New York, until the emigration from New England brought in the opinions and usages of the Puritans. Like the "bon homme de Noël," he arrives at each Christmas.

your coachman did pretend that he had tamed her before I took her in hand; but anybody could see that he lied—he was a great liar, that John—what's that, a buck?"—Richard abandoned the horses and ran to the spot where Marmaduke had thrown the deer. "It is a buck! I am amazed! Yes, here are two holes in him, he has fired both barrels and hit him each time. Ecod! How Marmaduke will brag! He is a prodigious bragger about any small matter like this now; well, to think that 'duke has killed a buck before Christmas! There will be no such thing as living with him—they are both bad shots though, mere chance—mere chance; now, I never fired twice at a cloven foot in my life—it is hit or miss with me—dead or runaway:—had it been a bear, or a wildcat, a man might have wanted both barrels. Here! you Aggy! How far off was the Judge when this buck was shot?"

"Eh! Massa Richard, maybe a ten rod," cried the black, bending under one of the horses with the pretense of fastening a buckle, but in reality to conceal the grin that opened a mouth from ear to ear.

"Ten rod!" echoed the other. "Why, Aggy, the deer I killed last winter was at twenty—yes! If anything it was nearer thirty than twenty. I wouldn't shoot at a deer at ten rod: besides, you may remember, Aggy, I only fired once."

"Yes, Massa Richard, I 'member 'em! Natty Bumppo fire t'oder gun. You know, sir, all 'e folk say Natty kill him."

"The folks lie, you black devil!" exclaimed Richard in great heat. "I have not shot even a gray squirrel these four years, to which that old rascal has not laid claim, or someone else for him. This is a damned envious world that we live in —people are always for dividing the credit of a thing in order to bring down merit to their own level. Now they have a story about the Patent * that Hiram Doolittle helped to plan the steeple to St. Paul's, when Hiram knows that it is entirely mine; a little taken from a print of its namesake in London, I own; but essentially, as to all points of genius, my own."

* The grants of land, made either by the crown or the state, were by letters patent under the great seal, and the term "patent" is usually applied to any district of extent, thus conceded; though under the crown, manorial rights being often granted with the soil, in the older counties, the word "manor" is frequently used. There are many "manors" in New York, though all political and judicial rights have ceased.

"I don't know where he come from," said the black, losing every mark of humor in an expression of admiration, "but eb'ry body say, he wonnerful hansome."

"And well they may say so, Aggy," cried Richard, leaving the buck and walking up to the Negro with the air of a man who has new interest awakened within him. "I think I may say, without bragging, that it is the handsomest and the most scientific country church in America. I know that the Connecticut settlers talk about their Westherfield meetinghouse; but I never believe more than half what they say, they are such unconscionable braggers. Just as you have got a thing done, if they see it likely to be successful, they are always for interfering; and then it's ten to one but they lay claim to half, or even all of the credit. You may remember, Aggy, when I painted the sign of the bold dragoon for Captain Hollister, there was that fellow who was about town laying brick dust on the houses came one day and offered to mix what I call the streaky black, for the tail and mane, and then, because it looks like horsehair, he tells everybody that the sign was painted by himself and Squire Jones. If Marmaduke don't send that fellow off the Patent, he may ornament his village with his own hands for me." Here Richard paused a moment, and cleared his throat by a loud hem, while the Negro, who was all this time busily engaged in preparing the sleigh, proceeded with his work in respectful silence. Owing to the religious scruples of the Judge, Aggy was the servant of Richard, who had his services for a *time*,* and who, of course, commanded a legal claim to the respect of the young Negro. But when any dispute between his lawful and his real master occurred, the black felt too much deference for both to express any opinion. In the meanwhile, Richard continued watching the Negro as he fastened buckle after buckle, until, stealing a look of consciousness towards the other, he con-

* The manumission of the slaves in New York has been gradual. When public opinion became strong in their favor, then grew up a custom of buying the services of a slave, for six or eight years, with a condition to liberate him at the end of the period. Then the law provided that all born after a certain day should be free, the males at twenty-eight, and the females at twenty-five. After this the owner was obliged to cause his servants to be taught to read and write before they reached the age of eighteen, and, finally, the few that remained were all unconditionally liberated in 1826, or after the publication of this tale. It was quite usual for men more or less connected with the Quakers, who never held slaves, to adopt the first expedient.

tinued, "Now, if that young man who was in your sleigh is a real Connecticut settler, he will be telling everybody how he saved my horses, when, if he had let them alone for half a minute longer, I would have brought them in much better, without upsetting, with the whip and rein—it spoils a horse to give him his head. I should not wonder if I had to sell the whole team, just for that one jerk he gave them." Richard paused, and hemmed; for his conscience smote him a little for censuring a man who had just saved his life. "Who is the lad, Aggy—I don't remember to have seen him before?"

The black recollected the hint about Santa Claus; and while he briefly explained how they had taken up the person in question on the top of the mountain, he forbore to add anything concerning the accident of the wound, only saying that he believed the youth was a stranger. It was so usual for men of the first rank to take into their sleighs anyone they found toiling through the snow, that Richard was perfectly satisfied with this explanation. He heard Aggy with great attention, and then remarked, "Well, if the lad has not been spoiled by the people in Templeton, he may be a modest young man, and as he certainly meant well, I shall take some notice of him—perhaps he is land-hunting—I say, Aggy, maybe he is out hunting?"

"Eh! Yes, Massa Richard," said the black, a little confused; for as Richard did all the flogging, he stood in great terror of his master, in the main. "Yes, sir, I b'lieve he be."

"Had he a pack and an ax?"

"No, sir, only he rifle."

"Rifle!" exclaimed Richard, observing the confusion of the Negro, which now amounted to terror. "By Jove, he killed the deer! I knew that Marmaduke couldn't kill a buck on the jump—how was it, Aggy? Tell me all about it, and I'll roast 'duke quicker than he can roast his saddle—How was it, Aggy? The lad shot the buck, and the Judge bought it, ha! And he is taking the youth down to get the pay?"

The pleasure of this discovery had put Richard in such a good humor that the Negro's fears in some measure vanished, and he remembered the stocking of Santa Claus. After a gulp or two, he made out to reply:

"You forgit a two shot, sir?"

"Don't lie, you black rascal!" cried Richard, stepping on the snowbank to measure the distance from his lash to the

Negro's back. "Speak truth, or I trounce you." While speaking, the stock was slowly rising in Richard's right hand, and
the lash drawing through his left, in the scientific manner
with which drummers apply the cat; and Agamemnon, after
turning each side of himself towards his master, and finding
both equally unwilling to remain there, fairly gave in. In a
very few words he made his master acquainted with the truth,
at the same time earnestly conjuring Richard to protect him
from the displeasure of the Judge.

"I'll do it, boy, I'll do it," cried the other, rubbing his
hands with delight; "say nothing, but leave me to manage
'duke. I have a great mind to leave the deer on the hill and
to make the fellow send for his own carcass: but no, I will let
Marmaduke tell a few bounces about it before I come out
upon him. Come, hurry in, Aggy, I must help to dress the
lad's wound: this Yankee * doctor knows nothing of surgery
—I had to hold old Milligan's leg for him while he cut it
off."—Richard was now seated on the stool again, and the
black taking the hind seat, the steeds were put in motion
towards home. As they dashed down the hill, on a fast trot,
the driver occasionally turned his face to Aggy, and continued speaking; for notwithstanding their recent rupture, the
most perfect cordiality was again existing between them.
"This goes to prove that I turned the horses with the reins,
for no man who is shot in the right shoulder can have
strength enough to bring round such obstinate devils. I knew
I did it from the first; but I did not want to multiply words
with Marmaduke about it.—Will you bite, you villain?—
Hip, boys, hip! Old Natty too, that is the best of it!—Well,
well—'duke will say no more about my deer—and the Judge
fired both barrels and hit nothing but a poor lad who was
behind a pine tree. I must help that quack to take out the
buckshot for the poor fellow." In this manner Richard descended the mountain; the bells ringing, and his tongue
going, until they entered the village, when the whole attention
of the driver was devoted to a display of his horsemanship,

* In America the term Yankee is of local meaning. It is thought
to be derived from the manner in which the Indians of New England pronounced the word "English" or "Yengeese." New York being
originally a Dutch province, the term of course was not known
there, and further south different dialects among the natives themselves probably produced a different pronunciation. Marmaduke and
his cousin being Pennsylvanians by birth were not Yankees in the
American sense of the word.

to the admiration of all the gaping women and children who thronged the windows to witness the arrival of their landlord and his daughter.

CHAPTER V

Nathaniel's coat, sir, was not fully made,
And Gabriel's pumps were all unpink'd i' th' heel;
There was no link to color Peter's hat,
And Walter's dagger was not come from sheathing;
There were none fine, but Adam, Ralph, and Gregory.
                                                  SHAKESPEARE

AFTER winding along the side of the mountain, the road, on reaching the gentle declivity which lay at the base of the hill, turned at a right angle to its former course and shot down an inclined plane directly into the village of Templeton. The rapid little stream that we have already mentioned was crossed by a bridge of hewn timber, which manifested, by its rude construction and the unnecessary size of its framework, both the value of labor and the abundance of materials. This little torrent, whose dark waters gushed over the limestones that lined its bottom, was nothing less than one of the many sources of the Susquehanna, a river to which the Atlantic herself has extended an arm in welcome. It was at this point that the powerful team of Mr. Jones brought him up to the more sober steeds of our travelers. A small hill was risen, and Elizabeth found herself at once amidst the incongruous dwellings of the village. The street was of the ordinary width, notwithstanding the eye might embrace, in one view, thousands and tens of thousands of acres that were yet tenanted only by the beasts of the forest. But such had been the will of her father, and such had also met the wishes of his followers. To them the road that made the most rapid approaches to the condition of the old, or, as they expressed it, the *down* countries, was the most pleasant; and surely nothing could look more like civilization than a city, even if it lay in a wilderness! The width of the street, for so it was called, might have been one hundred feet; but the track for the sleighs was much more limited. On either side of the highway were piled huge heaps of logs that were daily increasing rather than diminishing in size, notwithstanding the enormous fires that might be seen through every window.

The last object at which Elizabeth gazed when they renewed their journey, after the rencontre with Richard, was the sun, as it expanded in the refraction of the horizon, and over whose disk the dark umbrage of a pine was stealing, while it slowly sank behind the western hills. But his setting rays darted along the openings of the mountain she was on, and lighted the shining covering of the birches, until their smooth and glossy coats nearly rivaled the mountainsides in color. The outline of each dark pine was delineated far in the depths of the forest; and the rocks, too smooth and too perpendicular to retain the snow that had fallen, brightened, as if smiling at the leave-taking of the luminary. But at each step, as they descended, Elizabeth observed that they were leaving the day behind them. Even the heartless but bright rays of a December sun were missed, as they glided into the cold gloom of the valley. Along the summits of the mountains in the eastern range, it is true, the light still lingered, receding step by step from the earth into the clouds that were gathering, with the evening mist, about the limited horizon; but the frozen lake lay without a shadow on its bosom; the dwellings were becoming already gloomy and indistinct; and the woodcutters were shouldering their axes and preparing to enjoy, throughout the long evening before them, the comforts of those exhilarating fires that their labor had been supplying with fuel. They paused only to gaze at the passing sleighs, to lift their caps to Marmaduke, to exchange familiar nods with Richard, and each disappeared in his dwelling. The paper curtains dropped behind our travelers in every window, shutting from the air even the firelight of the cheerful apartments; and when the horses of her father turned, with a rapid whirl, into the open gate of the mansion house, and nothing stood before her but the cold dreary stone walls of the building, as she approached them through an avenue of young and leafless poplars, Elizabeth felt as if all the loveliness of the mountain view had vanished like the fancies of a dream. Marmaduke retained so much of his early habits as to reject the use of bells; but the equipage of Mr. Jones came dashing through the gate after them, sending its jingling sounds through every cranny of the building, and in a moment the dwelling was in an uproar.

On a stone platform of rather small proportions, considering the size of the building, Richard and Hiram had, conjointly, reared four little columns of wood, which in their turn supported the shingled roofs of the portico—this was the name that Mr. Jones had thought proper to give to a very plain, covered entrance. The ascent to the platform was by five or six stone steps, somewhat hastily laid together, and which the frost had already begun to move from their symmetrical positions. But the evils of a cold climate, and a superficial construction, did not end here. As the steps lowered, the platform necessarily fell also, and the foundations actually left the superstructure suspended in the air, leaving an open space of a foot between the base of the pillars and the stones on which they had originally been placed. It was lucky for the whole fabric that the carpenter who did the manual part of the labor had fastened the canopy of this classic entrance so firmly to the side of the house that, when the base deserted the superstructure in the manner we have described, and the pillars, for the want of a foundation, were no longer of service to support the roof, the roof was able to uphold the pillars. Here was, indeed, an unfortunate gap left in the ornamental part of Richard's column; but, like the window in Aladdin's palace, it seemed only left in order to prove the fertility of its master's resources. The composite order again offered its advantages, and a second edition of the base was given, as the booksellers say, with additions and improvements. It was necessarily larger, and it was properly ornamented with moldings: still the steps continued to yield, and, at the moment when Elizabeth returned to her father's door, a few rough wedges were driven under the pillars to keep them steady and to prevent their weight from separating them from the pediment which they ought to have supported.

From the great door which opened into the porch emerged two or three female domestics, and one male. The latter was bareheaded, but evidently more dressed than usual, and on the whole was of so singular a formation and attire as to deserve a more minute description. He was about five feet in height, of a square and athletic frame, with a pair of shoulders that would have fitted a grenadier. His low stature was rendered the more striking by a bend forward that he was in the habit of assuming, for no apparent reason, unless it might be to give greater freedom to his arms, in a particularly sweeping swing, that they constantly practiced when their master was in motion. His face was long, of a fair complexion, burnt to a fiery red; with a snub nose, cocked into an inveterate pug; a mouth of enormous dimensions, filled with fine teeth; and a pair of blue eyes, that seemed to look about them, on surrounding objects, with habitual contempt. His head composed full one-fourth of his whole length, and the queue that depended from its rear occupied another. He wore a coat of very light drab cloth, with buttons as large as dollars, bearing the impression of a "foul anchor." The skirts were extremely long, reaching quite to the calf, and were broad in proportion. Beneath, there were a vest and breeches of red plush, somewhat worn and soiled. He had shoes with large buckles, and stockings of blue and white stripes.

This odd-looking figure reported himself to be a native of the county of Cornwall, in the island of Great Britain. His boyhood had passed in the neighborhood of the tin mines, and his youth as the cabin boy of a smuggler, between Falmouth and Guernsey. From this trade he had been impressed into the service of his king, and, for the want of a better, had been taken into the cabin, first as a servant, and finally as steward to the captain. Here he acquired the art of making chowder, lobscouse, and one or two other sea dishes, and, as he was fond of saying, had an opportunity of seeing the world. With the exception of one or two outports in France, and an occasional visit to Portsmouth, Plymouth, and Deal, he had in reality seen no more of mankind, however, than if he had been riding a donkey in one of his native mines. But, being discharged from the navy at the peace of '83, he declared that, as he had seen all the civilized parts of the earth, he was inclined to make a trip to the wilds of America. We will not trace him in his brief wanderings, under the influence of that spirit of emigration that sometimes induces a dapper Cockney to quit his home, and lands him, before the sound of Bow bells is out of his ears, within the roar of the cataract of Niagara; but shall only add, that, at a very early day, even before Elizabeth had been sent to school, he had found his way into the family of Marmaduke Temple, where,

owing to a combination of qualities that will be developed
in the course of the tale, he held, under Mr. Jones, the office
of major-domo. The name of this worthy was Benjamin
Penguillan, according to his own pronunciation; but, owing
to a marvelous tale that he was in the habit of relating, concerning the length of time he had to labor to keep his ship
from sinking after Rodney's victory, he had universally acquired the nickname of Ben Pump.

By the side of Benjamin, and pressing forward as if a little
jealous of her station, stood a middle-aged woman, dressed in
calico, rather violently contrasted in color with a tall, meager
shapeless figure, sharp features, and a somewhat acute expression of her physiognomy. Her teeth were mostly gone,
and what did remain were of a light yellow. The skin of her
nose was drawn tightly over the member, to hang in large
wrinkles in her cheeks and about her mouth. She took snuff
in such quantities as to create the impression that she owed
the saffron of her lips and the adjacent parts to this circumstance; but it was the unvarying color of her whole face. She
presided over the female part of the domestic arrangements,
in the capacity of housekeeper; was a spinster, and bore the
name of Remarkable Pettibone. To Elizabeth she was an entire stranger, having been introduced into the family since
the death of her mother.

In addition to these were three or four subordinate
menials, mostly black, some appearing at the principal door,
and some running from the end of the building, where stood
the entrance to the cellar-kitchen.

Besides these, there was a general rush from Richard's
kennel, accompanied with every canine tone, from the howl
of the wolf dog to the petulant bark of the terrier. The
master received their boisterous salutations with a variety of
imitations from his own throat, when the dogs, probably
from shame of being outdone, ceased their outcry. One
stately, powerful mastiff, who wore round his neck a brass
collar with "M. T." engraved in large letters on the rim,
alone was silent. He walked majestically, amid the confusion, to the side of the Judge, where, receiving a kind pat
or two, he turned to Elizabeth, who even stooped to kiss him
as she called him kindly by the name of "Old Brave." The
animal seemed to know her, as she ascended the steps,
supported by Monsieur Le Quoi and her father, in order to

protect her from falling on the ice with which they were covered. He looked wistfully after her figure, and when the door closed on the whole party, he laid himself in a kennel that was placed nigh by, as if conscious that the house contained something of additional value to guard.

Elizabeth followed her father, who paused a moment to whisper a message to one of his domestics, into a large hall that was dimly lighted by two candles placed in high, old-fashioned, brass candlesticks. The door closed, and the party were at once removed from an atmosphere that was nearly at zero, to one of sixty degrees above. In the center of the hall stood an enormous stove, the sides of which appeared to be quivering with heat; from which a large, straight pipe, leading through the ceiling above, carried off the smoke. An iron basin, containing water, was placed on this furnace, for such only it could be called, in order to preserve a proper humidity in the apartment. The room was carpeted, and furnished with convenient, substantial furniture, some of which was brought from the city, and the remainder having been manufactured by the mechanics of Templeton. There was a sideboard of mahogany, inlaid with ivory, and bearing enormous handles of glittering brass, and groaning under the piles of silver plate. Near it stood a set of prodigious tables, made of the wild cherry, to imitate the imported wood of the sideboard, but plain, and without ornament of any kind. Opposite to these stood a smaller table, formed from a lighter-colored wood, through the grains of which the wavy lines of the curled maple of the mountains were beautifully undulating. Near to this, in a corner, stood a heavy, old-fashioned, brass-faced clock, encased in a high box, of the dark hue of the black walnut from the seashore. An enormous settee, or sofa, covered with light chintz, stretched along the walls for near twenty feet on one side of the hall; and chairs of wood, painted a light yellow, with black lines that were drawn by no very steady hand, were ranged opposite, and in the intervals between the other pieces of furniture. A Fahrenheit's thermometer, in a mahogany case and with a barometer annexed, was hung against the wall, at some little distance from the stove, which Benjamin consulted, every half-hour, with prodigious exactitude. Two small glass chandeliers were suspended at equal distances between the stove and the outer doors, one of which opened at each end of the hall, and gilt lusters were affixed to the framework of the numerous side doors that led from the apartment. Some little display in architecture had been made in constructing these frames and casings, which were surmounted with pediments that bore each a little pedestal in its center: on these pedestals were small busts in blacked plaster of Paris. The style of the pedestals, as well as the selection of the busts, were all due to the taste of Mr. Jones. On one stood Homer, a most striking likeness, Richard affirmed, "as any one might see, for it was blind." Another bore the image of a smooth-visaged gentleman with a pointed beard, whom he called Shakespeare. A third ornament was an urn, which from its shape, Richard was accustomed to say, intended to represent itself as holding the ashes of Dido. A fourth was certainly old Franklin, in his cap and spectacles. A fifth as surely bore the dignified composure of the face of Washington. A sixth was a nondescript, representing "a man with a shirt collar open," to use the language of Richard, "with a laurel on his head; it was Julius Cæsar or Dr. Faustus; there were good reasons for believing either."

The walls were hung with a dark, lead-colored English paper that represented Britannia weeping over the tomb of Wolfe. The hero himself stood at a little distance from the mourning goddess, and at the edge of the paper. Each width contained the figure, with the slight exception of one arm of the General, which ran over on the next piece, so that when Richard essayed, with his own hands, to put together this delicate outline, some difficulties occurred that prevented a nice conjunction; and Britannia had reason to lament, in addition to the loss of her favorite's life, numberless cruel amputations of his right arm.

The luckless cause of these unnatural divisions now announced his presence in the hall by a loud crack of his whip.

"Why, Benjamin! You Ben Pump! Is this the manner in which you receive the heiress?" he cried. "Excuse him, cousin Elizabeth. The arrangements were too intricate to be trusted to everyone; but now I am here, things will go on better. Come, light up, Mr. Penguillan, light up, light up, and let us see one another's faces. Well, 'duke, I have brought home your deer; what is to be done with it, ha?"

"By the Lord, Squire," commenced Benjamin in reply, first giving his mouth a wipe with the back of his hand, "if this here thing had been ordered sum'at earlier in the day, it might have been got up, d'ye see, to your liking. I had mustered all hands, and was exercising candles, when you hove in sight; but when the women heard your bells they started an end, as if they were riding the boatswain's colt; and, if so be there is that man in the house, who can bring up a parcel of women when they have got headway on them, until they've run out the end of their rope, his name is not Benjamin Pump. But Miss Betsey here must have altered more than a privateer in disguise, since she has got on her woman's duds, if she will take offense with an old fellow for the small matter of lighting a few candles."

Elizabeth and her father continued silent, for both experienced the same sensation on entering the hall. The former had resided one year in the building before she left home for school, and the figure of its lamented mistress was missed by both husband and child.

But candles had been placed in the chandeliers and lusters, and the attendants were so far recovered from surprise as to recollect their use; the oversight was immediately remedied, and in a minute the apartment was in a blaze of light.

The slight melancholy of our heroine and her father was banished by this brilliant interruption; and the whole party began to lay aside the numberless garments they had worn in the air.

During this operation, Richard kept up a desultory dialogue with the different domestics, occasionally throwing out a remark to the Judge concerning the deer; but as his conversation at such moments was much like an accompaniment on a piano, a thing that is heard without being attended to, we will not undertake the task of recording his diffuse discourse.

The instant that Remarkable Pettibone had executed her portion of the labor in illuminating, she returned to a position near Elizabeth, with the apparent motive of receiving the clothes that the other threw aside, but in reality to examine, with an air of curiosity—not unmixed with jealousy—the appearance of the lady who was to supplant her in the administration of their domestic economy. The housekeeper felt a little appalled, when, after cloaks, coats, shawls, and socks had been taken off in succession, the large black hood was removed, and the dark ringlets, shining like the raven's wing, fell from her head and left the sweet but commanding features of the young lady exposed to view. Nothing could be fairer and more spotless than the forehead of Elizabeth, and preserve the appearance of life and health. Her nose would have been called Grecian, but for a softly rounded swell that gave in character to the feature what it lost in beauty. Her mouth, at first sight, seemed only made for love; but the instant that its muscles moved, every expression that womanly dignity could utter played around it with the flexibility of female grace. It spoke not only to the ear but to the eye. So much added to a form of exquisite proportions, rather full and rounded for her years, and of the tallest medium height, she inherited from her mother. Even the color of her eye, the arched brows, and the long silken lashes, came from the same source; but its expression was her father's. Inert and composed, it was soft, benevolent, and attractive; but it could be roused, and that without much difficulty. At such moments it was still beautiful, though it was a little severe. As the last shawl fell aside, and she stood dressed in a rich blue riding habit that fitted her form with the nicest exactness, her cheeks burning with roses that bloomed the richer for the heat of the hall, and her eyes slightly suffused with moisture that rendered their ordinary beauty more dazzling, and with every feature of her speaking countenance illuminated by the lights that flared around her, Remarkable felt that her own power had ended.

The business of unrobing had been simultaneous. Marmaduke appeared in a suit of plain neat black; Monsieur Le Quoi, in a coat of snuff color, covering a vest of embroidery, with breeches, and silk stockings, and buckles—that were commonly thought to be of paste. Major Hartmann wore a coat of sky blue, with large brass buttons, a club wig, and boots; and Mr. Richard Jones had set off his dapper little form in a frock of bottle green, with bullet buttons, by one of which the sides were united over his well-rounded waist, opening above, so as to show a jacket of red cloth, with an undervest of flannel, faced with green velvet, and below, so as to exhibit a pair of buckskin breeches, with long, soiled, white top boots, and spurs; one of the latter a little bent, from its recent attacks on the stool.

When the young lady had extricated herself from her garments, she was at liberty to gaze about her and to examine not only the household over which she was to preside, but also the air and manner in which their domestic arrangements were conducted. Although there was much incongruity in the furniture and appearance of the hall, there was nothing mean. The floor was carpeted, even in its remotest corners. The brass candlesticks, the gilt lusters, and the glass chandeliers, whatever might be their *keeping* as to propriety and taste, were admirably kept as to all the purposes of use and comfort. They were clean and glittering in the strong light of the apartment. Compared with the chill aspect of the December night without, the warmth and brilliancy of the apartment produced an effect that was not unlike enchantment. Her eye had not time to detect in detail the little errors, which, in truth, existed, but was glancing around her in delight, when an object arrested her view, that was in strong contrast to the smiling faces and neatly attired personages who had thus assembled to do honor to the heiress of Templeton.

In a corner of the hall near the grand entrance stood the young hunter, unnoticed, and for the moment apparently forgotten. But even the forgetfulness of the Judge, which, under the influence of strong emotion, had banished the recollection of the wound of this stranger, seemed surpassed by the absence of mind in the youth himself. On entering the apartment he had mechanically lifted his cap and exposed a head covered with hair that rivaled in color and gloss the locks of Elizabeth. Nothing could have wrought a greater transformation than the single act of removing the rough foxskin cap. If there was much that was prepossessing in the countenance of the young hunter, there was something even noble in the rounded outlines of his head and brow. The very air and manner with which the member haughtily maintained itself over the coarse and even wild attire in which the rest of his frame was clad, bespoke not only familiarity with a splendor that in those new settlements was thought to be unequaled, but something very like contempt also.

The hand that held the cap rested lightly on the little

ivory-mounted piano of Elizabeth, with neither rustic restraint nor obtrusive vulgarity. A single finger touched the instrument as if accustomed to dwell on such places. His other arm was extended to its utmost length, and the hand grasped the barrel of his long rifle with something like convulsive energy. The act and the attitude were both involuntary, and evidently proceeded from a feeling much deeper than that of vulgar surprise. His appearance, connected as it was with the rough exterior of his dress, rendered him entirely distinct from the busy group that were moving across the other end of the long hall, occupied in receiving the travelers, and exchanging their welcomes; and Elizabeth continued to gaze at him in wonder. The contraction of the stranger's brows increased as his eyes moved slowly from one object to another. For moments the expression of his countenance was fierce, and then again it seemed to pass away in some painful emotion. The arm that was extended bent, and brought the hand nigh to his face, when his head dropped upon it, and concealed the wonderfully speaking lineaments.

"We forget, dear sir, the strange gentleman" (for her life Elizabeth could not call him otherwise), "whom we have brought here for assistance, and to whom we owe every attention."

All eyes were instantly turned in the direction of those of the speaker, and the youth rather proudly elevated his head again, while he answered:

"My wound is trifling, and I believe that Judge Temple sent for a physician the moment we arrived."

"Certainly," said Marmaduke; "I have not forgotten the object of thy visit, young man, nor the nature of my debt."

"Oh!" exclaimed Richard, with something of a waggish leer, "thou owest the lad for the venison, I suppose, that thou killed, cousin 'duke! Marmaduke! Marmaduke! That was a marvelous tale of thine about the buck! Here, young man, are two dollars for the deer, and Judge Temple can do no less than pay the doctor. I shall charge you nothing for my services, but you shall not fare the worse for that. Come, come, 'duke, don't be downhearted about it; if you missed the buck, you contrived to shoot this poor fellow through a pine tree. Now I own that you have beat me; I never did such a thing in all my life."

"And I hope never will," returned the Judge, "if you are to experience the uneasiness that I have suffered. But be of good cheer, my young friend, the injury must be small, as thou movest thy arm with apparent freedom."

"Don't make the matter worse, 'duke, by pretending to talk about surgery," interrupted Mr. Jones, with a contemptuous wave of the hand; "it is a science that can only be learnt by practice. You know that my grandfather was a doctor, but you haven't got a drop of medical blood in your veins. These kind of things run in families. All my family by the father's side had a knack at physic. There was my uncle that was killed at Brandywine—he died as easy again as any other man in the regiment, just from knowing how to hold his breath naturally. Few men know how to breathe naturally."

"I doubt not, Dickon," returned the Judge, meeting the bright smile which, in spite of himself, stole over the stranger's features, "that thy family thoroughly understood the art of letting life slip through their fingers."

Richard heard him quite coolly, and putting a hand in either pocket of his surtout, so as to press forward the skirts, began to whistle a tune; but the desire to reply overcame his philosophy, and with great heat he exclaimed:

"You may affect to smile, Judge Temple, at hereditary virtues, if you please; but there is not a man on your Patent who don't know better. Here, even this young man, who has never seen anything but bears, and deer, and woodchucks, knows better than to believe virtues are not transmitted in families. Don't you, friend?"

"I believe that vice is not," said the stranger abruptly, his eye glancing from the father to the daughter.

"The squire is right, Judge," observed Benjamin, with a knowing nod of his head towards Richard, that bespoke the cordiality between them. "Now, in the old country, the king's majesty touches for the evil, and that is a disorder that the greatest doctor in the fleet, or, for the matter of that, admiral either, can't cure; only the king's majesty, or a man that's been hanged. Yes, the squire is right; for if so be that he wasn't, how is it that the seventh son always is a doctor, whether he ships for the cockpit or not? Now, when we fell in with the mounsheers, under De Grasse, d'ye see, we had aboard of us a doctor——"

"Very well, Benjamin," interrupted Elizabeth, glancing her eyes from the hunter to Monsieur Le Quoi, who was most politely attending to what fell from each individual in succession, "you shall tell me of that, and all your entertaining adventures together; just now, a room must be prepared in which the arm of this gentleman can be dressed."

"I will attend to that myself, cousin Elizabeth," observed Richard, somewhat haughtily. "The young man shall not suffer because Marmaduke chooses to be a little obstinate. Follow me, my friend, and I will examine the hurt myself."

"It will be well to wait for the physician," said the hunter, coldly; "he cannot be distant."

Richard paused and looked at the speaker, a little astonished at the language, and a good deal appalled at the refusal. He construed the latter into an act of hostility, and placing his hands in the pockets again, he walked up to Mr. Grant, and putting his face close to the countenance of the divine, said in an undertone:

"Now, mark my words: there will be a story among the settlers, that all our necks would have been broken but for that fellow—as if I did not know how to drive. Why, you might have turned the horses yourself, sir; nothing was easier; it was only pulling hard on the nigh rein, and touching the off flank of the leader. I hope, my dear sir, you are not at all hurt by the upset the lad gave us?"

The reply was interrupted by the entrance of the village physician.

CHAPTER VI

> ————————*And about his shelves,*
> *A beggarly account of empty boxes,*
> *Green earthen pots, bladders, and musty seeds,*
> *Remnants of packthread, and old cakes of roses,*
> *Were thinly scattered to make up a show.*
>
> SHAKESPEARE

DOCTOR ELNATHAN TODD, for such was the name of the man of physic, was commonly thought to be, among the settlers, a gentleman of great mental endowments; and he was assuredly of rare personal proportions. In height he measured, without his shoes, exactly six feet and four inches. His hands, feet, and knees corresponded in every respect with this formidable stature; but every other part of his frame appeared to have been intended for a man several sizes smaller, if we except the length of the limbs. His shoulders were square, in one sense at least, being in a right line from one side to the other; but they were so narrow that the long dangling arms they supported seemed to issue out of his back. His neck possessed, in an eminent degree, the property of length to which we have alluded, and it was topped by a small bullethead that exhibited, on one side, a bush of bristling brown hair, and on the other, a short, twinkling visage that appeared to maintain a constant struggle with itself in order to look wise. He was the youngest son of a farmer in the western part of Massachusetts, who, being in somewhat easy circumstances, had allowed this boy to shoot up to the height we have mentioned without the ordinary interruptions of field labor, wood chopping, and such other toils as were imposed on his brothers. Elnathan was indebted for this exemption from labor in some measure to his extraordinary growth, which, leaving him pale, inanimate, and listless, induced his tender mother to pronounce him "a sickly boy, and one that was not equal to work, but who might earn a living, comfortably enough, by taking to pleading law, or turning minister, or doctoring, or some such like easy calling." Still there was great uncertainty which of these vocations the youth was best endowed to fill; but, having no other employment, the stripling was constantly lounging about the "homestead," munching green apples, and hunting for sorrel, when the same sagacious eye that had brought to light his latent talents seized upon this circumstance as a clue to his future path through the turmoils of the world. "Elnathan was cut out for a doctor, she knew, for he was forever digging for herbs, and tasting all kinds of things that grow'd about the lots. Then again he had a natural love for doctor-stuff, for when she had left the bilious pills out for her man, all nicely covered with maple sugar, just ready to take, Nathan had come in, and swallowed them, for all the world as if they were nothing, while Ichabod (her husband) could never get one down without making such desperate faces that it was awful to look on."

This discovery decided the matter. Elnathan, then about fifteen, was much like a wild colt, caught and trimmed by clipping his bushy locks; dressed in a suit of homespun dyed in the butternut bark; furnished with a "New Testament" and a "Webster's Spelling Book," and sent to school. As the boy was by nature quite shrewd enough, and had previously, at odd times, laid the foundations of reading, writing, and arithmetic, he was soon conspicuous in the school for his learning. The delighted mother had the gratification of hearing, from the lips of the master, that her son was a "prodigious boy, and far above all his class." He also thought that "the youth had a natural love for doctoring, as he had known him frequently advise the smaller children against eating too much; and once or twice, when the ignorant little things had persevered in opposition to Elnathan's advice, he had known her son empty the school baskets with his own mouth, to prevent the consequences."

Soon after this comfortable declaration from his schoolmaster, the lad was removed to the house of the village doctor, a gentleman whose early career had not been unlike that of our hero, where he was to be seen, sometimes watering a horse, at others watering medicines, blue, yellow, and red; then again he might be noticed, lolling under an apple tree, with Ruddiman's Latin Grammar in his hand and a corner of Denman's Midwifery sticking out of a pocket; for his instructor held it absurd to teach his pupil how to dispatch a patient regularly from this world before he knew how to bring him into it.

This kind of life continued for a twelvemonth, when he suddenly appeared at meeting in a long coat (and well did it deserve the name!) of black homespun, with little bootees, bound with uncolored calfskin, for the want of red morocco.

Soon after he was seen shaving with a dull razor. Three or four months had scarce elapsed before several elderly ladies were observed hastening towards the house of a poor woman in the village, while others were running to and fro in great apparent distress. One or two boys were mounted, bareback, on horses, and sent off at speed in various directions. Several indirect questions were put concerning the place where the physician was last seen; but all would not do; and at length Elnathan was seen issuing from his door with a very grave air, preceded by a little white-headed boy, out of breath, trotting before him. The following day the youth appeared in the street, as the highway was called, and the neighborhood was much edified by the additional gravity of his air. The same week he bought a new razor, and the succeeding Sunday he entered the meetinghouse with a red silk handkerchief in his hand, and with an extremely demure countenance. In the evening he called upon a young woman of his own class in life, for there were no others to be found, and, when he was left alone with the fair, he was called for the first time in his life, Doctor Todd, by her prudent mother. The ice once broken in this manner, Elnathan was greeted from every mouth with his official appellation.

Another year passed under the superintendence of the same master, during which the young physician had the credit of "riding with the old doctor," although they were generally observed to travel different roads. At the end of that period, Dr. Todd attained his legal majority. He then took a jaunt to Boston to purchase medicines, and, as some intimated, to walk the hospital; we know not how the latter might have been, but if true, he soon walked through it, for he returned within a fortnight, bringing with him a suspicious-looking box that smelled powerfully of brimstone.

The next Sunday he was married, and the following morning he entered a one-horse sleigh with his bride, having before him the box we have mentioned, with another filled with homemade household linen, a paper-covered trunk, with a red umbrella lashed to it, a pair of quite new saddlebags, and a bandbox. The next intelligence that his friends received of the bride and bridegroom was that the latter was "settled in the new countries, and well-to-do as a doctor, in Templeton, in York state!"

If a Templar would smile at the qualifications of Marmaduke to fill the judicial seat he occupied, we are certain that a graduate of Leyden or Edinburgh would be extremely amused with this true narration of the servitude of Elnathan in the temple of Aesculapius. But the same consolation was afforded to both the jurist and the leech; for Dr. Todd was quite as much on a level with his compeers of the profession, in that country, as was Marmaduke with his brethren on the bench.

Time and practice did wonders for the physician. He was naturally humane, but possessed of no small share of moral courage; or, in other words, he was chary of the lives of his patients, and never tried uncertain experiments on such members of society as were considered useful; but once or twice when a luckless vagrant had come under his care, he was a little addicted to trying the effects of every phial in his saddlebags on the stranger's constitution. Happily their number was small, and in most cases their natures innocent. By these means Elnathan had acquired a certain degree of knowledge in fevers and agues, and could talk with much judgment concerning intermittents, remittents, tertians, quotidians, etc. In certain cutaneous disorders very prevalent in new settlements, he was considered to be infallible; and there was no woman on the Patent, but would as soon think of becoming a mother without a husband as without the assistance of Dr. Todd. In short, he was rearing, on this foundation of sand, a superstructure, cemented by practice, though composed of somewhat brittle materials. He, however, occasionally renewed his elementary studies, and, with the observation of a shrewd mind, was comfortably applying his practice to his theory.

In surgery, having the least experience, and it being a business that spoke directly to the senses, he was most apt to distrust his own powers; but he had applied oils to several burns, cut round the roots of sundry defective teeth, and sewed up the wounds of numberless wood choppers, with considerable éclat, when an unfortunate jobber * suffered a fracture of his leg by the tree that he had been felling. It was on this occasion that our hero encountered the greatest trial his nerves and moral feeling had ever sustained. In the hour of need, however, he was not found wanting. Most of the amputations in the new settlements, and they were quite frequent, were performed by some one practitioner, who possessing originally a reputation, was enabled by this circumstance to acquire an experience that rendered him deserving of it; and Elnathan had been present at one or two of these operations. But on the present occasion the man of practice

---

* People who clear land by the acre or job are thus called.

was not to be obtained, and the duty fell, as a matter of course, to the share of Mr. Todd. He went to work with a kind of blind desperation, observing, at the same time, all the externals of decent gravity and great skill. The sufferer's name was Milligan, and it was to this event that Richard alluded when he spoke of assisting the Doctor at an amputation—by holding the leg! The limb was certainly cut off, and the patient survived the operation. It was, however, two years before poor Milligan ceased to complain that they had buried the leg in so narrow a box, that it was straitened for room; he could feel the pain shooting up from the inhumed fragment into the living members. Marmaduke suggested that the fault might lie in the arteries and nerves; but Richard, considering the amputation as part of his own handiwork, strongly repelled the insinuation, at the same time declaring that he had often heard of men who could tell when it was about to rain by the toes of amputated limbs. After two or three years, notwithstanding Milligan's complaints gradually diminished, the leg was dug up, and a larger box furnished, and from that hour no one had heard the sufferer utter another complaint on the subject. This gave the public great confidence in Dr. Todd, whose reputation was hourly increasing, and, luckily for his patients, his information also.

Notwithstanding Dr. Todd's practice, and his success with the leg, he was not a little appalled on entering the hall of the mansion house. It was glaring with the light of day; it looked so splendid and imposing, compared with the hastily built and scantily furnished apartments which he frequented in his ordinary practice, and contained so many well-dressed persons and anxious faces, that his usually firm nerves were a good deal discomposed. He had heard from the messenger who summoned him that it was a gunshot wound, and had come from his own home, wading through the snow, with his saddlebags thrown over his arm, while separated arteries, penetrated lungs, and injured vitals were whirling through his brain, as if he were stalking over a field of battle, instead of Judge Temple's peaceable enclosure.

The first object that met his eye, as he moved into the room, was Elizabeth in her riding habit, richly laced with gold cord, her fine form bending towards him, and her face expressing deep anxiety in every one of its beautiful features. The enormous bony knees of the physician struck each other

with a noise that was audible; for in the absent state of his
mind, he mistook her for a general officer, perforated with
bullets, hastening from the field of battle to implore assistance. The delusion, however, was but momentary, and his
eye glanced rapidly from the daughter to the earnest dignity
of the father's countenance: thence to the busy strut of Richard, who was cooling his impatience at the hunter's indifference to his assistance by pacing the hall and cracking his
whip; from him to the Frenchman, who had stood for several
minutes unheeded with a chair for the lady; thence to Major
Hartmann, who was very coolly lighting a pipe three feet
long by a candle in one of the chandeliers; thence to Mr.
Grant, who was turning over a manuscript with much earnestness at one of the lusters; thence to Remarkable, who
stood, with her arms demurely folded before her, surveying
with a look of admiration and envy the dress and beauty of
the young lady; and from her to Benjamin, who with his
feet standing wide apart, and his arms akimbo, was balancing his square little body with the indifference of one who is
accustomed to wounds and bloodshed. All of these seemed
to be unhurt, and the operator began to breathe more freely;
but before he had time to take a second look, the Judge, advancing, shook him kindly by the hand, and spoke.

"Thou art welcome, my good sir, quite welcome, indeed;
here is a youth whom I have unfortunately wounded in
shooting a deer this evening, and who requires some of thy
assistance."

"Shooting at a deer, 'duke," interrupted Richard, "shooting at a deer. Who do you think can prescribe, unless he
knows the truth of the case? It is always so with some people; they think a doctor can be deceived with the same impunity as another man."

"Shooting at a deer, truly," returned the Judge, smiling,
"although it is by no means certain that I did not aid in destroying the buck; but the youth is injured by my hand, be
that as it may; and it is thy skill that must cure him, and
my pocket shall amply reward thee for it."

"Two ver good tings to depend on," observed Monsieur Le
Quoi, bowing politely, with a sweep of his head, to the Judge
and the practitioner.

"I thank you, Monsieur," returned the Judge; "but we keep

the young man in pain. Remarkable, thou wilt please to provide linen for lint and bandages."

This remark caused a cessation of the compliments and induced the physician to turn an inquiring eye in the direction of his patient. During the dialogue the young hunter had thrown aside his overcoat, and now stood clad in a plain suit of the common, light-colored homespun of the country, that was evidently but recently made. His hand was on the lapels of his coat, in the attitude of removing the garment, when he suddenly suspended the movement and looked towards the commiserating Elizabeth, who was standing in an unchanged posture, too much absorbed with her anxious feelings to heed his actions. A slight color appeared on the brow of the youth.

"Possibly the sight of blood may alarm the lady; I will retire to another room while the wound is dressing."

"By no means," said Dr. Todd, who, having discovered that his patient was far from being a man of importance, felt much emboldened to perform the duty. "The strong light of these candles is favorable to the operation, and it is seldom that we hard students enjoy good eyesight."

While speaking, Elnathan placed a pair of large iron-rimmed spectacles on his face, where they dropped as it were by long practice, to the extremity of his slim pug nose; and if they were of no service as assistants to his eyes, neither were they any impediment to his vision; for his little gray organs were twinkling above them, like two stars emerging from the envious cover of a cloud. The action was unheeded by all but Remarkable, who observed to Benjamin:

"Dr. Todd is a comely man to look on, and dispu't pretty. How well he seems in spectacles! I declare, they give a grand look to a body's face. I have quite a great mind to try them myself."

The speech of the stranger recalled the recollection of Miss Temple, who started, as if from deep abstraction, and coloring excessively, she motioned to a young woman who served in the capacity of maid, and retired with an air of womanly reserve.

The field was now left to the physician and his patient, while the different personages who remained gathered around the latter, with faces expressing the various degrees of interest that each one felt in his condition. Major Hartmann alone retained his seat, where he continued to throw out vast quantities of smoke, now rolling his eyes up to the ceiling, as if musing on the uncertainty of life, and now bending them on the wounded man, with an expression that bespoke some consciousness of his situation.

In the meantime Elnathan, to whom the sight of a gunshot wound was a perfect novelty, commenced his preparations with a solemnity and care that were worthy of the occasion. An old shirt was procured by Benjamin and placed in the hands of the other, who tore divers bandages from it, with an exactitude that marked both his own skill and the importance of the operation.

When this preparatory measure was taken, Dr. Todd selected a piece of the shirt with great care, and handing it to Mr. Jones, without moving a muscle, said:

"Here, Squire Jones, you are well acquainted with these things; will you please to scrape the lint? It should be fine and soft, you know, my dear sir; and be cautious that no cotton gets in, or it may p'ison the wound. The shirt has been made with cotton thread, but you can easily pick it out."

Richard assumed the office, with a nod at his cousin that said quite plainly, "You see this fellow can't get along without me," and began to scrape the linen on his knee with great diligence.

A table was now spread with phials, boxes of salve, and divers surgical instruments. As the latter appeared in succession from a case of red morocco, their owner held up each implement to the strong light of the chandelier, near to which he stood, and examined it with the nicest care. A red silk handkerchief was frequently applied to the glittering steel, as if to remove from the polished surfaces the least impediment which might exist, to the most delicate operation. After the rather scantily furnished pocket case which contained these instruments was exhausted, the physician turned to his saddlebags and produced various phials, filled with liquids of the most radiant colors. These were arranged in due order, by the side of the murderous saws, knives, and scissors, when Elnathan stretched his long body to its utmost elevation, placing his hand on the small of his back, as if for support, and looked about him to discover what effect this display of professional skill was likely to produce on the spectators.

"Upon my wort, toctor," observed Major Hartmann, with a roguish roll of his little black eyes, but with every other feature of his face in a state of perfect rest, "put you have a very pretty pocketpook of tools tere, and your toctor-stuff glitters as if it was petter for ter eyes as for ter pelly."

Elnathan gave a hem—one that might have been equally taken for that kind of noise which cowards are said to make in order to awaken their dormant courage, or for a natural effort to clear the throat; if for the latter, it was successful; for turning his face to the veteran German, he said:

"Very true, Major Hartmann, very true, sir; a prudent man will always strive to make his remedies agreeable to the eyes, though they may not altogether suit the stomach. It is no small part of our art, sir," and he now spoke with the confidence of a man who understood his subject, "to reconcile the patient to what is for his own good, though at the same time it may be unpalatable."

"Sartain! Dr. Todd is right," said Remarkable, "and has Scripter for what he says. The Bible tells us how things may be sweet to the mouth, and bitter to the inwards."

"True, true," interrupted the Judge, a little impatiently; "but here is a youth who needs no deception to lure him to his own benefit. I see, by his eye, that he fears nothing more than delay."

The stranger had, without assistance, bared his own shoulder, when the slight perforation produced by the passage of the buckshot was plainly visible. The intense cold of the evening had stopped the bleeding, and Dr. Todd, casting a furtive glance at the wound, thought it by no means so formidable an affair as he had anticipated. Thus encouraged he approached his patient and made some indication of an intention to trace the route that had been taken by the lead.

Remarkable often found occasions, in after days, to recount the minutiae of that celebrated operation; and when she arrived at this point she commonly proceeded as follows: "And then the Doctor tuck out of the pocketbook a long thing, like a knitting needle, with a button fastened to the end on't; and then he pushed it into the wownd; and then the young man looked awful; and then I thought I should have swaned away—I felt in sitch a dispu't taking; and then the doctor had run it right through his shoulder, and shoved the bullet out on t'other side; and so Dr. Todd cured the young man—of a ball that the Judge had shot into him, for all the world, as easy as I could pick out a splinter with my darning needle."

Such were the impressions of Remarkable on the subject; and such doubtless were the opinions of most of those who felt it necessary to entertain a species of religious veneration for the skill of Elnathan; but such was far from the truth.

When the physician attempted to introduce the instrument described by Remarkable, he was repulsed by the stranger, with a good deal of decision, and some little contempt, in his manner.

"I believe, sir," he said, "that a probe is not necessary; the shot has missed the bone, and has passed directly through the arm to the opposite side, where it remains but skin-deep, and whence, I should think, it might be easily extracted."

"The gentleman knows best," said Dr. Todd, laying down the probe with the air of a man who had assumed it merely in compliance with forms; and turning to Richard, he fingered the lint with the appearance of great care and foresight. "Admirably well scraped, Squire Jones! It is about the best lint I have ever seen. I want your assistance, my good sir, to hold the patient's arm while I make an incision for the ball. Now, I rather guess there is not another gentleman present who could scrape the lint so well as Squire Jones."

"Such things run in families," observed Richard, rising with alacrity to render the desired assistance. "My father, and my grandfather before him, were both celebrated for their knowledge of surgery; they were not, like Marmaduke here, puffed up with an accidental thing, such as the time when he drew in the hip joint of the man who was thrown from his horse: that was the fall before you came into the settlement, Doctor; but they were men who were taught the thing regularly, spending half their lives in learning those little niceties; though for the matter of that, my grandfather was a college-bred physician, and the best in the colony, too —that is, in his neighborhood."

"So it goes with the world, Squire," cried Benjamin, "if so be that a man wants to walk the quarter-deck with credit, d'ye see, and with regular built swabs on his shoulders, he mustn't think to do it by getting in at the cabin windows. There are two ways to get into a top, besides the lubbershole. The true way to walk aft is to begin forrard; tho'f it be only in a humble way, like myself, d'ye see, which was, from being only a hander of topgallant sails, and a stower of the flying jib, to keeping the key of the Captain's locker."

"Benjamin speaks quite to the purpose," continued Richard. "I dare say that he has often seen shot extracted in the different ships in which he has served; suppose we get him to hold the basin; he must be used to the sight of blood."

"That he is, Squire, that he is," interrupted the *ci-devant* steward. "Many's the good shot, round, double-headed, and grape, that I've seen the doctors at work on. For the matter of that, I was in a boat, alongside the ship, when they cut out the twelve-pound shot from the thigh of the Captain of the Foody-rong, one of Mounsheer Ler Quaw's countrymen!" *

"A twelve-pound ball from the thigh of a human being?" exclaimed Mr. Grant, with great simplicity, dropping the sermon he was again reading and raising his spectacles to the top of his forehead.

"A twelve-pounder!" echoed Benjamin, staring around him with much confidence; "A twelve-pounder! Ay! A twenty-four pound shot can easily be taken from a man's body, if so be a doctor only knows how. There's Squire Jones, now, ask him, sir; he reads all the books; ask him if he never fell in with a page that keeps the reckoning of such things."

"Certainly, more important operations than that have been performed," observed Richard. "The Encyclopædia mentions much more incredible circumstances than that, as, I dare say, you know, Doctor Todd."

"Certainly, there are incredible tales told in the Encyclopaedias," returned Elnathan, "though I cannot say that I have ever seen, myself, anything larger than a musket bullet extracted."

During this discourse an incision had been made through the skin of the young hunter's shoulder, and the lead was laid bare. Elnathan took a pair of glittering forceps, and was in the act of applying them to the wound, when a sudden motion of the patient caused the shot to fall out of itself. The long arm and broad hand of the operator were now of

---

* It is possible that the reader may start at this declaration of Benjamin, but those who have lived in the new settlements of America are too much accustomed to hear of these European exploits to doubt it.

singular service; for the latter expanded itself and caught
the lead, while at the same time, an extremely ambiguous
motion was made by its brother, so as to leave it doubtful to
the spectators how great was its agency in releasing the shot.
Richard, however, put the matter at rest by exclaiming:

"Very neatly done, Doctor! I have never seen a shot more
neatly extracted; and, I dare say, Benjamin will say the
same."

"Why, considering," returned Benjamin, "I must say, that
it was shipshape and Brister-fashion. Now all that the Doctor
has to do is to clap a couple of plugs in the holes, and the
lad will float in any gale that blows in these here hills."

"I thank you, sir, for what you have done," said the youth,
with a little distance; "but here is a man who will take me
under his care, and spare you all, gentlemen, any further
trouble on my account."

The whole group turned their heads in surprise and beheld, standing at one of the distant doors of the hall, the
person of Indian John.

CHAPTER VII

From Susquehanna's utmost springs,
Where savage tribes pursue their game,
His blanket tied with yellow strings,
The shepherd of the forest came.

                                        FRENEAU

BEFORE the Europeans, or, to use a more significant term,
the Christians, dispossessed the original owners of the soil,
all that section of country which contains the New England
States and those of the Middle which lie east of the mountains was occupied by two great nations of Indians, from
whom had descended numberless tribes. But, as the original
distinctions between these nations were marked by a difference in language, as well as by repeated and bloody wars,
they never were known to amalgamate, until after the power
and inroads of the whites had reduced some of the tribes to a
state of dependence that rendered not only their political,

but, considering the wants and habits of a savage, their animal existence also, extremely precarious.

These two great divisions consisted, on the one side, of the Five, or as they were afterwards called, the Six Nations, and their allies; and, on the other, of the Lenni Lenape, or Delawares, with the numerous and powerful tribes that owned that nation as their grandfather. The former were generally called, by the Anglo-Americans, Iroquois, or the Six Nations, and sometimes Mingoes. Their appellation, among their rivals, seems generally to have been the Mengwe, or Maqua. They consisted of the tribes, or, as their allies were fond of asserting, in order to raise their consequence, of the several nations of the Mohawks, the Oneidas, the Onondagas, Cayugas, and Senecas; who ranked, in the confederation, in the order in which they are named. The Tuscaroras were admitted to this union, near a century after its formation, and thus completed the number to six.

Of the Lenni Lenape, or as they were called by the whites, from the circumstance of their holding their great council fire on the banks of that river, the Delaware nation, the principal tribes, besides that which bore the generic name, were the Mahicanni, Mohicans, or Mohegans, and the Nanticokes, or Nentigoes. Of these, the latter held the country along the waters of the Chesapeake and the seashore; while the Mohegans occupied the district between the Hudson and the ocean, including much of New England. Of course, these two tribes were the first who were dispossessed of their lands by the Europeans.

The wars of a portion of the latter are celebrated among us, as the wars of King Philip; but the peaceful policy of William Penn, or Miquon, as he was termed by the natives, effected its object with less difficulty, though not with less certainty. As the natives gradually disappeared from the country of the Mohegans, some scattering families sought a refuge around the council fire of the mother tribe, or the Delawares.

This people had been induced to suffer themselves to be called *women*, by their old enemies, the Mingoes, or Iroquois, after the latter, having in vain tried the effects of hostility, had recourse to artifice, in order to prevail over their rivals. According to this declaration, the Delawares were to cultivate the arts of peace and to entrust their defense entirely to the *men*, or warlike tribes of the Six Nations.

This state of things continued until the war of the revolution, when the Lenni Lenape formally asserted their independence, and fearlessly declared that they were again men. But in a government so peculiarly republican as the Indian polity, it was not at all times an easy task to restrain its members within the rules of the nation. Several fierce and renowned warriors of the Mohegans, finding the conflict with the whites to be in vain, sought a refuge with their grandfather and brought with them the feelings and principles that had so long distinguished them in their own tribe. These chieftains kept alive, in some measure, the martial spirit of the Delawares; and would, at times, lead small parties against their ancient enemies, or such other foes as incurred their resentment.

Among these warriors was one race particularly famous for their prowess, and for those qualities that render an Indian hero celebrated. But war, time, disease, and want had conspired to thin their number; and the sole representative of this once renowned family now stood in the hall of Marmaduke Temple. He had for a long time been an associate of the white men, particularly in their wars; and having been, at a season when his services were of importance, much noticed and flattered, he had turned Christian, and was baptized by the name of John. He had suffered severely in his family during the recent war, having had every soul to whom he was allied cut off by an inroad of the enemy; and when the last, lingering remnant of his nation extinguished their fires, among the hills of the Delaware, he alone had remained, with a determination of laying his bones in that country where his fathers had so long lived and governed.

It was only, however, within a few months, that he had appeared among the mountains that surrounded Templeton. To the hut of the old hunter he seemed peculiarly welcome; and, as the habits of the "Leatherstocking" were so nearly assimilated to those of the savages, the conjunction of their interests excited no surprise. They resided in the same cabin, ate of the same food, and were chiefly occupied in the same pursuits.

We have already mentioned the baptismal name of this ancient chief; but in his conversation with Natty, held in the language of the Delawares, he was heard uniformly to call himself Chingachgook, which, interpreted, means the "Great Snake." This name he had acquired in youth, by his skill and prowess in war; but when his brows began to wrinkle with time, and he stood alone, the last of his family and his particular tribe, the few Delawares who yet continued about the headwaters of their river gave him the mournful appellation of Mohegan. Perhaps there was something of deep feeling excited in the bosom of this inhabitant of the forest by the sound of a name that recalled the idea of his nation in ruins, for he seldom used it himself—never indeed, excepting on the most solemn occasions; but the settlers had united, according to the Christian custom, his baptismal with his national name, and to them he was generally known as John Mohegan or, more familiarly, as Indian John.

From his long association with the white men, the habits of Mohegan were a mixture of the civilized and savage states, though there was certainly a strong preponderance in favor of the latter. In common with all his people who dwelt within the influence of the Anglo-Americans, he had acquired new wants, and his dress was a mixture of his native and European fashions. Notwithstanding the intense cold without, his head was uncovered; but a profusion of long, black, coarse hair concealed his forehead, his crown, and even hung about his cheeks, so as to convey the idea, to one who knew his present and former conditions, that he encouraged its abundance, as a willing veil, to hide the shame of a noble soul, mourning for glory once known. His forehead, when it could be seen, appeared lofty, broad, and noble. His nose was high, and of the kind called Roman, with nostrils that expanded, in his seventieth year, with the freedom that had distinguished them in youth. His mouth was large, but compressed, and possessing a great share of expression and character; and, when opened, it discovered a perfect set of short, strong, and regular teeth. His chin was full, though not prominent; and his face bore the infallible mark of his people, in its square, high cheekbones. The eyes were not large, but their black orbs glittered in the rays of the candles, as he gazed intently down the hall, like two balls of fire.

The instant that Mohegan observed himself to be noticed by the group around the young stranger, he dropped the blanket which covered the upper part of his frame, from his shoulders, suffering it to fall over his leggings of untanned deer-skin, where it was retained by a belt of bark that confined it to his waist.

As he walked slowly down the long hall, the dignified and deliberate tread of the Indian surprised the spectators. His shoulders, and body to his waist, were entirely bare, with the exception of a silver medallion of Washington that was suspended from his neck by a thong of buckskin, and rested on his high chest, amidst many scars. His shoulders were rather broad and full; but the arms, though straight and graceful, wanted the muscular appearance that labor gives to a race of men. The medallion was the only ornament he wore, although enormous slits in the rim of either ear, which suffered the cartilages to fall two inches below the members, had evidently been used for the purposes of decoration in other days. In his hand he held a small basket of the ash-wood slips, colored in divers fantastical conceits, with red and black paints mingled with the white of the wood.

As this child of the forest approached them, the whole party stood aside and allowed him to confront the object of his visit. He did not speak, however, but stood fixing his glowing eyes on the shoulder of the young hunter, and then turning them intently on the countenance of the Judge. The latter was a good deal astonished at this unusual departure from the ordinarily subdued and quiet manner of the Indian; but he extended his hand, and said:

"Thou art welcome, John. This youth entertains a high opinion of thy skill, it seems, for he prefers thee to dress his wound even to our good friend, Dr. Todd."

Mohegan now spoke, in tolerable English, but in a low, monotonous, guttural tone:

"The children of Miquon do not love the sight of blood; and yet the Young Eagle has been struck by the hand that should do no evil!"

"Mohegan! Old John!" exclaimed the Judge. "Thinkest thou that my hand has ever drawn human blood willingly? For shame! For shame, old John! Thy religion should have taught thee better."

"The evil spirit sometimes lives in the best heart," returned John, "but my brother speaks the truth; his hand has never taken life, when awake. No! Not even when the children of the great English Father were making the waters red with the blood of his people."

"Surely, John," said Mr. Grant, with much earnestness, "you remember the divine command of our Saviour, 'Judge not, lest ye be judged.' What motive could Judge Temple have for injuring a youth like this; one to whom he is unknown, and from whom he can receive neither injury nor favor!"

John listened respectfully to the divine, and when he had concluded, he stretched out his arm, and said with energy—

"He is innocent—my brother has not done this."

Marmaduke received the offered hand of the other with a smile that showed however he might be astonished at his suspicion, he had ceased to resent it; while the wounded youth stood, gazing from his red friend to his host, with interest powerfully delineated in his countenance. No sooner was this act of pacification exchanged than John proceeded to discharge the duty on which he had come. Dr. Todd was far from manifesting any displeasure at this invasion of his rights, but made way for the new leech with an air that expressed a willingness to gratify the humors of his patient, now that the all-important part of the business was so successfully performed, and nothing remained to be done but what any child might effect. Indeed, he whispered as much to Monsieur Le Quoi, when he said:

"It was fortunate that the ball was extracted before this Indian came in; but any old woman can dress the wound. The young man, I hear, lives with John and Natty Bumppo, and it's always best to humor a patient, when it can be done discreetly—I say, discreetly, monsieur."

"Certainement," returned the Frenchman; "you seem ver happy, Mister Todd, in your pratique. I tink the elder lady might ver well finish vat you so skeelfully begin."

But Richard had, at the bottom, a great deal of veneration for the knowledge of Mohegan, especially in external wounds; and retaining all his desire for a participation in glory, he advanced nigh the Indian, and said:

"Sago, sago, Mohegan! Sago, my good fellow! I am glad you have come; give me a regular physician, like Dr. Todd, to cut into flesh, and a native to heal the wound. Do you remember, John, the time when I and you set the bone of Natty Bumppo's little finger, after he broke it by falling from the rock, when he was trying to get the partridge that fell on the cliffs. I never could tell yet, whether it was I or Natty who killed that bird: he fired first, and the bird stooped, and then it was rising again as I pulled trigger. I should have claimed it, for a certainty, but Natty said the hole was too big for shot, and he fired a single ball from his rifle; but the piece I carried then didn't scatter, and I have known it to bore a hole through a board, when I've been shooting at a mark, very much like rifle bullets. Shall I help you, John? You know I have a knack at these things."

Mohegan heard this disquisition quite patiently, and when Richard concluded, he held out the basket which contained his specifics, indicating, by a gesture, that he might hold it. Mr. Jones was quite satisfied with this commission; and, ever after, in speaking of the event, was used to say, that "Doctor Todd and I cut out the bullet, and I and Indian John dressed the wound."

The patient was much more deserving of that epithet while under the hands of Mohegan than while suffering under the practice of the physician. Indeed, the Indian gave him but little opportunity for the exercise of a forbearing temper, as he had come prepared for the occasion. His dressings were soon applied, and consisted only of some pounded bark, moistened with a fluid that he had expressed from some of the simples of the woods.

Among the native tribes of the forest, there were always two kinds of leeches to be met with. The one placed its whole dependence on the exercise of a supernatural power and was held in greater veneration than their practice could at all justify; but the other was really endowed with great skill in the ordinary complaints of the human body and was more particularly, as Natty had intimated, "curious in cuts and bruises."

While John and Richard were placing the dressings on the wound, Elnathan was acutely eying the contents of Mohegan's basket, which Mr. Jones, in his physical ardor, had transferred to the Doctor, in order to hold, himself, one end of the bandages. Here he was soon enabled to detect sundry fragments of wood and bark, of which he, quite coolly, took possession, very possibly without any intention of speaking at all upon the subject; but when he beheld the full blue eye of Marmaduke watching his movements, he whispered to the Judge:

"It is not to be denied, Judge Temple, but what the savages are knowing in small matters of physic. They hand these things down in their traditions. Now in cancers and hydrophoby, they are quite ingenious. I will just take this bark home and analyze it; for, though it can't be worth sixpence to the young man's shoulder, it may be good for the toothache, or rheumatism, or some of them complaints. A man should never be above learning, even if it be from an Indian."

It was fortunate for Dr. Todd that his principles were so liberal, as, coupled with his practice, they were the means by which he acquired all his knowledge, and by which he was gradually qualifying himself for the duties of his profession. The process to which he subjected the specific differed, however, greatly from the ordinary rules of chemistry; for, instead of separating, he afterwards united the component parts of Mohegan's remedy, and thus was able to discover the tree whence the Indian had taken it.

Some ten years after this event, when civilization and its refinements had crept, or rather rushed, into the settlements among these wild hills, an affair of honor occurred, and Elnathan was seen to apply a salve to the wound received by one of the parties, which had the flavor that was peculiar to the tree, or root, that Mohegan had used. Ten years later still, when England and the United States were again engaged in war, and the hordes of the western parts of the state of New York were rushing to the field, Elnathan, presuming on the reputation obtained by these two operations, followed in the rear of a brigade of militia as its surgeon.

When Mohegan had applied the bark, he freely relinquished to Richard the needle and thread that were used in sewing the bandages, for these were implements of which the native but little understood the use; and, stepping back, with decent gravity, awaited the completion of the business by the other.

"Reach me the scissors," said Mr. Jones, when he had finished, and finished for the second time, after tying the linen in every shape and form that it could be placed; "reach me the scissors, for here is a thread that must be cut off, or it might get under the dressings and inflame the wound. See, John, I have put the lint I scraped between two layers of the linen; for though the bark is certainly best for the flesh, yet the lint will serve to keep the cold air from the wound. If any lint will do it good, it is this lint; I scraped it myself, and I will not turn my back at scraping lint to any man on the Patent. I ought to know how, if anybody ought, for my grandfather was a doctor, and my father had a natural turn that way."

"Here, Squire, is the scissors," said Remarkable, producing from beneath her petticoat of green moreen a pair of dull-looking shears. "Well, upon my say-so, you *have* sewed on the rags as well as a woman."

"As well as a woman!" echoed Richard, with indignation. "What do women know of such matters? And you are proof of the truth of what I say. Who ever saw such a pair of shears used about a wound? Dr. Todd, I will thank you for the scissors from the case. Now, young man, I think you'll do. The shot has been very neatly taken out, although perhaps, seeing I had a hand in it, I ought not to say so; and the wound is admirably dressed. You will soon be well again; though the jerk you gave my leaders must have a tendency to inflame the shoulder, yet you will do, you will do. You were rather flurried, I suppose, and not used to horses; but I forgive the accident for the motive—no doubt you had the best of motives—yes, now you will do."

"Then, gentlemen," said the wounded stranger, rising, and resuming his clothes, "it will be unnecessary for me to trespass longer on your time and patience. There remains but one thing more to be settled, and that is, our respective rights to the deer, Judge Temple."

"I acknowledge it to be thine," said Marmaduke; "and much more deeply am I indebted to thee than for this piece of venison. But in the morning thou wilt call here, and we can adjust this, as well as more important matters. Elizabeth," —for the young lady, being apprised that the wound was dressed, had re-entered the hall,—"thou wilt order a repast for this youth before we proceed to the church; and Aggy will have a sleigh prepared, to convey him to his friend."

"But, sir, I cannot go without a part of the deer," returned the youth, seemingly struggling with his own feelings; "I have already told you that I needed the venison for myself."

"Oh! We will not be particular," exclaimed Richard; "the Judge will pay you in the morning for the whole deer; and

Remarkable, give the lad all the animal excepting the saddle; so, on the whole, I think you may consider yourself as a very lucky young man—you have been shot without being disabled; have had the wound dressed in the best possible manner here in the woods, as well as it would have been done in the Philadelphia hospital, if not better; have sold your deer at a high price, and yet can keep most of the carcass, with the skin in the bargain. 'Marky, tell Tom to give him the skin, too; and in the morning bring the skin to me, and I will give you half a dollar for it, or at least three and sixpence. I want just such a skin to cover the pillion that I am making for cousin Bess."

"I thank you, sir, for your liberality, and, I trust, am also thankful for my escape," returned the stranger; "but you reserve the very part of the animal that I wished for my own use. I must have the saddle myself."

"Must!" echoed Richard; "Must is harder to be swallowed than the horns of the buck."

"Yes, must," repeated the youth, when, turning his head proudly around him, as if to see who would dare to controvert his rights, he met the astonished gaze of Elizabeth and proceeded more mildly—"that is, if a man is allowed the possession of that which his hand hath killed, and the law will protect him in the enjoyment of his own."

"The law will do so," said Judge Temple, with an air of mortification mingled with surprise. "Benjamin, see that the whole deer is placed in the sleigh; and have this youth conveyed to the hut of Leatherstocking. But, young man, thou hast a name, and I shall see you again, in order to compensate thee for the wrong I have done thee?"

"I am called Edwards," returned the hunter; "Oliver Edwards. I am easily to be seen, sir, for I live nigh by, and am not afraid to show my face, having never injured any man."

"It is we who have injured you, sir," said Elizabeth; "and the knowledge that you decline our assistance would give my father great pain. He would gladly see you in the morning."

The young hunter gazed at the fair speaker until his earnest look brought the blood to her temples; when, recollecting himself, he bent his head, dropping his eyes to the carpet, and replied:

"In the morning, then, will I return, and see Judge Temple;

and I will accept his offer of the sleigh, in token of amity."

"Amity!" repeated Marmaduke; "There was no malice in the act that injured thee, young man; there should be none in the feelings which it may engender."

"Forgive our trespasses as we forgive those who trespass against us," observed Mr. Grant, "is the language used by our Divine Master himself, and it should be the golden rule of us, his humble followers."

The stranger stood a moment, lost in thought, and then glancing his dark eyes rather wildly around the hall, he bowed low to the divine, and moved from the apartment, with an air that would not admit of detention.

" 'Tis strange that one so young should harbor such feelings of resentment," said Marmaduke, when the door closed behind the stranger; "but while the pain is recent, and the sense of the injury so fresh, he must feel more strongly than in cooler moments. I doubt not we shall see him in the morning more tractable."

Elizabeth, to whom this speech was addressed, did not reply, but moved slowly up the hall, by herself, fixing her eyes on the little figure of the English ingrained carpet that covered the floor; while, on the other hand, Richard gave a loud crack with his whip, as the stranger disappeared, and cried—

"Well, 'duke, you are your own master, but I would have tried law for the saddle, before I would have given it to the fellow. Do you not own the mountains as well as the valleys? Are not the woods your own? What right has this chap, or the Leatherstocking, to shoot in your woods without your permission? Now, I have known a farmer in Pennsylvania order a sportsman off his farm with as little ceremony as I would order Benjamin to put a log in the stove. By the by, Benjamin, see how the thermometer stands. Now, if a man has a right to do this on a farm of a hundred acres, what power must a landlord have who owns sixty thousand—aye, for the matter of that, including the late purchases, a hundred thousand? There is Mohegan, to be sure, he may have some right, being a native; but it's little the poor fellow can do now with his rifle. How is this managed in France, Monsieur Le Quoi? Do you let everybody run over your land in that country, helter-skelter, as they do here, shooting the game, so that a gentleman has but little or no chance with his gun?"

"Bah! Diable, no, Meester Deeck," replied the Frenchman. "We give, in France, no liberty, except to the ladi."

"Yes, yes, to the women, I know," said Richard, "that is your Salic law. I read, sir, all kinds of books; of France, as well as England; of Greece, as well as Rome. But if I were in 'duke's place, I would stick up advertisements tomorrow morning, forbidding all persons to shoot, or trespass in any manner, on my woods. I could write such an advertisement myself, in an hour, as would put a stop to the thing at once."

"Richart," said Major Hartmann, very coolly knocking the ashes from his pipe into the spitting box by his side, "now listen; I have livet seventy-five years on ter Mohawk, and in ter woots.—You hat petter mettle as mit ter deyvel, as mit ter hunters. Tey live mit ter gun, and a rifle is petter as ter law."

"A'nt Marmaduke a judge?" said Richard, indignantly. "Where is the use of being a judge, or having a judge, if there is no law? Damn the fellow! I have a great mind to sue him in the morning myself, before Squire Doolittle, for meddling with my leaders. I am not afraid of his rifle. I can shoot, too. I have hit a dollar many a time at fifty rods."

"Thou hast missed more dollars than ever thou hast hit, Dickon," exclaimed the cheerful voice of the Judge. "But we will now take our evening's repast, which, I perceive by Remarkable's physiognomy, is ready. Monsieur Le Quoi, Miss Temple has a hand at your service. Will you lead the way, my child?"

"Ah! ma chère Mam'selle, comme je suis enchanté!" said the Frenchman. "Il ne manque que les dames de faire un paradis de Templeton."

Mr. Grant and Mohegan continued in the hall, while the remainder of the party withdrew to an eating parlor, if we except Benjamin, who civilly remained, to close the rear after the clergyman and to open the front door for the exit of the Indian.

"John," said the divine, when the figure of Judge Temple disappeared, the last of the group, "tomorrow is the festival of the nativity of our blessed Redeemer, when the church has appointed prayers and thanksgivings to be offered up by her children, and when all are invited to partake of the mystical elements. As you have taken up the cross and become a follower of good and an eschewer of evil, I trust I shall see you before the altar, with a contrite heart and a meek spirit."

"John will come," said the Indian, betraying no surprise; though he did not understand all the terms used by the other.

"Yes," continued Mr. Grant, laying his hand gently on the tawny shoulder of the aged chief, "but it is not enough to be there in the body; you must come in the spirit and in truth. The Redeemer died for all, for the poor Indian as well as for the white man. Heaven knows no difference in color; nor must earth witness a separation of the church. It is good and profitable, John, to freshen the understanding, and support the wavering, by the observance of our holy festivals; but all form is but stench in the nostrils of the Holy One, unless it be accompanied by a devout and humble spirit."

The Indian stepped back a little, and, raising his body to its utmost powers of erection, he stretched his right arm on high, and dropped his forefinger downward, as if pointing from the heavens, then striking his other hand on his naked breast, he said, with energy:

"The eye of the Great Spirit can see from the clouds;— the bosom of Mohegan is bare!"

"It is well, John, and I hope you will receive profit and consolation from the performance of this duty. The Great Spirit overlooks none of his children; and the man of the woods is as much an object of his care as he who dwells in a palace. I wish you a good night, and pray God to bless you."

The Indian bent his head, and they separated—the one to seek his hut, and the other to join the party at the supper table. While Benjamin was opening the door for the passage of the chief, he cried, in a tone that was meant to be encouraging:

"The parson says the word that is true, John. If so be that they took count of the color of the skin in heaven, why they might refuse to muster on their books a Christian-born, like myself, just for the matter of a little tan, from cruising in warm latitudes; though, for the matter of that, this damned

nor'wester is enough to whiten the skin of a blackamore. Let
the reef out of your blanket, man, or your red hide will hardly weather the night, without a touch from the frost."

CHAPTER VIII

For here the exile met from every clime,
And spoke, in friendship, every distant tongue. CAMPBELL

WE have made our readers acquainted with some variety in
character and nations in introducing the most important personages of this legend to their notice; but, in order to establish the fidelity of our narrative, we shall briefly attempt
to explain the reason why we have been obliged to present
so motley a dramatis personae.

Europe, at the period of our tale, was in the commencement of that commotion which afterwards shook her political institutions to the center. Louis the Sixteenth had been
beheaded, and a nation once esteemed the most refined among the civilized people of the world was changing
its character, and substituting cruelty for mercy, and subtlety
and ferocity for magnanimity and courage. Thousands of
Frenchmen were compelled to seek protection in distant
lands. Among the crowds who fled from France and her
islands to the United States of America was the gentleman
whom we have already mentioned as Monsieur Le Quoi. He
had been recommended to the favor of Judge Temple by the
head of an eminent mercantile house in New York, with
whom Marmaduke was in habits of intimacy and accustomed
to exchange good offices. At his first interview with the
Frenchman, our Judge had discovered him to be a man of
breeding, and one who had seen much more prosperous
days in his own country. From certain hints that had escaped
him, Monsieur Le Quoi was suspected of having been a
West India planter, great numbers of whom had fled from
St. Domingo and the other islands and were now living in
the Union in a state of comparative poverty, and some in
absolute want. The latter was not, however, the lot of Monsieur Le Quoi. He had but little, he acknowledged; but that

little was enough to furnish, in the language of the country, an assortment for a store.

The knowledge of Marmaduke was eminently practical, and there was no part of a *settler's* life with which he was not familiar. Under his direction, Monsieur Le Quoi made some purchases, consisting of a few cloths; some groceries, with a good deal of gunpowder and tobacco; a quantity of ironware, among which was a large proportion of Barlow's jackknives, potash kettles, and spiders; a very formidable collection of crockery, of the coarsest quality and most uncouth forms; together with every other common article that the art of man has devised for his wants, not forgetting the luxuries of looking glasses and jew's harps. With this collection of valuables, Monsieur Le Quoi had stepped behind a counter, and, with a wonderful pliability of temperament, had dropped into his assumed character as gracefully as he had ever moved in any other. The gentleness and suavity of his manners rendered him extremely popular; besides this, the women soon discovered that he had a taste. His calicoes were the finest, or, in other words, the most showy, of any that were brought into the country; and it was impossible to look at the prices asked for his goods by "so pretty a spoken man." Through these conjoint means, the affairs of Monsieur Le Quoi were again in a prosperous condition, and he was looked up to by the settlers as the second-best man on the "Patent."

The term "Patent," which we have already used, and for which we may have further occasion, meant the district of country that had been originally granted to old Major Effingham by the "king's letters patent," and which had now become, by purchase under the act of confiscation, the property of Marmaduke Temple. It was a term in common use throughout the *new* parts of the state; and was usually annexed to the landlord's name as "Temple's or Effingham's Patent."

Major Hartmann was the descendant of a man who, in company with a number of his countrymen, had emigrated, with their families, from the banks of the Rhine to those of the Mohawk. This migration had occurred as far back as the reign of Queen Anne; and their descendants were now living, in great peace and plenty, on the fertile borders of that beautiful stream.

The Germans, or "High Dutchers," as they were called to distinguish them from the original or Low Dutch colonists, were a very peculiar people. They possessed all the gravity of the latter, without any of their phlegm; and, like them, the "High Dutchers" were industrious, honest, and economical.

Fritz, or Frederick Hartmann, was an epitome of all the vices and virtues, foibles and excellences, of his race. He was passionate, though silent, obstinate, and a good deal suspicious of strangers; of immovable courage, inflexible honesty, and undeviating in his friendships. Indeed there was no change about him, unless it were from grave to gay. He was serious by months, and jolly by weeks. He had, early in their acquaintance, formed an attachment for Marmaduke Temple, who was the only man that could not speak High Dutch that ever gained his entire confidence. Four times in each year, at periods equidistant, he left his low stone dwelling on the banks of the Mohawk and traveled thirty miles, through the hills, to the door of the mansion house in Templeton. Here he generally stayed a week; and was reputed to spend much of that time in riotous living, greatly countenanced by Mr. Richard Jones. But everyone loved him, even to Remarkable Pettibone, to whom he occasioned some additional trouble, he was so frank, so sincere, and, at times, so mirthful. He was now on his regular Christmas visit, and had not been in the village an hour when Richard summoned him to fill a seat in the sleigh, to meet the landlord and his daughter.

Before explaining the character and situation of Mr. Grant, it will be necessary to recur to times far back in the brief history of the settlement.

There seems to be a tendency in human nature to endeavor to provide for the wants of this world before our attention is turned to the business of the other. Religion was a quality but little cultivated amid the stumps of Temple's Patent for the first few years of its settlement; but, as most of its inhabitants were from the moral states of Connecticut and Massachusetts, when the wants of nature were satisfied, they began seriously to turn their attention to the introduction of those customs and observances which had been the principal care of their forefathers. There was certainly a great variety of opinions on the subject of grace and free will among the tenantry of Marmaduke; and, when we take into consideration the variety of the religious instruction which they received, it can easily be seen that it could not well be otherwise.

Soon after the village had been formally laid out into the streets and *blocks* that resembled a city, a meeting of its inhabitants had been convened to take into consideration the propriety of establishing an academy. This measure originated with Richard, who, in truth, was much disposed to have the institution designated a university, or at least a college. Meeting after meeting was held, for this purpose, year after year. The *resolutions* of these assemblages appeared in the most conspicuous columns of a little, blue-looking newspaper, that was already issued weekly from the garret of a dwelling house in the village, and which the traveler might as often see stuck into the fissure of a stake, erected at the point where the footpath from the log cabin of some settler entered the highway, as a post office for an individual. Sometimes the stake supported a small box, and a whole neighborhood received a weekly supply for their literary wants, at this point, where the man who "rides post" regularly deposited a bundle of the precious commodity. To these flourishing resolutions, which briefly recounted the general utility of education, the political and geographical rights of the village of Templeton to a participation in the favors of the regents of the university, the salubrity of the air, and wholesomeness of the water, together with the cheapness of food and the superior state of morals in the neighborhood, were uniformly annexed, in large Roman capitals, the names of Marmaduke Temple as chairman and Richard Jones as Secretary.

Happily for the success of this undertaking, the regents were not accustomed to resist these appeals to their generosity, whenever there was the smallest prospect of a donation to second the request. Eventually Judge Temple concluded to bestow the necessary land and to erect the required edifice at his own expense. The skill of Mr., or, as he was now called, from the circumstance of having received the commission of a justice of the peace, Squire Doolittle, was again put in requisition; and the science of Mr. Jones was once more resorted to.

We shall not recount the different devices of the architects on the occasion; nor would it be decorous so to do, seeing that there was a convocation of the society of the ancient and honorable fraternity "of the Free and Accepted Masons," at the head of whom was Richard in the capacity of master, doubtless to approve or reject such of the plans as, in their wisdom, they deemed to be for the best. The knotty point was, however, soon decided; and, on the appointed day, the brotherhood marched in great state, displaying sundry banners and mysterious symbols, each man with a little mimic apron before him, from a most cunningly contrived apartment in the garret of the "Bold Dragoon," an inn kept by one Captain Hollister, to the site of the intended edifice. Here Richard laid the cornerstone, with suitable gravity, amidst an assemblage of more than half the men, and all the women, within ten miles of Templeton.

In the course of the succeeding week there was another meeting of the people, not omitting swarms of the gentler sex, when the abilities of Hiram at the "square rule" were put to the test of experiment. The frame fitted well; and the skeleton of the fabric was reared without a single accident, if we except a few falls from horses while the laborers were returning home in the evening. From this time the work advanced with great rapidity, and in the course of the season the labor was completed; the edifice standing, in all its beauty and proportions, the boast of the village, the study of young aspirants for architectural fame, and the admiration of every settler on the Patent.

It was a long, narrow house of wood, painted white, and more than half windows; and when the observer stood at the western side of the building, the edifice offered but a small obstacle to a full view of the rising sun. It was, in truth, but a very comfortless open place, through which the daylight shone with natural facility. On its front were divers ornaments in wood, designed by Richard, and executed by Hiram; but a window in the center of the second story, immediately over the door or grand entrance, and the "steeple" were the pride of the building. The former was, we believe, of the composite order; for it included in its composition a multitude of ornaments and a great variety of proportions. It consisted of an arched compartment in the center, with a square and small division on either side, the whole encased in heavy frames, deeply and laboriously molded in pine wood, and lighted with a vast number of blurred and green-looking glass, of those dimensions which are commonly called "eight by ten." Blinds, that were intended to be painted green, kept the window in a state of preservation; and probably might have contributed to the effect of the whole, had not the failure in the public funds, which seems always to be incidental to any undertaking of this kind, left them in the somber coat of lead color with which they had been originally clothed. The "steeple" was a little cupola, reared on the very center of the roof, on four tall pillars of pine, that were fluted with a gouge and loaded with moldings. On the tops of the columns was reared a dome or cupola, resembling in shape an inverted teacup without its bottom, from the center of which projected a spire, or shaft of wood, transfixed with two iron rods that bore on their ends the letters N. S. E. and W. in the same metal. The whole was surmounted by an imitation of one of the finny tribe, carved in wood by the hands of Richard, and painted what he called a "scale color." This animal Mr. Jones affirmed to be an admirable resemblance of a great favorite of the epicures in that country, which bore the title of "lake fish"; and doubtless the assertion was true, for, although intended to answer the purposes of a weathercock, the fish was observed invariably to look, with a longing eye, in the direction of the beautiful sheet of water that lay imbedded in the mountains of Templeton.

For a short time after the charter of the regents was received, the trustees of this institution employed a graduate of one of the eastern colleges to instruct such youth as aspired to knowledge within the walls of the edifice which we have described. The upper part of the building was in one apartment and was intended for gala days and exhibitions; and the lower contained two rooms that were intended for the great divisions of education, viz., the Latin and the English scholars. The former were never very numerous; though the sounds of "nominative, *pennaa*—genitive, *penny*," were soon heard to issue from the windows of the room, to the great delight and manifest edification of the passenger.

Only one laborer in this temple of Minerva, however, was known to get so far as to attempt a translation of Virgil. He, indeed, appeared at the annual exhibition, to the prodigious exultation of all his relatives, a farmer's family in

the vicinity, and repeated the whole of the first eclogue
from memory, observing the intonations of the dialogue
with much judgment and effect. The sounds, as they proceeded from his mouth, of

"Titty-ree too patty-lee ree-coo-bans sub teg-mi-nee faa-gy
Syl-ves-trem ten-oo-i moo-sam, med-i-taa-ris, aa-ve-ny"—

were the last that had been heard in that building, as probably they were the first that had ever been heard, in the
same language, there or anywhere else. By this time the
trustees discovered that they had anticipated the age, and
the *instructor,* or *principal,* was superseded by a *master,* who
went on to teach the more humble lesson of "the more
haste the worse speed," in good, plain English.

From this time, until the date of our incidents, the
academy was a common country school, and the great room
of the building was sometimes used as a courtroom, on
extraordinary trials; sometimes for conferences of the religious and the morally disposed, in the evening; at others
for a ball, in the afternoon, given under the auspices of
Richard; and on Sundays, invariably, as a place of public
worship.

When an itinerant priest of the persuasion of the Metho-
dists, Baptists, Universalists, or of the more numerous sect
of the Presbyterians, was accidentally in the neighborhood,
he was ordinarily invited to officiate, and was commonly rewarded for his services by a collection in a hat, before the
congregation separated. When no such regular minister offered, a kind of colloquial prayer or two was made by some
of the more gifted members, and a sermon was usually
read, from Sterne, by Mr. Richard Jones.

The consequence of this desultory kind of priesthood was,
as we have already intimated, a great diversity of opinion
on the more abstruse points of faith. Each sect had its adherents, though neither was regularly organized and disciplined. Of the religious education of Marmaduke we have
already written, nor was the doubtful character of his faith
completely removed by his marriage. The mother of Elizabeth was an Episcopalian, as, indeed, was the mother of
the Judge himself; and the good taste of Marmaduke revolted
at the familiar colloquies which the leaders of the con-

ferences held with the Deity, in their nightly meetings. In form, he was certainly an Episcopalian, though not a sectary of that denomination. On the other hand, Richard was as rigid in the observance of the canons of his church as he was inflexible in his opinions. Indeed, he had once or twice essayed to introduce the Episcopal form of service on the Sundays that the pulpit was vacant; but Richard was a good deal addicted to carrying things to an excess, and then there was something so papal in his air, that the greater part of his hearers deserted him on the second Sabbath—on the third his only auditor was Ben Pump, who had all the obstinate and enlightened orthodoxy of a high churchman.

Before the war of the revolution, the English church was supported in the colonies with much interest by some of its adherents in the mother country, and a few of the congregations were very amply endowed. But, for a season, after the independence of the States was established, this sect of Christians languished, for the want of the highest order of its priesthood. Pious and suitable divines were at length selected and sent to the mother country to receive that authority, which, it is understood, can only be transmitted directly from one to the other, and thus obtain, in order to preserve, that unity in their churches which properly belonged to a people of the same nation. But unexpected difficulties presented themselves in the oaths with which the policy of England had fettered their establishment; and much time was spent before a conscientious sense of duty would permit the prelates of Britain to delegate the authority so earnestly sought. Time, patience, and zeal, however, removed every impediment; and the venerable men, who had been set apart by the American churches, at length returned to their expecting dioceses, endowed with the most elevated functions of their earthly church. Priests and deacons were ordained, and missionaries provided, to keep alive the expiring flame of devotion in such members as were deprived of the ordinary administrations by dwelling in new and unorganized districts.

Of this number was Mr. Grant. He had been sent into the county of which Templeton was the capital, and had been kindly invited by Marmaduke, and officiously pressed by Richard, to take up his abode in the village. A small and humble dwelling was prepared for his family, and the divine had made his appearance in the place but a few days previously to the time of his introduction to the reader. As his forms were entirely new to most of the inhabitants, and a clergyman of another denomination had previously occupied the field by engaging the academy, the first Sunday after his arrival was suffered to pass in silence; but now that his rival had passed on, like a meteor, filling the air with the light of his wisdom, Richard was empowered to give notice that "Public worship, after the forms of the Protestant Episcopal Church, would be held on the night before Christmas, in the long room of the academy in Templeton, by the Rev. Mr. Grant."

This annunciation excited great commotion among the different sectaries. Some wondered as to the nature of the exhibition; others sneered; but a far greater part, recollecting the essays of Richard in that way, and mindful of the liberality, or rather laxity of Marmaduke's notions on the subject of sectarianism, thought it most prudent to be silent.

The expected evening was, however, the wonder of the hour; nor was the curiosity at all diminished, when Richard and Benjamin, on the morning of the eventful day, were seen to issue from the woods in the neighborhood of the village, each bearing on his shoulders a large bunch of evergreens. This worthy pair was observed to enter the academy, and carefully to fasten the door, after which their proceedings remained a profound secret to the rest of the village; Mr. Jones, before he commenced this mysterious business, having informed the schoolmaster, to the great delight of the white-headed flock he governed, that there could be no school that day. Marmaduke was apprised of all these preparations, by letter, and it was especially arranged, that he and Elizabeth should arrive in season, to participate in the solemnities of the evening.

After this digression, we shall return to our narrative.

CHAPTER IX

Now all admire, in each high-flavored dish,
The capabilities of flesh—fowl—fish;
In order due each guest assumes his station,
Throbs high his breast with fond anticipation,
And prelibates the joys of mastication.

HELIOGABALIAD

THE apartment to which Monsieur Le Quoi handed Eliza-beth communicated with the hall, through the door that led under the urn which was supposed to contain the ashes of Dido. The room was spacious, and of very just propor-tions; but in its ornaments and furniture, the same diversity of taste and imperfection of execution were to be observed as existed in the hall. Of furniture, there were a dozen green, wooden armchairs, with cushions of moreen, taken from the same piece as the petticoat of Remarkable. The tables were spread, and their materials and workmanship could not be seen; but they were heavy, and of great size. An enormous mirror in a gilt frame hung against the wall, and a cheerful fire, of the hard or sugar maple, was burning on the hearth. The latter was the first object that struck the attention of the Judge, who, on beholding it, exclaimed, rather angrily, to Richard:

"How often have I forbidden the use of the sugar maple in my dwelling! The sight of that sap, as it exudes with the heat, is painful to me, Richard. Really, it behoves the owner of woods so extensive as mine to be cautious what example he sets his people, who are already felling the forests as if no end could be found to their treasures, nor any limits to their extent. If we go on in this way, twenty years hence we shall want fuel."

"Fuel in these hills, cousin 'duke!" exclaimed Richard, in derision—"Fuel! Why, you might as well predict that the fish will die for the want of water in the lake, because I intend, when the frost gets out of the ground, to lead one or two of the springs, through logs, into the village. But you are always a little wild on such subjects, Marmaduke."

"Is it wildness," returned the Judge, earnestly, "to condemn a practice which devotes these jewels of the forest, these precious gifts of nature, these mines of comfort and wealth, to the common uses of a fireplace? But I must, and will, the instant the snow is off the earth, send out a party into the mountains to explore for coal."

"Coal!" echoed Richard; "Who the devil do you think will dig for coal, when in hunting for a bushel he would have to rip up more roots of trees than would keep him in fuel for a twelvemonth? Poh! poh! Marmaduke, you should leave the management of these things to me, who have a natural turn that way. It was I that ordered this fire, and a noble one it is, to warm the blood of my pretty cousin Bess."

"The motive, then, must be your apology, Dickon," said the Judge. "But, gentlemen, we are waiting. Elizabeth, my child, take the head of the table; Richard, I see, means to spare me the trouble of carving, by sitting opposite to you."

"To be sure I do," cried Richard; "here is a turkey to carve; and I flatter myself that I understand carving a turkey, or, for that matter, a goose, as well as any man alive. Mr. Grant! Where's Mr. Grant? Will you please to say grace, sir? Everything is getting cold. Take a thing from the fire, this cold weather, and it will freeze in five minutes. Mr. Grant! We want you to say grace. 'For what we are about to receive, the Lord make us thankful.' Come, sit down, sit down. Do you eat wing or breast, cousin Bess?"

But Elizabeth had not taken her seat, nor was she in readiness to receive either the wing or breast. Her laughing eyes were glancing at the arrangements of the table and the quality and selection of the food. The eyes of the father soon met the wondering looks of his daughter, and he said, with a smile:

"You perceive, my child, how much we are indebted to Remarkable for her skill in housewifery; she has indeed provided a noble repast; such as well might stop the cravings of hunger."

"Law!" said Remarkable, "I'm glad if the Judge is pleased; but I'm notional that you'll find the sa'ce overdone. I thought, as Elizabeth was coming home, that a body could do no less than make things agreeable."

"My daughter has now grown to woman's estate, and is from this moment mistress of my house," said the Judge;

"it is proper that all who live with me address her as Miss Temple."

"*Do* tell!" exclaimed Remarkable, a little aghast; "Well, who ever heerd of a young woman's being called Miss? If the Judge had a wife now, I shouldn't think of calling her anything but Miss Temple; but——"

"Having nothing but a daughter, you will observe that style to her, if you please, in future," interrupted Marmaduke.

As the Judge looked seriously displeased, and, at such moments, carried a particularly commanding air with him, the wary housekeeper made no reply; and, Mr. Grant entering the room, the whole party were soon seated at the table. As the arrangements of this repast were much in the prevailing taste of that period and country, we shall endeavor to give a short description of the appearance of the banquet.

The table linen was of the most beautiful damask, and the plates and dishes of real china, an article of great luxury at this early period in American commerce. The knives and forks were of exquisitely polished steel, and were set in unclouded ivory. So much, being furnished by the wealth of Marmaduke, was not only comfortable, but even elegant. The contents of the several dishes, and their positions, however, were the result of the sole judgment of Remarkable. Before Elizabeth was placed an enormous roasted turkey, and before Richard, one boiled. In the center of the table stood a pair of heavy silver casters, surrounded by four dishes; one a fricassee that consisted of gray squirrels; another of fish fried; a third of fish boiled; the last was a venison steak. Between these dishes and the turkeys stood, on the one side, a prodigious chine of roasted bear's meat, and on the other a boiled leg of delicious mutton. Interspersed among this load of meats was every species of vegetables that the season and country afforded. The four corners were garnished with plates of cake. On one was piled certain curiously twisted and complicated figures called "nutcakes." On another were heaps of a black-looking substance, which, receiving its hue from molasses, was properly termed "sweet cake," a wonderful favorite in the coterie of Remarkable. A third was filled, to use the language of the housekeeper, with "cards of gingerbread," and the last held a "plum cake," so called from the number of large raisins that were showing their black heads in a substance of a suspiciously similar color. At each corner of the table stood saucers, filled with a thick fluid, of somewhat equivocal color and consistence, variegated with small dark lumps of a substance that resembled nothing but itself, which Remarkable termed her "sweetmeats." At the side of each plate, which was placed bottom upwards, with its knife and fork most accurately crossed above it, stood another, of smaller size, containing a motley-looking pie, composed of triangular slices of apple, mince, pumpkin, cranberry, and *custard*, so arranged as to form an entire whole. Decanters of brandy, rum, gin, and wine, with sundry pitchers of cider, beer, and one hissing vessel of "flip," were put wherever an opening would admit of their introduction. Notwithstanding the size of the table, there was scarcely a spot where the rich damask could be seen, so crowded were the dishes, with their associated bottles, plates, and saucers. The object seemed to be profusion, and it was obtained entirely at the expense of order and elegance.

All the guests, as well as the Judge himself, seemed perfectly familiar with this description of fare, for each one commenced eating with an appetite that promised to do great honor to Remarkable's taste and skill. What rendered this attention to the repast a little surprising was the fact that both the German and Richard had been summoned from another table to meet the Judge; but Major Hartmann both ate and drank without any rule, when on his excursions; and Mr. Jones invariably made it a point to participate in the business in hand, let it be what it would. The host seemed to think some apology necessary for the warmth he had betrayed on the subject of the firewood, and when the party were comfortably seated, and engaged with their knives and forks, he observed:

"The wastefulness of the settlers, with the noble trees of this country, is shocking, Monsieur Le Quoi, as doubtless you have noticed. I have seen a man fell a pine, when he has been in want of fencing stuff, and roll his first cuts into the gap, where he left it to rot, though its top would have made rails enough to answer his purpose, and its butt would have sold in the Philadelphia market for twenty dollars."

"And how the devil—I beg your pardon, Mr. Grant," interrupted Richard; "but how is the poor devil to get his logs to the Philadelphia market, pray? Put them in his pocket,

ha! As you would a handful of chestnuts, or a bunch of
chickaberries? I should like to see you walking up High
Street, with a pine log in each pocket!—Poh! poh! cousin
'duke, there are trees enough for us all, and some to spare.
Why, I can hardly tell which way the wind blows, when I'm
out in the clearings, they are so thick, and so tall—I couldn't
at all, if it wasn't for the clouds, and I happen to know all
the points of the compass, as it were, by heart."

"Ay! ay! Squire," cried Benjamin, who had now entered
and taken his place behind the Judge's chair, a little aside
withal, in order to be ready for any observation like
the present. "Look aloft, sir, look aloft. The old seamen
say, 'that the devil wouldn't make a sailor, unless he look'd
aloft.' As for the compass, why, there is no such thing as
steering without one. I'm sure I never lose sight of the
maintop, as I call the Squire's lookout on the roof, but I set
my compass, d'ye see, and take the bearings and distance of
things, in order to work out my course, if so be that it should
cloud up, or the tops of the trees should shut out the light of
heaven. The steeple of St. Paul's, now that we have got it on
end, is a great help to the navigation of the woods, for, by
the Lord Harry, as I was—"

"It is well, Benjamin," interrupted Marmaduke, observing
that his daughter manifested displeasure at the major-domo's
familiarity; "but you forget there is a lady in company, and
the women love to do most of the talking themselves."

"The Judge says the true word," cried Benjamin, with one
of his discordant laughs. "Now here is Mistress Remarkable Prettybones; just take the stopper off her tongue, and
you'll hear a gabbling, worse like than if you should happen
to fall to leeward in crossing a French privateer, or some
such thing, mayhap, as a dozen monkeys stowed in one bag."

It were impossible to say how perfect an illustration of the
truth of Benjamin's assertion the housekeeper would have
furnished, if she had dared; but the Judge looked sternly at
her, and, unwilling to incur his resentment, yet unable to contain her anger, she threw herself out of the room, with a
toss of the body, that nearly separated her frail form in the
center.

"Richard," said Marmaduke, observing that his displeasure
had produced the desired effect, "can you inform me of
anything concerning the youth whom I so unfortunately

wounded? I found him on the mountain, hunting in company with the Leatherstocking, as if they were of the same family; but there is a manifest difference in their manners. The youth delivers himself in chosen language; such as is seldom heard in these hills, and such as occasions great surprise to me, how one so meanly clad, and following so lowly a pursuit, could attain. Mohegan also knew him. Doubtless he is a tenant of Natty's hut. Did you remark the language of the lad, Monsieur Le Quoi?"

"Certainement, Monsieur Templ'," returned the Frenchman. "He deed conovairse in de excellent Anglaise."

"The boy is no miracle," exclaimed Richard; "I've known children that were sent to school early, talk much better, before they were twelve years old. There was Zared Coe, old Nehemiah's son, who first settled on the beaver-dam meadow, he could write almost as good a hand as myself, when he was fourteen; though it's true, I helped to teach him a little, in the evenings. But this shooting gentleman ought to be put in the stocks if he ever takes a rein in his hand again. He is the most awkward fellow about a horse I ever met with. I dare say he never drove anything but oxen in his life."

"There I think, Dickon, you do the lad injustice," said the Judge; "he uses much discretion in critical moments. Dost thou not think so, Bess?"

There was nothing in this question particularly to excite blushes, but Elizabeth started from the reverie into which she had fallen and colored to her forehead, as she answered:

"To me, dear sir, he appeared extremely skillful, and prompt, and courageous; but perhaps cousin Richard will say I am as ignorant as the gentleman himself."

"Gentleman!" echoed Richard; "Do you call such chaps gentlemen at school, Elizabeth?"

"Every man is a gentleman that knows how to treat a woman with respect and consideration," returned the young lady, promptly, and a little smartly.

"So much for hesitating to appear before the heiress in his shirt sleeves," cried Richard, winking at Monsieur Le Quoi, who returned the wink with one eye, while he rolled the other, with an expression of sympathy, towards the young lady. "Well, well, to me he seemed anything but a gentleman. I must say, however, for the lad, that he draws a good trigger and has a true aim. He's good at shooting a buck, ha! Marmaduke?"

"Richart," said Major Hartmann, turning his grave countenance towards the gentleman he addressed, with much earnestness, "ter poy is goot. He savet your life, and my life, and ter life of Tominie Grant, and ter life of ter Frenchman; and, Richart, he shall never vont a pet to sleep in vile olt Fritz Hartmann has a shingle to cover his het mit."

"Well, well, as you please, old gentleman," returned Mr. Jones, endeavoring to look indifferent; "put him into your own stone house, if you will, Major. I dare say the lad never slept in anything better than a bark shanty in his life, unless it was some such hut as the cabin of Leatherstocking. I prophesy you will soon spoil him; anyone could see how proud he grew, in a short time, just because he stood by my horses' heads, while I turned them into the highway."

"No, no, my old friend," cried Marmaduke, "it shall be my task to provide in some manner for the youth; I owe him a debt of my own, besides the service he has done me, through my friends. And yet I anticipate some little trouble in inducing him to accept of my services. He showed a marked dislike, I thought, Bess, to my offer of a residence within these walls for life."

"Really, dear sir," said Elizabeth, projecting her beautiful underlip, "I have not studied the gentleman so closely as to read his feelings in his countenance. I thought he might very naturally feel pain from his wound, and therefore pitied him; but"—and as she spoke she glanced her eye, with suppressed curiosity, towards the major-domo—"I dare say, sir, that Benjamin can tell you something about him. He cannot have been in the village, and Benjamin not have seen him often."

"Ay! I have seen the boy before," said Benjamin, who wanted little encouragement to speak; "he has been backing and filling in the wake of Natty Bumppo, through the mountains, after deer, like a Dutch longboat in tow of an Albany sloop. He carries a good rifle, too. The Leatherstocking said, in my hearing, before Betty Hollister's barroom fire, no later than the Tuesday night, that the younker was certain death to the wild beasts. If so be he can kill the wildcat that has been heard moaning on the lake side since the hard frosts and deep snows have driven the deer to herd, he will be doing the thing that is good. Your wildcat is a bad ship-mate, and should be made to cruise out of the track of Christian men."

"Lives he in the hut of Bumppo?" asked Marmaduke, with some interest.

"Cheek by jowl; the Wednesday will be three weeks since he first hove in sight, in company with Leatherstocking. They had captured a wolf between them and had brought in his scalp for the bounty. That Mister Bump-ho has a handy turn with him, in taking off a scalp; and there's them, in this here village, who say he larnt the trade by working on Chris-tian men. If so be that there is truth in the saying, and I com-manded along shore here, as your honor does, why, d'ye see, I'd bring him to the gangway for it, yet. There's a very pretty post rigged alongside of the stocks; and for the matter of a cat, I can fit one with my own hands; ay! and use it, too, for the want of a better."

"You are not to credit the idle tales you hear of Natty; he has a kind of natural right to gain a livelihood in these mountains; and if the idlers in the village take it into their heads to annoy him, as they sometimes do reputed rogues, they shall find him protected by the strong arm of the law."

"Ter rifle is petter as ter law," said the Major, sententious-ly.

"That for his rifle!" exclaimed Richard, snapping his fin-gers; "Ben is right, and I——" He was stopped by the sounds of a common ship bell that had been elevated to the belfry of the academy, which now announced, by its incessant ring-ing, that the hour for the appointed service had arrived. " 'For this, and every other instance of his goodness'—I beg pardon, Mr. Grant, will you please to return thanks, sir? It is time we should be moving, as we are the only Episco-palians in the neighborhood; that is I, and Benjamin, and Elizabeth; for I count half-breeds, like Marmaduke, as bad as heretics."

The divine arose and performed the office meekly and fervently, and the whole party instantly prepared themselves for the church—or rather academy.

CHAPTER X

*"And, calling sinful man to pray,
Loud, long, and deep, the bell had tolled."*
SCOTT'S BURGHER

WHILE Richard and Monsieur Le Quoi, attended by Benjamin, proceeded to the academy by a footpath through the snow, the Judge, his daughter, the divine, and the Major took a more circuitous route to the same place by the streets of the village.

The moon had risen, and its orb was shedding a flood of light over the dark outline of pines which crowned the eastern mountain. In many climates the sky would have been thought clear and lucid for a noontide. The stars twinkled in the heavens, like the last glimmerings of distant fire, so much were they obscured by the overwhelming radiance of the atmosphere; the rays from the moon striking upon the smooth white surfaces of the lake and fields, reflecting upwards a light that was brightened by the spotless color of the immense bodies of snow which covered the earth.

Elizabeth employed herself with reading the signs, one of which appeared over almost every door; while the sleigh moved steadily, and at an easy gait, along the principal street. Not only new occupations, but names that were strangers to her ears, met her gaze at every step they proceeded. The very houses seemed changed. This had been altered by an addition; that had been painted; another had been erected on the site of an old acquaintance, which had been banished from the earth almost as soon as it made its appearance on it. All were, however, pouring forth their inmates, who uniformly held their way towards the point where the expected exhibition of the conjoint taste of Richard and Benjamin was to be made.

After viewing the buildings, which really appeared to some advantage, under the bright but mellow light of the moon, our heroine turned her eyes to a scrutiny of the different figures that they passed, in search of any form that she knew. But all seemed alike as, muffled in cloaks, hoods, coats, or tippets, they glided along the narrow passages in the snow which led under the houses, half hid by the bank that had been thrown up in excavating the deep path in which they trod. Once or twice she thought there was a stature or a gait that she recollected; but the person who owned it instantly disappeared behind one of those enormous piles of wood that lay before most of the doors. It was only as they turned from the main street into another that intersected it at right angles, and which led directly to the place of meeting, that she recognized a face and building that she knew.

The house stood at one of the principal corners in the village; and, by its well-trodden doorway, as well as the sign that was swinging with a kind of doleful sound in the blasts that occasionally swept down the lake, was clearly one of the most frequented inns in the place. The building was only of one story; but the dormer windows in the roof, the paint, the window shutters, and the cheerful fire that shone through the open door gave it an air of comfort that was not possessed by many of its neighbors. The sign was suspended from a common alehouse post and represented the figure of a horseman, armed with saber and pistols and surmounted by a bearskin cap, with a fiery animal that he bestrode "rampant." All these particulars were easily to be seen by the aid of the moon, together with a row of somewhat illegible writing in black paint, but in which Elizabeth, to whom the whole was familiar, read with facility, "The Bold Dragoon."

A man and a woman were issuing from the door of this habitation as the sleigh was passing. The former moved with a stiff, military step that was a good deal heightened by a limp in one leg; but the woman advanced with a measure and an air that seemed not particularly regardful of what she might encounter. The light of the moon fell directly upon her full, broad, and red visage, exhibiting her masculine countenance, under the mockery of a ruffled cap that was intended to soften the lineaments of features that were by no means squeamish. A small bonnet of black silk, and of a slightly formal cut, was placed on the back of her head, but so as not to shade her visage in the least. Her face, as it encountered the rays of the moon from the east, seemed not unlike a sun rising in the west. She advanced, with masculine strides, to intercept the sleigh; and the Judge, directing the namesake of the Grecian king, who held the lines, to check his horses, the parties were soon near to each other.

"Good luck to ye, and a wilcome home, Jooge!" cried the female, with a strong Irish accent; "and I'm sure it's to me that ye'r always wilcome. Sure! and there's Miss 'Lizzy, and a fine young woman is she grown. What a heartach would she be giving the young men now, if there was sich a thing as a rigiment in the town! Och! but it's idle to talk of sich vanities, while the bell is calling us to mateing, jist as we shall be call'd away unexpictedly, some day, when we are the laist calkilating. Good even, Major; will I make the bowl of gin toddy the night? or it's likely ye'll stay at the big house the Christmas Eve, and the very night of ye'r getting there?"

"I am glad to see you, Mrs. Hollister," returned Elizabeth. "I have been trying to find a face that I knew since we left the door of the mansion house; but none have I seen except your own. Your house, too, is unaltered; while all the others are so changed, that, but for the places where they stand, they would be utter strangers. I observe you also keep the dear sign that I saw cousin Richard paint; and even the name at the bottom, about which, you may remember, you had the disagreement."

"It is the bould dragoon ye mane? And what name would he have, who niver was known by any other, as my husband here, the Captain, can testify. He was a pleasure to wait upon, and was ever the foremost in need. Och! but he had a sudden end! But it's to be hoped that he was justified by the cause. And it's not Parson Grant there who'll gainsay that same. Yes, yes; the Squire would paint, and so I thought that we might have *his* face up there, who had so often shared good and evil wid us. The eyes is no so large nor so fiery as the Captain's own; but the whiskers and the cap is as like as two paes. Well, well, I'll not keep ye in the cowld, talking, but will drop in the morrow after sarvice, and ask ye how ye do. It's our bounden duty to make the most of this present, and to go to the house which is open to all; so God bless ye, and keep ye from evil! Will I make the gin twist the night, or no, Major?"

To this question the German replied, very sententiously, in the affirmative; and, after a few words had passed between the husband of this fiery-faced hostess and the

Judge, the sleigh moved on. It soon reached the door of the academy, where the party alighted and entered the building.

In the meantime, Mr. Jones and his two companions, having a much shorter distance to journey, had arrived before the appointed place several minutes sooner than the party in the sleigh. Instead of hastening into the room, in order to enjoy the astonishment of the settlers, Richard placed a hand in either pocket of his surtout and affected to walk about, in front of the academy, like one to whom the ceremonies were familiar.

The villagers proceeded uniformly into the building, with a decorum and gravity that nothing could move, on such occasions; but with a haste that was probably a little heightened by curiosity. Those who came in from the adjacent country spent some little time in placing certain blue and white blankets over their horses before they proceeded to indulge their desire to view the interior of the house. Most of these men Richard approached, and inquired after the health and condition of their families. The readiness with which he mentioned the names of even the children showed how very familiarly acquainted he was with their circumstances; and the nature of the answers he received proved that he was a general favorite.

At length one of the pedestrians from the village stopped also, and fixed an earnest gaze at a new brick edifice that was throwing a long shadow across the fields of snow, as it rose, with a beautiful gradation of light and shade, under the rays of a full moon. In front of the academy was a vacant piece of ground that was intended for a public square. On the side opposite to Mr. Jones, the new and as yet unfinished Church of St. Paul's was erected. This edifice had been reared during the preceding summer, by the aid of what was called a subscription; though all, or nearly all, of the money came from the pocket of the landlord. It had been built under a strong conviction of the necessity of a more seemly place of worship than "the long room of the academy," and under an implied agreement that, after its completion, the question should be fairly put to the people, that they might decide to what denomination it should belong. Of course, this expectation kept alive a strong excitement in some few of the sectaries who were interested in its decision; though but little was said openly on the sub-

ject. Had Judge Temple espoused the cause of any particular
sect, the question would have been immediately put at rest,
for his influence was too powerful to be opposed, but he declined interference in the matter, positively refusing to lend
even the weight of his name on the side of Richard, who had
secretly given an assurance to his diocesan, that both the
building and the congregation would cheerfully come within
the pale of the Protestant Episcopal Church. But when the
neutrality of the Judge was clearly ascertained, Mr. Jones
discovered that he had to contend with a stiff-necked people.
His first measure was to go among them and commence a
course of reasoning in order to bring them round to his own
way of thinking. They all heard him patiently, and not a
man uttered a word in reply, in the way of argument; and
Richard thought, by the time that he had gone through
the settlement, the point was conclusively decided in his
favor. Willing to strike while the iron was hot, he called a
meeting, through the newspaper, with a view to decide the
question by a vote, at once. Not a soul attended; and one of
the most anxious afternoons that he had ever known was
spent by Richard in a vain discussion with Mrs. Hollister,
who strongly contended that the Methodist (her own) church
was the best entitled to, and most deserving of, the possession of the new tabernacle. Richard now perceived that he
had been too sanguine and had fallen into the error of all
those who ignorantly deal with that wary and sagacious people. He assumed a disguise himself—that is, as well as he
knew how—and proceeded step by step to advance his purpose.

The task of erecting the building had been unanimously
transferred to Mr. Jones and Hiram Doolittle. Together they
had built the mansion house, the academy, and the jail; and
they alone knew how to plan and rear such a structure as was
now required. Early in the day, these architects had made an
equitable division of their duties. To the former was assigned the duty of making all the plans, and to the latter, the
labor of superintending the execution.

Availing himself of this advantage, Richard silently determined that the window should have the Roman arch, the
first positive step in effecting his wishes. As the building was
made of bricks, he was enabled to conceal his design until
the moment arrived for placing the frames, then, indeed, it

became necessary to act. He communicated his wishes to Hiram with great caution; and, without in the least adverting to the spiritual part of his project, he pressed the point a little warmly, on the score of architectural beauty. Hiram heard him patiently and without contradiction, but still Richard was unable to discover the views of his coadjutor on this interesting subject. As the right to plan was duly delegated to Mr. Jones, no direct objection was made in words, but numberless unexpected difficulties arose in the execution. At first there was a scarcity in the right kind of material necessary to form the frames; but this objection was instantly silenced by Richard running his pencil through two feet of their length at one stroke. Then the expense was mentioned; but Richard reminded Hiram that his cousin paid, and that *he* was his treasurer. This last intimation had great weight, and after a silent and protracted, but fruitless opposition, the work was suffered to proceed on the original plan.

The next difficulty occurred in the steeple, which Richard had modeled after one of the smaller of those spires that adorn the great London cathedral. The imitation was somewhat lame, it is true, the proportions being but indifferently observed; but, after much difficulty, Mr. Jones had the satisfaction of seeing an object reared that bore, in its outlines, a striking resemblance to a vinegar cruet. There was less opposition to this model than to the windows, for the settlers were fond of novelty, and their steeple was without a precedent.

Here the labor ceased for the season, and the difficult question of the interior remained for further deliberation. Richard well knew that when he came to propose a reading desk and a chancel, he must unmask; for these were arrangements known to no church in the country but his own. Presuming, however, on the advantages he had already obtained, he boldly styled the building St. Paul's, and Hiram prudently acquiesced in this appellation, making, however, the slight addition of calling it *"New* St. Paul's," feeling less aversion to a name taken from the English cathedral than from the saint.

The pedestrian whom we have already mentioned, as pausing to contemplate this edifice, was no other than the gentleman so frequently named as Mr., or Squire, Doolittle. He was of a tall, gaunt formation, with rather sharp features, and a face that expressed formal propriety, mingled with low cunning. Richard approached him, followed by Monsieur Le Quoi and the major-domo.

"Good evening, Squire," said Richard, bobbing his head, but without moving his hands from his pockets.

"Good evening, Squire," echoed Hiram, turning his body in order to turn his head also.

"A cold night, Mr. Doolittle, a cold night, sir."

"Coolish; a tedious spell on't."

"What, looking at our church, ha! It looks well, by moonlight; how the tin of the cupola glistens! I warrant you the dome of the other St. Paul's never shines so in the smoke of London."

"It is a pretty meetinghouse to look on," returned Hiram, "and I believe that Monshure Ler Quow and Mr. Penguillan will allow it."

"Sairtainlee!" exclaimed the complaisant Frenchman, "It ees ver fine."

"I thought the Monshure would say so. The last molasses that we had was excellent good. It isn't likely that you have any more of it on hand?"

"Ah! oui; ees, sair," returned Monsieur Le Quoi, with a slight shrug of his shoulder, and a trifling grimace. "Dere is more. I feel ver happi dat you love eet. I hope dat Madame Doleet' is in good 'ealth."

"Why, so as to be stirring," said Hiram. "The Squire hasn't finished the plans for the inside of the meetinghouse yet?"

"No—no—no," returned Richard, speaking quickly, but making a significant pause between each negative. "It requires reflection. There is a great deal of room to fill up, and I am afraid we shall not know how to dispose of it to advantage. There will be a large vacant spot around the pulpit, which I do not mean to place against the wall, like a sentry box stuck up on the side of a fort."

"It is rulable to put the deacon's box under the pulpit," said Hiram; and then, as if he had ventured too much, he added, "but there's different fashions in different countries."

"That there is," cried Benjamin. "Now, in running down the coast of Spain and Portingall, you may see a nunnery stuck out on every headland, with more steeples and outriggers, such as dogvanes and weathercocks, than you'll find aboard of a three-masted schooner. If so be that a well-built church is wanting, Old England, after all, is the country to go to after your models and fashion pieces. As to Paul's, thof I've never seen it, being that it's a long way up town from Radcliffe highway and the docks, yet everybody knows that it's the grandest place in the world. Now, I've no opinion but this here church over there is as like one end of it as a grampus is to a whale, and that's only a small difference in bulk. Mounsheer Ler Quaw, here, has been in foreign parts; and thof that is not the same as having been at home, yet he must have seen churches in France, too, and can form a small idee of what a church should be; now, I ask the Mounsheer to his face, if it is not a clever little thing, taking it by and large?"

"It ees ver apropos of saircumstance," said the Frenchman —"ver judgment—but it is in de Catholique country dat dey build de—vat you call—ah a ah-ha—la grande cathédrale —de big church. St. Paul, Londre, is ver fine; ver belle; ver grand—vat you call beeg; but, Monsieur Ben, pardonnez moi, it is no vort so much as Notre Dame."

"Ha! Mounsheer, what is that you say?" cried Benjamin. "St. Paul's Church not worth so much as a damn! Mayhap you may be thinking, too, that the Royal Billy isn't so good a ship as the Billy de Paris; but she would have licked two of her, any day, and in all weathers."

As Benjamin had assumed a very threatening kind of attitude, flourishing an arm, with a bunch at the end of it that was half as big as Monsieur Le Quoi's head, Richard thought it time to interpose his authority.

"Hush, Benjamin, hush," he said; "you both misunderstand Monsieur Le Quoi, and forget yourself. But here comes Mr. Grant, and the service will commence. Let us go in."

The Frenchman, who received Benjamin's reply with a well-bred good humor that would not admit of any feeling but pity for the other's ignorance, bowed in acquiescence, and followed his companion.

Hiram and the major-domo brought up the rear, the latter grumbling, as he entered the building:

"If so be that the King of France had so much as a house to live in that would lay alongside of Paul's, one might put up with their jaw. It's more than flesh and blood can bear, to hear a Frenchman run down an English church in this manner. Why, Squire Doolittle, I've been at the whipping of two of them in one day—clean-built, snug frigates, with standing royals, and them new-fashioned cannonades on their quarters —such as, if they had only Englishmen aboard of them, would have fout the devil."

With this ominous word in his mouth, Benjamin entered the church.

CHAPTER XI

And fools who came to scoff, remained to pray. GOLDSMITH

NOTWITHSTANDING the united labors of Richard and Benjamin, the "long room" was but an extremely inartificial temple. Benches, made in the coarsest manner, and entirely with a view to usefulness, were arranged in rows for the reception of the congregation; while a rough, unpainted box was placed against the wall, in the center of the length of the apartment, as an apology for a pulpit. Something like a reading desk was in front of this rostrum; and a small mahogany table from the mansion house, covered with a spotless damask cloth, stood a little on one side, by the way of an altar. Branches of pines and hemlocks were stuck in each of the fissures that offered, in the unseasoned and hastily completed woodwork, of both the building and its furniture; while festoons and hieroglyphics met the eye in vast profusion along the brown sides of the scratch-coated walls. As the room was only lighted by some ten or fifteen miserable candles, and the windows were without shutters, it would have been but a dreary, cheerless place for the solemnities of a Christmas Eve, had not the large fire that was crackling at each end of the apartment given an air of cheerfulness to the scene by throwing an occasional glare of light through the vistas of bushes and faces.

The two sexes were separated by an area in the center of the room immediately before the pulpit; and a few benches lined this space, that were occupied by the principal personages of the village and its vicinity. This distinction was rather a gratuitous concession, made by the poorer and less polished part of the population, than a right claimed by the favored few. One bench was occupied by the party of Judge Temple, including his daughter; and, with the exception of Dr. Todd, no one else appeared willing to incur the imputation of pride by taking a seat in what was, literally, the high place of the tabernacle.

Richard filled the chair that was placed behind another table, in the capacity of clerk; while Benjamin, after heaping sundry logs on the fire, posted himself nigh by, in reserve for any movement that might require cooperation.

It would greatly exceed our limits to attempt a description of the congregation, for the dresses were as various as the individuals. Some one article, of more than usual finery, and perhaps the relic of other days, was to be seen about most of the females, in connection with the coarse attire of the woods. This wore a faded silk, that had gone through at least three generations, over coarse, woolen black stockings; that, a shawl, whose dyes were as numerous as those of the rainbow, over an awkwardly fitting gown, of rough brown "woman's wear." In short, each one exhibited some favorite article, and all appeared in their best, both men and women; while the groundworks in dress, in either sex, were the coarse fabrics manufactured within their own dwellings. One man appeared in the dress of a volunteer company of artillery, of which he had been a member in the "down countries," precisely for no other reason than because it was the best suit he had. Several, particularly of the younger men, displayed pantaloons of blue, edged with red cloth down the seams, part of the equipments of the "Templeton Light Infantry," from a little vanity to be seen in "boughten clothes." There was also one man in a "rifle frock," with its fringes and folds of spotless white, striking a chill to the heart with the idea of its coolness; although the thick coat of brown "home made" that was concealed beneath preserved a proper degree of warmth.

There was a marked uniformity of expression in countenance, especially in that half of the congregation who did not enjoy the advantages of the polish of the village. A sallow skin, that indicated nothing but exposure, was common to all, as was an air of great decency and attention, mingled, generally, with an expression of shrewdness, and, in the present instance, of active curiosity. Now and then a face and dress were to be seen among the congregation that dif-

fered entirely from this description. If pockmarked and
florid, with gaitered legs, and a coat that snugly fitted the
person of the wearer, it was surely an English emigrant, who
had bent his steps to this retired quarter of the globe. If
hard-featured and without color, with high cheek bones, it
was a native of Scotland, in similar circumstances.

The short, black-eyed man, with a cast of the swarthy
Spaniard in his face, who rose repeatedly to make room for
the belles of the village as they entered, was a son of Erin
who had lately left off his pack and become a stationary
trader in Templeton. In short, half the nations in the north of
Europe had their representatives in this assembly, though all
had closely assimilated themselves to the Americans in dress
and appearance, except the Englishman. He, indeed, not only
adhered to his native customs in attire and living, but usually
drove his plow among the stumps in the same manner as
he had before done on the plains of Norfolk, until dear-
bought experience taught him the useful lesson that a sagacious people knew what was suited to their circumstances
better than a casual observer; or a sojourner, who was, perhaps, too much prejudiced to compare, and, peradventure,
too conceited to learn.

Elizabeth soon discovered that she divided the attention of
the congregation with Mr. Grant. Timidity, therefore, confined her observation of the appearances which we have described to stolen glances; but, as the stamping of feet was
now becoming less frequent, and even the coughing, and
other little preliminaries of a congregation settling themselves down into reverential attention were ceasing, she felt
emboldened to look around her. Gradually all noises diminished, until the suppressed cough denoted that it was necessary to avoid singularity, and the most profound stillness
pervaded the apartment. The snapping of the fires, as they
threw a powerful heat into the room, was alone heard, and
each face, and every eye, were turned on the divine.

At this moment, a heavy stamping of feet was heard in
the passage below, as if a newcomer was releasing his limbs
from the snow that was necessarily clinging to the legs of a
pedestrian. It was succeeded by no audible tread; but directly
Mohegan, followed by the Leatherstocking and the young
hunter, made his appearance. Their footsteps would not have

been heard, as they trod the apartment in their moccasins, but for the silence which prevailed.

The Indian moved with great gravity across the floor, and, observing a vacant seat next to the Judge, he took it, in a manner that manifested his sense of his own dignity. Here, drawing his blanket closely around him, so as partly to conceal his countenance, he remained, during the service, immovable, but deeply attentive. Natty passed the place that was so freely taken by his red companion and seated himself on one end of a log that was lying near the fire, where he continued, with his rifle standing between his legs, absorbed in reflections, seemingly of no very pleasing nature. The youth found a seat among the congregation, and another silence prevailed.

Mr. Grant now arose, and commenced his service, with the sublime declaration of the Hebrew prophet—"The Lord is in his holy temple; let all the earth keep silence before him." The example of Mr. Jones was unnecessary to teach the congregation to rise; the solemnity of the divine effected this as by magic. After a short pause, Mr. Grant proceeded with the solemn and winning exhortation of his service. Nothing was heard but the deep, though affectionate, tones of the reader, as he slowly went through this exordium, until, something unfortunately striking the mind of Richard as incomplete, he left his place and walked on tiptoe from the room.

When the clergyman bent his knees in prayer and confession, the congregation so far imitated his example as to resume their seats; whence no succeeding effort of the divine, during the evening, was able to remove them in a body. Some rose at times; but by far the larger part continued unbending; observant, it is true, but it was the kind of observation that regarded the ceremony as a spectacle rather than a worship in which they were to participate. Thus deserted by his clerk, Mr. Grant continued to read, but no response was audible. The short and solemn pause that succeeded each petition was made; still no voice repeated the eloquent language of the prayer.

The lips of Elizabeth moved, but they moved in vain; and, accustomed as she was to the service in the churches of the metropolis, she was beginning to feel the awkwardness of the circumstance most painfully, when a soft, low, female voice repeated after the priest, "We have left undone those things which we ought to have done." Startled at finding one of her own sex in that place, who could rise superior to natural timidity, Miss Temple turned her eyes in the direction of the penitent. She observed a young female on her knees, but a short distance from her, with her meek face humbly bent over her book.

The appearance of this stranger, for such she was, entirely, to Elizabeth, was light and fragile. Her dress was neat and becoming, and her countenance, though pale and slightly agitated, excited deep interest by its sweet and melancholy expression. A second and third response were made by this juvenile assistant, when the manly sounds of a male voice proceeded from the opposite part of the room. Miss Temple knew the tones of the young hunter instantly, and struggling to overcome her own diffidence, she added her low voice to the number.

All this time Benjamin stood thumbing the leaves of a prayer book with great industry, but some unexpected difficulties prevented his finding the place. Before the divine reached the close of the confession, however, Richard reappeared at the door, and, as he moved lightly across the room, he took up the response in a voice that betrayed no other concern than that of not being heard. In his hand he carried a small open box, with the figures "8 by 10" written in black paint on one of its sides; which, having placed in the pulpit, apparently as a footstool for the divine, he returned to his station in time to say, sonorously, "Amen." The eyes of the congregation, very naturally, were turned to the windows, as Mr. Jones entered with this singular load; and then, as if accustomed to his "general agency," were again bent on the priest, in close and curious attention.

The long experience of Mr. Grant admirably qualified him to perform his present duty. He well understood the character of his listeners, who were mostly a primitive people in their habits, and who, being a good deal addicted to subtleties and nice distinctions in their religious opinions, viewed the introduction of any such temporal assistance as form into their spiritual worship, not only with jealousy, but frequently with disgust. He had acquired much of his knowledge from studying the great book of human nature, as it lay open in the world; and, knowing how dangerous it was to contend with ignorance, uniformly endeavored to avoid dictating where his better reason taught him it was the most prudent to attempt to lead. His orthodoxy had no dependence on his cassock; he could pray with fervor and with faith, if circumstances required it, without the assistance of his clerk; and he had even been known to preach a most evangelical sermon, in the winning manner of native eloquence, without the aid of a cambric handkerchief.

In the present instance he yielded, in many places, to the prejudices of his congregation; and when he had ended, there was not one of his new hearers who did not think the ceremonies less papal and offensive, and more conformant to his or her own notions of devout worship, than they had been led to expect from a service of forms. Richard found in the divine, during the evening, a most powerful cooperator in his religious schemes. In preaching, Mr. Grant endeavored to steer a middle course between the mystical doctrines of those sublimated creeds which daily involve their professors in the most absurd contradictions, and those fluent rules of moral government, which would reduce the Saviour to a level with the teacher of a school of ethics. Doctrine it was necessary to preach, for nothing less would have satisfied the disputatious people who were his listeners, and who would have interpreted silence on his part into a tacit acknowledgment of the superficial nature of his creed. We have already said that, among the endless variety of religious instructors, the settlers were accustomed to hear every denomination urge its own distinctive precepts; and to have found one indifferent to this interesting subject would have been destructive to his influence. But Mr. Grant so happily blended the universally received opinions of the Christian faith with the dogmas of his own church that, although none were entirely exempt from the influence of his reasons, very few took any alarm at the innovation.

"When we consider the great diversity of the human character, influenced as it is by education, by opportunity, and by the physical and moral conditions of the creature, my dear hearers," he earnestly concluded, "it can excite no surprise that creeds so very different in their tendencies should grow out of a religion, revealed, it is true, but whose revelations are obscured by the lapse of ages, and whose doctrines were, after the fashion of the countries in which they were first promulgated, frequently delivered in parables, and in a language abounding in metaphors, and loaded with figures. On points where the learned have, in purity of heart, been compelled to differ, the unlettered will necessarily be at variance. But, happily for us, my brethren, the fountain of divine love flows from a source too pure to admit of pollution in its course; it extends to those who drink of its vivifying waters, the peace of the righteous, and life everlasting; it endures through all time, and it pervades creation. If there be mystery in its workings, it is the mystery of a Divinity. With a clear knowledge of the nature, the might, and majesty of God, there might be conviction, but there could be no faith. If we are required to believe in doctrines that seem not in conformity with the deductions of human wisdom, let us never forget that such is the mandate of a wisdom that is infinite. It is sufficient for us that enough is developed to point our path aright, and to direct our wandering steps to that portal which shall open on the light of an eternal day. Then, indeed, it may be humbly hoped that the film which has been spread by the subtleties of earthly arguments will be dissipated by the spiritual light of Heaven; and that our hour of probation, by the aid of divine grace, being once passed in triumph, will be followed by an eternity of intelligence, and endless ages of fruition. All that is now obscure shall become plain to our expanded faculties; and what to our present senses may seem irreconcilable to our limited notions of mercy, of justice, and of love shall stand, irradiated by the light of truth, confessedly the suggestions of Omniscience, and the acts of an All-powerful Benevolence.

"What a lesson of humility, my brethren, might not each of us obtain from a review of his infant hours, and the recollection of his juvenile passions! How differently do the same acts of parental rigor appear, in the eyes of the suffering child, and of the chastened man! When the sophist would supplant, with the wild theories of his worldly wisdom, the positive mandates of inspiration, let him remember the expansion of his own feeble intellects and pause—let him feel the wisdom of God in what is partially concealed, as well as in that which is revealed; in short, let him substitute humility for pride of reason—let him have faith, and live!

"The consideration of this subject is full of consolation, my hearers, and does not fail to bring with it lessons of humility and of profit, that, duly improved, would both chasten the heart and strengthen the feeble-minded man in his course. It is a blessed consolation to be able to lay the misdoubtings of our arrogant nature at the threshold of the dwelling place of the Deity, from whence they shall be swept away, at the great opening of the portal, like the mists of the morning before the rising sun. It teaches us a lesson of humility, by impressing us with the imperfection of human powers, and by warning us of the many weak points where we are open to the attacks of the great enemy of our race; it proves to us that we are in danger of being weak, when our vanity would fain soothe us into the belief that we are most strong; it forcibly points out to us the vainglory of intellect, and shows us the vast difference between a saving faith and the corollaries of a philosophical theology, and it teaches us to reduce our self-examination to the test of good works. By good works must be understood the fruits of repentance, the chiefest of which is charity. Not that charity only, which causes us to help the needy and comfort the suffering, but that feeling of universal philanthropy, which, by teaching us to love, causes us to judge with lenity, all men; striking at the root of self-righteousness, and warning us to be sparing of our condemnation of others, while our own salvation is not yet secure.

"The lesson of expediency, my brethren, which I would gather from the consideration of this subject, is most strongly inculcated by humility. On the leading and essential points of our faith, there is but little difference, among those classes of Christians who acknowledge the attributes of the Saviour and depend on his mediation. But heresies have polluted every church, and schisms are the fruits of disputation. In order to arrest these dangers, and to insure the union of his followers, it would seem that Christ had established his visible church, and delegated the ministry. Wise and holy men, the fathers of our religion, have expended their labors in clearing what was revealed from the obscurities of language, and the results of their experience and researches have been embodied in the form of evangelical discipline. That this discipline must be salutary is evident from the view of the weakness of human nature that we have already taken; and that it may be profitable to us, and all who listen to its precepts and its liturgy, may God, in his infinite wisdom, grant. And now to," etc.

With this ingenious reference to his own forms and ministry, Mr. Grant concluded the discourse. The most profound attention had been paid to the sermon during the whole of its delivery, although the prayers had not been received with so perfect a demonstration of respect. This was by no means an intended slight of that liturgy to which the divine alluded, but was the habit of a people who owed their very existence as a distinct nation to the doctrinal character of their ancestors. Sundry looks of private dissatisfaction were exchanged between Hiram and one or two of the leading members of the *conference,* but the feeling went no further at that time; and the congregation, after receiving the blessing of Mr. Grant, dispersed in silence, and with great decorum.

CHAPTER XII

Your creeds and dogmas of a learned church
May build a fabric, fair with moral beauty;
But it would seem, that the strong hand of God
Can, only, 'rase the devil from the heart.

DUO

WHILE the congregation was separating, Mr. Grant approached the place where Elizabeth and her father were seated, leading the youthful female whom we have mentioned in the preceding chapter, and presented her as his daughter. Her reception was as cordial and frank as the manners of the country, and the value of good society, could render it; the two young women feeling, instantly, that they were necessary to the comfort of each other. The Judge, to whom the clergyman's daughter was also a stranger, was pleased to find one who, from habits, sex, and years, could probably contribute largely to the pleasures of his own child, during her first privations, on her removal from the associations of a city to the solitude of Templeton; while Elizabeth, who had been forcibly struck with the sweetness and devotion of the youthful suppliant, removed the slight embarrassment of the timid stranger by the ease of her own manners. They were at once acquainted; and, during the ten minutes that the "academy" was clearing, engagements were made between the young people, not only for the succeeding day, but they would probably have embraced in their arrangements half of the winter had not the divine interrupted them by saying:

"Gently, gently, my dear Miss Temple, or you will make my girl too dissipated. You forget that she is my housekeeper, and that my domestic affairs must remain unattended to, should Louisa accept of half the kind offers you are so good as to make her."

"And why should they not be neglected entirely, sir?" interrupted Elizabeth. "There are but two of you; and certain I am that my father's house will not only contain you both, but will open its doors spontaneously, to receive such guests. Society is a good not to be rejected on account of cold forms in this wilderness, sir; and I have often heard my father say, that hospitality is not a virtue in a new country, the favor being conferred by the guest."

"The manner in which Judge Temple exercises its rites would confirm this opinion, but we must not trespass too freely. Doubt not that you will see us often, my child particularly, during the frequent visits that I shall be compelled to make to the distant parts of the country. But to obtain an influence with such a people," he continued, glancing his eyes towards the few who were still lingering, curious observers of the interview, "a clergyman must not awaken envy or distrust by dwelling under so splendid a roof as that of Judge Temple."

"You like the roof, then, Mr. Grant," cried Richard, who had been directing the extinguishment of the fires, and other little necessary duties, and who approached in time to hear the close of the divine's speech. "I am glad to find one man of taste at last. Here's 'duke, now, pretends to call it by every abusive name he can invent; but though 'duke is a very tolerable judge, he is a very poor carpenter, let me tell him. Well, sir, well, I think we may say, without boasting, that the service was as well performed this evening as you often see; I think, quite as well as I ever knew it to be done in old Trinity—that is, if we except the organ. But there is the schoolmaster leads the psalm with a very good air. I used to lead myself, but latterly I have sung nothing but bass. There is a good deal of science to be shown in the bass, and it affords a fine opportunity to show off a full, deep voice. Benjamin, too, sings a good bass, though he is often out in the words. Did you ever hear Benjamin sing the 'Bay of Biscay, O'?"

"I believe he gave us part of it this evening," said Marmaduke, laughing. "There was, now and then, a fearful quaver in his voice, and it seems that Mr. Pengullan is like most others who do one thing particularly well; he knows nothing else. He has, certainly, a wonderful partiality to one tune, and he has a prodigious self-confidence in that one, for he delivers himself like a northwester sweeping across the lake. But come, gentlemen, our way is clear, and the sleigh waits. Good evening, Mr. Grant. Good night, young lady— remember that you dine beneath the Corinthian roof tomorrow with Elizabeth."

The parties separated, Richard holding a close dissertation with Mr. Le Quoi, as they descended the stairs, on the subject of psalmody, which he closed by a violent eulogium on the air of the "Bay of Biscay, O," as particularly connected with his friend Benjamin's execution.

During the preceding dialogue, Mohegan retained his seat, with his head shrouded in his blanket, as seemingly inattentive to surrounding objects as the departing congregation was, itself, to the presence of the aged chief. Natty, also, continued on the log where he had first placed himself, with his head resting on one of his hands, while the other held the rifle, which was thrown carelessly across his lap. His countenance expressed uneasiness, and the occasional unquiet glances that he had thrown around him during the service plainly indicated some unusual causes for unhappiness. His continuing seated was, however, out of respect to the Indian chief, to whom he paid the utmost deference on all occasions, although it was mingled with the rough manner of a hunter.

The young companion of these two ancient inhabitants of the forest remained also, standing before the extinguished brands, probably from an unwillingness to depart without his comrades. The room was now deserted by all but this group, the divine, and his daughter. As the party from the mansion house disappeared, John arose, and dropping the blanket from his head, he shook back the mass of black hair from his face, and approaching Mr. Grant, he extended his hand and said solemnly:

"Father, I thank you. The words that have been said, since the rising moon, have gone upward and the Great Spirit is glad. What you have told your children, they will remember, and be good." He paused a moment, and then, elevating himself with the grandeur of an Indian chief, he added, "If Chingachgook lives to travel towards the setting sun, after his tribe, and the Great Spirit carries him over the lakes and mountains with the breath in his body, he will tell his people the good talk he has heard; and they will believe him; for who can say that Mohegan has ever lied?"

"Let him place his dependence on the goodness of Divine mercy," said Mr. Grant, to whom the proud consciousness of the Indian sounded a little heterodox, "and it never will desert him. When the heart is filled with love to God, there is no room for sin. But, young man, to you I owe not only an obligation, in common with those you saved this evening on the mountain, but my thanks, for your respectful and pious manner in assisting in the service at a most embarrassing moment. I should be happy to see you sometimes at my dwelling, when, perhaps, my conversation may strengthen you in the path which you appear to have chosen. It is so unusual to find one of your age and appearance, in these woods, at all acquainted with our holy liturgy, that it lessens at once the distance between us, and I feel that we are no longer strangers. You seem quite at home in the service; I did not perceive that you had even a book, although good Mr. Jones had laid several in different parts of the room."

"It would be strange if I were ignorant of the service of our church, sir," returned the youth modestly; "for I was baptized in its communion, and I have never yet attended public worship elsewhere. For me to use the forms of any other denomination would be as singular as our own have proved to the people here this evening."

"You give me great pleasure, my dear sir," cried the divine, seizing the other by the hand and shaking it cordially. "You will go home with me now—indeed you must— my child has yet to thank you for saving my life. I will listen to no apologies. This worthy Indian, and your friend, there, will accompany us. Bless me! to think that he has arrived at manhood in this country, without entering a dissenting * meetinghouse!"

"No, no," interrupted the Leatherstocking, "I must away to the wigwam; there's work there that mustn't be forgotten for all your churchings and merrymakings. Let the lad go with you in welcome; he is used to keeping company with ministers, and talking of such matters; so is old John, who was Christianized by the Moravians about the time of the old war. But I am a plain, unlarned man that has sarved both the king and his country, in his day, ag'in the French and savages, but never so much as looked into a book, or larnt a letter of scholarship, in my born days. I've never seen the use of such indoor work, though I have lived to be partly bald, and in my time have killed two hundred beaver in a season, and that without counting the other game. If you mistrust what I am telling you, you can ask Chingachgook there, for I did it in the heart of the Delaware country, and the old man is knowing to the truth of every word I say."

"I doubt not, my friend, that you have been both a valiant soldier and skillful hunter in your day," said the divine; "but more is wanting to prepare you for that end which approaches. You may have heard the maxim, that 'young men *may* die, but that old men *must*.'"

"I'm sure I never was so great a fool as to expect to live forever," said Natty, giving one of his silent laughs; "no man need do that, who trails the savages through the woods, as I have done, and lives, for the hot months, on the lake streams. I've a strong constitution, I must say that for myself, as is plain to be seen; for I've drunk the Onondaga water a hundred times, while I've been watching the deer licks, when the fever-an-agy seeds was to be seen in it as plain and as plenty as you can see the rattlesnakes on old Crumhorn. But then, I never expected to hold out forever; though there's them living who have seen the Jarman flats a wilderness; ay! and them that's larned, and acquainted with religion, too; though you might look a week, now, and not find even the stump of a pine on them; and that's a wood that lasts in the ground the better part of a hundred years after the tree is dead."

---

* The divines of the Protestant Episcopal Church of the United States, commonly call other denominations *Dissenters,* though there never was an established church in their own country!

"This is but time, my good friend," returned Mr. Grant, who began to take an interest in the welfare of his new acquaintance, "but I would have you prepare for eternity. It is incumbent on you to attend places of public worship, as I am pleased to see that you have done this evening. Would it not be heedless in you to start on a day's toil of hard hunting, and leave your ramrod and flint behind?"

"It must be a young hand in the woods," interrupted Natty, with another laugh, "that didn't know how to dress a rod out of an ash sapling, or find a firestone in the mountains. No, no, I never expected to live forever; but I see, times be altering in these mountains from what they was thirty years ago, or, for that matter, ten years. But might makes right, and the law is stronger than an old man, whether he is one that has much larning, or only one like me, that is better now at standing at the passes than in following the hounds, as I once used to could. Heigh-ho! I never know'd preaching come into a settlement but it made game scarce, and raised the price of gunpowder; and that's a thing that's not as easily made as a ramrod or an Indian flint."

The divine, perceiving that he had given his opponent an argument by his own unfortunate selection of a comparison, very prudently relinquished the controversy; although he was fully determined to resume it at a more happy moment. Repeating his request to the young hunter, with great earnestness, the youth and Indian consented to accompany him and his daughter to the dwelling that the care of Mr. Jones had provided for their temporary residence. Leatherstocking persevered in his intention of returning to the hut, and at the door of the building they separated.

After following the course of one of the streets of the village a short distance, Mr. Grant, who led the way, turned into a field, through a pair of open bars, and entered a footpath, of but sufficient width to admit one person to walk in it at a time. The moon had gained a height that enabled her to throw her rays perpendicularly on the valley; and the distinct shadows of the party flitted along on the banks of the silver snow, like the presence of aerial figures, gliding to their appointed .place of meeting. The night still continued intensely cold, although not a breath of wind was felt. The path was beaten so hard, that the gentle female, who made one of the party, moved with ease along its windings; though the frost emitted a low creaking at the impression of even her light footsteps.

The clergyman in his dark dress of broadcloth, with his mild, benevolent countenance, occasionally turned towards his companions, expressing that look of subdued care which was its characteristic, presented the first object in this singular group. Next to him moved the Indian, his hair falling about his face, his head uncovered, and the rest of his form concealed beneath his blanket. As his swarthy visage, with its muscles fixed in rigid composure, was seen under the light of the moon which struck his face obliquely, he seemed a picture of resigned old age on whom the storms of winter had beaten in vain for the greater part of a century; but when, in turning his head, the rays fell directly on his dark, fiery eyes, they told a tale of passions unrestrained, and of thoughts free as air. The slight person of Miss Grant, which followed next, and which was but too thinly clad for the severity of the season, formed a marked contrast to the wild attire and uneasy glances of the Delaware chief; and more than once during their walk, the young hunter, himself no insignificant figure in the group, was led to consider the difference in the human form, as the face of Mohegan, and the gentle countenance of Miss Grant, with eyes that rivaled the soft hue of the sky, met his view at the instant that each turned to throw a glance at the splendid orb which lighted their path. Their way, which led through fields that lay at some distance in the rear of the houses, was cheered by a conversation that flagged or became animated with the subject. The first to speak was the divine.

"Really," he said, "it is so singular a circumstance to meet with one of your age, that has not been induced by idle curiosity to visit any other church than the one in which he has been educated, that I feel a strong curiosity to know the history of a life so fortunately regulated. Your education must have been excellent; as indeed is evident from your manners and language. Of which of the States are you a native, Mr. Edwards? For such, I believe, was the name that you gave Judge Temple."

"Of this."

"Of this! I was at a loss to conjecture, from your dialect, which does not partake, particularly, of the peculiarities of

any country with which I am acquainted. You have, then,
resided much in the cities, for no other part of this country is
so fortunate as to possess the constant enjoyment of our excellent liturgy."

The young hunter smiled, as he listened to the divine while
he so clearly betrayed from what part of the country he had
come himself; but for reasons probably connected with his
present situation, he made no answer.

"I am delighted to meet with you, my young friend, for I
think an ingenuous mind, such as I doubt not yours must be,
will exhibit all the advantages of a settled doctrine and
devout liturgy. You perceive how I was compelled to bend to
the humors of my hearers this evening. Good Mr. Jones wished
me to read the communion, and, in fact, all the morning
service; but, happily, the canons do not require this of an
evening. It would have wearied a new congregation: but tomorrow I purpose administering the sacrament. Do you
commune, my young friend?"

"I believe not, sir," returned the youth, with a little embarrassment, that was not at all diminished by Miss Grant's
pausing involuntarily and turning her eyes on him in surprise. "I fear that I am not qualified; I have never yet approached the altar; neither would I wish to do it, while I
find so much of the world clinging to my heart."

"Each must judge for himself," said Mr. Grant; "though
I should think that a youth who had never been blown about
by the wind of false doctrines, and who has enjoyed the advantages of our liturgy for so many years in its purity,
might safely come. Yet, sir, it is a solemn festival, which
none should celebrate until there is reason to hope it is not
mockery. I observed this evening, in your manner to Judge
Temple, a resentment that bordered on one of the worst
of human passions. We will cross this brook on the ice; it
must bear us all, I think, in safety. Be careful not to slip, my
child." While speaking, he descended a little bank by the
path and crossed one of the small streams that poured their
waters into the lake; and, turning to see his daughter pass,
observed that the youth had advanced and was kindly directing her footsteps. When all were safely over, he moved up
the opposite bank and continued his discourse. "It was wrong,
my dear sir, very wrong, to suffer such feelings to rise, under

any circumstances, and especially in the present, where the evil was not intended."

"There is good in the talk of my father," said Mohegan, stopping short, and causing those who were behind him to pause also; "it is the talk of Miquon. The white man may do as his fathers have told him; but the 'Young Eagle' has the blood of a Delaware chief in his veins: it is red, and the stain it makes can only be washed out with the blood of a Mingo."

Mr. Grant was surprised by the interruption of the Indian, and, stopping, faced the speaker. His mild features were confronted to the fierce and determined looks of the chief, and expressed the horror he felt at hearing such sentiments from one who professed the religion of his Saviour. Raising his hands to a level with his head, he exclaimed:

"John, John! Is this the religion that you have learned from the Moravians? But no—I will not be so uncharitable as to suppose it. They are a pious, a gentle, and a mild people, and could never tolerate these passions. Listen to the language of the Redeemer—'But I say unto you, love your enemies; bless them that curse you; do good to them that hate you; pray for them that despitefully use you and persecute you.' —This is the command of God, John, and without striving to cultivate such feelings, no man can see him."

The Indian heard the divine with attention; the unusual fire of his eye gradually softened, and his muscles relaxed into their ordinary composure; but, slightly shaking his head, he motioned with dignity for Mr. Grant to resume his walk, and followed himself in silence. The agitation of the divine caused him to move with unusual rapidity along the deep path, and the Indian, without any apparent exertion, kept an equal pace; but the young hunter observed the female to linger in her steps, until a trifling distance intervened between the two former and the latter. Struck by the circumstance, and not perceiving any new impediment to retard her footsteps, the youth made a tender of his assistance.

"You are fatigued, Miss Grant," he said; "the snow yields to the foot, and you are unequal to the strides of us men. Step on the crust, I entreat you, and take the help of my arm. Yonder light is, I believe, the house of your father; but it seems yet at some distance."

"I am quite equal to the walk," returned a low tremulous

voice; "but I am startled by the manner of that Indian. Oh! His eye was horrid, as he turned to the moon, in speaking to my father. But I forget, sir; he is your friend, and by his language may be your relative; and yet of you I do not feel afraid."

The young man stepped on the bank of snow, which firmly sustained his weight, and by a gentle effort induced his companion to follow. Drawing her arm through his own, he lifted his cap from his head, allowing the dark locks to flow in rich curls over his open brow, and walked by her side with an air of conscious pride, as if inviting an examination of his inmost thoughts. Louisa took but a furtive glance at his person, and moved quietly along, at a rate that was greatly quickened by the aid of his arm.

"You are but little acquainted with this peculiar people, Miss Grant," he said, "or you would know that revenge is a virtue with an Indian. They are taught from infancy upwards to believe it a duty never to allow an injury to pass unrevenged; and nothing but the stronger claims of hospitality can guard one against their resentments, where they have power."

"Surely, sir," said Miss Grant, involuntarily withdrawing her arm from his, "you have not been educated with such unholy sentiments."

"It might be a sufficient answer to your excellent father to say that I was educated in the church," he returned; "but to you I will add that I have been taught deep and practical lessons of forgiveness. I believe that, on this subject, I have but little cause to reproach myself; it shall be my endeavor that there yet be less."

While speaking, he stopped, and stood with his arm again proffered to her assistance. As he ended, she quietly accepted his offer, and they resumed their walk.

Mr. Grant and Mohegan had reached the door of the former's residence and stood waiting near its theshold for the arrival of their young companions. The former was earnestly occupied in endeavoring to correct, by his precepts, the evil propensities that he had discovered in the Indian during their conversation; to which the latter listened in profound, but respectful attention. On the arrival of the young hunter and the lady, they entered the building. The house stood at some distance from the village, in the center of a field, surrounded by stumps that were peering above the snow, bearing caps of pure white, nearly two feet in thickness. Not a tree nor a shrub was nigh it; but the house externally exhibited that cheerless, unfinished aspect which is so common to the hastily erected dwellings of a new country. The uninviting character of its outside was, however, happily relieved by the exquisite neatness and comfortable warmth within.

They entered an apartment that was fitted as a parlor, though the large fireplace, with its culinary arrangements, betrayed the domestic uses to which it was occasionally applied. The bright blaze from the hearth rendered the light that proceeded from the candle Louisa produced unnecessary, for the scanty furniture of the room was easily seen and examined by the former. The floor was covered in the center by a carpet made of rags, a species of manufacture that was then, and yet continues to be, much in use in the interior; while its edges that were exposed to view were of unspotted cleanliness. There was a trifling air of better life in a tea table and workstand, as well as in an old-fashioned mahogany bookcase; but the chairs, the dining table, and the rest of the furniture were of the plainest and cheapest construction. Against the walls were hung a few specimens of needlework and drawing, the former executed with great neatness, though of somewhat equivocal merit in their designs, while the latter were strikingly deficient in both.

One of the former represented a tomb, with a youthful female weeping over it, exhibiting a church with arched windows in the background. On the tomb were the names, with the dates of the births and deaths, of several individuals, all of whom bore the name of Grant. An extremely cursory glance at this record was sufficient to discover to the young hunter the domestic state of the divine. He there read that he was a widower; and that the innocent and timid maiden, who had been his companion, was the only survivor of six children. The knowledge of the dependence which each of these meek Christians had on the other for happiness threw an additional charm around the gentle, but kind attentions, which the daughter paid to the father.

These observations occurred while the party were seating themselves before the cheerful fire, during which time there

was a suspension of discourse. But when each was comfortably arranged, and Louisa, after laying aside a thin coat
of faded silk and a gypsy hat that was more becoming to her
modest, ingenuous countenance than appropriate to the season, had taken a chair between her father and the youth,
the former resumed the conversation.

"I trust, my young friend," he said, "that the education
you have received has eradicated most of those revengeful
principles which you may have inherited by descent, for I
understand from the expressions of John that you have some
of the blood of the Delaware tribe. Do not mistake me, I beg,
for it is not color, nor lineage, that constitutes merit; and
I know not that he who claims affinity to the proper owners
of this soil has not the best right to tread these hills with
the lightest conscience."

Mohegan turned solemnly to the speaker, and, with the
peculiarly significant gestures of an Indian, he spoke:

"Father, you are not yet past the summer of life; your
limbs are young. Go to the highest hill, and look around you.
All that you see from the rising to the setting sun, from the
headwaters of the great spring to where the 'crooked
river' * is hid by the hills, is his. He has Delaware blood,
and his right is strong. But the brother of Miquon is just: he
will cut the country in two parts, as the river cuts the lowlands, and will say to the 'Young Eagle,' Child of the Delawares! Take it—keep it—and be a chief in the land of your
fathers."

"Never!" exclaimed the young hunter, with a vehemence
that destroyed the rapt attention with which the divine and
his daughter were listening to the Indian. "The wolf of the
forest is not more rapacious for his prey, than that man
is greedy of gold; and yet his glidings into wealth are subtle
as the movements of a serpent."

"Forbear, forbear, my son, forbear," interrupted Mr. Grant.
"These angry passions must be subdued. The accidental injury you have received from Judge Temple has heightened
the sense of your hereditary wrongs. But remember that the
one was unintentional, and that the other is the effect of
political changes, which have, in their course, greatly low

* The Susquehannah means crooked river; "hannah," or hannock,
meant "river," in many of the native dialects. Thus we find Rappahannock as far south as Virginia.

ered the pride of kings, and swept mighty nations from the face of the earth. Where now are the Philistines, who so often held the children of Israel in bondage? or that city of Babylon, which rioted in luxury and vice, and who styled herself the Queen of Nations in the drunkenness of her pride? Remember the prayer of our holy litany, where we implore the Divine Power—'that it may please thee to forgive our enemies, persecutors, and slanderers, and to turn their hearts.' The sin of the wrongs which have been done to the natives is shared by Judge Temple only in common with a whole people, and your arm will speedily be restored to its strength."

"This arm!" repeated the youth, pacing the floor in violent agitation. "Think you, sir, that I believe the man a murderer? Oh, no! He is too wily, too cowardly for such a crime. But let him and his daughter riot in their wealth—a day of retribution will come. No, no, no," he continued, as he trod the floor more calmly—"it is for Mohegan to suspect him of an intent to injure me, but the trifle is not worth a second thought."

He seated himself and hid his face between his hands, as they rested on his knees.

"It is the hereditary violence of a native's passion, my child," said Mr. Grant in a low tone, to his affrighted daughter, who was clinging in terror to his arm. "He is mixed with the blood of the Indians, you have heard; and neither the refinements of education, nor the advantages of our excellent liturgy, have been able entirely to eradicate the evil. But care and time will do much for him yet."

Although the divine spoke in a low tone, yet what he uttered was heard by the youth, who raised his head, with a smile of indefinite expression, and spoke more calmly.

"Be not alarmed, Miss Grant, at either the wildness of my manner or that of my dress. I have been carried away by passions that I should struggle to repress. I must attribute it with your father, to the blood in my veins, although I would not impeach my lineage willingly; for it is all that is left me to boast of. Yes! I am proud of my descent from a Delaware chief, who was a warrior that ennobled human nature. Old Mohegan was his friend and will vouch for his virtues."

Mr. Grant here took up the discourse, and, finding the

young man more calm, and the aged chief attentive, he
entered into a full and theological discussion of the duty of
forgiveness. The conversation lasted for more than an hour,
when the visitors arose, and, after exchanging good wishes
with their entertainers, they departed. At the door they separated, Mohegan taking the direct route to the village, while
the youth moved towards the lake. The divine stood at the
entrance of his dwelling, regarding the figure of the aged
chief as it glided, at an astonishing gait for his years,
along the deep path; his black, straight hair just visible
over the bundle formed by his blanket, which was sometimes
blended with the snow, under the silvery light of the moon.
From the rear of the house was a window that overlooked
the lake; and here Louisa was found by her father, when
he entered, gazing intently on some object in the direction
of the eastern mountain. He approached the spot and saw
the figure of the young hunter, at the distance of half a
mile, walking with prodigious steps across the wide fields of
frozen snow that covered the ice, towards the point where he
knew the hut inhabited by the Leatherstocking was situated
on the margin of the lake, under a rock that was crowned by
pines and hemlocks. At the next instant, the wildly looking
form entered the shadow cast from the overhanging trees
and was lost to view.

"It is marvelous how long the propensities of the savage
continue in that remarkable race," said the good divine; "but
if he persevere as he has commenced, his triumph shall yet
be complete. Put me in mind, Louisa, to lend him the homily
'against peril of idolatry,' at his next visit."

"Surely, father, you do not think him in danger of re-
lapsing into the worship of his ancestors!"

"No, my child," returned the clergyman, laying his hand
affectionately on her flaxen locks, and smiling; "his white
blood would prevent it; but there is such a thing as the
idolatry of our passions."

Chapter XIII

And I'll drink out of the quart pot,—
Here's a health to the barley mow.
Drinking Song

On one of the corners, where the two principal streets of Templeton intersected each other, stood, as we have already mentioned, the inn called the "Bold Dragoon." In the original plan, it was ordained that the village should stretch along the little stream that rushed down the valley; and the street which led from the lake to the academy was intended to be its western boundary. But convenience frequently frustrates the best regulated plans. The house of Mr., or as, in consequence of commanding the militia of that vicinity, he was called, Captain Hollister, had, at an early day, been erected directly facing the main street and ostensibly interposed a barrier to its further progress. Horsemen, and subsequently teamsters, however, availed themselves of an opening, at the end of the building, to shorten their passage westward, until, in time, the regular highway was laid out along this course, and houses were gradually built on either side, so as effectually to prevent any subsequent correction of the evil.

Two material consequences followed this change in the regular plans of Marmaduke. The main street, after running about half its length, was suddenly reduced to precisely that difference in its width; and the "Bold Dragoon" became, next to the mansion house, by far the most conspicuous edifice in the place.

This conspicuousness, aided by the characters of the host and hostess, gave the tavern an advantage over all its future competitors, that no circumstances could conquer. An effort was, however, made to do so; and at the corner diagonally opposite, stood a new building that was intended, by its occupants, to look down all opposition. It was a house of wood, ornamented in the prevailing style of architecture, and about the roof and balustrades was one of the three imitators of the mansion house. The upper windows were filled with

138

rough boards secured by nails, to keep out the cold air—for the edifice was far from finished, although glass was to be seen in the lower apartments, and the light of the powerful fires within denoted that it was already inhabited. The exterior was painted white on the front, and on the end which was exposed to the street; but in the rear, and on the side which was intended to join the neighboring house, it was coarsely smeared with Spanish brown. Before the door stood two lofty posts, connected at the top by a beam, from which was suspended an enormous sign, ornamented around its edges with certain curious carvings in pine boards, and on its faces loaded with Masonic emblems. Over these mysterious figures was written, in large letters, "The Templeton Coffeehouse, and Travelers' Hotel," and beneath them, "by Habakkuk Foote and Joshua Knapp." This was a fearful rival to the "Bold Dragoon," as our readers will the more readily perceive, when we add that the same sonorous names were to be seen over the door of a newly erected store in the village, a hatter's shop, and the gates of a tanyard. But, either because too much was attempted to be executed well, or that the "Bold Dragoon" had established a reputation which could not be easily shaken, not only Judge Temple and his friends, but most of the villagers also, who were not in debt to the powerful firm we have named, frequented the inn of Captain Hollister on all occasions where such a house was necessary.

On the present evening the limping veteran and his consort were hardly housed after their return from the academy, when the sounds of stamping feet at their threshold announced the approach of visitors, who were probably assembling with a view to compare opinions on the subject of the ceremonies they had witnessed.

The public, or as it was called, the "barroom," of the "Bold Dragoon" was a spacious apartment, lined on three sides with benches and on the fourth by fireplaces. Of the latter there were two of such size as to occupy, with their enormous jambs, the whole of that side of the apartment where they were placed, excepting room enough for a door or two, and a little apartment in one corner, which was protected by miniature palisadoes and profusely garnished with bottles and glasses. In the entrance to this sanctuary, Mrs. Hollister was seated, with great gravity in her air, while her husband occupied himself with stirring the fires, moving the logs with a large stake burnt to a point at one end.

"There, Sargeant, dear," said the landlady, after she thought the veteran had got the logs arranged in the most judicious manner, "give over poking, for it's no good ye'll be doing, now that they burn so convaniently. There's the glasses on the table there, and the mug that the Doctor was taking his cider and ginger in, before the fire here—just put them in the bar, will ye? for we'll be having the Jooge, and the Major, and Mr. Jones down the night, without reckoning Benjamin Poomp, and the lawyers: so ye'll be fixing the room tidy; and put both flip irons in the coals; and tell Jude, the lazy black baste, that if she's no be claneing up the kitchen I'll turn her out of the house, and she may live wid the jontlemen that kape the 'Coffeehouse,' good luck to 'em. Och! Sargeant, sure it's a great privilege to go to a mateing where a body can sit asy, widout joomping up and down so often, as this Mr. Grant is doing that same."

"It's a privilege at all times, Mrs. Hollister, whether we stand or be seated; or, as good Mr. Whitefield used to do after he had made a wearisome day's march, get on our knees and pray, like Moses of old, with a flanker to the right and left, to lift his hands to heaven," returned her husband, who composedly performed what she had directed to be done. "It was a very pretty fight, Betty, that the Israelites had on that day with the Amalekites. It seems that they fout on a plain, for Moses is mentioned as having gone on to the heights to overlook the battle, and wrestle in prayer; and if I should judge, with my little larning, the Israelites depended mainly on their horse, for it is written that Joshua cut up the enemy with the edge of the sword; from which I infer, not only that they were horse, but well-disciplyn'd troops. Indeed, it says as much as that they were chosen men; quite likely volunteers; for raw dragoons seldom strike with the *edge* of their swords, particularly if the weapon be any way crooked."

"Pshaw! Why do ye bother yourself wid taxts, man, about so small a matter," interrupted the landlady. "Sure, it was the Lord who was with 'em; for he always sided wid the Jews, before they fell away; and it's but little matter what kind of men Joshua commanded, so that he was doing the right bidding. Aven them cursed millaishy, the Lord forgive me for swearing, that was the death of him, wid their cowardice, would have carried the day in old times. There's no rason to be thinking that the soldiers were used to the drill."

"I must say, Mrs. Hollister, that I have not often seen raw troops fight better than the left flank of the militia, at the time you mention. They rallied handsomely, and that without beat of drum, which is no easy thing to do under fire, and were very steady till he fell. But the Scriptures contain no unnecessary words; and I will maintain that horse, who know how to strike with the *edge* of the sword, must be well disciplyn'd. Many a good sarmon has been preached about smaller matters than that one word! If the text was not meant to be particular, why wasn't it written with the sword, and not with the edge? Now, a backhanded stroke, on the edge, takes long practice. Goodness! What an argument would Mr. Whitefield make of that word edge! As to the Captain, if he had only called up the guard of dragoons when he rallied the foot, they would have shown the inimy what the edge of a sword was; for, although there was no commissioned officer with them, yet I think I may say," the veteran continued, stiffening his cravat about the throat, and raising himself up, with the air of a drill sergeant, "they were led by a man who know'd how to bring them on, in spite of the ravine."

"Is it lade on ye would," cried the landlady, "when ye know yourself, Mr. Hollister, that the baste he rode was but little able to joomp from one rock to another, and the animal was as spry as a squirrel? Och! But it's useless to talk, for he's gone this many a year. I would that he had lived to see the true light; but there's mercy for a brave sowl, that died in the saddle, fighting for the liberty. It is a poor tombstone they have given him, anyway, and many a good one that died like himself; but the sign is very like, and I will be kapeing it up, while the blacksmith can make a hook for it to swing on, for all the 'coffeehouses' betwane this and Albany."

There is no saying where this desultory conversation would have led the worthy couple had not the men who were stamping the snow off their feet on the little platform before the door suddenly ceased their occupation, and entered the barroom.

For ten or fifteen minutes, the different individuals, who intended either to bestow or receive edification before the fires of the "Bold Dragoon" on that evening, were collecting, until the benches were nearly filled with men of different occupations. Dr. Todd and a slovenly-looking, shabby-genteel young man, who took tobacco profusely, wore a coat of imported cloth, cut with something like a fashionable air, frequently exhibited a large French silver watch, with a chain of woven hair and a silver key, and who, altogether, seemed as much above the artisans around him as he was himself inferior to the real gentleman, occupied a high-back wooden settee, in the most comfortable corner in the apartment.

Sundry brown mugs, containing cider or beer, were placed between the heavy andirons, and little groups were formed among the guests, as subjects arose, or the liquor was passed from one to the other. No man was seen to drink by himself, nor in any instance was more than one vessel considered necessary for the same beverage; but the glass, or the mug, was passed from hand to hand, until a chasm in the line, or a regard to the rights of ownership, would regularly restore the dregs of the potation to him who defrayed the cost.

Toasts were uniformly drunk; and, occasionally, someone who conceived himself peculiarly endowed by nature to shine in the way of wit would attempt some such sentiment as "hoping that he" who treated "might make a better man than his father," or, "live till all his friends wished him dead"; while the more humble pot companion contented himself by saying, with a most imposing gravity in his air, "come, here's luck," or by expressing some other equally comprehensive desire. In every instance, the veteran landlord was requested to imitate the custom of the cupbearers to kings, and taste the liquor he presented, by the invitation of "after you is manners," with which request he ordinarily complied, by wetting his lips, first expressing the wish of "here's hoping," leaving it to the imagination of the hearers to fill the vacuum by whatever good each thought most desirable. During these movements, the landlady was busily occupied with mixing the various compounds required by her customers, with her own hands, and occasionally exchanging greetings and inquiries concerning the conditions of their respective families, with such of the villagers as approached the bar.

At length the common thirst being in some measure assuaged, conversation of a more general nature became the order of the hour. The physician, and his companion, who was one of the two lawyers of the village, being considered the best qualified to maintain a public discourse with credit, were the principal speakers, though a remark was hazarded, now and then, by Mr. Doolittle, who was thought to be their inferior only in the enviable point of education. A general silence was produced on all but the two speakers by the following observation from the practitioner of the law:

"So, Dr. Todd, I understand that you have been performing an important operation, this evening, by cutting a charge of buckshot from the shoulder of the son of Leatherstocking?"

"Yes, sir," returned the other, elevating his little head with an air of importance. "I had a small job up at the Judge's in that way; it was, however, but a trifle to what it might have been, had it gone through the body. The shoulder is not a very vital part; and I think the young man will soon be well. But I did not know that the patient was a son of Leatherstocking: it is news to me to hear that Natty had a wife."

"It is by no means a necessary consequence," returned the other, winking, with a shrewd look around the barroom; "there is such a thing, I suppose you know, in law, as a 'filius nullius.'"

"Spake it out, man," exclaimed the landlady; "spake it out in king's English; what for should ye be talking Indian in a room full of Christian folks, though it is about a poor hunter, who is but a little better in his ways than the wild savages themselves? Och! It's to be hoped that the missionaries will, in his own time, make a convarsion of the poor divils; and then it will matter little of what color is the skin, or wedder there be wool or hair on the head."

"Oh! It is Latin, not Indian, Miss Hollister," returned the lawyer, repeating his winks and shrewd looks; "and Dr. Todd understands Latin, or how would he read the labels on his gallipots and drawers? No, no, Miss Hollister, the Doctor understands me; don't you, Doctor?"

"Hem—why I guess I am not far out of the way," returned Elnathan, endeavoring to imitate the expression of the other's countenance by looking jocular. "Latin is a queer language, gentlemen; now I rather guess there is no one in the room except Squire Lippet, who can believe that 'Far. Av.' means oatmeal in English."

The lawyer in his turn was a good deal embarrassed by this display of learning; for, although he actually had taken his first degree at one of the eastern universities, he was somewhat puzzled with the terms used by his companion. It was dangerous, however, to appear to be outdone in learning in a public barroom, and before so many of his clients; he therefore put the best face on the matter and laughed knowingly, as if there were a good joke concealed under it, that was understood only by the physician and himself. All this was attentively observed by the listeners, who exchanged looks of approbation; and the expressions of "tonguey man," and "I guess Squire Lippet knows, if anybody doos," were heard in different parts of the room, as vouchers for the admiration of his auditors. Thus encouraged, the lawyer rose from his chair, and turning his back to the fire, and facing the company, he continued:

"The son of Natty, or the son of nobody, I hope the young man is not going to let the matter drop. This is a country of laws; and I should like to see it fairly tried, whether a man who owns, or says he owns, a hundred thousand acres of land has any more right to shoot a body than another. What do you think of it, Dr. Todd?"

"Oh! Sir, I am of opinion that the gentleman will soon be well, as I said before; the wound isn't in a vital part; and as the ball was extracted so soon, and the shoulder was what I call well attended to, I do not think there is as much danger as there might have been."

"I say, Squire Doolittle," continued the attorney, raising his voice, "you are a magistrate and know what is law, and what is not law. I ask you, sir, if shooting a man is a thing that is to be settled so very easily? Suppose, sir, that the young man had a wife and family; and suppose that he was a mechanic like yourself, sir; and suppose that his family depended on him for bread; and suppose that the ball, instead of merely going through the flesh, had broken the shoulder blade and crippled him forever; I ask you all, gentlemen, supposing this to be the case, whether a jury wouldn't give what I call handsome damages?"

As the close of this supposititious case was addressed to the company generally, Hiram did not, at first, consider himself called on for a reply; but finding the eyes of the listeners bent on him in expectation, he remembered his character for judicial discrimination and spoke, observing a due degree of deliberation and dignity.

"Why, if a man should shoot another," he said, "and if he should do it on purpose, and if the law took notice on't, and if a jury should find him guilty, it would be likely to turn out a state-prison matter."

"It would so, sir," returned the attorney. "The law, gentlemen, is no respecter of persons in a free country. It is one of the great blessings that has been handed down to us from our ancestors that all men are equal in the eye of the law as they are by nater. Though some may get property, no one knows how, yet they are not privileged to transgress the laws any more than the poorest citizen in the state. This is my notion, gentlemen; and I think that if a man had a mind to bring this matter up, something might be made out of it that would help pay for the salve—ha! Doctor?"

"Why, sir," returned the physician, who appeared a little uneasy at the turn the conversation was taking, "I have the promise of Judge Temple before men—not but what I would take his word as soon as his note of hand—but it was before men. Let me see—there was Mounshier Ler Quow, and Squire Jones, and Major Hartmann, and Miss Pettibone, and one or two of the blacks by, when he said that his pocket would amply reward me for what I did."

"Was the promise made before or after the service was performed?" asked the attorney.

"It might have been both," returned the discreet physician; "though I'm certain he said so before I undertook the dressing."

"But it seems that he said his pocket should reward you, Doctor," observed Hiram. "Now I don't know that the law will hold a man to such a promise; he might give you his pocket with sixpence in't, and tell you to take your pay out on't."

"That would not be a reward in the eye of the law," interrupted the attorney—"not what is called a 'quid pro quo';

nor is the pocket to be considered as an agent, but as part of a man's own person, that is, in this particular. I am of opinion that an action would lie on that promise, and I will undertake to bear him out, free of costs, if he don't recover."

To this proposition the physician made no reply; but he was observed to cast his eyes around him, as if to enumerate the witnesses, in order to substantiate this promise also, at a future day, should it prove necessary. A subject so momentous as that of suing Judge Temple was not very palatable to the present company in so public a place; and a short silence ensued, that was only interrupted by the opening of the door, and the entrance of Natty himself.

The old hunter carried in his hand his never failing companion, the rifle; and although all of the company were uncovered excepting the lawyer, who wore his hat on one side, with a certain dam'me air, Natty moved to the front of one of the fires, without in the least altering any part of his dress or appearance. Several questions were addressed to him, on the subject of the game he had killed, which he answered readily, and with some little interest; and the landlord, between whom and Natty there existed much cordiality, on account of their both having been soldiers in youth, offered him a glass of a liquid, which, if we might judge from its reception, was no unwelcome guest. When the forester had got his potation also, he quietly took his seat on the end of one of the logs that lay nigh the fires, and the slight interruption produced by his entrance seemed to be forgotten.

"The testimony of the blacks could not be taken, sir," continued the lawyer, "for they are all the property of Mr. Jones, who owns their time. But there is a way by which Judge Temple, or any other man, might be made to pay for shooting another, and for the cure in the bargain. There is a way, I say, and that without going into the 'court of errors,' too."

"And a mighty big error ye would make of it, Mister Todd," cried the landlady, "should ye be putting the matter into the law at all, with Joodge Temple, who has a purse as long as one of them pines on the hill, and who is an asy man to dale wid, if yees but mind the humor of him. He's a good man is Joodge Temple, and a kind one, and one who will be no the likelier to do the pratty thing, becase ye would

wish to tarrify him wid the law. I know of but one objaction
to the same, which is an over carelessness about his sowl. It's
neither a Methodie, nor a Papish, or Prasbetyrian, that he is,
but just nothing at all; and it's hard to think that he, 'who
will not fight the good fight, under the banners of a rig'lar
church, in this world, will be mustered among the chosen in
heaven,' as my husband, the captain there, as ye call him,
says—though there is but one captain that I 'know, who de-
saarves the name. I hopes Latherstocking, ye'll no be foolish,
and putting the boy up to try the law in the matter; for
'twill be an evil day to ye both, when ye first turn the skin of
so paceable an animal as a sheep into a bone of contention.
The lad is wilcome to his drink for nothing, until his shoul-
ther will bear the rifle ag'in."

"Well, that's gin'rous," was heard from several mouths at
once, for this was a company in which a liberal offer was
not thrown away; while the hunter, instead of expressing any
of that indignation which he might be supposed to feel at
hearing the hurt of his young companion alluded to, opened
his mouth, with the silent laugh for which he was so remarkable; and after he had indulged his humor, made this
reply:

"I know'd the Judge would do nothing with his smoothbore when he got out of his sleigh. I never saw but one
smoothbore that would carry at all, and that was a French-
ducking piece, upon the big lakes: it had a barrel half as long
ag'in as my rifle and would throw fine shot into a goose at
100 yards; but it made dreadful work with the game, and you
wanted a boat to carry it about in. When I went with Sir
William ag'in the French, at Fort Niagara, all the rangers
used the rifle; and a dreadful weapon it is, in the hands of
one who knows how to charge it and keep a steady aim.
The Captain knows, for he says he was a soldier in Shir-
ley's; and though they were nothing but baggonet men, he
must know how we cut up the French and Iroquois in the
scrimmages in that war. Chingachgook, which means 'Big
Sarpent' in English, old John Mohegan, who lives up at the
hut with me, was a great warrior then, and was out with us;
he can tell all about it, too; though he was overhand for
the tomahawk, never firing more than once or twice, before
he was running in for the scalps. Ah! times is dreadfully altered since then. Why, Doctor, there was nothing but a foot-

path, or at the most a track for pack horses, along the Mohawk, from the Jarman Flats up to the forts. Now, they say,
they talk of running one of them wide roads with gates on
it along the river; first making a road, and then fencing it
up! I hunted one season back of the Catskills, nigh hand
to the settlements, and the dogs often lost the scent, when
they came to them highways, there was so much travel on
them; though I can't say that the brutes was of a very good
breed. Old Hector will wind a deer in the fall of the year,
across the broadest place in the Otsego, and that is a
mile and a half, for I paced it myself on the ice, when the
tract was first surveyed, under the Indian grant."

"It sames to me, Natty, but a sorry compliment, to call
your comrade after the evil one," said the landlady; "and it's
no much like a snake that old John is looking now. Nimrod
would be a more besameing name for the lad, and a more
Christian, too, seeing that it comes from the Bible. The sargeant read me the chapter about him, the night before my
christening, and a mighty asement it was, to listen to anything from the book."

"Old John and Chingachgook were very different men to
look on," returned the hunter, shaking his head at his melancholy recollections. "In the 'fifty-eighth war' he was in the
middle of manhood, and taller than now by three inches.
If you had seen him, as I did, the morning we beat Dieskau,
from behind our log walls, you would have called him as
comely a redskin as ye ever set eyes on. He was naked all to
his breechcloth and leggins; and you never seed a creater so
handsomely painted. One side of his face was red, and the
other black. His head was shaved clean, all to a few hairs on
the crown, where he wore a tuft of eagle's feathers, as bright
as if they had come from a peacock's tail. He had colored
his sides so that they looked like an atomy, ribs and all; for
Chingachgook had a great taste in such things; so that,
what with his bold, fiery countenance, his knife, and his
tomahawk, I have never seen a fiercer warrior on the
ground. He played his part, too, like a man; for I saw him
next day, with thirteen scalps on his pole. And I will say this
for the 'Big Snake,' that he always dealt fair, and never
scalped any that he didn't kill with his own hands."

"Well, well," cried the landlady; "fighting is fighting,
anyway, and there is different fashions in the thing;

though I can't say that I relish mangling a body after the breath is out of it; neither do I think it can be uphild by doctrine. I hope, sargeant, ye niver was helping in sich evil worrek."

"It was my duty to keep my ranks, and to stand or fall by the baggonet or lead," returned the veteran. "I was then in the fort, and seldom leaving my place, saw but little of the savages, who kept on the flanks or in front, scrimmaging. I remember, howsomever, to have heard mention made of the 'Great Snake,' as he was called, for he was a chief of renown; but little did I ever expect to see him enlisted in the cause of Christianity, and civilized like old John."

"Oh! He was Christianized by the Moravians, who were always overintimate with the Delawares," said Leatherstocking. "It's my opinion that, had they been left to themselves, there would be no such doings now, about the headwaters of the two rivers, and that these hills mought have been kept as good hunting ground by their right owner, who is not too old to carry a rifle, and whose sight is as true as a fish hawk hovering——"

He was interrupted by more stamping at the door, and presently the party from the mansion house entered, followed by the Indian himself.

CHAPTER XIV

"There's quart-pot, pint-pot, half-pint,
Gill-pot, half gill, nipperkin,
And the brown bowl——.
Here's a health to the barley mow,
My brave boys,
Here's a health to the barley mow."
DRINKING SONG

SOME little commotion was produced by the appearance of the new guests, during which the lawyer slunk from the room. Most of the men approached Marmaduke and shook his offered hand, hoping "that the Judge was well"; while Major Hartmann, having laid aside his hat and wig and substituted for the latter a warm, peaked woolen nightcap, took his seat very quietly on one end of the settee, which was relinquished by its former occupants. His tobacco box was next produced, and a clean pipe was handed him by the landlord. When he had succeeded in raising a smoke, the Major gave a long whiff, and turning his head towards the bar, he said:

"Petty, pring in ter toddy."

In the meantime the Judge had exchanged his salutations with most of the company and taken a place by the side of the Major, and Richard had bustled himself into the most comfortable seat in the room. Mr. Le Quoi was the last seated, nor did he venture to place his chair finally, until by frequent removals, he had ascertained that he could not possibly intercept a ray of heat from any individual present. Mohegan found a place on an end of one of the benches, and somewhat approximated to the bar. When these movements had subsided, the Judge remarked pleasantly:

"Well, Betty, I find you retain your popularity through all weathers, against all rivals, and among all religions. How liked you the sermon?"

"Is it the sarmon?" exclaimed the landlady. "I can't say but it was rasonable; but the prayers is mighty unasy. It's no small a matter for a body in their fifty-nint' year, to be moving so much in church. Mr. Grant sames a godly man, anyway, and his garrel is a hoomble one, and a devout.— Here, John, is a mug of cider, laced with whiskey. An Indian will drink cider, though he niver be athirst."

"I must say," observed Hiram, with due deliberation, "that it was a tonguey thing, and I rather guess that it gave considerable satisfaction. There was one part, though, which might have been left out, or something else put in; but then I s'pose that, as it was a written discourse, it is not so easily altered as where a minister preaches without notes."

"Ay! There's the rub, Jooge," cried the landlady. "How can a man stand up and be praching his word, when all that he is saying is written down, and he is as much tied to it as iver a thaving dragoon was to the pickets?"

"Well, well," cried Marmaduke, waving his hand for silence, "there is enough said; as Mr. Grant told us, there are different sentiments on such subjects, and in my opinion he spoke most sensibly. So, Jotham, I am told you have sold your betterments to a new settler and have moved into the village and opened a school. Was it cash or dicker?"

The man who was thus addressed occupied a seat immediately behind Marmaduke; and one who was ignorant of the extent of the Judge's observation might have thought he would have escaped notice. He was of a thin, shapeless figure, with a discontented expression of countenance, and with something extremely shiftless in his whole air. Thus spoken to, after turning and twisting a little, by way of preparation, he made a reply.

"Why, part cash, and part dicker. I sold out to a Pumfretman who was so'thin forehanded. He was to give me ten dollars an acre for the clearin', and one dollar an acre over the first cost, on the woodland; and we agreed to leave the buildin's to men. So I tuck Asa Montagu, and he tuck Absalom Bement, and they two tuck old Squire Napthali Green. And so they had a meetin', and made out a vardict of eighty dollars for the buildins. There was twelve acres of clearin', at ten dollars, and eighty-eight at one, and the whull came to two hundred and eighty-six dollars and a half, after paying the men."

"Hum," said Marmaduke, "what did you give for the place?"

"Why, besides what's comin' to the Judge, I gi'n my brother Tim a hundred dollars for his bargain; but then there's a new house on't, that cost me sixty more; and I paid Moses a hundred dollars for choppin' and loggin' and sowin'; so that the whull stood me in about two hundred and sixty dollars. But then I had a great crop off on't, and as I got twenty-six dollars and a half more than it cost, I conclude I made a pretty good trade on't."

"Yes, but you forgot that the crop was yours without the trade, and you have turned yourself out of doors for twenty-six dollars."

"Oh! The Judge is clean out," said the man, with a look of sagacious calculation. "He turned out a span of horses, that is wuth a hundred and fifty dollars of any man's money, with a bran-new wagon; fifty dollars in cash; and a good note for eighty more; and a sidesaddle that was valued at seven and a half—so there was jist twelve shillings betwixt us. I wanted him to turn out a set of harness, and take the cow and the sap troughs. He wouldn't—but I saw through it; he thought I should have to buy the tacklin' afore I could use the wagon and horses; but I know'd a thing or two myself; I should like to know of what use is the tacklin' to him! I offered him to trade back ag'in, for one hundred and fifty-five. But my woman said she wanted a churn, so I tuck a churn for the change."

"And what do you mean to do with your time this winter? You must remember that time is money."

"Why, as the master is gone down country, to see his mother, who, they say, is going to make a die on't, I agreed to take the school in hand till he comes back. If times doosn't get worse in the spring, I've some notion of going into trade, or maybe I may move off to the Genesee; they say they are carryin' on a great stroke of business that-a-way. If the wust comes to the wust, I can but work at my trade, for I was brought up in a shoe manufactory."

It would seem that Marmaduke did not think his society of sufficient value to attempt inducing him to remain where he was; for he addressed no further discourse to the man, but turned his attention to other subjects. After a short pause, Hiram ventured a question:

"What news does the Judge bring us from the Legislature? It's not likely that Congress has done much this session: or maybe the French haven't fit any more battles lately?"

"The French since they have beheaded their king have done nothing but fight," returned the Judge. "The character of the nation seems changed. I knew many French gentlemen, during our war, and they all appeared to me to be men of great humanity and goodness of heart; but these Jacobins are as bloodthirsty as bulldogs."

"There was one Roshambow wid us, down at Yorrektown," cried the landlady; "a mighty pratty man he was, too; and their horse was the very same. It was there that the sargeant got the hurt in the leg, from the English batteries, bad luck to 'em."

"Ah! Mon pauvre Roi!" murmured Monsieur Le Quoi.

"The Legislature have been passing laws," continued Marmaduke, "that the country much required. Among others, there is an act prohibiting the drawing of seines, at any other than proper seasons, in certain of our streams and small lakes; and another, to prohibit the killing of deer in the teeming months. These are laws that were loudly called for, by judicious men; nor do I despair of getting an act to make the unlawful felling of timber a criminal offense."

The hunter listened to this detail with breathless attention, and when the Judge had ended, he laughed in open derision.

"You may make your laws, Judge," he cried, "but who will you find to watch the mountains through the long summer days, or the lakes at night? Game is game, and he who finds may kill; that has been the law in these mountains for forty years, to my sartain knowledge; and I think one old law is worth two new ones. None but a green one would wish to kill a doe with a fa'n by its side, unless his moccasins were getting old, or his leggins ragged, for the flesh is lean and coarse. But a rifle rings among the rocks along the lake shore, sometimes, as if fifty pieces were fired at once—it would be hard to tell where the man stood who pulled the trigger."

"Armed with the dignity of the law, Mr. Bumppo," returned the Judge, gravely, "a vigilant magistrate can prevent much of the evil that has hitherto prevailed, and which is already rendering the game scarce. I hope to live to see the day when a man's rights in his game shall be as much respected as his title to his farm."

"Your titles and your farms are all new together," cried Natty; "but laws should be equal, and not more for one than another. I shot a deer, last Wednesday was a fortnight, and it floundered through the snowbanks till it got over a brush fence; I catch'd the lock of my rifle in the twigs in following, and was kept back, until finally the creater got off. Now I want to know who is to pay me for that deer; and a fine buck it was. If there hadn't been a fence I should have gotten another shot into it; and I never draw'd upon anything that hadn't wings three times running, in my born days.— No, no, Judge, it's the farmers that makes the game scarce, and not the hunters."

"Ter teer is not so plenty as in ter old war, Pumppo," said the Major, who had been an attentive listener, amidst clouds of smoke; "put ter lant is not mate as for ter teer to live on, put for Christians."

"Why, Major, I believe you're a friend to justice and the right, though you go so often to the grand house; but it's a hard case to a man to have his honest calling for a livelihood stopped by laws, and that too when, if right was done, he mought hunt or fish on any day in the week, or on the best flat in the Patent, if he was so minded."

"I unstertant you, Letterstockint," returned the Major, fixing his black eyes, with a look of peculiar meaning, on the hunter; "put you didn't use to be so prutent, as to look ahet mit so much care."

"Maybe there wasn't so much occasion," said the hunter, a little sulkily; when he sank into a silence from which he was not roused for some time.

"The Judge was saying so'thin about the French," Hiram observed, when the pause in the conversation had continued a decent time.

"Yes, sir," returned Marmaduke, "the Jacobins of France seem rushing from one act of licentiousness to another. They continue those murders which are dignified by the name of executions. You have heard that they have added the death of their Queen to the long list of their crimes."

"Les Monstres!" again murmured Monsieur Le Quoi, turning himself suddenly in his chair with a convulsive start.

"The province of La Vendée is laid waste by the troops of the Republic, and hundreds of its inhabitants, who are Royalists in their sentiments, are shot at a time. La Vendée is a district in the southwest of France that continues yet much attached to the family of the Bourbons; doubtless Monsieur Le Quoi is acquainted with it, and can describe it more faithfully."

"Non, non, non, mon cher ami," returned the Frenchman, in a suppressed voice, but speaking rapidly, and gesticulating with his right hand, as if for mercy, while with his left he concealed his eyes.

"There have been many battles fought lately," continued Marmaduke, "and the infuriated republicans are too often victorious. I cannot say, however, that I am sorry they have captured Toulon from the English, for it is a place to which they have a just right."

"Ah—ha!" exclaimed Monsieur Le Quoi, springing on his feet, and flourishing both arms with great animation; "ces Anglais!"

The Frenchman continued to move about the room with great alacrity for a few minutes, repeating his exclamations to himself; when, overcome by the contradictory nature of his emotions, he suddenly burst out of the house, and was seen wading through the snow towards his little shop, waving his arms on high, as if to pluck down honor from the moon. His departure excited but little surprise, for the villagers were used to his manner; but Major Hartmann laughed out-right for the first time during his visit as he lifted the mug and observed:

"Ter Frenchman is mat—put he is goot as for notting to trink; he is trunk mit joy."

"The French are good soldiers," said Captain Hollister; "they stood us in hand a good turn, down at Yorktown; nor do I think, although I am an ignorant man about the great movements of the army, that his Excellency would have been able to march against Cornwallis, without their reinforcements."

"Ye spake the trut', sargeant," interrupted his wife, "and I would iver have ye be doing the same. It's varry pratty men is the French; and jist when I stopt the cart, the time when ye was pushing on in front it was, to kape the rig'lers in, a rigiment of the jontlemen marched by, and so I dealt them out to their liking. Was it pay I got? Sure did I, and in good solid crowns: the divil a bit of continental could they muster among them all, for love nor money. Och! The Lord forgive me for swearing and spakeing of such vanities: but this I will say for the French, that they paid in good silver; and one glass would go a great way wid 'em, for they gin'rally handed it back wid a drop in the cup; and that's a brisk trade, Joodge, where the pay is good, and the men not overpartic'lar."

"A thriving trade, Mrs. Hollister," said Marmaduke. "But what has become of Richard? He jumped up as soon as seated, and has been absent so long that I am fearful he has frozen."

"No fear of that, cousin 'duke," cried the gentleman himself; "business will sometimes keep a man warm the coldest night that ever snapt in the mountains. Betty, your husband told me, as we came out of church, that your hogs were getting mangy, so I have been out to take a look at them, and found it true. I stepped across, Doctor, and got your boy to weigh me out a pound of salts, and have been mixing it with their swill. I'll bet a saddle of venison against a gray squirrel, that they are better in a week. And now, Mrs. Hollister, I'm ready for a hissing mug of flip."

"Sure I know'd yee'd be wanting that same," said the landlady; "it's mixt and ready to the boiling. Sargeant, dear, be handing up the iron, will ye?—no, the one in the far fire, it's black, ye will see. Ah! You've the thing now; look if it's not as red as a cherry."

The beverage was heated, and Richard took that kind of draught which men are apt to indulge in who think that they have just executed a clever thing, especially when they like the liquor.

"Oh! You have a hand, Betty, that was formed to mix flip," cried Richard, when he paused for breath. "The very iron has a flavor in it. Here, John, drink, man, drink. I and you and Dr. Todd have done a good thing with the shoulder of that lad this very night. 'Duke, I made a song while you were gone—one day when I had nothing to do; so I'll sing you a verse or two, though I haven't really determined on the tune yet:

> What is life but a scene of care,
>   Where each one must foil in his way?
> Then let us be jolly, and prove that we are
> A set of good fellows, who seem very rare,
>   And can laugh and sing all the day.
>   Then let us be jolly,
>   And cast away folly,
> For grief turns a black head to gray.

There, 'duke, what do you think of that? There is another verse of it, all but the last line. I haven't got a rhyme for the last line yet. Well, old John, what do you think of the music? as good as one of your war songs, ha?"

"Good!" said Mohegan, who had been sharing deeply in the potations of the landlady, besides paying a proper respect to the passing mugs of the Major and Marmaduke.

"Pravo! pravo! Richart," cried the Major, whose black eyes were beginning to swim in moisture. "Pravissimo! It is a goot song; put Natty Pumppo hast a petter. Letterstockint, vilt sing? Say, olt poy, vilt sing ter song, as apout ter woots?"

"No, no, Major," returned the hunter, with a melancholy shake of the head, "I have lived to see what I thought eyes could never behold in these hills, and I have no heart left for singing. If he, that has a right to be master and ruler here, is forced to squinch his thirst, when adry, with snow water, it ill becomes them that have lived by his bounty to be making merry, as if there was nothing in the world but sunshine and summer."

When he had spoken, Leatherstocking again dropped his head on his knees, and concealed his hard and wrinkled features with his hands. The change from the excessive cold without to the heat of the barroom, coupled with the depth and frequency of Richard's draughts, had already leveled whatever inequality there might have existed between him and the other guests on the score of spirits; and he now held out a pair of swimming mugs of foaming flip towards the hunter, as he cried:

"Merry! Ay! Merry Christmas to you, old boy! Sunshine and summer! No! You are blind, Leatherstocking, 'tis moonshine and winter; take these spectacles and open your eyes:

> So let us be jolly,
> And cast away folly,
> For grief turns a black head to gray.

"Hear how old John turns his quavers. What damned dull music an Indian song is, after all, Major! I wonder if they ever sing by note."

While Richard was singing and talking, Mohegan was uttering dull, monotonous tones, keeping time by a gentle motion of his head and body. He made use of but few words, and such as he did utter were in his native language, and consequently only understood by himself and Natty. Without heeding Richard, he continued to sing a kind of wild, melancholy air, that rose, at times, in sudden and quite elevated notes, and then fell again into the low, quavering sounds that seemed to compose the character of his music.

The attention of the company was now much divided, the men in the rear having formed themselves into little groups, where they were discussing various matters; among the principal of which were the treatment of mangy hogs and Parson Grant's preaching; while Dr. Todd was endeavoring to explain to Marmaduke the nature of the hurt received by the young hunter. Mohegan continued to sing, while his countenance was becoming vacant, though, coupled with his thick bushy hair, it was assuming an expression very much like brutal ferocity. His notes were gradually growing louder and soon rose to a height that caused a general cessation in the discourse. The hunter now raised his head again and addressed the old warrior, warmly, in the Delaware language, which, for the benefit of our readers, we shall render freely into English.

"Why do you sing of your battles, Chingachgook, and of the warriors you have slain, when the worst enemy of all is near you, and keeps the Young Eagle from his rights? I have fought in as many battles as any warrior in your tribe, but cannot boast of my deeds at such a time as this."

"Hawkeye," said the Indian, tottering with a doubtful step from his place, "I am the Great Snake of the Delawares; I can track the Mingoes like an adder that is stealing on the whippoorwill's eggs, and strike them like the rattlesnake, dead at a blow. The white man made the tomahawk of Chingachgook bright as the waters of Otsego, when the last sun is shining; but it is red with the blood of the Maquas."

"And why have you slain the Mingo warriors? Was it not to keep these hunting grounds and lakes to your father's children? And were they not given in solemn council to the Fire-eater? And does not the blood of a warrior run in the veins of a young chief, who should speak aloud, where his voice is now too low to be heard?"

The appeal of the hunter seemed in some measure to recall the confused faculties of the Indian, who turned his face towards the listeners and gazed intently on the Judge. He shook his head, throwing his hair back from his countenance, and exposed eyes that were glaring with an expression of wild resentment. But the man was not himself. His hand seemed to make a fruitless effort to release his tomahawk, which was confined by its handle to his belt, while his eyes gradually became vacant. Richard at that instant thrusting a mug before him, his features changed to the grin of idiocy, and seizing the vessel with both hands, he sank backward on the bench and drank until satiated, when he made an effort to lay aside the mug with the helplessness of total inebriety.

"Shed not blood!" exclaimed the hunter, as he watched the countenance of the Indian in its moment of ferocity. "But he is drunk and can do no harm. This is the way with all the savages; give them liquor, and they make dogs of themselves. Well, well—the time will come when right will be done; and we must have patience."

Natty still spoke in the Delaware language, and of course was not understood. He had hardly concluded before Richard cried:

"Well, old John is soon sowed up. Give him a berth, Captain, in the barn, and I will pay for it. I am rich tonight, ten times richer than 'duke, with all his lands, and military lots, and funded debts, and bonds, and mortgages.

> Come let us be jolly,
> And cast away folly,
> For grief——

Drink, King Hiram—drink, Mr. Doonothing—drink, sir, I say. This is a Christmas eve, which comes, you know, but once a year."

"He! he! he! The squire is quite moosical tonight," said Hiram, whose visage began to give marvelous signs of relaxation. "I rather guess we shall make a church on't yet. Squire?"

"A church, Mr. Doolittle! We will make a cathedral of it! Bishops, priests, deacons, wardens, vestry, and choir: organ, organist, and bellows! By the Lord Harry, as Benjamin says, we will clap a steeple on the other end of it, and make two churches of it. What say you, 'duke, will you pay? Ha! My cousin Judge, wil't pay!"

"Thou makest such a noise, Dickon," returned Marmaduke, "it is impossible that I can hear what Dr. Todd is saying—I think thou observedst, it is probable the wound will fester, so as to occasion danger to the limb in this cold weather?"

"Out of nater, sir, quite out of nater," said Elnathan, attempting to expectorate, but succeeding only in throwing a light, frothy substance, like a flake of snow, into the fire— "quite out of nater, that a wound so well dressed, and with the ball in my pocket, should fester. I s'pose, as the Judge talks of taking the young man into his house, it will be most convenient if I make but one charge on't."

"I should think one would do," returned Marmaduke, with that arch smile that so often beamed on his face; leaving the beholder in doubt whether he most enjoyed the character of his companion, or his own covert humor. The landlord had succeeded in placing the Indian on some straw in one of his outbuildings, where, covered with his own blanket, John continued for the remainder of the night.

In the meantime, Major Hartmann began to grow noisy and jocular; glass succeeded glass, and mug after mug was introduced, until the carousal had run deep into the night, or rather morning; when the veteran German expressed an inclination to return to the mansion house. Most of the party had already retired, but Marmaduke knew the habits of his friend too well to suggest an earlier adjournment. So soon, however, as the proposal was made, the Judge eagerly availed himself of it, and the trio prepared to depart. Mrs. Hollister attended them to the door in person, cautioning her guests as to the safest manner of leaving her premises.

"Lane on Mister Jones, Major," said she, "he's young, and will be a support to ye. Well, it's a charming sight to see ye, anyway, at the Bould Dragoon; and sure it's no harm to be kaping a Christmas Eve wid a light heart, for it's no telling when we may have sorrow come upon us. So good night, Joodge, and a Merry Christmas to ye all, tomorrow morning."

The gentlemen made their adieus as well as they could, and taking the middle of the road, which was a fine, wide, and well-beaten path, they did tolerably well until they reached the gate of the mansion house: but on entering the Judge's domains, they encountered some slight difficulties. We shall not stop to relate them, but will just mention that, in the morning, sundry diverging paths were to be seen in the snow; and that once during their progress to the door, Marmaduke, missing his companions, was enabled to trace them, by one of these paths, to a spot where he discovered them with nothing visible but their heads: Richard singing in a most vivacious strain,

> "Come, let us be jolly,
> And cast away folly,
> For grief turns a black head to gray."

CHAPTER XV

"As she lay, on that day, in the Bay of Biscay, O!"

PREVIOUSLY to the occurrence of the scene at the "Bold Dragoon," Elizabeth had been safely reconducted to the mansion house, where she was left as its mistress, either to amuse or employ herself during the evening as best suited her own inclinations. Most of the lights were extinguished; but as Benjamin adjusted, with great care and regularity, four large candles, in as many massive candlesticks of brass, in a row on the sideboard, the hall possessed a peculiar air of comfort and warmth, contrasted with the cheerless aspect of the room she had left in the academy.

Remarkable had been one of the listeners to Mr. Grant, and returned with her resentment, which had been not a little excited by the language of the Judge, somewhat softened by reflection and the worship. She recollected the youth of Elizabeth, and thought it no difficult task, under present appearances, to exercise that power indirectly, which hitherto she had enjoyed undisputed. The idea of being governed, or of being compelled to pay the deference of servitude, was absolutely intolerable; and she had already determined within herself, some half dozen times, to make an effort, that should at once bring to an issue the delicate point of her domestic condition. But as often as she met the dark, proud eye of Elizabeth, who was walking up and down the apartment, musing on the scenes of her youth, and the change in her condition, and perhaps the events of the day, the house-keeper experienced an awe that she would not own to herself could be excited by anything mortal. It, however, checked her advances, and for some time held her tongue-tied. At length she determined to commence the discourse by entering on a subject that was apt to level all human distinctions, and in which she might display her own abilities.

"It was quite a wordy sarmon that Parson Grant gave us tonight," said Remarkable. "The Church ministers be commonly smart sarmonizers; but they write down their idees, which is a great privilege. I don't think that by nater, they are as tonguey speakers, for an offhand discourse, as the standing-order ministers."

"And what denomination do you distinguish as the standing order?" inquired Miss Temple, with some surprise.

"Why, the Presbyter'ans and Congregationals, and Baptists, too, for-ti'-now; and all sitch as don't go on their knees to prayer."

"By that rule, then, you would call those who belong to the persuasion of my father, the sitting order," observed Elizabeth.

"I'm sure I've never heard 'em spoken of by any other name than Quakers, so called," returned Remarkable, betraying a slight uneasiness. "I should be the last to call them otherwise, for I never in my life used a disparaging tarm of the Judge, or any of his family. I've always set store by the Quakers, they are so pretty-spoken, clever people; and it's a wonderment to me how your father come to marry into a church family; for they are as contrary in religion as can be. One sits still, and for the most part, says nothing, while the church folks practyse all kinds of ways, so that I sometimes think it quite moosical to see them; for I went to a church meeting once before, down country."

"You have found an excellence in the church liturgy that has hitherto escaped me. I will thank you to inquire whether the fire in my room burns: I feel fatigued with my journey, and will retire."

Remarkable felt a wonderful inclination to tell the young mistress of the mansion, that by opening a door she might see for herself; but prudence got the better of resentment, and after pausing some little time, as a salvo to her dignity, she did as desired. The report was favorable, and the young lady, wishing Benjamin, who was filling the stove with wood, and the housekeeper, each a good night, withdrew.

The instant the door closed on Miss Temple, Remarkable commenced a sort of mysterious, ambiguous discourse, that was neither abusive nor commendatory of the qualities of the absent personage; but which seemed to be drawing nigh, by regular degrees, to a most dissatisfied description. The major-domo made no reply, but continued his occupation with great industry, which being happily completed, he took a look at the thermometer, and then, opening a drawer of the sideboard, he produced a supply of stimulants that would have served to keep the warmth in his system without the aid of the enormous fire he had been building. A small stand was drawn up near the stove, and the bottles and the glasses necessary for convenience were quietly arranged. Two chairs were placed by the side of this comfortable situation, when Benjamin, for the first time, appeared to observe his companion.

"Come," he cried, "come, Mistress Remarkable, bring yourself to an anchor in this chair. It's a peeler without, I can tell you, good woman; but what cares I? Blow high or blow low, d'ye see, it's all the same thing to Ben. The niggers are snug stowed below before a fire that would roast an ox whole. The thermometer stands now at fifty-five, but if there's any vartue in good maple wood, I'll weather upon it, before one glass, as much as ten points more, so that the Squire, when he comes home from Betty Hollister's warm room, will feel as hot as a hand that has given the rigging a lick with bad tar. Come, mistress, bring up in this here chair, and tell me how you like our new heiress."

"Why, to my notion, Mr. Penguillan——"

"Pump, Pump," interrupted Benjamin; "it's Christmas Eve, Mistress Remarkable, and so, d'ye see, you had better call me Pump. It's a shorter name, and as I mean to pump this here pecanter till it sucks, why you may as well call me Pump."

"Did you ever!" cried Remarkable, with a laugh that seemed to unhinge every joint in her body. "You're a moosical creater, Benjamin, when the notion takes you. But as I was saying, I rather guess that times will be altered now in this house."

"Altered!" exclaimed the major-domo, eying the bottle that was assuming the clear aspect of cut glass with astonishing rapidity; "it don't matter much, Mistress Remarkable, so long as I keep the keys of the lockers in my pocket."

"I can't say," continued the housekeeper, "but there's good eatables and drinkables enough in the house for a body's content—a little more sugar, Benjamin, in the glass—for Squire Jones is an excellent provider. But new lords, new laws; and I shouldn't wonder if you and I had an unsartain time on't in footer."

"Life is as unsartain as the wind that blows," said Benjamin, with a moralizing air; "and nothing is more vari'ble than the wind, Mistress Remarkable, unless you happen to fall in with the trades, d'ye see, and then you may run for the matter of a month at a time, with studding sails on both sides, alow and aloft, and with the cabin boy at the wheel."

"I know that life is disp'ut unsartain," said Remarkable, compressing her features to the humor of her companion; "but I expect there will be great changes made in the house to rights; and that you will find a young man put over your head, as there is one that wants to be over mine; and after having been settled as long as you have, Benjamin, I should judge that to be hard."

"Promotion should go according to length of sarvice," said the major-domo; "and if so be that they ship a hand for my berth, or place a new steward aft, I shall throw up my commission in less time than you can put a pilot boat in stays. Thof Squire Dickens"—this was a common misnomer with Benjamin—"is a nice gentleman, and as good a man to sail with as heart could wish, yet I shall tell the Squire, d'ye see, in plain English, and that's my native tongue, that if so be he is thinking of putting any Johnny Raw over my head, why I shall resign. I began forrard, Mistress Prettybones, and worked my way aft, like a man. I was six months aboard a Garnsey lugger, hauling in the slack of the lee sheet, and coiling up rigging. From that I went a few trips in a fore-and-after, in the same trade, which, after all, was but a blind kind of sailing in the dark, where a man larns but little, excepting how to steer by the stars. Well, then, d'ye see, I larnt how a topmast should be slushed, and how a top-gallant sail was to be becketted; and then I did small jobs in the cabin, such as mixing the skipper's grog. 'Twas there I got my taste, which, you must have often seen, is excellent. Well, here's better acquaintance to us."

Remarkable nodded a return to the compliment and took a sip of the beverage before her; for, provided it was well sweetened, she had no objection to a small potation now and then. After this observance of courtesy between the worthy couple, the dialogue proceeded.

"You have had great experiences in life, Benjamin; for, as the Scripter says, 'They that go down to the sea in ships see the works of the Lord.'"

"Ay! For that matter, they in brigs and schooners, too; and it mought say, the works of the devil. The sea, Mistress

Remarkable, is a great advantage to a man, in the way of knowledge, for he sees the fashions of nations, and the shape of a country. Now, I suppose, for myself here, who is but an unlarned man to some that follows the seas, I suppose that, taking the coast from Cape Ler Hogue, as low down as Cape Finish-there, there isn't so much as a headland, or an island, that I don't know either the name of it, or something more or less about it. Take enough, woman, to color the water. Here's sugar. It's a sweet tooth, that fellow that you hold on upon yet, Mistress Prettybones. But, as I was saying, take the whole coast along I know it as well as the way from here to the Bold Dragoon; and a devil of an acquaintance is that Bay of Biscay. Whew! I wish you could but hear the wind blow there. It sometimes takes two to hold one man's hair on his head. Scudding through the Bay is pretty much the same thing as traveling the roads in this country, up one side of a mountain, and down the other."

"Do tell!" exclaimed Remarkable; "And does the sea run as high as mountains, Benjamin?"

"Well, I will tell; but first let's taste the grog. Hem! It's the right kind of stuff, I must say, that you keep in this country, but then you're so close aboard the West Indies, you make but a small run of it. By the Lord Harry, woman, if Garnsey only lay somewhere between Cape Hatteras and the Bite of Logann, but you'd see rum cheap! As to the seas, they runs more in uppers in the Bay of Biscay, unless it may be in a souwester, when they tumble about quite handsomely; tho'f it's not in the narrow sea that you are to look for a swell; just go off the Western Islands, in a westerly blow, keeping the land on your larboard hand, with the ship's head to the south'ard, and bring to, under a close-reef'd topsail; or, mayhap, a reef'd foresail, with a fore-topmast staysail, and mizzen staysail, to keep her up to the sea, if she will bear it; and lay there for the matter of two watches, if you want to see mountains. Why, good woman, I've been off there in the Boadishey frigate, when you could see nothing but some such matter as a piece of sky, mayhap, as big as the mainsail; and then again, there was a hole under your lee quarter big enough to hold the whole British navy."

"Oh! For massy's sake! And wan't you afeard, Benjamin? And how did you get off?"

"Afeard! Who the devil do you think was to be frightened at a little salt water tumbling about his head? As for getting off, when we had enough of it, and had washed our decks down pretty well, we called all hands, for, d'ye see, the watch below was in their hammocks, all the same as if they were in one of your best bedrooms; and so we watched for a smooth time; clapt her helm hard a weather, let fall the foresail, and got the tack aboard; and so, when we got her afore it, I ask you, Mistress Prettybones, if she didn't walk? Didn't she? I'm no liar, good woman, when I say that I saw that ship jump from the top of one seat to another, just like one of these squirrels, that can fly, jumps from tree to tree."

"What, clean out of the water!" exclaimed Remarkable, lifting her two lank arms, with their bony hands spread in astonishment.

"It was no such easy matter to get out of the water, good woman; for the spray flew so that you couldn't tell which was sea and which was cloud. So there we kept her afore it for the matter of two glasses. The first lieutenant he cun'd the ship himself, and there was four quartermasters at the wheel, besides the master with six forecastle men in the gun room, at the relieving tackles. But then she behaved herself so well! Oh! She was a sweet ship, mistress! That one frigate was well worth more, to live in, than the best house in the island. If I was King of England, I'd have her hauled up above Lon'on Bridge and fit her up for a palace; because why? If anybody can afford to live comfortably, his Majesty can."

"Well! But, Benjamin," cried the listener, who was in an ecstasy of astonishment at this relation of the steward's dangers, "What *did* you do?"

"Do! Why we did our duty like hearty fellows. Now if the countrymen of Mounsheer Ler Quaw had been aboard of her, they would have just struck her ashore on some of them small islands; but we run along the land, until we found her dead to leeward off the mountains of Pico, and dam'me if I know to this day how we got there; whether we jumped over the island, or hauled round it; but there we was, and there we lay, under easy sail, forereaching first upon one tack and then upon t'other, so as to poke her nose out now and then, and take a look to wind'ard, till the gale blow'd its pipe out."

"I wonder now!" exclaimed Remarkable, to whom most of the terms used by Benjamin were perfectly unintelligible, but who had got a confused idea of a raging tempest. "It must be an awful life, that going to sea! and I don't feel astonishment that you are so affronted with the thoughts of being forced to quit a comfortable home like this. Not that a body cares much for't, as there's more houses than one to live in. Why, when the Judge agreed with me to come and live with him, I'd no more notion of stopping any time than anything. I happened in, just to see how the family did, about a week after Miss Temple died, thinking to be back home agin night; but the family was in sitch a distressed way, that I couldn't but stop awhile, and help 'em on. I thought the situation a good one, seeing that I was an unmarried body, and they were so much in want of help; so I tarried."

"And a long time have you left your anchors down in the same place, mistress. I think you must find that the ship rides easy."

"How you talk, Benjamin! There's no believing a word you say. I must say that the Judge and Squire Jones have both acted quite clever, so long; but I see that now we shall have a specimen to the contrary. I heer'n say that the Judge was gone a great 'broad, and that he meant to bring his darter hum, but I didn't calculate on sitch carrins on. To my notion, Benjamin, she's likely to turn out a desput ugly gal."

"Ugly!" echoed the major-domo, opening eyes, that were beginning to close in a very suspicious sleepiness, in wide amazement. "By the Lord Harry, woman, I should as soon think of calling the Boadishey a clumsy frigate. What the devil would you have? Arn't her eyes as bright as the morning and evening stars? And isn't her hair as black and glistening as rigging that has just had a lick of tar? Doesn't she move as stately as a first rate in smooth water, on a bowline? Why, woman, the figurehead of the Boadishey was a fool to her, and that, as I've often heard the captain say, was an image of a great queen; and arn't queens always comely, woman? For who do you think would be a king, and not choose a handsome bedfellow?"

"Talk decent, Benjamin," said the housekeeper, "or I won't keep your company. I don't gainsay her being comely to look

on, but I will maintain that she's likely to show poor conduct. She seems to think herself too good to talk to a body.
From what Squire Jones had tell'd me, I some expected to be
quite captivated by her company. Now, to my reckoning,
Lowizy Grant is much more pritty behaved than Betsey
Temple. She wouldn't so much as hold discourse with me,
when I wanted to ask her how she felt on coming home and
missing her mammy."

"Perhaps she didn't understand you, woman; you are none
of the best linguister; and then Miss Lizzy has been exercising
the king's English under a great Lon'on lady, and, for that
matter, can talk the language almost as well as myself, or
any native-born British subject. You've forgot your schooling,
and the young mistress is a great scollard."

"Mistress!" cried Remarkable. "Don't make one out to be
a nigger, Benjamin. She's no mistress of mine and never
will be. And as to speech, I hold myself as second to nobody
out of New England. I was born and raised in Essex county;
and I've always heer'n say that the Bay State was provarbal
for pronounsation!"

"I've often heard of that Bay of State," said Benjamin,
"but can't say that I've ever been in it, nor do I know
exactly whereaway it is that it lays; but I suppose there is
good anchorage in it, and that it's no bad place for the
taking of ling; but for size, it can't be so much as a yawl to a
sloop of war, compared with the Bay of Biscay, or, mayhap, Torbay. And as for language, if you want to hear the
dictionary overhauled, like a long line in a blow, you
must go to Wapping, and listen to the Lon'oners, as they deal
out their lingo. Howsomever, I see no such mighty matter
that Miss Lizzy has been doing to you, good woman, so take
another drop of your brew, and forgive and forget, like an
honest soul."

"No, indeed! And I shan't do sitch a thing, Benjamin.
This treatment is a newity to me, and what I won't put up
with. I have a hundred and fifty dollars at use, besides a bed
and twenty sheep, to good; and I don't crave to live in a
house where a body mustn't call a young woman by her
given name to her face. I *will* call her Betsey as much as I
please: it's a free country, and no one can stop me. I did
intend to stop while summer, but I shall quit tomorrow
morning; and I will talk just as I please."

"For that matter, Mistress Remarkable," said Benjamin, "there's none here who will contradict you; for I'm of opinion that it would be as easy to stop a hurricane with a Barcelony handkerchy, as to bring up your tongue when the stopper is off. I say, good woman, do they grow many monkeys along the shores of that Bay of State?"

"You're a monkey yourself, Mr. Penguillan," cried the enraged housekeeper, "or a bear! A black, beastly bear! And an't fit for a decent woman to stay with. I'll never keep your company again, sir, if I should live thirty years with the Judge. Sitch talk is more befitting the kitchen than the keeping room of a house of one who is well to do in the world."

"Look you, Mistress Pitty—Patty—Prettybones, mayhap I'm some such matter as a bear, as they will find who come to grapple with me; but dam'me if I'm a monkey—a thing that chatters without knowing a word of what it says—a parrot, that will hold a dialogue, for what an honest man knows, in a dozen languages; mayhap in the Bay of State lingo; mayhap in Greek or High Dutch. But dost it know what it means itself? Canst answer me that, good woman? Your midshipman can sing out, and pass the word, when the captain gives the order, but just set him adrift by himself, and let him work the ship of his own head, and stop my grog, if you don't find all the Johnny Raws laughing at him."

"Stop your grog, indeed!" said Remarkable, rising with great indignation, and seizing a candle; "You're groggy now, Benjamin, and I'll quit the room before I hear any misbecoming words from you."

The housekeeper retired, with a manner but little less dignified, as she thought, than the air of the heiress, muttering, as she drew the door after her, with a noise like the report of a musket, the opprobrious terms of "drunkard," "sot," and "beast."

"Who's that you say is drunk?" cried Benjamin, fiercely, rising and making a movement towards Remarkable. "You talk of mustering yourself with a lady! You're just fit to grumble and find fault. Where the devil should you larn behavior and dictionary? In your damned Bay of State, ha?"

Benjamin here fell back in his chair, and soon gave vent to certain ominous sounds, which resembled not a little the growling of his favorite animal, the bear itself. Before, however, he was quite locked—to use the language that would suit

the Della-Cruscan humor of certain refined minds of the
present day—"in the arms of Morpheus," he spoke aloud,
observing due pauses between his epithets, the impressive
terms of "monkey," "parrot," "picnic," "tarpot," and "lin-
guisters."

We shall not attempt to explain his meaning, nor connect
his sentences; and our readers must be satisfied with our in-
forming them that they were expressed with all that coolness
of contempt that a man might well be supposed to feel for a
monkey.

Nearly two hours passed in this sleep before the major-
domo was awakened by the noisy entrance of Richard,
Major Hartmann, and the master of the mansion. Benjamin so
far rallied his confused faculties, as to shape the course of
the two former to their respective apartments, when he disappeared himself, leaving the task of securing the house to
him who was most interested in its safety. Locks and bars
were but little attended to in the early day of that settlement; and so soon as Marmaduke had given an eye to the
enormous fires of his dwelling, he retired. With this act of
prudence closes the first night of our tale.

CHAPTER XVI

Watch. (aside) Some treason, masters—
Yet stand close.

MUCH ADO ABOUT NOTHING

IT was fortunate for more than one of the bacchanalians
who left the "Bold Dragoon" late in the evening, that the
severe cold of the season was becoming rapidly less dangerous, as they threaded the different mazes through the snowbanks that led to their respective dwellings. Thin, driving
clouds began towards morning to flit across the heavens, and
the moon set behind a volume of vapor that was impelled
furiously towards the north, carrying with it the softer atmosphere from the distant ocean. The rising sun was obscured by
denser and increasing columns of clouds, while the southerly
wind that rushed up the valley, brought the never-failing
symptoms of a thaw.

It was quite late in the morning before Elizabeth, observing the faint glow which appeared on the eastern mountain, long after the light of the sun had struck the opposite hills, ventured from the house, with a view to gratify her curiosity with a glance by daylight at the surrounding objects, before the tardy revelers of the Christmas Eve should make their appearance at the breakfast table. While she was drawing the folds of her pelisse more closely around her form, to guard against a cold that was yet great, though rapidly yielding, in the small enclosure that opened in the rear of the house on a little thicket of low pines, that were springing up where trees of a mightier growth had lately stood, she was surprised at the voice of Mr. Jones.

"Merry Christmas, Merry Christmas to you, cousin Bess," he shouted. "Ah, ha! an early riser, I see; but I knew I should steal a march on you. I never was in a house yet, where I didn't get the first Christmas greeting on every soul in it, man, woman, and child; great and small; black, white, and yellow. But stop a minute, till I can just slip on my coat; you are about to look at the improvements, I see, which no one can explain so well as I, who planned them all. It will be an hour before 'duke and the Major can sleep off Mrs. Hollister's confounded distillations, and so I'll come down and go with you."

Elizabeth turned, and observed her cousin in his nightcap, with his head out of his bedroom window, where his zeal for pre-eminence, in defiance of the weather, had impelled him to thrust it. She laughed, and promising to wait for his company, re-entered the house, making her appearance again, holding in her hand a packet that was secured by several large and important seals, just in time to meet the gentleman.

"Come, Bessy, come," he cried, drawing one of her arms through his own; "the snow begins to give, but it will bear us yet. Don't you snuff old Pennsylvania in the very air? This is a vile climate, girl; now at sunset, last evening, it was cold enough to freeze a man's zeal, and that, I can tell you, takes a thermometer near zero for me; then about nine or ten it began to moderate; at twelve it was quite mild, and here all the rest of the night I have been so hot, as not to bear a blanket on the bed.—Holla! Aggy—Merry Christmas, Aggy —I say, do you hear me, you black dog! there's a dollar for you; and if the gentlemen get up before I come back, do you come out and let me know. I wouldn't have 'duke get the start of me for the worth of your head."

The black caught the money from the snow, and promising a due degree of watchfulness, he gave the dollar a whirl of twenty feet in the air, and catching it as it fell, in the palm of his hand, he withdrew to the kitchen, to exhibit his present, with a heart as light as his face was happy in his expression.

"Oh, rest easy, my dear coz," said the young lady; "I took a look in at my father, who is likely to sleep an hour; and, by using due vigilance, you will secure all the honors of the season."

"Why, 'duke is your father, Elizabeth; but 'duke is a man who likes to be foremost, even in trifles. Now, as for myself, I care for no such things, except in the way of competition; for a thing which is of no moment in itself may be made of importance in the way of competition. So it is with your father—he loves to be first; but I only struggle with him as a competitor."

"It's all very clear, sir," said Elizabeth; "you would not care a fig for distinction if there were no one in the world but yourself; but as there happen to be a great many others, why you must struggle with them all—in the way of competition."

"Exactly so; I see you are a clever girl, Bess, and one who does credit to her masters. It was my plan to send you to that school; for when your father first mentioned the thing, I wrote a private letter for advice to a judicious friend in the city, who recommended the very school you went to. 'Duke was a little obstinate at first, as usual, but when he heard the truth, he was obliged to send you."

"Well, a truce to 'duke's foibles, sir; he is my father; and if you knew what he has been doing for you while we were in Albany, you would deal more tenderly with his character."

"For me!" cried Richard, pausing a moment in his walk to reflect. "Oh! He got the plans of the new Dutch meeting-house for me, I suppose; but I care very little about it, for a man of a certain kind of talent is seldom aided by any foreign suggestions: his own brain is the best architect."

"No such thing," said Elizabeth, looking provokingly knowing.

"No! Let me see—perhaps he had my name put in the bill for the new turnpike, as a director."

"He might possibly; but it is not to such an appointment that I allude."

"Such an appointment!" repeated Mr. Jones, who began to fidget with curiosity; "then it is an appointment. If it is in the militia, I won't take it."

"No, no, it is not in the militia," cried Elizabeth, showing the packet in her hand, and then drawing it back with a coquettish air; "it is an office of both honor and emolument."

"Honor and emolument!" echoed Richard, in painful suspense; "show me the paper, girl. Say, is it an office where there is anything to *do?*"

"You have hit it, cousin Dickon; it is the executive office of the county; at least so said my father when he gave me this packet to offer you as a Christmas box. 'Surely if anything will please Dickon,' he said, 'it will be to fill the executive chair of the county.'"

"Executive chair! What nonsense!" cried the impatient gentleman, snatching the packet from her hand. "There is no such office in the county. Eh! What! It is, I declare, a commission, appointing Richard Jones, Esquire, sheriff of the county. Well, this is kind in 'duke, positively. I must say 'duke has a warm heart and never forgets his friends. Sheriff! High Sheriff of ———! It sounds well, Bess, but it shall execute better. 'Duke is a judicious man, after all, and knows human nature thoroughly. I'm much obliged to him," continued Richard, using the skirt of his coat unconsciously to wipe his eyes; "though I would do as much for him any day, as he shall see, if I have an opportunity to perform any of the duties of my office on him. It shall be done, cousin Bess—it shall be done, I say.—How this cursed south wind makes one's eyes water!"

"Now, Richard," said the laughing maiden, "now I think you will find something to do. I have often heard you complain of old, that there was nothing to do in this new country, while to my eyes it seemed as if everything remained to be done."

"Do!" echoed Richard, who blew his nose, raised his little form to its greatest elevation, and looked serious. "Everything depends on system, girl. I shall sit down this afternoon, and systematize the county. I must have deputies, you know. I will divide the county into districts, over which I will place my deputies; and I will have one for the village, which I will call my home department. Let me see—oh! Benjamin! Yes, Benjamin will make a good deputy; he has been naturalized, and would answer admirably, if he could only ride on horseback."

"Yes, Mr. Sheriff," said his companion; "and as he understands ropes so well, he would be very expert, should occasion happen for his services, in another way."

"No," interrupted the other, "I flatter myself that no man could hang a man better than—that is—ha—oh! yes, Benjamin would do extremely well, in such an unfortunate dilemma, if he could be persuaded to attempt it. But I should despair of the thing. I never could induce him to hang, or teach him to ride on horseback. I must seek another deputy."

"Well, sir, as you have abundant leisure for all these important affairs, I beg that you will forget that you are High Sheriff, and devote some little of your time to gallantry. Where are the beauties and improvements which you were to show me?"

"Where? Why everywhere. Here I have laid out some new streets; and when they are opened, and the trees felled, and they are all built up, will they not make a fine town? Well, 'duke is a liberal-hearted fellow, with all his stubbornness. —Yes, yes, I must have at least four deputies, besides a jailor."

"I see no streets in the direction of our walk," said Elizabeth, "unless you call the short avenues through these pine bushes by that name. Surely you do not contemplate building houses, very soon, in that forest before us, and in those swamps."

"We must run our streets by the compass, coz, and disregard trees, hills, ponds, stumps, or, in fact, anything but posterity. Such is the will of your father, and your father, you know——"

"Had you made Sheriff, Mr. Jones," interrupted the lady, with a tone that said very plainly to the gentleman, that he was touching a forbidden subject.

"I know it, I know it," cried Richard; "and if it were in my power, I'd make 'duke a king. He is a noble-hearted fellow and would make an excellent king; that is, if he had a good prime minister.—But who have we here? Voices in the bushes—a combination about mischief, I'll wager my commission. Let us draw near, and examine a little into the matter."

During this dialogue, as the parties had kept in motion, Richard and his cousin advanced some distance from the house, into the open space in the rear of the village, where, as may be gathered from the conversation, streets were planned, and future dwellings contemplated; but where, in truth, the only mark of improvement that was to be seen was a neglected clearing along the skirt of a dark forest of mighty pines, over which the bushes or sprouts of the same tree had sprung up, to a height that interspersed the fields of snow with little thickets of evergreen. The rushing of the wind, as it whistled through the tops of these mimic trees, prevented the footsteps of the pair from being heard, while the branches concealed their persons. Thus aided, the listeners drew nigh to a spot where the young hunter, Leatherstocking, and the Indian chief were collected in an earnest consultation. The former was urgent in his manner and seemed to think the subject of deep importance, while Natty appeared to listen with more than his usual attention to what the other was saying. Mohegan stood a little on one side, with his head sunken on his chest, his hair falling forward, so as to conceal most of his features, and his whole attitude expressive of deep dejection, if not of shame.

"Let us withdraw," whispered Elizabeth; "we are intruders, and can have no right to listen to the secrets of these men."

"No right!" returned Richard, a little impatiently, in the same tone, and drawing her arm so forcibly through his own as to prevent her retreat; "you forget, cousin, that it is my duty to preserve the peace of the county, and see the laws executed. These wanderers frequently commit depredations; though I do not think John would do anything secretly. Poor fellow! He was quite boozy last night, and hardly seems to be over it yet. Let us draw nigher, and hear what they say."

Notwithstanding the lady's reluctance, Richard, stimulated doubtless by his nice sense of duty, prevailed; and they were soon so near as distinctly to hear sounds.

"The bird must be had," said Natty, "by fair means or foul. Heigh-ho! I've known the time, lad, when the wild turkeys wasn't over scarce in the country; though you must go into the Virginy gaps, if you want them now. To be sure, there is a different taste to a partridge, and a well-fatted turkey; though, to my eating, beaver's tail and bear's hams makes the best of food. But then everyone has his own appetite. I gave the last farthing, all to that shilling, to the French trader, this very morning, as I came through the town, for powder; so, as you have nothing, we can have but one shot for it. I know that Billy Kirby is out, and means to have a pull of the trigger at that very turkey. John has a true eye for a single fire, and somehow, my hand shakes so whenever I have to do anything extrawnary that I often lose my aim. Now, when I killed the she-bear this fall, with her cubs, though they were so mighty ravenous, I knocked them over one at a shot, and loaded while I dodged the trees in the bargain; but this is a very different thing, Mr. Oliver."

"This," cried the young man with an accent that sounded as if he took a bitter pleasure in his poverty, while he held a shilling up before his eyes—"This is all the treasure that I possess—this and my rifle! Now, indeed, I have become a man of the woods, and must place my sole dependence on the chase. Come, Natty, let us stake the last penny for the bird; with your aim, it cannot fail to be successful."

"I would rather it should be John, lad; my heart jumps into my mouth, because you set your mind so much on't; and I'm sartain that I shall miss the bird. Them Indians can shoot one time as well as another; nothing ever troubles them. I say, John, here's a shilling; take my rifle, and get a shot at the big turkey they've put up at the stump. Mr. Oliver is over-anxious for the creater, and I'm sure to do nothing when I have overanxiety about it."

The Indian turned his head gloomily, and after looking keenly for a moment, in profound silence, at his companions, he replied:

"When John was young, eyesight was not straighter than his bullet. The Mingo squaws cried out at the sound of his rifle. The Mingo warriors were made squaws. When did he ever shoot twice! The eagle went above the clouds, when he passed the wigwam of Chingachgook; his feathers were plenty with the women. But see," he said, raising his voice from the low, mournful tones in which he had spoken to a pitch of keen excitement, and stretching forth both hands—"they shake like a deer at the wolf's howl. Is John old? When was a Mohican a squaw, with seventy winters! No! the white man brings old age with him—rum is his tomahawk!"

"Why then do you use it, old man?" exclaimed the young hunter; "why will one, so noble by nature, aid the devices of the devil by making himself a beast!"

"Beast! Is John a beast?" replied the Indian, slowly; "Yes; you say no lie, child of the Fire-eater! John is a beast. The smokes were once few in these hills. The deer would lick the hand of a white man, and the birds rest on his head. They were strangers to him. My fathers came from the shores of the salt lake. They fled before rum. They came to their grandfather, and they lived in peace; or, when they did raise the hatchet, it was to strike it into the brain of a Mingo. They gathered around the council fire, and what they said was done. Then John was the man. But warriors and traders with light eyes followed them. One brought the long knife, and one brought rum. They were more than the pines on the mountains; and they broke up the councils, and took the lands. The evil spirit was in their jugs, and they let him loose. Yes, yes—you say no lie, Young Eagle; John is a Christian beast."

"Forgive me, old warrior," cried the youth, grasping his hand; "I should be the last to reproach you. The curses of heaven light on the cupidity that has destroyed such a race. Remember, John, that I am of your family, and it is now my greatest pride."

The muscles of Mohegan relaxed a little, and he said, more mildly:

"You are a Delaware, my son; your words are not heard—John cannot shoot."

"I thought that lad had Indian blood in him," whispered Richard, "by the awkward way he handled my horses last night. You see, coz, they never use harness. But the poor fellow shall have two shots at the turkey, if he wants it, for I'll give him another shilling myself; though, perhaps, I had better offer to shoot for him. They have got up their Christmas sports, I find, in the bushes yonder, where you hear the laughter; though it is a queer taste this chap has for turkey; not but what it is good eating too."

"Hold, cousin Richard," exclaimed Elizabeth, clinging to his arm, "would it be delicate to offer a shilling to that gentleman?"

"Gentleman again! Do you think a half-breed, like him, will refuse money? No, no, girl, he will take the shilling; ay! and even rum, too, notwithstanding he moralizes so much about it. But I'll give the lad a chance for his turkey, for that Billy Kirby is one of the best marksmen in the country; that is, if we except the—the gentleman."

"Then," said Elizabeth, who found her strength unequal to her will, "then, sir, I will speak." She advanced, with an air of determination, in front of her cousin, and entered the little circle of bushes that surrounded the trio of hunters. Her appearance startled the youth, who at first made an unequivocal motion towards retiring, but, recollecting himself, bowed, by lifting his cap, and resumed his attitude of leaning on his rifle. Neither Natty nor Mohegan betrayed any emotion, though the appearance of Elizabeth was so entirely unexpected.

"I find," she said, "that the old Christmas sport of shooting the turkey is yet in use among you. I feel inclined to try my chance for a bird. Which of you will take this money, and, after paying my fee, give me the aid of his rifle?"

"Is this a sport for a lady?" exclaimed the young hunter, with an emphasis that could not well be mistaken, and with a rapidity that showed he spoke without consulting anything but feeling.

"Why not, sir? If it be inhuman, the sin is not confined to one sex only. But I have my humor as well as others. I ask not your assistance; but"—turning to Natty, and dropping a dollar in his hand—"this old veteran of the forest will not be so ungallant as to refuse one fire for a lady."

Leatherstocking dropped the money into his pouch, and throwing up the end of his rifle, he freshened his priming; and, first laughing in his usual manner, he threw the piece over his shoulder, and said:

"If Billy Kirby don't get the bird before me, and the Frenchman's powder don't hang fire this damp morning, you'll see as fine a turkey dead, in a few minutes, as ever was eaten in the Judge's shanty. I have know'd the Dutch women, on the Mohawk and Schoharie, count greatly on coming to the merrymakings; and so, lad, you shouldn't be short with the lady. Come, let us go forward, for if we wait, the finest bird will be gone."

"But I have a right before you, Natty, and shall try my own

luck first. You will excuse me, Miss Temple; I have much reason to wish that bird, and may seem ungallant, but I must claim my privileges."

"Claim anything that is justly your own, sir," returned the lady; "we are both adventurers; and this is my knight. I trust my fortune to his hand and eye. Lead on, Sir Leatherstocking, and we will follow."

Natty, who seemed pleased with the frank address of the young and beauteous Elizabeth, who had so singularly entrusted him with such a commission, returned the bright smile with which she had addressed him, by his own peculiar mark of mirth, and moved across the snow, towards the spot whence the sounds of boisterous mirth proceeded, with the long strides of a hunter. His companions followed in silence, the youth casting frequent and uneasy glances towards Elizabeth, who was detained by a motion from Richard.

"I should think, Miss Temple," he said, so soon as the others were out of hearing, "that if you really wished a turkey, you would not have taken a stranger for the office, and such a one as Leatherstocking. But I can hardly believe that you are serious, for I have fifty at this moment shut up in the coops, in every stage of fat, so that you might choose any quality you pleased. There are six that I am trying an experiment on, by giving them brickbats with——"

"Enough, cousin Dickon," interrupted the lady; "I do wish the bird, and it is because I so wish, that I commissioned this Mr. Leatherstocking."

"Did you ever hear of the great shot that I made at the wolf, cousin Elizabeth, who was carrying off your father's sheep?" said Richard, drawing himself up into an air of displeasure. "He had the sheep on his back; and had the head of the wolf been on the other side, I should have killed him dead; as it was——"

"You killed the sheep—I know it all, dear coz. But would it have been decorous for the High Sheriff of —— to mingle in such sports as these?"

"Surely you did not think that I intended actually to fire with my own hands?" said Mr. Jones. "But let us follow, and see the shooting. There is no fear of anything unpleasant occurring to a female in this new country, especially to your father's daughter, and in my presence."

"My father's daughter fears nothing, sir, more especially when escorted by the highest executive officer in the county."

She took his arm, and he led her through the mazes of the bushes to the spot where most of the young men of the village were collected for the sports of shooting a Christmas match, and whither Natty and his companions had already preceded them.

CHAPTER XVII

I guess, by all this quaint array,
The burghers hold their sports to-day.

SCOTT

THE ancient amusement of shooting the Christmas turkey is one of the few sports that the settlers of a new country seldom or never neglect to observe. It was connected with the daily practices of a people who often laid aside the ax or the scythe to seize the rifle, as the deer glided through the forests they were felling, or the bear entered their rough meadows to scent the air of a clearing, and to scan, with a look of sagacity, the progress of the invader.

On the present occasion, the usual amusement of the day had been a little hastened, in order to allow a fair opportunity to Mr. Grant, whose exhibition was not less a treat to the young sportsmen, than the one which engaged their present attention. The owner of the birds was a free black, who had prepared for the occasion a collection of game that was admirably qualified to inflame the appetite of an epicure, and was well adapted to the means and skill of the different competitors, who were of all ages. He had offered to the younger and more humble marksmen divers birds of an inferior quality, and some shooting had already taken place, much to the pecuniary advantage of the sable owner of the game. The order of the sports was extremely simple, and well understood. The bird was fastened by a string to the stump of a large pine, the side of which, towards the point where the marksmen were placed, had been flattened with an ax, in order that it might serve the purpose of a target by which the merit of each individual might be ascertained. The distance between the stump and shooting stand was one hundred measured yards: a foot more or a foot less being thought an invasion of the right of one of the parties. The Negro affixed his own price to every bird, and the terms of the chance; but when these were once established, he was obliged by the strict principles of public justice that prevailed in the country, to admit any adventurer who might offer.

The throng consisted of some twenty or thirty young men, most of whom had rifles, and a collection of all the boys in the village. The little urchins, clad in coarse but warm garments, stood gathered around the more distinguished marksmen, with their hands stuck under their waistbands, listening eagerly to the boastful stories of skill that had been exhibited on former occasions, and were already emulating in their hearts these wonderful deeds in gunnery.

The chief speaker was the man who had been mentioned by Natty as Billy Kirby. This fellow, whose occupation when he did labor, was that of clearing lands, or chopping jobs, was of great stature, and carried, in his very air, the index of his character. He was a noisy, boisterous, reckless lad, whose good-natured eye contradicted the bluntness and bullying tenor of his speech. For weeks he would lounge around the taverns of the county, in a state of perfect idleness, or doing small jobs for his liquor and his meals, and caviling with applicants about the prices of his labor: frequently preferring idleness to an abatement of a tittle of his independence, or a cent in his wages. But when these embarrassing points were satisfactorily arranged, he would shoulder his ax and his rifle, slip his arms through the straps of his pack, and enter the woods with the tread of a Hercules. His first object was to learn his limits, round which he would pace, occasionally freshening, with a blow of his ax, the marks on the boundary trees; and then he would proceed with an air of great deliberation to the center of his premises, and, throwing aside his superfluous garments, measure, with a knowing eye, one or two of the nearest trees that were towering apparently into the very clouds as he gazed upwards. Commonly selecting one of the most noble for the first trial of his power, he would approach it with a listless air, whistling a low tune; and wielding his ax with a certain flourish, not unlike the salutes of a fencing master, he would strike a light blow into the bark, and measure his distance. The pause that followed was ominous of the fall of the forest which had flourished there for centuries. The heavy and brisk blows that he struck were soon succeeded by the thundering report of the tree, as it came, first cracking and threatening, with the separation of its own last ligaments, then threshing and tearing with its branches the tops of its surrounding brethren, and finally meeting the ground with a shock but little inferior to an earthquake. From that moment the sounds of the ax were ceaseless, while the falling of the trees was like a distant cannonading; and the daylight broke into the depths of the woods with the suddenness of a winter morning.

For days, weeks, nay months, Billy Kirby would toil with an ardor that evinced his native spirit, and with an effect that seemed magical, until, his chopping being ended, his stentorian lungs could be heard emitting sounds, as he called to his patient oxen, which rang through the hills like the cries of an alarm. He had been often heard, on a mild summer's evening, a long mile across the vale of Templeton; when the echoes from the mountains would take up his cries, until they died away in feeble sounds from the distant rocks that overhung the lake. His piles, or to use the language of the country, his logging, ended, with a dispatch that could only accompany his dexterity and Herculean strength, the jobber would collect together his implements of labor, light the heaps of timber, and march away under the blaze of the prostrate forest, like the conqueror of some city, who, having first prevailed over his adversary, applies the torch as the finishing blow to his conquest. For a long time Billy Kirby would then be seen, sauntering around the taverns, the rider of scrub races, the bully of cockfights, and not unfrequently the hero of such sports as the one in hand.

Between him and the Leatherstocking, there had long existed a jealous rivalry on the point of skill with the rifle. Notwithstanding the long practice of Natty, it was commonly supposed that the steady nerves and quick eye of the wood chopper rendered him his equal. The competition had, however, been confined hitherto to boastings and comparisons made from their success in various hunting excursions; but this was the first time that they had ever come in open collision. A good deal of higgling about the price of the choicest bird had taken place between Billy Kirby and its owner before Natty and his companions rejoined the sportsmen. It had, however, been settled at one shilling * a shot, which was the highest sum ever exacted, the black taking care to protect himself from losses as much as possible, by the conditions of the sport. The turkey was already fastened at the "mark," but its body was entirely hid by the surrounding snow, nothing being visible but its red swelling head and its long neck. If the bird was injured by any bullet that struck below the snow, it was to continue the property of its present owner; but if a feather was touched in a visible part, the animal became the prize of the successful adventurer.

These terms were loudly proclaimed by the Negro, who was seated in the snow in a somewhat hazardous vicinity to his favorite bird, when Elizabeth and her cousin approached the noisy sportsmen. The sounds of mirth and contention sensibly lowered at this unexpected visit; but, after a moment's pause, the curious interest exhibited in the face of the young lady, together with her smiling air, restored the freedom of the morning; though it was somewhat chastened, both in language and vehemence, by the presence of such a spectator.

"Stand out of the way there, boys!" cried the wood chopper, who was placing himself at the shooting point—"stand out of the way, you little rascals, or I will shoot through you. Now Brom, take leave of your turkey."

"Stop!" cried the young hunter; "I am a candidate for a chance. Here is my shilling, Brom; I wish a shot too."

"You may wish it in welcome," cried Kirby, "but if I ruffle the gobbler's feathers, how are you to get it? Is money so plenty in your deerskin pocket that you pay for a chance that you may never have?"

"How know you, sir, how plenty money is in my pocket?" said the youth fiercely. "Here is my shilling, Brom, and I claim a right to shoot."

"Don't be crabbed, my boy," said the other, who was very coolly fixing his flint. "They say you have a hole in your left shoulder, yourself: so I think Brom may give you a fire for half price. It will take a keen one to hit that bird, I

---

* Before the revolution, each province had its own money of account, though neither coined any but copper pieces. In New York the Spanish dollar was divided into eight shillings, each of the value of a fraction more than sixpence sterling. At present the Union has provided a decimal system, with coins to represent it.

can tell you, my lad, even if I give you a chance, which is what I have no mind to do."

"Don't be boasting, Billy Kirby," said Natty, throwing the breech of his rifle into the snow and leaning on its barrel; "you'll get but one shot at the creater, for if the lad misses his aim, which wouldn't be a wonder if he did, with his arm so stiff and sore, you'll find a good piece and an old eye coming a'ter you. Maybe it's true that I can't shoot as I used to could, but a hundred yards is a short distance for a long rifle."

"What, old Leatherstocking, are you out this morning?" cried his reckless opponent. "Well, fair play's a jewel. I've the lead of you, old fellow; so here goes for a dry throat or a good dinner."

The countenance of the Negro evinced not only all the interest which his pecuniary adventure might occasion, but also the keen excitement that the sport produced in the others, though with a very different wish as to the result. While the wood chopper was slowly and steadily raising his rifle, he bawled:

"Fair play, Billy Kirby—stand back—make 'em stand back, boys—gib a nibber fair play—poss-up, gobbler; shake a head, fool; don't you see 'em taking aim?"

These cries, which were intended as much to distract the attention of the marksman as for anything else, were fruitless.

The nerves of the wood chopper were not so easily shaken, and he took his aim with the utmost deliberation. Stillness prevailed for a moment, and he fired. The head of the turkey was seen to dash on one side, and its wings were spread in momentary fluttering; but it settled itself down calmly into its bed of snow, and glanced its eyes uneasily around. For a time long enough to draw a deep breath, not a sound was heard. The silence was then broken by the noise of the Negro, who laughed, and shook his body, with all kinds of antics, rolling over in the snow in the excess of delight.

"Well done a gobbler," he cried, jumping up and affecting to embrace his bird; "I tell 'em to poss-up, and you see 'em dodge. Gib anoder shillin', Billy, and hab anoder shot."

"No—the shot is mine," said the young hunter; "you have my money already. Leave the mark, and let me try my luck."

"Ah! It's but money thrown away, lad," said Leather-stocking. "A turkey's head and neck is but a small mark for a new hand and a lame shoulder. You'd best let me take the fire, and maybe we can make some settlement with the lady about the bird."

"The chance is mine," said the young hunter. "Clear the ground, that I may take it."

The discussions and disputes concerning the last shot were now abating, it having been determined that if the turkey's head had been anywhere but just where it was at the moment, the bird must certainly have been killed. There was not much excitement produced by the preparations of the youth, who proceeded in a hurried manner to take his aim, and was in the act of pulling the trigger, when he was stopped by Natty.

"Your hand shakes, lad," he said, "and you seem over-eager. Bullet wounds are apt to weaken flesh, and to my judgment, you'll not shoot so well as in common. If you will fire, you should shoot quick, before there is time to shake off the aim."

"Fair play," again shouted the Negro; "fair play—gib a nigger fair play. What right a Nat-Bumppo advise a young man? Let 'em shoot—clear a ground."

The youth fired with great rapidity, but no motion was made by the turkey; and when the examiners for the ball returned from the "mark," they declared that he had missed the stump.

Elizabeth observed the change in his countenance, and could not help feeling surprise, that one so evidently superior to his companions should feel a trifling loss so sensibly. But her own champion was now preparing to enter the lists.

The mirth of Brom, which had been again excited, though in a much smaller degree than before, by the failure of the second adventurer, vanished the instant Natty took his stand. His skin became mottled with large brown spots, that fearfully sullied the luster of his native ebony, while his enormous lips gradually compressed around two rows of ivory that had hitherto been shining in his visage, like pearls set in jet. His nostrils, at all times the most conspicuous features of his face, dilated, until they covered the greater part of the diameter of his countenance; while his brown and bony hands unconsciously grasped the snowcrust near him, the excitement of the moment completely overcoming his native dread of cold.

While these indications of apprehension were exhibited in the sable owner of the turkey, the man who gave rise to this extraordinary emotion was as calm and collected as if there was not to be a single spectator of his skill.

"I was down in the Dutch settlements on the Schoharie," said Natty, carefully removing the leather guard from the lock of his rifle, "just before the breaking out of the last war, and there was a shooting match among the boys; so I took a hand. I think I opened a good many Dutch eyes that day; for I won the powder horn, three bars of lead, and a pound of as good powder as ever flashed in pan. Lord! How they did swear in Jarman! They did tell me of one drunken Dutchman who said he'd have the life of me before I got back to the lake ag'in. But if he had put his rifle to his shoulder with evil intent God would have punished him for it; and even if the Lord didn't, and he had missed his aim, I know one that would have given him as good as he sent, and better too, if good shooting could come into the 'count."

By this time the old hunter was ready for his business, and throwing his right leg far behind him, and stretching his left arm along the barrel of his piece, he raised it towards the bird. Every eye glanced rapidly from the marksman to the mark; but at the moment when each ear was expecting the report of the rifle, they were disappointed by the ticking sound of the flint.

"A snap, a snap!" shouted the Negro, springing from his crouching posture like a madman, before his bird. "A snap good as fire—Natty Bumppo gun he snap—Natty Bumppo miss a turkey!"

"Natty Bumppo hit a nigger," said the indignant old hunter, "if you don't get out of the way, Brom. It's contrary to the reason of the thing, boy, that a snap should count for a fire, when one is nothing more than a firestone striking a steel pan, and the other is sudden death; so get out of my way, boy, and let me show Billy Kirby how to shoot a Christmas turkey."

"Gib a nigger fair play!" cried the black, who continued resolutely to maintain his post, and making that appeal to the justice of his auditors, which the degraded condition of his caste so naturally suggested. "Ebery body know dat snap as good as fire. Leab it to Massa Jone—leab it to lady."

"Sartain," said the wood chopper; "it's the law of the game in this part of the country, Leatherstocking. If you fire ag'in you must pay up the other shilling. I b'lieve I'll try luck once more myself; so Brom, here's my money, and I take the next fire."

"It's likely you know the laws of the woods better than I do, Billy Kirby," returned Natty. "You come in with the settlers, with an oxgoad in your hand, and I come in with moccasins on my feet, and with a good rifle on my shoulder, so long back as afore the old war. Which is likely to know the best? I say no man need tell me that snapping is as good as firing when I pull the trigger."

"Leab it to Massa Jone," said the alarmed Negro; "he know ebery ting."

This appeal to the knowledge of Richard was too flattering to be unheeded. He therefore advanced a little from the spot whither the delicacy of Elizabeth had induced her to withdraw, and gave the following opinion, with the gravity that the subject and his own rank demanded:

"There seems to be a difference in opinion," he said, "on the subject of Nathaniel Bumppo's right to shoot at Abraham Freeborn's turkey, without the said Nathaniel paying one shilling for the privilege." This fact was too evident to be denied, and after pausing a moment, that the audience might digest his premises, Richard proceeded. "It seems proper that I should decide this question, as I am bound to preserve the peace of the county; and men with deadly weapons in their hands should not be heedlessly left to contention and their own malignant passions. It appears that there was no agreement, either in writing or in words, on the disputed point; therefore we must reason from analogy, which is, as it were, comparing one thing with another. Now, in duels, where both parties shoot, it is generally the rule that a snap is a fire; and if such is the rule, where the party has a right to fire back again, it seems to me unreasonable to say that a man may stand snapping at a defenseless turkey all day. I therefore am of opinion that Nathaniel Bumppo has lost his chance, and must pay another shilling before he renews his right."

As this opinion came from so high a quarter, and was de-

livered with effect, it silenced all murmurs—for the whole
of the spectators had begun to take sides with great warmth
—except from the Leatherstocking himself.

"I think Miss Elizabeth's thoughts should be taken," said
Natty. "I've known the squaws give very good counsel when
the Indians have been dumbfoundered. If she says that I
ought to lose, I agree to give it up."

"Then I adjudge you to be a loser for this time," said
Miss Temple; "but pay your money and renew your chance;
unless Brom will sell me the bird for a dollar. I will give
him the money and save the life of the poor victim."

This proposition was evidently but little relished by any
of the listeners, even the Negro feeling the evil excitement
of the chances. In the meanwhile, as Billy Kirby was preparing himself for another shot, Natty left the stand, with an
extremely dissatisfied manner, muttering:

"There hasn't been such a thing as a good flint sold at
the foot of the lake since the Indian traders used to come
into the country; and if a body should go into the flats
along the streams in the hills to hunt for such a thing, it's
ten to one but they will be all covered up with the plow.
Heigh-ho! It seems to me that just as the game grows scarce,
and a body wants the best ammunition to get a livelihood,
everything that's bad falls on him, like a judgment. But I'll
change the stone, for Billy Kirby hasn't the eye for such a
mark, I know."

The wood chopper seemed now entirely sensible that his
reputation depended on his care; nor did he neglect any
means to insure success. He drew up his rifle and renewed
his aim again and again, still appearing reluctant to fire.
No sound was heard from even Brom, during these por-
tentous movements, until Kirby discharged his piece, with
the same want of success as before. Then, indeed, the shouts
of the Negro rang through the bushes and sounded among
the trees of the neighboring forest like the outcries of a
tribe of Indians. He laughed, rolling his head first on one
side, then on the other, until nature seemed exhausted with
mirth. He danced until his legs were wearied with motion,
in the snow; and, in short, he exhibited all that violence of
joy that characterizes the mirth of a thoughtless Negro.

The wood chopper had exerted all his art, and felt a
proportionate degree of disappointment at the failure. He

first examined the bird with the utmost attention, and more than once suggested that he had touched its feathers; but the voice of the multitude was against him, for it felt disposed to listen to the often repeated cries of the black, to "gib a nigger fair play."

Finding it impossible to make out a title to the bird, Kirby turned fiercely to the black, and said:

"Shut your oven, you crow! Where is the man that can hit a turkey's head at a hundred yards? I was a fool for trying. You needn't make an uproar, like a falling pine tree, about it. Show me the man who can do it."

"Look this-a-way, Billy Kirby," said Leatherstocking, "and let them clear the mark, and I'll show you a man who's made better shots afore now, and that when he's been hard pressed by the savages and wild beasts."

"Perhaps there is one whose rights come before ours, Leatherstocking," said Miss Temple; "if so, we will waive our privilege."

"If it be me that you have reference to," said the young hunter, "I shall decline another chance. My shoulder is yet weak, I find."

Elizabeth regarded his manner, and thought that she could discern a tinge on his cheek that spoke the shame of conscious poverty. She said no more, but suffered her own champion to make a trial. Although Natty Bumppo had certainly made hundreds of more momentous shots at his enemies or his game, yet he never exerted himself more to excel. He raised his piece three several times; once to get his range; once to calculate his distance; and once because the bird, alarmed by the deathlike stillness, turned its head quickly to examine its foes. But the fourth time he fired. The smoke, the report, and the momentary shock prevented most of the spectators from instantly knowing the result; but Elizabeth, when she saw her champion drop the end of his rifle in the snow and open his mouth in one of its silent laughs, and then proceed very coolly to recharge his piece, knew that he had been successful. The boys rushed to the mark and lifted the turkey on high, lifeless, and with nothing but the remnant of a head.

"Bring in the creater," said Leatherstocking, "and put it at the feet of the lady. I was her deputy in the matter, and the bird is her property."

"And a good deputy you have proved yourself," returned Elizabeth,—"so good, cousin Richard, that I would advise you to remember his qualities." She paused, and the gaiety that beamed on her face gave place to a more serious earnestness. She even blushed a little as she turned to the young hunter, and, with the charm of a woman's manner, added—"But it was only to see an exhibition of the far-famed skill of Leatherstocking that I tried my fortunes. Will you, sir, accept the bird as a small peace offering for the hurt that prevented your own success?"

The expression with which the youth received this present was indescribable. He appeared to yield to the blandishment of her air, in opposition to a strong inward impulse to the contrary. He bowed and raised the victim silently from her feet, but continued silent.

Elizabeth handed the black a piece of silver as a remuneration for his loss, which had some effect in again unbending his muscles, and then expressed to her companion her readiness to return homeward.

"Wait a minute, cousin Bess," cried Richard; "there is an uncertainty about the rules of this sport that it is proper I should remove. If you will appoint a committee, gentlemen, to wait on me this morning, I will draw up in writing a set of regulations——" He stopped, with some indignation, for at that instant a hand was laid familiarly on the shoulder of the High Sheriff of——.

"A Merry Christmas to you, cousin Dickon," said Judge Temple, who had approached the party unperceived: "I must have a vigilant eye to my daughter, sir, if you are to be seized daily with these gallant fits. I admire the taste which would introduce a lady to such scenes!"

"It is her own perversity, 'duke," cried the disappointed Sheriff, who felt the loss of the first salutation as grievously as many a man would a much greater misfortune; "and I must say that she comes honestly by it. I led her out to show her the improvements, but away she scampered, through the snow, at the first sound of firearms, the same as if she had been brought up in a camp, instead of a first-rate boarding school. I do think, Judge Temple, that such dangerous amusements should be suppressed by statute; nay, I doubt whether they are not already indictable at common law."

"Well, sir, as you are Sheriff of the county, it becomes your duty to examine into the matter," returned the smiling Marmaduke. "I perceive that Bess has executed her commission, and I hope it met with a favorable reception." Richard glanced his eye at the packet which he held in his hand, and the slight anger produced by disappointment vanished instantly.

"Ah! 'duke, my dear cousin," he said, "step a little on one side; I have something I would say to you." Marmaduke complied, and the Sheriff led him to a little distance in the bushes and continued—"First, 'duke, let me thank you for your friendly interest with the Council and the Governor, without which, I am confident that the greatest merit would avail but little. But we are sisters' children—we are sisters' children; and you may use me like one of your horses; ride me or drive me, 'duke, I am wholly yours. But in my humble opinion, this young companion of Leatherstocking requires looking after. He has a very dangerous propensity for turkey."

"Leave him to my management, Dickon," said the Judge, "and I will cure his appetite by indulgence. It is with him that I would speak. Let us rejoin the sportsmen."

Chapter XVIII

Poor wretch! the mother that him bare,
If she had been in presence there,
In his wan face, and sunburnt hair,
*   She had not known her child.*

                                        Scott

It diminished, in no degree, the effect produced by the conversation which passed between Judge Temple and the young hunter, that the former took the arm of his daughter and drew it through his own, when he advanced from the spot whither Richard had led him to that where the youth was standing, leaning on his rifle, and contemplating the dead bird at his feet. The presence of Marmaduke did not interrupt the sports, which were resumed, by loud and clamorous disputes concerning the conditions of a chance, that involved the life of a bird of much inferior quality to the last. Leatherstocking and Mohegan had alone drawn aside to their youthful companion; and, although in the immediate vicinity of such a throng, the following conversation was heard only by those who were interested in it.

"I have greatly injured you, Mr. Edwards," said the Judge; but the sudden and inexplicable start, with which the person spoken to received this unexpected address, caused him to pause a moment. As no answer was given, and the strong emotion exhibited in the countenance of the youth gradually passed away, he continued—"But, fortunately, it is in some measure in my power to compensate you for what I have done. My kinsman, Richard Jones, has received an appointment that will, in future, deprive me of his assistance, and leaves me, just now, destitute of one who might greatly aid me with his pen. Your manner, notwithstanding appearances, is a sufficient proof of your education, nor will thy shoulder suffer thee to labor, for some time to come." (Marmaduke insensibly relapsed into the language of the Friends as he grew warm.) "My doors are open to thee, my young friend, for in this infant country we harbor no suspicions: little offering to tempt the cupidity of the evil disposed. Become my assistant, for at least a season, and receive such compensation as thy services will deserve."

There was nothing in the manner or the offer of the Judge to justify the reluctance, amounting nearly to loathing, with which the youth listened to his speech: but after a powerful effort for self-command, he replied:

"I would serve you, sir, or any other man, for an honest support, for I do not affect to conceal that my necessities are very great, even beyond what appearances would indicate; but I am fearful that such new duties would interfere too much with more important business: so that I must decline your offer, and depend on my rifle, as before, for subsistence."

Richard here took occasion to whisper to the young lady, who had shrunk a little from the foreground of the picture:

"This, you see, cousin Bess, is the natural reluctance of a half-breed to leave the savage state. Their attachment to a wandering life is, I verily believe, unconquerable."

"It is a precarious life," observed Marmaduke, without hearing the Sheriff's observation, "and one that brings more evils with it than present suffering. Trust me, young friend, my experience is greater than thine, when I tell thee, that the unsettled life of these hunters is of vast disadvantage for temporal purposes, and it totally removes one from the influence of more sacred things."

"No, no, Judge," interrupted the Leatherstocking, who was hitherto unseen, or disregarded; "take him into your shanty in welcome, but tell him truth. I have lived in the woods for forty long years, and have spent five at a time without seeing the light of a clearing bigger than a windrow in the trees; and I should like to know where you'll find a man, in his sixty-eighth year, who can get an easier living, for all your betterments and your deer laws: and, as for honesty, or doing what's right between man and man, I'll not turn my back to the longest winded deacon on your Patent."

"Thou art an exception, Leatherstocking," returned the Judge, nodding good-naturedly at the hunter; "for thou hast a temperance unusual in thy class, and a hardihood exceeding thy years. But this youth is made of materials too precious to be wasted in the forest. I entreat thee to join my family, if it be but till thy arm be healed. My daughter here, who is mistress of my dwelling, will tell thee that thou art welcome."

"Certainly," said Elizabeth, whose earnestness was a little checked by female reserve. "The unfortunate would be welcome at any time, but doubly so when we feel that we have occasioned the evil ourselves."

"Yes," said Richard, "and if you relish turkey, young man, there are plenty in the coops, and of the best kind, I can assure you."

Finding himself thus ably seconded, Marmaduke pushed his advantage to the utmost. He entered into a detail of the duties that would attend the situation, and circumstantially mentioned the reward, and all those points which are deemed of importance among men of business. The youth listened in extreme agitation. There was an evident contest in his feelings; at times he appeared to wish eagerly for the change, and then again the incomprehensible expression of disgust would cross his features, like a dark cloud obscuring a noonday sun.

The Indian, in whose manner the depression of self-abasement was most powerfully exhibited, listened to the offers of the Judge with an interest that increased with each syllable. Gradually he drew nigher to the group; and when, with his keen glance, he detected the most marked evidence of yielding in the countenance of his young companion, he changed at once from his attitude and look of shame to the front of an Indian warrior, and moving, with great dignity, closer to the parties, he spoke:

"Listen to your Father," he said; "his words are old. Let the Young Eagle and the Great Land Chief eat together; let them sleep, without fear, near each other. The children of Miquon love not blood; they are just and will do right. The sun must rise and set often, before men can make one family; it is not the work of a day, but of many winters. The Mingoes and the Delawares are born enemies; their blood can never mix in the wigwam: it never will run in the same stream in the battle. What makes the brother of Miquon and the Young Eagle foes? They are of the same tribe: their fathers and mothers are one. Learn to wait, my son: you are a Delaware, and an Indian warrior knows how to be patient."

This figurative address seemed to have great weight with the young man, who gradually yielded to the representations of Marmaduke, and eventually consented to his proposal. It was, however, to be an experiment only; and if either of the parties thought fit to rescind the engagement, it was left at his option so to do. The remarkable and ill-concealed reluctance of the youth to accept of an offer, which most men in his situation would consider as an unhoped-for elevation, occasioned no little surprise in those to whom he was a stranger; and it left a slight impression to his disadvantage. When the parties separated, they very naturally made the subject the topic of a conversation, which we shall relate; first commencing with the Judge, his daughter, and Richard, who were slowly pursuing the way back to the mansion house.

"I have surely endeavored to remember the holy mandates of our Redeemer, when he bids us 'love them who despitefully use you,' in my intercourse with this incomprehensible boy," said Marmaduke. "I know not what there is in my dwelling to frighten a lad of his years, unless it may be thy presence and visage, Bess."

"No, no," said Richard, with great simplicity; "it is not cousin Bess. But when did you ever know a half-breed, 'duke, who could bear civilization? For that matter, they are worse than the savages themselves? Did you notice how knock-kneed he stood, Elizabeth, and what a wild look he had in his eyes?"

"I heeded not his eyes, nor his knees, which would be all the better for a little humbling. Really, my dear sir, I think you did exercise the Christian virtue of patience to the utmost. I was disgusted with his airs, long before he consented to make one of our family. Truly, we are much honored by the association! In what apartment is he to be placed, sir; and at what table is he to receive his nectar and ambrosia?"

"With Benjamin and Remarkable," interrupted Mr. Jones; "you surely would not make the youth eat with the blacks! He is part Indian, it is true; but the natives hold the Negroes in great contempt. No, no; he would starve before he would break a crust with the Negroes."

"I am but too happy, Dickon, to tempt him to eat with ourselves," said Marmaduke, "to think of offering even the indignity you propose."

"Then, sir," said Elizabeth, with an air that was slightly affected, as if submitting to her father's orders in opposition to her own will, "it is your pleasure that he be a gentleman."

"Certainly; he is to fill the station of one. Let him receive the treatment that is due to his place, until we find him unworthy of it."

"Well, well, 'duke," cried the Sheriff, "you will find it no easy matter to make a gentleman of him. The old proverb says 'that it takes three generations to make a gentleman.' There was my father, whom everybody knew; my grandfather was an M.D., and his father a D.D.; and his father came from England. I never could come at the truth of his origin; but he was either a great merchant in London, or a great country lawyer, or the youngest son of a bishop."

"Here is a true American genealogy for you," said Marmaduke, laughing. "It does very well till you get across the water, where, as everything is obscure, it is certain to deal in the superlative. You are sure that your English progenitor was great, Dickon, whatever his profession might have been?"

"To be sure I am," returned the other. "I have heard my old aunt talk of him by the month. We are of a good family, Judge Temple, and have never filled any but honorable stations in life."

"I marvel that you should be satisfied with so scanty a provision of gentility in the olden time, Dickon. Most of the American genealogists commence their traditions, like the stories for children, with three brothers, taking especial care that one of the triumvirate shall be the progenitor of any of the same name who may happen to be better furnished with worldly gear than themselves. But, here all are equal who know how to conduct themselves with propriety; and Oliver Edwards comes into my family on a footing with both the High Sheriff and the Judge."

"Well, 'duke, I call this democracy, not republicanism; but I say nothing; only let him keep within the law, or I shall show him that the freedom of even this country is under wholesome restraint."

"Surely, Dickon, you will not execute till I condemn! But what says Bess to the new inmate? We must pay a deference to the ladies in this matter, after all."

"Oh, sir!" returned Elizabeth, "I believe I am much like a certain Judge Temple in this particular—not easily to be turned from my opinion. But, to be serious, although I must think the introduction of a demisavage into the family a somewhat startling event, whomsoever you think proper to countenance may be sure of my respect."

The Judge drew her arm more closely in his own and smiled, while Richard led the way through the gate of the little courtyard in the rear of the dwelling, dealing out his ambiguous warnings with his accustomed loquacity.

On the other hand, the foresters—for the three hunters, notwithstanding their difference in character, well deserved this common name—pursued their course along the skirts of the village in silence. It was not until they had reached the lake, and were moving over its frozen surface towards the foot of the mountain, where the hut stood, that the youth exclaimed:

"Who could have foreseen this a month since! I have consented to serve Marmaduke Temple—to be an inmate in the dwelling of the greatest enemy of my race; yet what better could I do? The servitude cannot be long; and when the motive for submitting to it ceases to exist, I will shake it off, like the dust from my feet."

"Is he a Mingo, that you will call him enemy?" said Mohegan. "The Delaware warrior sits still and waits the time of the Great Spirit. He is no woman, to cry out like a child."

"Well, I'm mistrustful, John," said Leatherstocking, in whose air there had been, during the whole business, a strong expression of doubt and uncertainty. "They say that there's new laws in the land, and I am sartain that there's new ways in the mountains. One hardly knows the lakes and streams, they've altered the country so much. I must say I'm mistrustful of such smooth speakers; for I've known the whites talk fair when they wanted the Indian lands most. This I will say, though I'm white myself, and was born nigh York, and of honest parents, too."

"I will submit," said the youth; "I will forget who I am. Cease to remember, old Mohegan, that I am the descendant of a Delaware chief, who once was master of these noble hills, these beautiful vales, and of this water over which we tread. Yes, yes; I will become his bondsman—his slave. Is it not an honorable servitude, old man?"

"Old man!" repeated the Indian, solemnly, and pausing in his walk, as usual, when much excited: "yes; John is old. Son of my brother! if Mohegan was young, when would his rifle be still? Where would the deer hide, and he not find him? But John is old; his hand is the hand of a squaw; his tomahawk is a hatchet; brooms and baskets are his enemies— he strikes no other. Hunger and old age come together. See, Hawkeye! when young, he would go days and eat nothing; but should he not put the brush on the fire now, the blaze would go out. Take the son of Miquon by the hand, and he will help you."

"I'm not the man I was, I'll own, Chingachgook," returned the Leatherstocking; "but I can go without a meal now, on occasion. When we tracked the Iroquois through the 'Beech woods,' they drove the game afore them, for I hadn't a morsel to eat from Monday morning come Wednesday sundown; and then I shot as fat a buck, on the Pennsylvany line, as ever mortal laid eyes on. It would have done your heart good to have seen the Delaware eat; for I was out scouting and scrimmaging with their tribe at the time. Lord! The Indians, lad, lay still, and just waited till Providence should send them their game; but I foraged about, and put a deer up, and put him down too, afore he had made a dozen jumps. I was too weak and too ravenous to stop for his flesh; so I took a good drink of his blood, and the Indians ate of his meat raw. John was there, and John knows. But then starvation would be apt to be too much for me now, I will own, though I'm no great eater at any time."

"Enough is said, my friends," cried the youth. "I feel that everywhere the sacrifice is required at my hands, and it shall be made; but say no more, I entreat you; I cannot bear this subject now."

His companions were silent; and they soon reached the hut, which they entered, after removing certain complicated and ingenious fastenings that were put there apparently to guard a property of but very little value. Immense piles of snow lay against the log walls of this secluded habitation, on one side; while fragments of small trees and branches of oak and chestnut that had been torn from their parent stems by the winds were thrown into a pile, on the other. A small column of smoke rose through a chimney of sticks, cemented with clay, along the side of the rock; and had marked the snow above with its dark tinges, in a wavy line, from the point of emission to another, where the hill receded from the brow of a precipice, and held a soil that nourished trees of a gigantic growth, that overhung the little bottom beneath.

The remainder of the day passed off as such days are commonly spent in a new country. The settlers thronged to the academy again, to witness the second effort of Mr. Grant; and Mohegan was one of his hearers. But, notwithstanding the divine fixed his eyes intently on the Indian, when he invited his congregation to advance to the table, the shame of last night's abasement was yet too keen in the old chief to suffer him to move.

When the people were dispersing, the clouds that had been gathering all the morning were dense and dirty; and before half of the curious congregation had reached their different cabins, that were placed in every glen and hollow of the mountains, or perched on the summits of the hills themselves, the rain was falling in torrents. The dark edges of the stumps began to exhibit themselves, as the snow settled rapidly; the fences of logs and brush, which before had been only traced by long lines of white mounds that ran across the valley and up the mountains peeped out from their covering, and the black stubs were momentarily becoming more distinct, as large masses of snow and ice fell from their sides, under the influence of the thaw.

Sheltered in the warm hall of her father's comfortable mansion, Elizabeth, accompanied by Louisa Grant, looked abroad with admiration of the ever-varying face of things without. Even the village, which had just before been glittering with the color of the frozen element, reluctantly dropped its mask, and the houses exposed their dark roofs and smoked chimneys. The pines shook off the covering of snow, and everything seemed to be assuming its proper hue, with a transition that bordered on the supernatural.

CHAPTER XIX

And yet, poor Edwin was no vulgar boy.

BEATTIE

THE close of Christmas Day, A.D. 1793, was tempestuous, but comparatively warm. When darkness had again hid the objects in the village from the gaze of Elizabeth, she turned from the window, where she had remained while the least vestige of light lingered over the tops of the dark pines, with a curiosity that was rather excited than appeased by the passing glimpses of woodland scenery that she had caught during the day.

With her arm locked in that of Miss Grant, the young mistress of the mansion walked slowly up and down the hall, musing on scenes that were rapidly recurring to her memory, and possibly dwelling, at times, in the sanctuary of her thoughts, on the strange occurrences that had led to the introduction to her father's family of one whose manners so singularly contradicted the inferences to be drawn from his situation. The expiring heat of the apartment—for its great size required a day to reduce its temperature—had given to her cheeks a bloom that exceeded their natural color, while the mild and melancholy features of Louisa were brightened with a faint tinge, that, like the hectic of disease, gave a painful interest to her beauty.

The eyes of the gentlemen, who were yet seated around the rich wines of Judge Temple, frequently wandered from the table that was placed at one end of the hall to the forms that were silently moving over its length. Much mirth, and that, at times, of a boisterous kind, proceeded from the mouth of Richard; but Major Hartmann was not yet excited to his pitch of merriment, and Marmaduke respected the presence of his clerical guest too much to indulge in even the innocent humor that formed no small ingredient in his character.

Such were, and such continued to be, the pursuits of the party for half an hour after the shutters were closed, and candles were placed in various parts of the hall as substitutes for the departing daylight. The appearance of Benjamin, staggering under the burden of an armful of wood, was the first interruption to the scene.

"How now, Master Pump!" roared the newly appointed sheriff; "is there not warmth enough in 'duke's best Madeira to keep up the animal heat through this thaw? Remember, old boy, that the Judge is particular with his beech and maple, beginning to dread already a scarcity of the precious articles. Ha! ha! ha! 'duke, you are a good, warmhearted relation, I will own, as in duty bound, but you have some queer notions about you, after all. 'Come let us be jolly, and cast away folly.' "

The notes gradually sank into a hum, while the major-domo threw down his load and, turning to his interrogator with an air of earnestness, replied:

"Why, look you, Squire Dickens, mayhap there's a warm latitude round about the table there, tho'f it's not the stuff to raise the heat in my body, neither; the raal Jamaiky being the only thing to do that, besides good wood, or some such matter as Newcastle coal. But, if I know anything of weather, d'ye see, it's time to be getting all snug, and for putting the ports in, and stirring the fires a bit. Mayhap I've not followed the seas twenty-seven years, and lived another seven in these here woods, for nothing, gemmen."

"Why, does it bid fair for a change in the weather, Benjamin?" inquired the master of the house.

"There's a shift of wind, your honor," returned the steward; "and when there's a shift of wind, you may look for a change in this here climate. I was aboard of one of Rodney's fleet, d'ye see, about the time we licked De Grasse, Mounsheer Ler Quaw's countryman, there; and the wind was here at the south'ard and east'ard; and I was below, mixing a toothful of hot stuff for the captain of marines, who dined, d'ye see, in the cabin, that there very same day; and I suppose he wanted to put out the Captain's fire with a gun-room ingyne: and so, just as I got it to my own liking, after tasting pretty often, for the soldier was difficult to please, slap came the foresail ag'in the mast, whiz went the ship round on her heel, like a whirligig. And a lucky thing was it that our helm was down; for as she gathered starnway she paid off, which was more than every ship in the fleet did, or could do. But she strained herself in the trough of the sea, and she shipped a deal of water over her quarter. I never swallowed so much clear water at a time in my life, as I did then, for I was looking up the afterhatch at the instant."

"I wonder, Benjamin, that you did not die with a dropsy!" said Marmaduke.

"I mought, Judge," said the old tar, with a broad grin; "but there was no need of the med'cine chest for a cure; for, as I thought the brew was spoilt for the marine's taste, and there was no telling when another sea might come and spoil it for mine, I finished the mug on the spot. So then all hands was called to the pumps, and there we began to ply the pumps——"

"Well, but the weather?" interrupted Marmaduke; "what of the weather without doors?"

"Why, here the wind has been all day at the south, and now there's a lull, as if the last blast was out of the bellows; and there's a streak along the mountains, to the north'ard, that, just now, wasn't wider than the bigness of your hand; and then the clouds drive afore it as you'd brail a mainsail, and the stars are heaving in sight, like so many lights and beacons, put there to warn us to pile on the wood; and, if so be that I'm a judge of weather, it's getting to be time to build on a fire; or you'll have half of them there porter bottles, and them dimmyjohns of wine, in the locker here, breaking with the frost, afore the morning watch is called."

"Thou art a prudent sentinel," said the Judge. "Act thy pleasure with the forests, for this night at least."

Benjamin did as he was ordered; nor had two hours elapsed, before the prudence of his precautions became very visible. The south wind had, indeed, blown itself out, and it was succeeded by the calmness that usually gave warning of a serious change in the weather. Long before the family retired to rest, the cold had become cuttingly severe; and when Monsieur Le Quoi sallied forth, under a bright moon, to seek his own abode, he was compelled to beg a blanket, in which he might envelop his form, in addition to the numerous garments that his sagacity had provided for the occasion. The divine and his daughter remained as inmates of the mansion house during the night, and the excess of last night's merriment induced the gentlemen to make an early retreat to their several apartments. Long before midnight, the whole family were invisible.

Elizabeth and her friend had not yet lost their senses in sleep, when the howlings of the northwest wind were heard around the buildings, and brought with them that exquisite sense of comfort that is ever excited under such circumstances, in an apartment where the fire has not yet ceased to glimmer; and curtains, and shutters, and feathers unite to preserve the desired temperature. Once, just as her eyes had opened, apparently in the last stage of drowsiness, the roaring winds brought with them a long and plaintive howl that seemed too wild for a dog, and yet resembled the cries of that faithful animal, when night awakens his vigilance and gives sweetness and solemnity to his alarms. The form of Louisa Grant instinctively pressed nearer to that of the young heiress, who, finding her companion was yet awake, said, in a low tone, as if afraid to break a charm with her voice:

"Those distant cries are plaintive, and even beautiful. Can they be the hounds from the hut of Leatherstocking?"

"They are wolves, who have ventured from the mountain, on the lake," whispered Louisa, "and who are only kept from the village by the lights. One night, since we have been here, hunger drove them to our very door. Oh, what a dreadful night it was! But the riches of Judge Temple have given him too many safeguards to leave room for fear in this house."

"The enterprise of Judge Temple is taming the very forests!" exclaimed Elizabeth, throwing off the covering and partly rising in the bed. "How rapidly is civilization treading on the footsteps of nature!" she continued, as her eye glanced over, not only the comforts, but the luxuries of her apartment, and her ear again listened to the distant, but often repeated howls from the lake. Finding, however, that the timidity of her companion rendered the sounds painful to her, Elizabeth resumed her place, and soon forgot the changes in the country, with those in her own condition, in a deep sleep.

The following morning, the noise of the female servant, who entered the apartment to light the fire, awoke the females. They arose, and finished the slight preparations of their toilets in a clear, cold atmosphere that penetrated through all the defenses of even Miss Temple's warm room. When Elizabeth was attired, she approached a window and drew its curtain, and throwing open its shutters, she endeavored to look abroad on the village and the lake. But a thick covering of frost on the glass, while it admitted the light, shut out the view. She raised the sash, and then, indeed, a glorious scene met her delighted eye.

The lake had exchanged its covering of unspotted snow for a face of dark ice that reflected the rays of the rising sun like a polished mirror. The houses were clothed in a dress of the same description, but which, owing to its position, shone like bright steel; while the enormous icicles that were pendent from every roof caught the brilliant light, apparently throwing it from one to the other, as each glittered, on the side next the luminary, with a golden luster that melted away, on its opposite, into the dusky shades of a background. But it was the appearance of the boundless forests that covered the hills as they rose, in the distance, one over the other, that most attracted the gaze of Miss Temple. The huge branches of the pines and hemlocks bent with the weight of the ice they supported, while their summits rose above the swelling tops of the oaks, beeches, and maples like spires of burnished silver issuing from domes of the same material. The limits of the view, in the west, were marked by an undulating outline of bright light, as if, reversing the order of nature, numberless suns might momentarily be expected to heave above the horizon. In the foreground of the picture, along the shores of the lake, and near to the village, each tree seemed studded with diamonds. Even the sides of the mountains where the rays of the sun could not yet fall were decorated with a glassy coat that presented every gradation of brilliancy, from the first touch of the luminary to the dark foliage of the hemlock, glistening through its coat of crystal. In short, the whole view was one scene of quivering radiancy, as lake, mountains, village, and woods, each emitted a portion of light, tinged with its peculiar hue, and varied by its position and its magnitude.

"See!" cried Elizabeth—"see, Louisa: hasten to the window, and observe the miraculous change!"

Miss Grant complied; and, after bending for a moment in silence, from the opening, she observed, in a low tone, as if afraid to trust the sound of her voice:

"The change is indeed wonderful! I am surprised that he should be able to effect it so soon."

Elizabeth turned in amazement to hear so skeptical a sentiment from one educated like her companion; but was surprised to find that, instead of looking at the view, the mild blue eyes of Miss Grant were dwelling on the form of a well-dressed young man, who was standing before the door of the building, in earnest conversation with her father. A second look was necessary, before she was able to recognize the person of the young hunter, in a plain, but assuredly, the ordinary, garb of a gentleman.

"Everything in this magical country seems to border on the marvelous," said Elizabeth; "and among all the changes, this is certainly not the least wonderful. The actors are as unique as the scenery."

Miss Grant colored, and drew in her head.

"I am a simple country girl, Miss Temple, and I am afraid you will find me but a poor companion," she said. "I—I am not sure that I understand all you say. But I really thought that you wished me to notice the alteration in Mr. Edwards. Is it not more wonderful when we recollect his origin? They say he is part Indian."

"He is a genteel savage: but let us go down, and give the Sachem his tea—for I suppose he is a descendant of King Philip, if not a grandson of Pocahontas."

The ladies were met in the hall by Judge Temple, who took his daughter aside to apprise her of that alternation in the appearance of their new inmate with which she was already acquainted.

"He appears reluctant to converse on his former situation," continued Marmaduke; "but I gather from his discourse, as is apparent from his manner, that he has seen better days; and I really am inclining to the opinion of Richard, as to his origin; for it was no unusual thing for the Indian agents to rear their children in a laudable manner, and——"

"Very well, my dear sir," interrupted his daughter, laughing and averting her eyes; "it is all well enough, I dare say; but as I do not understand a word of the Mohawk language, he must be content to speak English; and as for his behavior, I trust to your discernment to control it."

"Ay! but, Bess," said the Judge, detaining her gently with his hand, "nothing must be said to him of his past life. This he has begged particularly of me, as a favor. He is, perhaps, a little soured, just now, with his wounded arm; the injury seems very light, and another time he may be more communicative."

"Oh! I am not much troubled, sir, with that laudable thirst after knowledge that is called curiosity. I shall believe him to be the child of Cornstalk, or Corn-planter, or some other renowned chieftain; possibly of the Big Snake himself; and shall treat him as such until he sees fit to shave his good-looking head, borrow some half-dozen pair of my best earrings, shoulder his rifle again, and disappear as suddenly as he made his entrance. So come, my dear sir, and let us not forget the rites of hospitality for the short time he is to remain with us."

Judge Temple smiled at the playfulness of his child, and taking her arm, they entered the breakfast parlor, where the young hunter was seated, with an air that showed his determination to domesticate himself in the family with as little parade as possible.

Such were the incidents that led to this extraordinary increase in the family of Judge Temple, where, having once established the youth, the subject of our tale requires us to leave him, for a time, to pursue with diligence and intelligence the employments that were assigned him by Marmaduke.

Major Hartmann made his customary visit, and took his leave of the party for the next three months. Mr. Grant was compelled to be absent much of his time in remote parts of the country, and his daughter became almost a constant visitor at the mansion house. Richard entered, with his constitutional eagerness, on the duties of his new office; and, as

Marmaduke was much employed with the constant applications of adventurers for farms, the winter passed swiftly away. The lake was a principal scene for the amusements of the young people; where the ladies, in their one-horse cutter, driven by Richard, and attended, when the snow would admit of it, by young Edwards, on his skates, spent many hours, taking the benefit of exercise in the clear air of the hills. The reserve of the youth gradually gave way to time and his situation, though it was still evident, to a close observer, that he had frequent moments of bitter and intense feeling.

Elizabeth saw many large openings appear in the sides of the mountains during the three succeeding months, where different settlers had, in the language of the country, "made their pitch"; while the numberless sleighs that passed through the village, loaded with wheat and barrels of potashes, afforded a clear demonstration that all these labors were not undertaken in vain. In short, the whole country was exhibiting the bustle of a thriving settlement, where the highways were thronged with sleighs, bearing piles of rough household furniture; studded, here and there, with the smiling faces of women and children, happy in the excitement of novelty; or with loads of produce, hastening to the common market at Albany, that served as so many snares to induce the emigrants to enter into those wild mountains in search of competence and happiness.

The village was alive with business; the artisans increasing in wealth with the prosperity of the country, and each day witnessing some nearer approach to the manners and usages of an old-settled town. The man who carried the mail, or "the post," as he was called, talked much of running a stage, and, once or twice during the winter, he was seen taking a single passenger, in his cutter, through the snowbanks, towards the Mohawk, along which a regular vehicle glided, semiweekly, with the velocity of lightning, and under the direction of a knowing whip from the "down countries." Towards spring, divers families, who had been into the "old states" to see their relatives, returned in time to save the snow, frequently bringing with them whole neighborhoods, who were tempted by their representations to leave the farms of Connecticut and Massachusetts, to make a trial of fortune in the woods.

During all this time, Oliver Edwards, whose sudden elevation excited no surprise in that changeful country, was earnestly engaged in the service of Marmaduke, during the days; but his nights were often spent in the hut of Leatherstocking. The intercourse between the three hunters was maintained with a certain air of mystery, it is true, but with much zeal and apparent interest to all the parties. Even Mohegan seldom came to the mansion house, and Natty, never; but Edwards sought every leisure moment to visit his former abode, from which he would often return in the gloomy hours of night, through the snow, or, if detained beyond the time at which the family retired to rest, with the morning sun. These visits certainly excited much speculation in those to whom they were known, but no comments were made, excepting occasionally, in whispers from Richard, who would say:

"It is not at all remarkable—a half-breed can never be weaned from the savage ways—and for one of his lineage, the boy is much nearer civilization than could, in reason, be expected."

Chapter XX

Away! nor let me loiter in my song,
For we have many a mountain path to tread. BYRON

As the spring gradually approached, the immense piles of snow, that by alternate thaws and frosts, and repeated storms, had obtained a firmness which threatened a tiresome durability, began to yield to the influence of milder breezes and a warmer sun. The gates of Heaven at times seemed to open, and a bland air diffused itself over the earth, when animate and inanimate nature would awaken, and, for a few hours, the gaiety of spring shone in every eye, and smiled on every field. But the shivering blasts from the north would carry their chill influence over the scene again, and the dark and gloomy clouds that intercepted the rays of the sun were not more cold and dreary than the reaction. These struggles between the seasons became daily more frequent, while the earth, like a victim to contention, slowly lost the animated brilliancy of winter, without obtaining the aspect of spring.

Several weeks were consumed in this cheerless manner, during which the inhabitants of the country gradually changed their pursuits from the social and bustling movements of the time of snow to the laborious and domestic engagements of the coming season. The village was no longer thronged with visitors; the trade that had enlivened the shops for several months began to disappear; the highways lost their shining coats of beaten snow in impassable sloughs, and were deserted by the gay and noisy travelers who, in sleighs, had, during the winter, glided along their windings; and, in short, everything seemed indicative of a mighty change, not only in the earth, but in those who derived their sources of comfort and happiness from its bosom.

The younger members of the family in the mansion house, of which Louisa Grant was now habitually one, were by no means indifferent observers of these fluctuating and tardy changes. While the snow rendered the roads passable, they had partaken largely in the amusements of the winter, which included not only daily rides over the mountains, and through every valley within twenty miles of them, but divers ingenious and varied sources of pleasure, on the bosom of their frozen lake. There had been excursions in the equipage of Richard, when, with his four horses, he had outstripped the winds, as it flew over the glassy ice which invariably succeeded a thaw. Then the exciting and dangerous whirligig would be suffered to possess its moment of notice. Cutters, drawn by a single horse, and hand sleds, impelled by the gentlemen, on skates, would each in turn be used; and, in short, every source of relief against the tediousness of a winter in the mountains was resorted to by the family. Elizabeth was compelled to acknowledge to her father, that the season, with the aid of his library, was much less irksome than she had anticipated.

As exercise in the open air was in some degree necessary to the habits of the family, when the constant recurrence of frosts and thaws rendered the roads, which were dangerous at the most favorable times, utterly impassable for wheels, saddle horses were used as substitutes for other conveyances. Mounted on small and sure-footed beasts, the ladies would again attempt the passages of the mountains, and penetrate into every retired glen, where the enterprise of a settler had induced him to establish himself. In these excursions they were attended by some one or all of the gentlemen of the family, as their different pursuits admitted. Young Edwards was hourly becoming more familiarized to his situation, and not unfrequently mingled in the parties with an unconcern and gaiety that for a short time would expel all unpleasant recollections from his mind. Habit, and the buoyancy of youth, seemed to be getting the ascendancy over the secret causes of his uneasiness; though there were moments, when the same remarkable expression of disgust would cross his intercourse with Marmaduke, that had distinguished their conversations in the first days of their acquaintance.

It was at the close of the month of March, that the Sheriff succeeded in persuading his cousin and her young friend to accompany him in a ride to a hill that was said to overhang the lake in a manner peculiar to itself.

"Besides, cousin Bess," continued the indefatigable Richard, "we will stop and see the 'sugarbush' of Billy Kirby: he is on the east end of the Ransom lot, making sugar for Jared Ransom. There is not a better hand over a kettle in the county than that same Kirby. You remember, 'duke, that I had him his first season, in our own camp; and it is not a wonder that he knows something of his trade."

"He's a good chopper, is Billy," observed Benjamin, who held the bridle of the horse while the Sheriff mounted; "and he handles an ax much the same as a forecastleman does his marlinespike, or a tailor his goose. They say he'll lift a potash kettle off the arch alone, tho' I can't say that I've ever seen him do it with my eyes; but that is the say. And I've seen sugar of his making, which, maybe, wasn't as white as an old topgallant sail, but which my friend Mistress Prettybones, within there, said had the true molasses smack to it; and you are not the one, Squire Dickens, to be told that Mistress Remarkable has a remarkable tooth for sweet things, in her nut grinder."

The loud laugh that succeeded the wit of Benjamin, and in which he participated, with no very harmonious sounds, himself very fully illustrated the congenial temper which existed between the pair. Most of its point was, however, lost on the rest of the party, who were either mounting their horses or assisting the ladies at the moment. When all were safely in their saddles, they moved through the village in great order.

They paused for a moment before the door of Monsieur Le Quoi, until he could bestride his steed, and then issuing from the little cluster of houses, they took one of the principal of those highways that centered in the village.

As each night brought with it a severe frost, which the heat of the succeeding day served to dissipate the equestrians were compelled to proceed singly along the margin of the road, where the turf, and firmness of the ground, gave the horses a secure footing. Very trifling indications of vegetation were to be seen, the surface of the earth presenting a cold, wet, and cheerless aspect that chilled the blood. The snow yet lay scattered over most of those distant clearings that were visible in different parts of the mountains; though here and there an opening might be seen, where, as the white covering yielded to the season, the bright and lively green of the wheat served to enkindle the hopes of the husbandman. Nothing could be more marked than the contrast between the earth and the heavens; for, while the former presented the dreary view that we have described, a warm and invigorating sun was dispensing his heats from a sky that contained but a solitary cloud, and through an atmosphere that softened the colors of the sensible horizon until it shone like a sea of blue.

Richard led the way, on this, as on all other occasions that did not require the exercise of unusual abilities; and as he moved along, he essayed to enliven the party with the sounds of his experienced voice.

"This is your true sugar weather, 'duke," he cried; "a frosty night and a sunshiny day. I warrant me that the sap runs like a milltail up the maples this warm morning. It is a pity, Judge, that you do not introduce a little more science into the manufactory of sugar among your tenants. It might be done, sir, without knowing as much as Doctor Franklin—it might be done, Judge Temple."

"The first object of my solicitude, friend Jones," returned Marmaduke, "is to protect the sources of this great mine of comfort and wealth from the extravagance of the people themselves. When this important point shall be achieved, it will be in season to turn our attention to an improvement in the manufacture of the article. But thou knowest, Richard, that I have already subjected our sugar to the process of the refiner, and that the result has produced loaves as white as the snow on yon fields, and possessing the saccharine quality in its utmost purity."

"Saccharine, or turpentine, or any other 'ine, Judge Temple, you have never made a loaf larger than a good sized sugarplum," returned the Sheriff. "Now, sir, I assert that no experiment is fairly tried until it be reduced to practical purposes. If, sir, I owned a hundred, or, for that matter, two hundred thousand acres of land, as you do, I would build a sugarhouse in the village; I would invite learned men to an investigation of the subject—and such are easily to be found, sir; yes, sir, they are not difficult to find—men who unite theory with practice; and I would select a wood of young and thrifty trees; and instead of making loaves of the size of a lump of candy, dam'me, 'duke, but I'd have them as big as a haycock."

"And purchase the cargo of one of those ships that they say are going to China," cried Elizabeth; "turn your potash kettles into teacups, the scows on the lake into saucers; bake your cake in yonder limekiln, and invite the county to a tea party. How wonderful are the projects of genius! Really, sir, the world is of opinion that Judge Temple has tried the experiment fairly, though he did not cause his loaves to be cast in molds of the magnitude that would suit your magnificent conceptions."

"You may laugh, cousin Elizabeth—you may laugh, madam," retorted Richard, turning himself so much in his saddle as to face the party, and making dignified gestures with his whip; "but I appeal to common sense, good sense, or, what is of more importance than either, to the sense of taste, which is one of the five natural senses, whether a big loaf of sugar is not likely to contain a better illustration of a proposition than such a lump as one of your Dutch women puts under her tongue when she drinks her tea. There are two ways of doing everything; the right way, and the wrong way. You make sugar now, I will admit, and you may, possibly, make loaf sugar; but I take the question to be, whether you make the best possible sugar, and in the best possible loaves."

"Thou art very right, Richard," observed Marmaduke, with a gravity in his air that proved how much he was interested in the subject. "It is very true that we manufacture sugar, and the inquiry is quite useful, how much? and in what manner?

I hope to live to see the day when farms and plantations shall be devoted to this branch of business. Little is known concerning the properties of the tree itself, the source of all this wealth; how much it may be improved by cultivation, by the use of the hoe and plow."

"Hoe and plow!" roared the Sheriff. "Would you set a man hoeing round the root of a maple like this?"—pointing to one of the noble trees that occur so frequently in that part of the country. "Hoeing trees! Are you mad, 'duke? This is next to hunting for coal! Poh! My dear cousin, hear reason, and leave the management of the sugarbush to me. Here is Mr. Le Quoi, he has been in the West Indies and has seen sugar made. Let him give an account of how it is made there, and you will hear the philosophy of the thing.—Well, Monsieur, how is it that you make sugar in the West Indies; anything in Judge Temple's fashion?"

The gentleman to whom this query was put was mounted on a small horse, of no very fiery temperament, and was riding with his stirrups so short, as to bring his knees, while the animal rose a small ascent in the wood path they were now traveling, into a somewhat hazardous vicinity to his chin. There was no room for gesticulation or grace in the delivery of his reply, for the mountain was steep and slippery; and although the Frenchman had an eye of uncommon magnitude on either side of his face, they did not seem to be half competent to forewarn him of the impediments of bushes, twigs, and fallen trees that were momentarily crossing his path. With one hand employed in averting these dangers, and the other grasping his bridle, to check an untoward speed that his horse was assuming, the native of France responded as follows—

"Sucre! Dey do make sucre in Martinique: mais—mais ce n'est pas one tree—ah—ah—vat you call—Je voudrois que ces chemins fussent au diable—vat you call—steeck pour le promenade."

"Cane," said Elizabeth, smiling at the imprecation which the wary Frenchman supposed was understood only by himself.

"Oui, mam'selle, cane."

"Yes, yes," cried Richard, "cane is the vulgar name for it, but the real term is *Saccharum officinarum;* and what we call the sugar, or hard maple, is *Acer saccharum.* These are the learned names, Monsieur, and are such as, doubtless, you well understand."

"Is this Greek or Latin, Mr. Edwards?" whispered Elizabeth to the youth who was opening a passage for herself and her companions through the bushes—"or perhaps it is a still more learned language, for an interpretation of which we must look to you."

The dark eye of the young man glanced towards the speaker, but its resentful expression changed in a moment.

"I shall remember your doubts, Miss Temple, when next I visit my old friend Mohegan, and either his skill, or that of Leatherstocking, shall solve them."

"And are you, then, really ignorant of their language?"

"Not absolutely; but the deep learning of Mr. Jones is more familiar to me, or even the polite masquerade of Monsieur Le Quoi."

"Do you speak French?" said the lady, with quickness.

"It is a common language with the Iroquois, and through the Canadas," he answered, smiling.

"Ah! But they are Mingoes, and your enemies."

"It will be well for me if I have no worse," said the youth, dashing ahead with his horse, and putting an end to the evasive dialogue.

The discourse, however, was maintained with great vigor by Richard, until they reached an open wood on the summit of the mountain, where the hemlocks and pines totally disappeared, and a grove of the very trees that formed the subject of debate covered the earth with their tall, straight trunks and spreading branches, in stately pride. The underwood had been entirely removed from this grove, or bush, as in conjunction with the simple arrangements for boiling, it was called, and a wide space of many acres was cleared, which might be likened to the dome of a mighty temple, to which the maples formed the columns, their tops composing the capitals, and the heavens the arch. A deep and careless incision had been made into each tree, near its root, into which little sprouts, formed of the bark of the alder, or of the sumac, were fastened; and a trough, roughly dug out of the linden, or basswood, was lying at the root of each tree, to catch the sap that flowed from this extremely wasteful and inartificial arrangement.

The party paused a moment, on gaining the flat, to breathe

their horses, and, as the scene was entirely new to several of their number, to view the manner of collecting the fluid. A fine powerful voice aroused them from their momentary silence, as it rang under the branches of the trees, singing the following words of that inimitable doggerel, whose verses, if extended, would reach from the waters of the Connecticut to the shores of Ontario. The tune was, of course, that familiar air, which, although it is said to have been first applied to his nation in derision, circumstances have since rendered so glorious, that no American ever hears its jingling cadence without feeling a thrill at his heart.

> "The Eastern States be full of men,
>   The Western full of woods, sir,
> The hills be like a cattle pen,
>   The roads be full of goods, sir!
>   Then flow away, my sweety sap,
>   And I will make you boily;
>   Nor catch a woodman's hasty nap,
>   For fear you should get roily.

> "The maple tree's a precious one,
>   'Tis fuel, food, and timber;
> And when your stiff day's work is done,
>   Its juice will make you limber,
>   Then flow away, etc.

> "And what's a man without his glass,
>   His wife without her tea, sir?
> But neither cup nor mug will pass,
>   Without this honeybee, sir!
>   Then flow away," etc.

During the execution of this sonorous doggerel, Richard kept time with his whip on the mane of his charger, accompanying the gestures with a corresponding movement of his head and body. Towards the close of the song, he was overheard humming the chorus, and at its last repetition, to strike in at "sweety sap," and carry a second through, with a prodigious addition to the "effect" of the noise, if not to that of the harmony.

"Well done us!" roared the Sheriff, on the same key with

the tune; "a very good song, Billy Kirby, and very well sung. Where got you the words, lad? Is there more of it, and can you furnish me with a copy?"

The sugar boiler, who was busy in his "camp," at a short distance from the equestrians, turned his head with great indifference and surveyed the party, as they approached, with admirable coolness. To each individual, as he or she rode close by him, he gave a nod that was extremely good-natured and affable, but which partook largely of the virtue of equality, for not even to the ladies did he in the least vary his mode of salutation, by touching the apology for a hat that he wore, or by any other motion than the one we have mentioned.

"How goes it, how goes it, Sheriff?" said the wood chopper. "What's the good word in the village?"

"Why, much as usual, Billy," returned Richard. "But how is this? Where are your four kettles, and your troughs, and your iron coolers? Do you make sugar in this slovenly way? I thought you were one of the best sugar boilers in the county."

"I'm all that, Squire Jones," said Kirby, who continued his occupation; "I'll turn my back to no man in the Otsego hills, for chopping and logging, for boiling down the maple sap, for tending brickkiln, splitting out rails, making potash, and parling too, or hoeing corn; though I keep myself pretty much to the first business, seeing that the ax comes most natural to me."

"You be von Jack All-trade, Mister Beel," said Monsieur Le Quoi.

"How?" said Kirby, looking up, with a simplicity which, coupled with his gigantic frame and manly face, was a little ridiculous. "If you be for trade, Mounshere, here is some as good sugar as you'll find the season through. It's as clear from dirt as the Jarman Flats is free from stumps, and it has the raal maple flavor. Such stuff would sell in York for candy."

The Frenchman approached the place where Kirby had deposited his cakes of sugar, under the cover of a bark roof, and commenced the examination of the article, with the eye of one who well understood its value. Marmaduke had dismounted, and was viewing the works and the trees very closely, and not without frequent expressions of dissatisfaction at the careless manner in which the manufacture was conducted.

"You have much experience in these things, Kirby," he said; "what course do you pursue in making your sugar? I see you have but two kettles."

"Two is as good as two thousand, Judge. I'm none of your polite sugar makers, that boils for the great folks; but if the raal sweet maple is wanted, I can answer your turn. First, I choose, and then I tap my trees; say along about the last of February, or in these mountains may be not afore the middle of March; but anyway, just as the sap begins to cleverly run——"

"Well, in this choice," interrupted Marmaduke, "are you governed by any outward signs that prove the quality of the tree?"

"Why, there's judgment in all things," said Kirby, stirring the liquor in his kettles briskly. "There's something in knowing when and how much to stir the pot. It's a thing that must be larnt. Rome wasn't built in a day, nor for that matter Templetown either, though it may be said to be a quick-growing place. I never put my ax into a stunty tree, or one that hasn't a good, fresh-looking bark; for trees have disorders, like creaters; and where's the policy of taking a tree that's sickly, any more than you'd choose a foundered horse to ride post, or an over-heated ox to do your logging."

"All this is true. But what are the signs of illness? How do you distinguish a tree that is well from one that is diseased?"

"How does the doctor tell who has fever, and who colds?" interrupted Richard. "By examining the skin, and feeling the pulse, to be sure."

"Sartain," continued Billy; "the Squire an't far out of the way. It's by the look of the thing, sure enough. Well, when the sap begins to get a free run, I hang over the kettles, and set up thé bush. My first boiling I push pretty smartly, till I get the virtue of the sap; but when it begins to grow of a molasses nater, like this in the kettle, one mustn't drive the fires too hard, or you'll burn the sugar; and burny sugar is bad to the taste, let it be never so sweet. So you ladle out from one kettle into the other till it gets so, when you put the stirring stick into it, that it will draw into a thread—when it takes a kerful hand to manage it. There is a way to drain it off, after it has grained, by putting clay into the pans; but it isn't always practiced: some doos, and some doosn't. Well, Mounsher, be we likely to make a trade?"

"I will give you, Mister Beel, for von pound, dix sous."

"No, I expect cash for't: I never dicker my sugar. But, seeing that it's you, Mounsher," said Billy, with a coaxing smile, "I'll agree to receive a gallon of rum, and cloth enough for two shirts, if you will take the molasses in the bargain. It's raal good. I wouldn't deceive you or any man; and to my drinking it's about the best molasses that come out of a sugarbush."

"Mr. Le Quoi has offered you ten pence," said young Edwards.

The manufacturer stared at the speaker with an air of great freedom, but made no reply.

"Oui," said the Frenchman, "ten penny. Je vous remercie, Monsieur: ah! mon Anglois! je l'oublie toujours."

The wood chopper looked from one to the other with some displeasure; and evidently imbibed the opinion that they were amusing themselves at his expense. He seized the enormous ladle, which was lying in one of his kettles, and began to stir the boiling liquid with great diligence. After a moment passed in dipping the ladle full, and then raising it on high, as the thick rich fluid fell back into the kettle, he suddenly gave it a whirl, as if to cool what yet remained, and offered the bowl to Mr. Le Quoi, saying:

"Taste that, Mounsher, and you will say it is worth more than you offer. The molasses itself would fetch the money."

The complaisant Frenchman, after several timid efforts to trust his lips in contact with the bowl of the ladle, got a good swallow of the scalding liquid. He clapped his hand on his breast, and looked most piteously at the ladies, for a single instant; and then, to use the language of Billy, when he afterwards recounted the tale, "no drumsticks ever went faster on the skin of a sheep, than the Frenchman's legs, for a round or two: and then such swearing and spitting in French you never saw. But it's a knowing one, from the old countries, that thinks to get his jokes smoothly over a wood chopper."

The air of innocence with which Kirby resumed the occupation of stirring the contents of his kettle would have completely deceived the spectators as to his agency in the temporary suffering of Mr. Le Quoi, had not the reckless fellow thrust his tongue into his cheek, and cast his eyes over the party, with a simplicity of expression that was too exquisite to be natural. Mr. Le Quoi soon recovered his presence of mind, and his decorum; he briefly apologized to the ladies for one or two very intemperate expressions that had escaped him in a moment of extraordinary excitement, and remounting his horse, he continued in the background during the remainder of the visit, the wit of Kirby putting a violent termination, at once, to all negotiations on the subject of trade. During all this time, Marmaduke had been wandering about the grove, making observations on his favorite trees, and the wasteful manner in which the wood chopper conducted his manufacture.

"It grieves me to witness the extravagance that pervades this country," said the Judge, "where the settlers trifle with the blessings they might enjoy, with the prodigality of successful adventurers. You are not exempt from the censure yourself, Kirby, for you make dreadful wounds in these trees where a small incision would effect the same object. I earnestly beg you will remember, that they are the growth of centuries, and when once gone, none living will see their loss remedied."

"Why, I don't know, Judge," returned the man he addressed: "it seems to me, if there's a plenty of anything in this mountaynious country, it's the trees. If there's any sin in chopping them, I've a pretty heavy account to settle; for I've chopped over the best half of a thousand acres, with my own hands, counting both Varmount and York states; and I hope to live to finish the whull, before I lay up my ax. Chopping comes quite natural to me, and I wish no other employment; but Jared Ransom said that he thought the sugar was likely to be scurce this season, seeing that so many folks was coming into the settlement, and so I concluded to take the 'bush' on sheares, for this one spring. What's the best news, Judge, consarning ashes? Do pots hold so that a man can live by them still? I s'pose they will, if they keep on fighting across the water."

"Thou reasonest with judgment, William," returned Marmaduke. "So long as the old world is to be convulsed with wars, so long will the harvest of America continue."

"Well, it's an ill wind, Judge, that blows nobody any good. I'm sure the country is in a thriving way; and, though I know you calkilate greatly on the trees, setting as much store by them as some men would by their children, yet to my eyes they are a sore sight at any time, unless I'm privileged to work my will on them; in which case I can't say but they are more to my liking. I have heard the settlers from the old countries say that their rich men keep great oaks and elms, that would make a barrel of pots to the tree, standing round their doors and humsteads, and scattered over their farms, just to look at. Now, I call no country much improved, that is pretty well covered with trees. Stumps are a different thing, for they don't shade the land; and besides, if you dig them, they make a fence that will turn anything bigger than a hog, being grand for breachy cattle."

"Opinions on such subjects vary much in different countries," said Marmaduke; "but it is not as ornaments that I value the noble trees of this country; it is for their usefulness. We are stripping the forests, as if a single year would replace what we destroy. But the hour approaches when the laws will take notice of not only the woods, but the game they contain also."

With this consoling reflection, Marmaduke remounted, and the equestrians passed the sugar camp on their way to the promised landscape of Richard. The wood chopper was left alone, in the bosom of the forest, to pursue his labors. Elizabeth turned her head when they reached the point where they were to descend the mountain, and thought that the slow fires that were glimmering under his enormous kettles, his little brush shelter, covered with pieces of hemlock bark, his gigantic size, as he wielded his ladle with a steady and knowing air, aided by the background of stately trees, with their sprouts and troughs, formed, altogether, no unreal picture of human life in its first stages of civilization. Perhaps whatever the scene possessed of a romantic character was not injured by the powerful tones of Kirby's voice ringing through the woods, as he again awoke his strains to another tune, which was but little more scientific than th former. All that she understood of the words were:

> "And when the proud forest is falling,
>   To my oxen cheerfully calling.
> From morn until night I am bawling,
>   Woe, back there, and hoy and gee;

Till our labor is mutually ended,
By my strength and cattle befriended,
And against the mosquitoes defended,
    By the bark of the walnut tree.

"Away! then, you lads who would buy land,
Choose the oak that grows on the high land,
Or the silvery pine on the dry land,
    It matters but little to me."

CHAPTER XXI

*Speed! Malise, speed! Such cause of haste
Thine active sinews never braced.*

SCOTT

THE roads of Otsego, if we except the principal highways, were, at the early day of our tale, but little better than wood paths. The high trees that were growing on the very verge of the wheel tracks excluded the sun's rays, unless at meridian; and the slowness of the evaporation, united with the rich mold of vegetable decomposition that covered the whole country to the depth of several inches, occasioned but an indifferent foundation for the footing of travelers. Added to these were the inequalities of a natural surface, and the constant recurrence of enormous and slippery roots that were laid bare by the removal of the light soil, together with stumps of trees, to make a passage not only difficult but dangerous. Yet the riders, among these numerous obstructions, which were such as would terrify an unpracticed eye, gave no demonstrations of uneasiness, as their horses toiled through the sloughs, or trotted with uncertain paces along the dark route. In many places, the marks on the trees were the only indications of a road, with perhaps an occasional remnant of a pine, that, by being cut close to the earth, so as to leave nothing visible but its base of roots, spreading for twenty feet in every direction, was apparently placed there as a beacon to warn the traveler that it was the center of a highway.

Into one of these roads the active sheriff led the way, first striking out of the footpath, by which they had descended from the sugarbush, across a little bridge, formed of round logs laid loosely on sleepers of pine, in which large openings of a formidable width were frequent. The nag of Richard, when it reached one of these gaps, laid its nose along the logs, and stepped across the difficult passage with the sagacity of a man; but the blooded filly which Miss Temple rode disdained so humble a movement. She made a step or two with an unusual caution, and then on reaching the broadest opening, obedient to the curb and whip of her fearless mistress, she bounded across the dangerous pass with the activity of a squirrel.

"Gently, gently, my child," said Marmaduke, who was following in the manner of Richard, "this is not a country for equestrian feats. Much prudence is requisite to journey through our rough paths with safety. Thou mayst practice thy skill in horsemanship on the plains of New Jersey with safety; but in the hills of Otsego they may be suspended for a time."

"I may as well then relinquish my saddle at once, dear sir," returned his daughter; "for if it is to be laid aside until this wild country be improved, old age will overtake me, and put an end to what you term my equestrian feats."

"Say not so, my child," returned her father; "but if thou venturest again, as in crossing this bridge, old age will never overtake thee, but I shall be left to mourn thee, cut off in thy pride, my Elizabeth. If thou hadst seen this district of country, as I did, when it lay in the sleep of nature, and had witnessed its rapid changes, as it awoke to supply the wants of man, thou wouldst curb thy impatience for a little time, though thou shouldst not check thy steed."

"I recollect hearing you speak of your first visit to these woods, but the impression is faint, and blended with the confused images of childhood. Wild and unsettled as it may yet seem, it must have been a thousand times more dreary then. Will you repeat, dear sir, what you then thought of your enterprise, and what you felt?"

During this speech of Elizabeth, which was uttered with the fervor of affection, young Edwards rode more closely to the side of the Judge, and bent his dark eyes on his countenance with an expression that seemed to read his thoughts.

"Thou wast then young, my child, but must remember

when I left thee and thy mother, to take my first survey of these uninhabited mountains," said Marmaduke. "But thou dost not feel all the secret motives that can urge a man to endure privations in order to accumulate wealth. In my case they have not been trifling, and God has been pleased to smile on my efforts. If I have encountered pain, famine, and disease, in accomplishing the settlement of this rough territory, I have not the misery of failure to add to the grievances."

"Famine!" echoed Elizabeth; "I thought this was the land of abundance! Had you famine to contend with?"

"Even so, my child," said her father. "Those who look around them now, and see the loads of produce that issue out of every wild path in these mountains, during the season of traveling, will hardly credit that no more than five years have elapsed, since the tenants of these woods were compelled to eat the scanty fruits of the forest to sustain life, and, with their unpracticed skill, to hunt the beasts as food for their starving families."

"Ay!" cried Richard, who happened to overhear the last of this speech, between the notes of the wood chopper's song, which he was endeavoring to breathe aloud; "that was the starving time,* cousin Bess. I grew as lank as a weasel that fall, and my face was as pale as one of your fever-and-ague visages. Monsieur Le Quoi, there, fell away like a pumpkin in drying; nor do I think you have got fairly over it yet, Monsieur. Benjamin, I thought, bore it with a worse grace than any of the family; for he swore it was harder to endure than a short allowance in the calm latitudes. Benjamin is a sad fellow to swear, if you starve him ever so little. I had half a mind to quit you then, 'duke, and go into Pennsylvania to fatten; but, damn it, thinks I, we are sisters' children, and I will live or die with him, after all."

* The author has no better apology for interrupting the interest of a work of fiction by these desultory dialogues, than that, they have reference to facts. In reviewing his work, after so many years, he is compelled to confess it is injured by too many allusions to incidents that are not at all suited to satisfy the just expectations of the general reader. One of these events is slightly touched on, in the commencement of this chapter.

More than thirty years since, a very near and dear relative of the writer, an elder sister and a second mother, was killed by a fall from a horse, in a ride among the very mountains mentioned in this tale. Few of her sex and years were more extensively known, or more universally beloved, than the admirable woman who thus fell a victim to the chances of the wilderness.

"I do not forget thy kindness," said Marmaduke, "nor that we are of one blood."

"But, my dear father," cried the wondering Elizabeth, "was there actual suffering? Where were the beautiful and fertile vales of the Mohawk? Could they not furnish food for your wants?"

"It was a season of scarcity; the necessities of life commanded a high price in Europe, and were greedily sought after by the speculators. The emigrants, from the east to the west, invariably passed along the valley of the Mohawk, and swept away the means of subsistence, like a swarm of locusts. Nor were the people on the Flats in a much better condition. They were in want themselves, but they spared the little excess of provisions that nature did not absolutely require, with the justice of the German character. There was no grinding of the poor. The word speculator was then unknown to them. I have seen many a stout man, bending under the load of the bag of meal, which he was carrying from the Mills of the Mohawk, through the rugged passes of these mountains, to feed his half-famished children, with a heart so light, as he approached his hut, that the thirty miles he had passed seemed nothing. Remember, my child, it was in our very infancy; we had neither mills, nor grain, nor roads, nor often clearings; we had nothing of increase, but the mouths that were to be fed; for, even at that inauspicious moment, the restless spirit of emigration was not idle; nay, the general scarcity which extended to the east tended to increase the number of adventurers."

"And how, dearest father, didst thou encounter this dreadful evil?" said Elizabeth, unconsciously adopting the dialect of her parent in the warmth of her sympathy. "Upon thee must have fallen the responsibility, if not the suffering."

"It did, Elizabeth," returned the Judge, pausing for a single moment, as if musing on his former feelings. "I had hundreds, at that dreadful time, daily looking up to me for bread. The sufferings of their families, and the gloomy prospect before them, had paralyzed the enterprise and efforts of my settlers; hunger drove them to the woods for food, but despair sent them at night, enfeebled and wan, to a sleepless pillow. It was not a moment for inaction. I purchased cargoes of wheat from the granaries of Pennsylvania; they were landed at Albany, and brought up the Mohawk in boats; from thence it was transported on pack horses into the wilderness, and distributed among my people. Seines were made, and the lakes and rivers were dragged for fish. Something like a miracle was wrought in our favor, for enormous shoals of herrings were discovered to have wandered five hundred miles, through the windings of the impetuous Susquehanna, and the lake was alive with their numbers. These were at length caught, and dealt out to the people, with proper portions of salt; and from that moment we again began to prosper." *

"Yes," cried Richard, "and I was the man who served out the fish and the salt. When the poor devils came to receive their rations, Benjamin, who was my deputy, was obliged to keep them off by stretching ropes around me, for they smelt so of garlic, from eating nothing but the wild onion, that the fumes put me out often in my measurement. You were a child then, Bess, and knew nothing of the matter, for great care was observed to keep both you and your mother from suffering. That year put me back dreadfully, both in the breed of my hogs and of my turkeys."

"No, Bess," cried the Judge, in a more cheerful tone, disregarding the interruption of his cousin, "he who hears of the settlement of a country knows but little of the toil and suffering by which it is accomplished. Unimproved and wild as this district now seems to your eyes, what was it when I first entered the hills! I left my party, the morning of my arrival, near the farms of the Cherry Valley, and, following a deer path, rode to the summit of the mountain that I have since called Mount Vision; for the sight that there met my eyes seemed to me as the deceptions of a dream. The fire had run over the pinnacle, and, in a great measure, laid open the view, the leaves were fallen, and I mounted a tree, and sat for an hour looking on the silent wilderness. Not an opening was to be seen in the boundless forest, except where the lake lay, like a mirror of glass. The water was covered by myriads of the wild fowl that migrate with the changes in the season; and, while in my situation on the branch of the beech, I saw a bear, with her cubs, descend to the shore to drink. I had met many deer, gliding through the woods, in my journey; but not the vestige of a

---

* All this was literally true.

man could I trace during my progress, not from my elevated observatory. No clearing, no hut, none of the winding roads that are now to be seen, were there; nothing but mountains rising behind mountains; and the valley, with its surface of branches, enlivened here and there with the faded foliage of some tree, that parted from its leaves with more than ordinary reluctance. Even the Susquehanna was then hid, by the height and density of the forest."

"And were you alone?" asked Elizabeth. "Passed you the night in that solitary state?"

"Not so, my child," returned her father. "After musing on the scene for an hour, with a mingled feeling of pleasure and desolation, I left my perch and descended the mountain. My horse was left to browse on the twigs that grew within his reach, while I explored the shores of the lake, and the spot where Templeton stands. A pine of more than ordinary growth stood where my dwelling is now placed! A windrow had been opened through the trees from thence to the lake, and my view was but little impeded. Under the branches of that tree I made my solitary dinner; I had just finished my repast as I saw a smoke curling from under the mountain, near the eastern bank of the lake. It was the only indication of the vicinity of man that I had then seen. After much toil I made my way to the spot and found a rough cabin of logs, built against the foot of a rock, and bearing the marks of a tenant, though I found no one within it——"

"It was the hut of Leatherstocking," said Edwards, quickly.

"It was; though I first supposed it to be a habitation of the Indians. But while I was lingering around the spot, Natty made his appearance, staggering under the carcass of a buck that he had slain. Our acquaintance commenced at that time; before, I had never heard that such a being tenanted the woods. He launched his bark canoe, and set me across the foot of the lake to the place where I had fastened my horse, and pointed out a spot where he might get a scanty browsing until the morning; when I returned and passed the night in the cabin of the hunter."

Miss Temple was so much struck by the deep attention of young Edwards during this speech that she forgot to resume her interrogatories; but the youth himself continued the discourse, by asking:

"And how did the Leatherstocking discharge the duties of a host, sir?"

"Why, simply but kindly, until late in the evening, when he discovered my name and object, and the cordiality of his manner very sensibly diminished, or, I might better say, disappeared. He considered the introduction of the settlers as an innovation on his rights, I believe; for he expressed much dissatisfaction at the measure, though it was in his confused and ambiguous manner. I hardly understood his objections myself, but supposed they referred chiefly to an interruption of the hunting."

"Had you then purchased the estate, or were you examining it with an intent to buy?" asked Edwards, a little abruptly.

"It had been mine for several years. It was with a view to people the land that I visited the lake. Natty treated me hospitably, but coldly, I thought, after he learned the nature of my journey. I slept on his own bearskin, however, and in the morning joined my surveyors again."

"Said he nothing of the Indian rights, sir? The Leatherstocking is much given to impeach the justice of the tenure by which the whites hold the country."

"I remember that he spoke of them, but I did not clearly comprehend him and may have forgotten what he said; for the Indian title was extinguished so far back as the close of the old war; and if it had not been at all, I hold under the patents of the Royal Governors, confirmed by an act of our own State Legislature, and no court in the country can affect my title."

"Doubtless, sir, your title is both legal and equitable," returned the youth, coldly, reining his horse back, and remaining silent till the subject was changed.

It was seldom Mr. Jones suffered any conversation to continue for a great length of time without his participation. It seems that he was of the party that Judge Temple had designated as his surveyors; and he embraced the opportunity of the pause that succeeded the retreat of young Edwards to take up the discourse, and with it a narration of their further proceedings, after his own manner. As it wanted, however, the interest that had accompanied the description of the Judge, we must decline the task of committing his sentences to paper.

They soon reached the point where the promised view

was to be seen. It was one of those picturesque and peculiar scenes that belong to the Otsego, but which required the absence of the ice and the softness of a summer's landscape to be enjoyed in all its beauty. Marmaduke had early forewarned his daughter of the season, and of its effect on the prospect; and after casting a cursory glance at its capabilities, the party returned homeward, perfectly satisfied that its beauties would repay them for the toil of a second ride, at a more propitious season.

"The spring is the gloomy time of the American year," said the Judge; "and it is more peculiarly the case in these mountains. The winter seems to retreat to the fastnesses of the hills, as to the citadel of its dominion, and is only expelled after a tedious siege, in which either party, at times, would seem to be gaining the victory."

"A very just and apposite figure, Judge Temple," observed the Sheriff; "and the garrison under the command of Jack Frost make formidable sorties—you understand what I mean by sorties, Monsieur; sallies in English—and sometimes drive General Spring and his troops back again into the low countries."

"Yes, sair," returned the Frenchman, whose prominent eyes were watching the precarious footsteps of the beast he rode, as it picked its dangerous way among the roots of trees, holes, log bridges, and sloughs that formed the aggregate of the highway. "Je vous entend; de low countrie is freeze up for half de year."

The error of Mr. Le Quoi was not noticed by the Sheriff; and the rest of the party were yielding to the influence of the changeful season, which was already teaching the equestrians that a continuance of its mildness was not to be expected for any length of time. Silence and thoughtfulness succeeded the gaiety and conversation that had prevailed during the commencement of the ride, as clouds began to gather about the heavens, apparently collecting from every quarter, in quick motion, without the agency of a breath of air.

While riding over one of the cleared eminences that occurred in their route, the watchful eye of Judge Temple pointed out to his daughter the approach of a tempest. Flurries of snow already obscured the mountain that formed the northern boundary of the lake, and the genial sensation which had quickened the blood through their veins was already succeeded by the deadening influence of an approaching northwester.

All of the party were now busily engaged in making the best of their way to the village, though the badness of the roads frequently compelled them to check the impatience of their animals, which often carried them over places that would not admit of any gait faster than a walk.

Richard continued in advance, followed by Mr. Le Quoi; next to whom rode Elizabeth, who seemed to have imbibed the distance which pervaded the manner of young Edwards, since the termination of the discourse between the latter and her father. Marmaduke followed his daughter, giving her frequent and tender warnings as to the management of her horse. It was, possibly, the evident dependence that Louisa Grant placed on his assistance which induced the youth to continue by her side, as they pursued their way through a dreary and dark wood, where the rays of the sun could but rarely penetrate, and where even the daylight was obscured and rendered gloomy by the deep forests that surrounded them. No wind had yet reached the spot where the equestrians were in motion, but that dead stillness that often precedes a storm contributed to render their situation more irksome than if they were already subject to the fury of the tempest. Suddenly the voice of young Edwards was heard shouting in those appalling tones that carry alarm to the very soul, and which curdle the blood of those that hear them:

"A tree! a tree! Whip—spur for your lives! a tree! a tree!"

"A tree! a tree!" echoed Richard, giving his horse a blow that caused the alarmed beast to jump nearly a rod, throwing the mud and water into the air like a hurricane.

"Von tree! von tree!" shouted the Frenchman, bending his body on the neck of his charger, shutting his eyes, and playing on the ribs of his beast with his heels at a rate that caused him to be conveyed on the crupper of the Sheriff with a marvelous speed.

Elizabeth checked her filly and looked up with an unconscious but alarmed air at the very cause of their danger, while she listened to the crackling sounds that awoke the stillness of the forest; but the next instant, her bridle was seized by her father, who cried:

"God protect my child!" and she felt herself hurried onward, impelled by the vigor of his nervous arm.

Each one of the party bowed to his saddlebows, as the tearing of branches was succeeded by a sound like the rushing of the winds, which was followed by a thundering report and a shock that caused the very earth to tremble, as one of the noblest ruins of the forest fell directly across their path.

One glance was enough to assure Judge Temple that his daughter, and those in front of him, were safe, and he turned his eyes, in dreadful anxiety, to learn the fate of the others. Young Edwards was on the opposite side of the tree, his form thrown back in his saddle to its utmost distance, his left hand drawing up his bridle with its greatest force, while the right grasped that of Miss Grant, so as to draw the head of her horse under its body. Both the animals stood shaking in every joint with terror, and snorting fearfully. Louisa herself had relinquished her reins, and with her hands pressed on her face, sat bending forward in her saddle, in an attitude of despair, mingled strangely with resignation.

"Are you safe?" cried the Judge, first breaking the awful silence of the moment.

"By God's blessing," returned the youth; "but if there had been branches to the tree we must have been lost——"

He was interrupted by the figure of Louisa slowly yielding in her saddle; and but for his arm she would have sunk to the earth. Terror, however, was the only injury that the clergyman's daughter had sustained, and with the aid of Elizabeth, she was soon restored to her senses. After some little time was lost in recovering her strength, the young lady was replaced in her saddle, and supported on either side by Judge Temple and Mr. Edwards, she was enabled to follow the party in their slow progress.

"The sudden fallings of the trees," said Marmaduke, "are the most dangerous accidents in the forest, for they are not to be foreseen, being impelled by no winds, nor any extraneous or visible cause against which we can guard."

"The reason of their falling, Judge Temple, is very obvious," said the Sheriff. "The tree is old and decayed, and it is gradually weakened by the frosts, until a line drawn from the center of gravity falls without its base, and then the tree comes of a certainty; and I should like to know what greater compulsion there can be for anything than a mathematical certainty. I studied mathe———"

"Very true, Richard," interrupted Marmaduke; "thy reasoning is true, and if my memory be not over treacherous, was furnished by myself on a former occasion. But how is one to guard against the danger? Canst thou go through the forests, measuring the bases, and calculating the centers of the oaks? Answer me that, friend Jones, and I will say thou wilt do the country a service."

"Answer thee that, friend Temple!" returned Richard. "A well-educated man can answer thee anything, sir. Do any trees fall in this manner but such as are decayed? Take care not to approach the roots of a rotten tree, and you will be safe enough."

"That would be excluding us entirely from the forests," said Marmaduke. "But, happily, the winds usually force down most of these dangerous ruins, as their currents are admitted into the woods by the surrounding clearings, and such a fall as this has been is very rare."

Louisa, by this time, had recovered so much strength as to allow the party to proceed at a quicker pace, but long before they were safely housed, they were overtaken by the storm; and when they dismounted at the door of the mansion house, the black plumes of Miss Temple's hat were drooping with the weight of a load of damp snow, and the coats of the gentlemen were powdered with the same material.

While Edwards was assisting Louisa from her horse, the warmhearted girl caught his hand with fervor and whispered:

"Now, Mr. Edwards, both father and daughter owe their lives to you."

A driving northwesterly storm succeeded, and before the sun was set, every vestige of spring had vanished; the lake, the mountains, the village, and the fields being again hidden under one dazzling coat of snow.

Chapter XXII

Men, boys, and girls,
Desert th' unpeopled village; and wild crowds
Spread o'er the plain, by the sweet phrensy driven.
                                                SOMERVILLE

FROM this time to the close of April the weather continued to be a succession of great and rapid changes. One day, the soft airs of spring seemed to be stealing along the valley, and in unison with an invigorating sun, attempting covertly to rouse the dormant powers of the vegetable world; while on the next, the surly blasts from the north would sweep across the lake and erase every impression left by their gentle adversaries. The snow, however, finally disappeared, and the green wheat fields were seen in every direction, spotted with the dark and charred stumps that had, the preceding season, supported some of the proudest trees of the forest. Plows were in motion, wherever those useful implements could be used, and the smokes of the sugar camps were no longer seen issuing from the woods of maple. The lake had lost the beauty of a field of ice, but still a dark and gloomy covering concealed its waters, for the absence of currents left them yet hidden under a porous crust, which, saturated with the fluid, barely retained enough strength to preserve the contiguity of its parts. Large flocks of wild geese were seen passing over the country, which hovered, for a time, around the hidden sheet of water, apparently searching for a resting place; and then, on finding themselves excluded by the chill covering, would soar away to the north, filling the air with discordant screams, as if venting their complaints at the tardy operations of nature.

For a week, the dark covering of the Otsego was left to the undisturbed possession of two eagles, who alighted on the center of its field and sat eying their undisputed territory. During the presence of these monarchs of the air, the flocks of migrating birds avoided crossing the plain of ice by turning into the hills, apparently seeking the protection of the forests, while the white and bald heads of the tenants

231

of the lake were turned upwards, with a look of contempt. But the time had come, when even these kings of birds were to be dispossessed. An opening had been gradually increasing at the lower extremity of the lake, and around the dark spot where the current of the river prevented the formation of ice, during even the coldest weather; and the fresh southerly winds that now breathed freely upon the valley made an impression on the waters. Mimic waves began to curl over the margin of the frozen field, which exhibited an outline of crystallizations that slowly receded towards the north. At each step the power of the winds and the waves increased, until, after a struggle of a few hours, the turbulent little billows succeeded in setting the whole field in motion, when it was driven beyond the reach of the eye, with a rapidity that was as magical as the change produced in the scene by this expulsion of the lingering remnant of winter. Just as the last sheet of agitated ice was disappearing in the distance, the eagles rose and soared with a wide sweep above the clouds, while the waves tossed their little caps of snow into the air, as if rioting in their release from a thralldom of five months' duration.

The following morning Elizabeth was awakened by the exhilarating sounds of the martins, who were quarreling and chattering around the little boxes suspended above her windows, and the cries of Richard, who was calling in tones animating as the signs of the season itself:

"Awake! awake! my fair lady! The gulls are hovering over the lake already, and the heavens are alive with pigeons. You may look an hour before you can find a hole through which to get a peep at the sun. Awake! awake! lazy ones! Benjamin is overhauling the ammunition, and we only wait for our breakfast, and away for the mountains and pigeon shooting."

There was no resisting this animated appeal, and in a few minutes Miss Temple and her friend descended to the parlor. The doors of the hall were thrown open, and the mild, balmy air of a clear spring morning was ventilating the apartment, where the vigilance of the ex-steward had been so long maintaining an artificial heat with such unremitted diligence. The gentlemen were impatiently waiting for their morning's repast, each equipped in the garb of a sportsman.

Mr. Jones made many visits to the southern door, and would cry:

"See, cousin Bess! See, 'duke, the pigeon roosts of the south have broken up! They are growing more thick every instant. Here is a flock that the eye cannot see the end of. There is food enough in it to keep the army of Xerxes for a month, and feathers enough to make beds for the whole country. Xerxes, Mr. Edwards, was a Grecian king, who— no, he was a Turk, or a Persian, who wanted to conquer Greece, just the same as these rascals will overrun our wheat fields, when they come back in the fall. Away! away! Bess; I long to pepper them."

In this wish both Marmaduke and young Edwards seemed equally to participate, for the sight was exhilarating to a sportsman; and the ladies soon dismissed the party after a hasty breakfast.

If the heavens were alive with pigeons, the whole village seemed equally in motion, with men, women, and children. Every species of firearms, from the French ducking gun with a barrel near six feet in length, to the common horseman's pistol, was to be seen in the hands of the men and boys; while bows and arrows, some made of the simple stick of a walnut sapling, and others in a rude imitation of the ancient crossbows, were carried by many of the latter.

The houses and the signs of life apparent in the village drove the alarmed birds from the direct line of their flight, towards the mountains, along the sides and near the bases of which they were glancing in dense masses, equally wonderful by the rapidity of their motion and their incredible numbers.

We have already said, that across the inclined plane which fell from the steep ascent of the mountain to the banks of the Susquehanna, ran the highway, on either side of which a clearing of many acres had been made at a very early day. Over those clearings, and up the eastern mountain, and along the dangerous path that was cut into its side, the different individuals posted themselves, and in a few moments the attack commenced.

Among the sportsmen was the tall, gaunt form of Leatherstocking, walking over the field, with his rifle hanging on his arm, his dogs at his heels; the latter now scenting the dead or wounded birds that were beginning to tumble from the flocks, and then crouching under the legs of their master, as if they participated in his feelings at this wasteful and unsportsmanlike execution.

The reports of the firearms became rapid, whole volleys rising from the plain, as flocks of more than ordinary numbers darted over the opening, shadowing the field like a cloud; and then the light smoke of a single piece would issue from among the leafless bushes on the mountain, as death was hurled on the retreat of the affrighted birds, who were rising from a volley, in a vain effort to escape. Arrows, and missiles of every kind, were in the midst of the flocks; and so numerous were the birds, and so low did they take their flight, that even long poles, in the hands of those on the sides of the mountain, were used to strike them to the earth.

During all this time, Mr. Jones, who disdained the humble and ordinary means of destruction used by his companions, was busily occupied, aided by Benjamin, in making arrangements for an assault of more than ordinarily fatal character. Among the relics of the old military excursions that occasionally are discovered throughout the different districts of the western part of New York, there had been found in Templeton, at its settlement, a small swivel, which would carry a ball of a pound weight. It was thought to have been deserted by a war party of the whites, in one of their inroads into the Indian settlements, when, perhaps, convenience or their necessity induced them to leave such an encumbrance behind them in the woods. This miniature cannon had been released from the rust, and being mounted on little wheels, was now in a state for actual service. For several years, it was the sole organ for extraordinary rejoicings used in those mountains. On the mornings of the Fourths of July, it would be heard ringing among the hills; and even Captain Hollister, who was the highest authority in that part of the country on all such occasions, affirmed that, considering its dimensions, it was no despicable gun for a salute. It was somewhat the worse for the service it had performed, it is true, there being but a trifling difference in size between the touchhole and the muzzle. Still, the grand conceptions of Richard had suggested the importance of such an instrument in hurling death at his nimble enemies. The swivel was dragged by a horse into a part of the open space that the Sheriff thought most eligible for planting a battery of the kind, and Mr. Pump proceeded to load it. Several handfuls of duck shot were placed on top of the powder, and the major-domo announced that his piece was ready for service.

The sight of such an implement collected all the idle spectators to the spot, who, being mostly boys, filled the air with cries of exultation and delight. The gun was pointed high, and Richard, holding a coal of fire in a pair of tongs, patiently took his seat on a stump, awaiting the appearance of a flock worthy of his notice.

So prodigious was the number of the birds, that the scattering fire of the guns, with the hurling of missiles, and the cries of the boys, had no other effect than to break off small flocks from the immense masses that continued to dart along the valley, as if the whole of the feathered tribe were pouring through that one pass. None pretended to collect the game, which lay scattered over the fields in such profusion as to cover the very ground with the fluttering victims.

Leatherstocking was a silent, but uneasy spectator of all these proceedings, but was able to keep his sentiments to himself until he saw the introduction of the swivel into the sport.

"This comes of settling a country!" he said. "Here have I known the pigeons to fly for forty long years, and, till you made your clearings, there was nobody to skear or to hurt them. I loved to see them come into the woods, for they were company to a body; hurting nothing; being, as it was, as harmless as a garter snake. But now it gives me sore thoughts when I hear the frighty things whizzing through the air, for I know it's only a motion to bring out all the brats in the village. Well! the Lord won't see the waste of his creatures for nothing, and right will be done to the pigeons, as well as others, by and by. There's Mr. Oliver, as bad as the rest of them, firing into the flocks, as if he was shooting down nothing but Mingo warriors."

Among the sportsmen was Billy Kirby, who, armed with an old musket, was loading, and without even looking into the air, was firing and shouting as his victims fell even on his own person. He heard the speech of Natty and took upon himself to reply:

"What! old Leatherstocking," he cried, "grumbling at the

loss of a few pigeons! If you had to sow your wheat twice, and three times, as I have done, you wouldn't be so massy-fully feeling towards the divils. Hurrah, boys! scatter the feathers! This is better than shooting at a turkey's head and neck, old fellow."

"It's better for you, maybe, Billy Kirby," replied the indignant old hunter, "and all them that don't know how to put a ball down a rifle barrel, or how to bring it up again with a true aim; but it's wicked to be shooting into flocks in this wasty manner; and none do it, who know how to knock over a single bird. If a body has a craving for pigeon's flesh, why, it's made the same as all other creatures, for man's eating; but not to kill twenty and eat one. When I want such a thing I go into the woods till I find one to my liking, and then I shoot him off the branches, without touching the feather of another, though there might be a hundred on the same tree. You couldn't do such a thing, Billy Kirby—you couldn't do it, if you tried."

"What's that, old cornstalk! You sapless stub!" cried the wood chopper. "You have grown wordy, since the affair of the turkey; but if you are for a single shot, here goes at that bird which comes on by himself."

The fire from the distant part of the field had driven a single pigeon below the flock to which it belonged, and, frightened with the constant reports of the muskets, it was approaching the spot where the disputants stood, darting first from one side and then to the other, cutting the air with the swiftness of lightning, and making a noise with its wings, not unlike the rushing of a bullet. Unfortunately for the wood chopper, notwithstanding his vaunt, he did not see this bird until it was too late to fire as it approached, and he pulled his trigger at the unlucky moment when it was darting immediately over his head. The bird continued its course with the usual velocity.

Natty lowered the rifle from his arm when the challenge was made, and waiting a moment, until the terrified victim had got in a line with his eye, and had dropped near the bank of the lake, he raised it again with uncommon rapidity, and fired. It might have been chance, or it might have been skill, that produced the result; it was probably a union of both; but the pigeon whirled over in the air, and fell into the lake, with a broken wing. At the sound of his rifle, both his dogs started from his feet, and in a few minutes the "slut" brought out the bird, still alive.

The wonderful exploit of Leatherstocking was noised through the field with great rapidity, and the sportsmen gathered in, to learn the truth of the report.

"What!" said young Edwards, "have you really killed a pigeon on the wing, Natty, with a single ball?"

"Haven't I killed loons before now, lad, that dive at the flash?" returned the hunter. "It's much better to kill only such as you want, without wasting your powder and lead, than to be firing into God's creatures in this wicked manner. But I came out for a bird, and you know the reason why I like small game, Mr. Oliver, and now I have got one I will go home, for I don't relish to see these wasty ways that you are all practysing, as if the least thing wasn't made for use, and not to destroy."

"Thou sayest well, Leatherstocking," cried Marmaduke, "and I begin to think it time to put an end to this work of destruction."

"Put an ind, Judge, to your clearings. An't the woods his work as well as the pigeons? Use, but don't waste. Wasn't the woods made for the beasts and birds to harbor in? And when man wanted their flesh, their skins, or their feathers there's the place to seek them. But I'll go to the hut with my own game, for I wouldn't touch one of the harmless things that cover the ground here, looking up with their eyes on me, as if they only wanted tongues to say their thoughts."

With this sentiment in his mouth, Leatherstocking threw his rifle over his arm, and followed by his dogs, stepped across the clearing with great caution, taking care not to tread on one of the wounded birds in his path. He soon entered the bushes on the margin of the lake and was hid from view.

Whatever impression the morality of Natty made on the Judge, it was utterly lost on Richard. He availed himself of the gathering of the sportsmen to lay a plan for one "fell swoop" of destruction. The musket men were drawn up in battle array, in a line extending on each side of his artillery, with orders to await the signal of firing from himself.

"Stand by, my lads," said Benjamin, who acted as an aide-de-camp on this occasion, "stand by, my hearties, and when Squire Dickens heaves out the signal to begin firing,

d'ye see, you may open upon them in a broadside. Take care
and fire low, boys, and you'll be sure to hull the flock."

"Fire low!" shouted Kirby. "Hear the old fool! If we fire
low, we may hit the stumps, but not ruffle a pigeon."

"How should you know, you lubber?" cried Benjamin,
with a very unbecoming heat for an officer on the eve of
battle. "How should you know, you grampus? Haven't I
sailed aboard of the Boadishey for five years? And wasn't it a
standing order to fire low, and to hull your enemy? Keep
silence at your guns, boys, and mind the order that is
passed."

The loud laughs of the musket men were silenced by the
more authoritative voice of Richard, who called for attention and obedience to his signals.

Some millions of pigeons were supposed to have already
passed that morning over the valley of Templeton; but nothing like the flock that was now approaching had been seen
before. It extended from mountain to mountain in one solid
blue mass, and the eye looked in vain, over the southern
hills, to find its termination. The front of this living column
was distinctly marked by a line but very slightly indented,
so regular and even was the flight. Even Marmaduke forgot
the morality of Leatherstocking as it approached, and, in
common with the rest, brought his musket to a poise.

"Fire!" cried the Sheriff, clapping a coal to the priming of
the cannon. As half of Benjamin's charge escaped through the
touchhole, the whole volley of the musketry preceded the
report of the swivel. On receiving this united discharge of
small arms, the front of the flock darted upwards, while, at
the same instant, myriads of those in the rear rushed with
amazing rapidity into their places, so that when the column
of white smoke gushed from the mouth of the little cannon, an accumulated mass of objects was gliding over its
point of direction. The roar of the gun echoed along the
mountains and died away to the north, like distant thunder,
while the whole flock of alarmed birds seemed, for a moment, thrown into one disorderly and agitated mass. The air
was filled with their irregular flight, layer rising above layer,
far above the tops of the highest pines, none daring to advance beyond the dangerous pass; when, suddenly, some of
the leaders of the feathered tribe shot across the valley,
taking their flight directly over the village, and hundreds of

thousands in their rear followed the example, deserting the eastern side of the plain to their persecutors and the slain.

"Victory!" shouted Richard, "victory! We have driven the enemy from the field."

"Not so, Dickon," said Marmaduke. "The field is covered with them; and, like the Leatherstocking, I see nothing but eyes, in every direction, as the innocent sufferers turn their heads in terror. Full one half of those that have fallen are yet alive; and I think it is time to end the sport, if sport it be."

"Sport!" cried the Sheriff; "it is princely sport! There are some thousands of the blue-coated boys on the ground, so that every old woman in the village may have a potpie for the asking."

"Well, we have happily frightened the birds from this side of the valley," said Marmaduke, "and the carnage must of necessity end, for the present. Boys, I will give you sixpence a hundred for the pigeons' heads only: so go to work, and bring them into the village."

This expedient produced the desired effect, for every urchin on the ground went industriously to work to wring the necks of the wounded birds. Judge Temple retired towards his dwelling with that kind of feeling that many a man has experienced before him, who discovers, after the excitement of the moment has passed, that he has purchased pleasure at the price of misery to others. Horses were loaded with the dead; and, after this first burst of sporting, the shooting of pigeons became a business, with a few idlers, for the remainder of the season. Richard, however, boasted for many a year, of his shot with the "cricket"; and Benjamin gravely asserted that he thought they killed nearly as many pigeons on that day, as there were Frenchmen destroyed on the memorable occasion of Rodney's victory.

Chapter XXIII

Help, masters, help; here's a fish hangs in the net, like a poor man's right in the law.

Pericles of Tyre

The advance of the season now became as rapid as its first approach had been tedious and lingering. The days were uniformly mild, while the nights, though cool, were no longer chilled by frosts. The whippoorwill was heard whistling his melancholy notes along the margin of the lake, and the ponds and meadows were sending forth the music of their thousand tenants. The leaf of the native poplar was seen quivering in the woods; the sides of the mountains began to lose their hue of brown, as the lively green of the different members of the forest blended their shades with the permanent colors of the pine and hemlock; and even the buds of the tardy oak were swelling with the promise of the coming summer. The gay and fluttering bluebird, the social robin, and the industrious little wren were all to be seen enlivening the fields with their presence and their songs; while the soaring fish hawk was already hovering over the waters of the Otsego, watching, with native voracity, for the appearance of his prey.

The tenants of the lake were far-famed for both their quantities and their quality, and the ice had hardly disappeared, before numberless little boats were launched from the shores, and the lines of the fishermen were dropped into the inmost recesses of its deepest caverns, tempting the unwary animals with every variety of bait that the ingenuity or the art of man had invented. But the slow, though certain adventures with hook and line were ill-suited to the profusion and impatience of the settlers. More destructive means were resorted to; and as the season had now arrived when the bass fisheries were allowed by the provisions of the law that Judge Temple had procured, the Sheriff declared his intention, by availing himself of the first dark night, to enjoy the sport in person.

"And you shall be present, cousin Bess," he added, when he announced this design, "and Miss Grant, and Mr. Edwards; and I will show you what I call fishing—not nibble, nibble,

nibble, as 'duke does when he goes after the salmon trout. There he will sit for hours, in a broiling sun, or, perhaps, over a hole in the ice, in the coldest days in winter, under the lee of a few bushes, and not a fish will he catch, after all this mortification of the flesh. No, no—give me a good seine that's fifty or sixty fathoms in length, with a jolly parcel of boatmen to crack their jokes the while, with Benjamin to steer, and let us haul them in by thousands; I call that fishing."

"Ah! Dickon," cried Marmaduke, "thou knowest but little of the pleasure there is in playing with the hook and line, or thou wouldst be more saving of the game. I have known thee to leave fragments enough behind thee, when thou hast headed a night party on the lake, to feed a dozen famishing families."

"I shall not dispute the matter, Judge Temple: this night will I go; and I invite the company to attend, and then let them decide between us."

Richard was busy during most of the afternoon making his preparations for the important occasion. Just as the light of the setting sun had disappeared, and a new moon had begun to throw its shadows on the earth, the fishermen took their departure in a boat, for a point that was situated on the western shore of the lake, at the distance of rather more than half a mile from the village. The ground had become settled, and the walking was good and dry. Marmaduke, with his daughter, her friend, and young Edwards, continued on the high grassy banks at the outlet of the placid sheet of water, watching the dark object that was moving across the lake, until it entered the shade of the western hills and was lost to the eye. The distance round by land to the point of destination was a mile, and he observed:

"It is time for us to be moving: the moon will be down ere we reach the point, and then the miraculous hauls of Dickon will commence."

The evening was warm, and, after the long and dreary winter from which they had just escaped, delightfully invigorating. Inspirited by the scene and their anticipated amusement, the youthful companions of the Judge followed his steps, as he led them along the shores of the Otsego and through the skirts of the village.

"See!" said young Edwards, "they are building their fire

already; it glimmers for a moment and dies again like the light of a firefly."

"Now it blazes," cried Elizabeth: "you can perceive figures moving around the light. Oh! I would bet my jewels against the gold beads of Remarkable, that my impatient cousin Dickon had an agency in raising that bright flame—and see; it fades again, like most of his brilliant schemes."

"Thou hast guessed the truth, Bess," said her father; "he has thrown an armful of brush on the pile, which has burnt out as soon as lighted. But it has enabled them to find a better fuel, for their fire begins to blaze with a more steady flame. It is the true fisherman's beacon now; observe how beautifully it throws its little circle of light on the water!"

The appearance of the fire urged the pedestrians on, for even the ladies had become eager to witness the miraculous draught. By the time they reached the bank, which rose above the low point where the fishermen had landed, the moon had sunk behind the tops of the western pines, and, as most of the stars were obscured by clouds, there was but little other light than that which proceeded from the fire. At the suggestion of Marmaduke, his companions paused to listen to the conversation of those below them, and examine the party for a moment before they descended to the shore.

The whole group were seated around the fire, with the exception of Richard and Benjamin; the former of whom occupied the root of a decayed stump, that had been drawn to the spot as part of their fuel, and the latter was standing, with his arms akimbo, so near to the flame that the smoke occasionally obscured his solemn visage, as it waved around the pile, in obedience to the night airs that swept gently over the water.

"Why, look you, Squire," said the major-domo, "you may call a lake fish that will weigh twenty or thirty pounds a serious matter; but to a man who has hauled in a shovel-nosed shirk, d'ye see, it's but a poor kind of fishing after all."

"I don't know, Benjamin," returned the Sheriff: "a haul of one thousand Otsego bass, without counting pike, pickerel, perch, bullpouts, salmon trouts, and suckers, is no bad fishing, let me tell you. There may be sport in sticking a shark, but what is he good for after you have got him? Now, any one of the fish that I have named is fit to set before a king."

"Well, Squire," returned Benjamin, "just listen to the philosophy of the thing. Would it stand to reason, that such fish should live and be catched in this here little pond of water, where it's hardly deep enough to drown a man, as you'll find in the wide ocean, where, as everybody knows, that is, everybody that has followed the seas, whales and grampuses are to be seen that are as long as one of the pine trees on yonder mountain?"

"Softly, softly, Benjamin," said the Sheriff, as if he wished to save the credit of his favorite; "why some of the pines will measure two hundred feet, and even more."

"Two hundred or two thousand, it's all the same thing," cried Benjamin, with an air which manifested that he was not easily to be bullied out of his opinion, on a subject like the present. "Haven't I been there, and haven't I seen? I have said that you fall in with whales as long as one of them there pines; and what I have once said I'll stand to!"

During this dialogue, which was evidently but the close of a much longer discussion, the huge frame of Billy Kirby was seen extended on one side of the fire, where he was picking his teeth with splinters of the chips near him and occasionally shaking his head with distrust of Benjamin's assertions.

"I've a notion," said the wood chopper, "that there's water in this lake to swim the biggest whale that ever was invented; and, as to the pines, I think I ought to know so'thing consarning them; I have chopped many a one that was sixty times the length of my helve, without counting the eye: and I believe, Benny, that if the old pine that stands in the hollow of the Vision Mountain, just over the village—you may see the tree itself by looking up, for the moon is on its top yet —well, now I believe, if that same tree was planted out in the deepest part of the lake, there would be water enough for the biggest ship that ever was built to float over it without touching its upper branches, I do."

"Did'ee ever see a ship, Master Kirby?" roared the steward. "Did'ee ever see a ship, man? Or any craft bigger than a lime scow, or a wood boat, on this here small bit of fresh water?"

"Yes, I have," said the wood chopper, stoutly; "I can say that I have, and tell no lie."

"Did'ee ever see a British ship, Master Kirby? An English line-of-battle ship, boy? Where away did'ee ever fall in with a regular built vessel, with starnpost and cutwater, garboard streak and plank-shear, gangways, and hatchways, and water-ways, quarter-deck and forecastle, ay, and flush deck?—tell me that, man, if you can; where away did'ee ever fall in with a full rigged, regular built, decked vessel?"

The whole company were a good deal astounded with this overwhelming question, and even Richard afterwards remarked, that it "was a thousand pities that Benjamin could not read, or he must have made a valuable officer to the British marine. It is no wonder that they overcame the French so easily on the water, when even the lowest sailor so well understood the different parts of a vessel." But Billy Kirby was a fearless wight, and had great jealousy of foreign dictation; he had arisen on his feet and turned his back to the fire during the voluble delivery of this interrogatory; and when the steward ended, contrary to all expectation, he gave the following spirited reply:

"Where! Why on the North River, and maybe on Champlain. There's sloops on the river, boy, that would give a hard time on't to the stoutest vessel King George owns. They carry masts of ninety feet in the clear of good solid pine, for I've been at the chopping of many a one in Varmount state. I wish I was captain in one of them, and you was in that Board-dish that you talk so much about; and we'd soon see what good Yankee stuff is made on, and whether a Varmounter's hide an't as thick as an Englishman's."

The echoes from the opposite hills, which were more than half a mile from the fishing point, sent back the discordant laugh that Benjamin gave forth at this challenge; and the woods that covered their sides seemed, by the noise that issued from their shades, to be full of mocking demons.

"Let us descend to the shore," whispered Marmaduke, "or there will soon be ill blood between them. Benjamin is a fearless boaster; and Kirby, though good-natured, is a careless son of the forest, who thinks one American more than a match for six Englishmen. I marvel that Dickon is silent where there is such a trial of skill in the superlative!"

The appearance of Judge Temple and the ladies produced, if not a pacification, at least a cessation of hostilities. Obedient to the directions of Mr. Jones, the fishermen prepared to launch their boat, which had been seen in the background of the view, with the net carefully disposed on a little platform in its stern, ready for service. Richard gave vent to his reproaches at the tardiness of the pedestrians, when all the turbulent passions of the party were succeeded by a calm, as mild and as placid as that which prevailed over the beautiful sheet of water that they were about to rifle of its best treasures.

The night had now become so dark as to render objects, without the reach of the light of the fire, not only indistinct, but in most cases invisible. For a little distance the water was discernible, glistening, as the glare from the fire danced over its surface, touching it here and there with red quivering streaks, but at a hundred feet from the shore, there lay a boundary of impenetrable gloom. One or two stars were shining through the openings of the clouds, and the lights were seen in the village, glimmering faintly, as if at an immeasurable distance. At times as the fire lowered, or as the horizon cleared, the outline of the mountain, on the other side of the lake, might be traced by its undulations; but its shadow was cast, wide and dense, on the bosom of the water, rendering the darkness in that direction trebly deep.

Benjamin Pump was invariably the coxswain and net caster of Richard's boat, unless the Sheriff saw fit to preside in person; and, on the present occasion, Billy Kirby and a youth of about half his strength were assigned to the oars. The remainder of the assistants were stationed at the dragropes. The arrangements were speedily made, and Richard gave the signal to "shove off."

Elizabeth watched the motion of the bateau as it pulled from the shore, letting loose its rope as it went, but it soon disappeared in the darkness, when the ear was her only guide to its evolutions. There was great affectation of stillness during all these maneuvers, in order, as Richard assured them, "not to frighten the bass, who were running into the shoal waters, and who would approach the light if not disturbed by the sounds from the fishermen."

The hoarse voice of Benjamin was alone heard issuing out of the gloom, as he uttered, in authoritative tones, "pull larboard oar," "pull starboard," "give way together, boys," and such other dictative mandates as were necessary for the right disposition of his seine. A long time was passed in this necessary part of the process, for Benjamin prided himself greatly on his skill in throwing the net, and, in fact, most of the success of the sport depended on its being done with judgment. At length a loud splash in the water, as he threw away the "staff," or "stretcher," with a hoarse call from the steward of "clear," announced that the boat was returning; when Richard seized a brand from the fire and ran to a point as far above the center of the fishing ground as the one from which the bateau had started was below it.

"Stick her in dead for the Squire, boys," said the steward, "and we'll have a look at what grows in this here pond."

In place of the falling net were now to be heard the quick strokes of the oars and the noise of the rope running out of the boat. Presently the bateau shot into the circle of light, and in an instant she was pulled to shore. Several eager hands were extended to receive the line, and both ropes being equally well-manned, the fishermen commenced hauling in with slow and steady drags, Richard standing in the center, giving orders, first to one party, and then to the other, to increase or slacken their efforts, as occasion required. The visitors were posted near him and enjoyed a fair view of the whole operation, which was slowly advancing to an end.

Opinions as to the result of their adventure were now freely hazarded by all the men, some declaring that the net came in as light as a feather, and others affirming that it seemed to be full of logs. As the ropes were many hundred feet in length, these opposing sentiments were thought to be of little moment by the Sheriff, who would go first to one line and then to the other, giving each a small pull in order to enable him to form an opinion for himself.

"Why, Benjamin," he cried, as he made his first effort in this way, "you did not throw the net clear. I can move it with my little finger. The rope slackens in my hand."

"Did you ever see a whale, Squire?" responded the steward. "I say that if that there net is foul, the devil is in the lake in the shape of a fish, for I cast it as fair as ever rigging was rove over the quarter-deck of a flagship."

But Richard discovered his mistake when he saw Billy Kirby before him, standing with his feet in the water, at an angle of forty-five degrees, inclining shorewards and expending his gigantic strength in sustaining himself in that posture. He ceased his remonstrances and proceeded to the party at the other line.

"I see the 'staffs,'" shouted Mr. Jones; "gather in, boys, and away with it; to shore with her!—to shore with her!"

At this cheerful sound, Elizabeth strained her eyes and saw the ends of the two sticks on the seine emerging from the darkness, while the men closed near to each other and formed a deep bag of their net. The exertions of the fishermen sensibly increased, and the voice of Richard was heard encouraging them to make their greatest efforts at the present moment.

"Now's the time, my lads," he cried; "let us get the ends to land, and all we have will be our own—away with her!"

"Away with her, it is," echoed Benjamin!—"Hurrah! Ho-a-hoy, ho-a-hoy, ho-a!"

"In with her," shouted Kirby, exerting himself in a manner that left nothing for those in his rear to do, but to gather up the slack of the rope which passed through his hands.

"Staff, ho!" shouted the steward.

"Staff, ho!" echoed Kirby, from the other rope.

The men rushed to the water's edge, some seizing the upper rope, and some the lower, or lead rope, and began to haul with great activity and zeal. A deep semicircular sweep of the little balls that supported the seine in its perpendicular position was plainly visible to the spectators, and, as it rapidly lessened in size, the bag of the net appeared, while an occasional flutter on the water announced the uneasiness of the prisoners it contained.

"Haul in, my lads," shouted Richard. "I can see the dogs kicking to get free. Haul in, and here's a cast that will pay for the labor."

Fishes of various sorts were now to be seen, entangled in the meshes of the net, as it was passed through the hands of the laborers; and the water, at a little distance from the shore, was alive with the movements of the alarmed victims. Hundreds of white sides were glancing up to the surface of the water, and glistening in the firelight, when, frightened at the uproar and the change, the fish would again dart to the bottom, in fruitless efforts for freedom.

"Hurrah!" shouted Richard; "one or two more heavy drags, boys, and we are safe."

"Cheerily, boys, cheerily!" cried Benjamin; "I see a salmon trout that is big enough for a chowder."

"Away with you, you varmint!" said Billy Kirby, plucking a bullpout from the meshes, and casting the animal back into the lake with contempt. "Pull, boys, pull; here's all kinds, and the Lord condemn me for a liar, if there an't a thousand bass!"

Inflamed beyond the bounds of discretion at the sight, and forgetful of the season, the wood chopper rushed to his middle into the water and began to drive the reluctant animals before him from their native element.

"Pull heartily, boys," cried Marmaduke, yielding to the excitement of the moment, and laying his hands to the net, with no trifling addition to the force. Edwards had preceded him; for the sight of the immense piles of fish that were slowly rolling over on the gravelly beach had impelled him also to leave the ladies, and join the fishermen.

Great care was observed in bringing the net to land, and, after much toil, the whole shoal of victims was safely deposited in a hollow of the bank, where they were left to flutter away their brief existence in the new and fatal element.

Even Elizabeth and Louisa were greatly excited and highly gratified by seeing two thousand captives thus drawn from the bosom of the lake, and laid prisoners at their feet. But when the feelings of the moment were passing away, Marmaduke took in his hands a bass that might have weighed two pounds, and after viewing it a moment, in melancholy musing, he turned to his daughter, and observed:

"This is a fearful expenditure of the choicest gifts of Providence. These fish, Bess, which thou seest lying in such piles before thee, and which by tomorrow evening will be rejected food on the meanest table in Templeton, are of a quality and flavor that, in other countries, would make them esteemed a luxury on the tables of princes or epicures. The world has no better fish than the bass of Otsego: it unites the richness of the shad * to the firmness of the salmon."

"But surely, dear sir," cried Elizabeth, "they must prove a great blessing to the country, and a powerful friend to the poor."

"The poor are always prodigal, my child, where there is plenty, and seldom think of a provision against the morrow. But if there can be any excuse for destroying animals in this manner, it is in taking the bass. During the winter, you know, they are entirely protected from our assaults by the ice, for they refuse the hook; and during the hot months they

---

* Of all the fish the writer has ever tasted, he thinks the one in question the best.

are not seen. It is supposed they retreat to the deep and cool waters of the lake, at that season; and it is only in the spring and autumn, that, for a few days, they are to be found around the points where they are within the reach of a seine. But, like all the other treasures of the wilderness, they already begin to disappear before the wasteful extravagance of man."

"Disappear, 'duke! disappear!" exclaimed the Sheriff; "if you don't call this appearing, I know not what you will. Here are a good thousand of the shiners, some hundreds of suckers, and a powerful quantity of other fry. But this is always the way with you, Marmaduke; first it's the trees, then it's the deer, after that it's the maple sugar, and so on to the end of the chapter. One day you talk of canals through a country where there's a river or a lake every half-mile, just because the water won't run the way you wish it to go; and the next, you say something about mines of coal, though any man who has good eyes like myself—I say with good eyes—can see more wood than would keep the city of London in fuel for fifty years; wouldn't it, Benjamin?"

"Why, for that, Squire," said the steward, "Lon'on is no small place. If it was stretched an end, all the same as a town on one side of a river, it would cover some such matter as this here lake. Tho'f I dar'st to say, that the wood in sight might sarve them a good turn, seeing that the Lon'oners mainly burn coal."

"Now we are on the subject of coal, Judge Temple," interrupted the Sheriff, "I have a thing of much importance to communicate to you; but I will defer it until tomorrow. I know that you intend riding into the eastern part of the Patent, and I will accompany you, and conduct you to a spot where some of your projects may be realized. We will say no more now, for there are listeners; but a secret has this evening been revealed to me, 'duke, that is of more consequence to your welfare than all your estate united."

Marmaduke laughed at the important intelligence, to which in a variety of shapes he was accustomed, and the Sheriff, with an air of great dignity, as if pitying his want of faith, proceeded in the business more immediately before them. As the labor of drawing the net had been very great, he directed one party of his men to commence throwing the fish into piles, preparatory to the usual division, while another, under the superintendence of Benjamin, prepared the seine for a second haul.

CHAPTER XXIV

While from its margin, terrible to tell!
Three sailors with their gallant boatswain fell. FALCONER

WHILE the fishermen were employed in making the preparations for an equitable division of the spoil, Elizabeth and her friend strolled a short distance from the group, along the shore of the lake. After reaching a point to which even the brightest of the occasional gleams of the fire did not extend, they turned, and paused a moment, in contemplation of the busy and lively party they had left, and of the obscurity, which, like the gloom of oblivion, seemed to envelop the rest of the creation.

"This is indeed a subject for the pencil!" exclaimed Elizabeth. "Observe the countenance of that wood chopper, while he exults in presenting a larger fish than common to my cousin Sheriff; and see, Louisa, how handsome and considerate my dear father looks, by the light of that fire, where he stands viewing the havoc of the game. He seems melancholy, as if he actually thought that a day of retribution was to follow this hour of abundance and prodigality! Would they not make a picture, Louisa?"

"You know that I am ignorant of all such accomplishments, Miss Temple."

"Call me by my Christian name," interrupted Elizabeth; "this is not a place, neither is this a scene, for forms."

"Well, then, if I may venture an opinion," said Louisa, timidly, "I should think it might indeed make a picture. The selfish earnestness of that Kirby over his fish would contrast finely with the—the—expression of Mr. Edwards's face. I hardly know what to call it; but it is—a—is—you know what I would say, dear Elizabeth."

"You do me too much credit, Miss Grant," said the heiress; "I am no diviner of thoughts, or interpreter of expressions."

There was certainly nothing harsh, or even cold, in the manner of the speaker, but still it repressed the conversation, and they continued to stroll still further from the party, retaining each other's arm, but observing a profound silence. Elizabeth perhaps conscious of the improper phraseology of her last speech, or perhaps excited by the new object that met her gaze, was the first to break the awkward cessation in the discourse, by exclaiming:

"Look, Louisa! we are not alone; there are fishermen lighting a fire on the other side of the lake, immediately opposite to us; it must be in front of the cabin of Leatherstocking!"

Through the obscurity, which prevailed most immediately under the eastern mountain, a small and uncertain light was plainly to be seen, though, as it was occasionally lost to the eye, it seemed struggling for existence. They observed it to move, and sensibly to lower, as if carried down the descent of the bank to the shore. Here, in a very short time, its flame gradually expanded, and grew brighter, until it became of the size of a man's head, when it continued to shine a steady ball of fire.

Such an object, lighted as it were by magic, under the brow of the mountain, and in that retired and unfrequented place, gave double interest to the beauty and singularity of its appearance. It did not at all resemble the large and unsteady light of their own fire, being much more clear and bright, and retaining its size and shape with perfect uniformity.

There are moments when the best regulated minds are more or less subjected to the injurious impressions which few have escaped in infancy; and Elizabeth smiled at her own weakness, while she remembered the idle tales which were circulated through the village at the expense of the Leatherstocking. The same ideas seized her companion, and at the same instant, for Louisa pressed nearer to her friend, as she said in a low voice, stealing a timid glance towards the bushes and trees that overhung the bank near them:

"Did you ever hear the singular ways of this Natty spoken of, Miss Temple? They say that, in his youth, he was an Indian warrior; or, what is the same thing, a white man leagued with the savages; and it is thought he has been concerned in many of their inroads, in the old wars."

"The thing is not at all improbable," returned Elizabeth; "he is not alone in that particular."

"No, surely; but is it not strange that he is so cautious with his hut? He never leaves it without fastening it in a remarkable manner; and in several instances, when the children, or even the men of the village, have wished to seek a shelter there from the storms, he has been known to drive them from his door with rudeness and threats. That, surely, is singular in this country!"

"It is certainly not very hospitable; but we must remember his aversion to the customs of civilized life. You heard my father say, a few days since, how kindly he was treated by him on his first visit to this place." Elizabeth paused, and smiled, with an expression of peculiar archness, though the darkness hid its meaning from her companion, as she continued—"Besides, he certainly admits the visits of Mr. Edwards, whom we both know to be far from a savage."

To this speech Louisa made no reply but continued gazing on the object which had elicited her remarks. In addition to the bright and circular flame, was now to be seen a fainter, though a vivid light, of an equal diameter to the other at the upper end; but which, after extending downwards for many feet, gradually tapered to a point at its lower extremity. A dark space was plainly visible between the two; and the new illumination was placed beneath the other; the whole forming an appearance not unlike an inverted note of admiration. It was soon evident that the latter was nothing but the reflection, from the water, of the former; and that the object, whatever it might be, was advancing across, or rather over, the lake, for it seemed to be several feet above its surface, in a direct line with themselves. Its motion was amazingly rapid, the ladies having hardly discovered that it was moving at all, before the waving light of a flame was discerned, losing its regular shape, while it increased in size, as it approached.

"It appears to be supernatural!" whispered Louisa, beginning to retrace her steps towards the party.

"It is beautiful!" exclaimed Elizabeth.

A brilliant, though waving flame, was now plainly visible, gracefully gliding over the lake and throwing its light on the water in such a manner as to tinge it slightly; though in the air, so strong was the contrast, the darkness seemed to have the distinctness of material substances, as if the fire were imbedded in a setting of ebony. This appearance, however, gradually wore off; and the rays from the torch struck out, and enlightened the atmosphere in front of it, leaving the background in a darkness that was more impenetrable than ever.

"Ho! Natty, is that you?" shouted the Sheriff. "Paddle in, old boy, and I'll give you a mess of fish that is fit to place before the Governor."

The light suddenly changed its direction, and a long and slightly built boat hove up out of the gloom, while the red glare fell on the weather-beaten features of the Leatherstocking, whose tall person was seen erect in the frail vessel, wielding, with the grace of an experienced boatman, a long fishing spear, which he held by its center, first dropping one end and then the other into the water, to aid in propelling the little canoe of bark, we will not say through, but over, the water. At the further end of the vessel a form was faintly seen, guiding its motions, and using a paddle with the ease of one who felt there was no necessity for exertion. The Leatherstocking struck his spear lightly against the short staff which upheld, on a rude grating framed of old hoops of iron, the knots of pine that composed the fuel, and the light, which glared high, for an instant fell on the swarthy features and dark, glancing eyes of Mohegan.

The boat glided along the shore until it arrived opposite the fishing ground, when it again changed its direction, and moved on to the land, with a motion so graceful, and yet so rapid, that it seemed to possess the power of regulating its own progress. The water in front of the canoe was hardly ruffled by its passage, and no sound betrayed the collision, when the light fabric shot on the gravelly beach for nearly half its length, Natty receding a step or two from its bow, in order to facilitate the landing.

"Approach, Mohegan," said Marmaduke; "approach, Leatherstocking, and load your canoe with bass. It would be a shame to assail the animals with the spear, when such multitudes of victims lie here, that will be lost as food for the want of mouths to consume them."

"No, no, Judge," returned Natty, his tall figure stalking over the narrow beach, and ascending to the little grassy bottom where the fish were laid in piles: "I eat of no man's wasty ways. I strike my spear into the eels or the trout, when

I crave the creaters; but I wouldn't be helping to such a sinful kind of fishing for the best rifle that was ever brought out from the old countries. If they had fur, like a beaver, or you could tan their hides, like a buck, something might be said in favor of taking them by the thousands with your nets; but as God made them for man's food, and for no other disarnable reason, I call it sinful and wasty to catch more than can be eat."

"Your reasoning is mine: for once, old hunter, we agree in opinion; and I heartily wish we could make a convert of the Sheriff. A net of half the size of this would supply the whole village with fish for a week at one haul."

The Leatherstocking did not relish this alliance in sentiment; and he shook his head doubtingly, as he answered:

"No, no; we are not much of one mind, Judge, or you'd never turn good hunting grounds into stumpy pastures. And you fish and hunt out of rule; but, to me, the flesh is sweeter where the creater has some chance for its life: for that reason, I always use a single ball, even if it be at a bird or a squirrel. Besides, it saves lead; for, when a body knows how to shoot, one piece of lead is enough for all, except hard-lived animals."

The Sheriff heard these opinions with great indignation; and when he completed the last arrangement for the division, by carrying, with his own hands, a trout of a large size, and placing it on four different piles in succession, as his vacillating ideas of justice required, he gave vent to his spleen.

"A very pretty confederacy, indeed! Judge Temple, the landlord and owner of a township, with Nathaniel Bumppo, a lawless squatter and professed deer killer, in order to preserve the game of the county! But, 'duke, when I fish I fish; so, away, boys, for another haul, and we'll send out wagons and carts in the morning to bring in our prizes."

Marmaduke appeared to understand that all opposition to the will of the Sheriff would be useless; and he strolled from the fire to the place where the canoe of the hunters lay, whither the ladies and Oliver Edwards had already preceded him.

Curiosity induced the females to approach this spot; but it was a different motive that led the youth thither. Elizabeth examined the light ashen timbers and thin bark covering of the canoe, in admiration of its neat but simple execution, and with wonder that any human being could be so daring as to trust his life in so frail a vessel. But the youth explained to her the buoyant properties of the boat and its perfect safety when under proper management; adding, in such glowing terms, a description of the manner in which the fish were struck with the spear, that she changed suddenly, from an apprehension of the danger of the excursion, to a desire to participate in its pleasures. She even ventured a proposition to that effect to her father, laughing at the same time at her own wish and accusing herself of acting under a woman's caprice.

"Say not so, Bess," returned the Judge. "I would have you above the idle fears of a silly girl. These canoes are the safest kind of boats to those who have skill and steady nerves. I have crossed the broadest part of the Oneida in one much smaller than this."

"And I the Ontary," interrupted the Leatherstocking; "and that with squaws in the canoe, too. But the Delaware women are used to the paddle and are good hands in a boat of this nater. If the young lady would like to see an old man strike a trout for his breakfast, she is welcome to a seat. John will say the same, seeing that he built the canoe, which was only launched yesterday; for I'm not overcurous at such small work as brooms, and basketmaking, and other like Indian trades."

Natty gave Elizabeth one of his significant laughs, with a kind nod of the head, when he concluded his invitation: but Mohegan, with the native grace of an Indian, approached, and taking her soft white hand into his own swarthy and wrinkled palm, said:

"Come, granddaughter of Miquon, and John will be glad. Trust the Indian; his head is old, though his hand is not steady. The young Eagle will go and see that no harm hurts his sister."

"Mr. Edwards," said Elizabeth, blushing slightly, "your friend Mohegan has given a promise for you. Do you redeem the pledge?"

"With my life, if necessary, Miss Temple," cried the youth, with fervor. "The sight is worth some little apprehension; for of real danger there is none. I will go with you and Miss Grant, however, to save appearances."

"With me!" exclaimed Louisa. "No, not with me, Mr.

Edwards; nor, surely, do you mean to trust yourself in that slight canoe."

"But I shall; for I have no apprehensions any longer," said Elizabeth, stepping into the boat, and taking a seat where the Indian directed. "Mr. Edwards, you may remain, as three do seem to be enough for such an eggshell."

"It shall hold a fourth," cried the young man, springing to her side with a violence that nearly shook the weak fabric of the vessel asunder. "Pardon me, Miss Temple, that I do not permit these venerable Charons to take you to the shades unattended by your genius."

"Is it a good or evil spirit?" asked Elizabeth.

"Good to you."

"And mine," added the maiden, with an air that strangely blended pique with satisfaction. But the motion of the canoe gave rise to new ideas, and fortunately afforded a good excuse to the young man to change the discourse.

It appeared to Elizabeth that they glided over the water by magic, so easy and graceful was the manner in which Mohegan guided his little bark. A slight gesture with his spear indicated the way in which the Leatherstocking wished to go, and a profound silence was preserved by the whole party, as a precaution necessary to the success of their fishery. At that point of the lake, the water shoaled regularly, differing in this particular, altogether, from those parts where the mountains rose, nearly in perpendicular precipices, from the beach. There, the largest vessels could have lain, with their yards interlocked with the pines; while here a scanty growth of rushes lifted their tops above the lake, gently curling the waters, as their bending heads waved with the passing breath of the night air. It was at the shallow points, only, that the bass could be found, or the net cast with success.

Elizabeth saw thousands of these fish swimming in shoals along the shallow and warm waters of the shore; for the flaring light of their torch laid bare the mysteries of the lake, as plainly as if the limpid sheet of the Otsego was but another atmosphere. Every instant she expected to see the impending spear of Leatherstocking darting into the thronging hosts that were rushing beneath her, where it would seem that a blow could not go amiss; and where, as her father had already said, the prize that would be obtained was worthy any epicure. But Natty had his peculiar habits, and, it would seem, his peculiar tastes also. His tall stature and his erect posture enabled him to see much further than those who were seated in the bottom of the canoe; and he turned his head warily in every direction, frequently bending his body forward, and straining his vision, as if desirous of penetrating the water that surrounded their boundary of light. At length his anxious scrutiny was rewarded with success, and, waving his spear from the shore, he said in a cautious tone:

"Send her outside the bass, John; I see a laker there that has run out of the school. It's seldom one finds such a creater in shallow water, where a spear can touch it."

Mohegan gave a wave of assent with his hand, and in the next instant the canoe was without the "run of the bass," and in water nearly twenty feet in depth. A few additional knots were laid on the grating, and the light penetrated to the bottom. Elizabeth then saw a fish of unusual size floating above small pieces of logs and sticks. The animal was only distinguishable, at that distance, by a slight, but almost imperceptible motion of its fins and tail. The curiosity excited by this unusual exposure of the secrets of the lake seemed to be mutual between the heiress of the land and the lord of these waters, for the "salmon trout" soon announced his interest by raising his head and body for a few degrees above a horizontal line, and then dropping them again into a horizontal position.

"Whist! whist!" said Natty, in a low voice, on hearing a slight sound made by Elizabeth in bending over the side of the canoe in curiosity. " 'Tis a skeary animal, and it's a far stroke for a spear. My handle is but fourteen foot, and the creater lies a good eighteen from the top of the water; but I'll try him, for he's a ten-pounder."

While speaking, the Leatherstocking was poising and directing his weapon. Elizabeth saw the bright, polished tines, as they slowly and silently entered the water, where the refraction pointed them many degrees from the true direction of the fish; and she thought that the intended victim saw them also, as he seemed to increase the play of his tail and fins, though without moving his station. At the next instant the tall body of Natty bent to the water's edge, and the handle of his spear disappeared in the lake. The long, dark streak of the gliding weapon, and the little bubbling vortex which followed its rapid flight, were easily to be seen; but it was not until the handle shot again into the air by its own reaction, and its master catching it in his hand, threw its tines uppermost, that Elizabeth was acquainted with the success of the blow. A fish of great size was transfixed by the barbed steel, and was very soon shaken from its impaled situation into the bottom of the canoe.

"That will do, John," said Natty, raising his prize by one of his fingers and exhibiting it before the torch; "I shall not strike another blow tonight."

The Indian again waved his hand, and replied with the simple and energetic monosyllable of:

"Good."

Elizabeth was awakened from the trance created by this scene, and by gazing in that unusual manner at the bottom of the lake, by the hoarse sounds of Benjamin's voice, and the dashing of oars, as the heavier boat of the seine drawers approached the spot where the canoe lay, dragging after it the folds of the net.

"Haul off, haul off, Master Bumppo," cried Benjamin; "your top light frightens the fish, who see the net and sheer off soundings. A fish knows as much as a horse, or, for that matter, more, seeing that it's brought up on the water. Haul off, Master Bumppo, haul off, I say, and give a wide berth to the seine."

Mohegan guided their little canoe to a point where the movements of the fishermen could be observed, without interruption to the business, and then suffered it to lie quietly on the water, looking like an imaginary vessel floating in air. There appeared to be much ill-humor among the party in the bateau, for the directions of Benjamin were not only frequent, but issued in a voice that partook largely of dissatisfaction.

"Pull larboard oar, will ye, Master Kirby?" cried the old seaman. "Pull larboard best. It would puzzle the oldest admiral in the British fleet to cast this here net fair, with a wake like a corkscrew. Pull starboard, boy, pull starboard oar, with a will."

"Harkee, Mister Pump," said Kirby, ceasing to row, and speaking with some spirit; "I'm a man that likes civil language and decent treatment, such as is right 'twixt man and man. If you want us to go hoy, say so, and hoy I'll go, for the benefit of the company; but I'm not used to being ordered about like dumb cattle."

"Who's dumb cattle?" echoed Benjamin fiercely, turning his forbidding face to the glare of light from the canoe, and exhibiting every feature teeming with the expression of disgust. "If you want to come aft and cund the boat round, come and be damned, and pretty steerage you'll make of it. There's but another heave of the net in the stern sheets, and we're clear of the thing. Give way, will ye? And shoot her ahead for a fathom or two, and if you catch me afloat again with such a horse marine as yourself, why rate me a ship's jackass, that's all."

Probably encouraged by the prospect of a speedy termination to his labor, the wood chopper resumed his oar, and, under strong excitement, gave a stroke, that not only cleared the boat of the net, but of the steward, at the same instant. Benjamin had stood on the little platform that held the seine, in the stern of the boat, and the violent whirl occasioned by the vigor of the wood chopper's arm completely destroyed his balance. The position of the lights rendered objects in the bateau distinguishable, both from the canoe and the shore; and the heavy fall on the water drew all eyes to the steward, as he lay struggling, for a moment, in sight.

A loud burst of merriment, to which the lungs of Kirby contributed no small part, broke out like a chorus of laughter and rang along the eastern mountain, in echoes, until it died away in distant, mocking mirth, among the rocks and woods. The body of the steward was seen slowly to disappear, as was expected; but when the light waves, which had been raised by his fall, began to sink in calmness, and the water finally closed over his head, unbroken and still, a very different feeling pervaded the spectators.

"How fare you, Benjamin?" shouted Richard from the shore.

"The dumb devil can't swim a stroke!" exclaimed Kirby, rising, and beginning to throw aside his clothes.

"Paddle up, Mohegan," cried young Edwards, "the light will show us where he lies, and I will dive for the body."

"Oh! save him! For God's sake, save him!" exclaimed Elizabeth, bowing her head on the side of the canoe in horror.

A powerful and dexterous sweep of Mohegan's paddle sent

the canoe directly over the spot where the steward had fallen, and a loud shout from the Leatherstocking announced that he saw the body.

"Steady the boat while I dive," again cried Edwards.

"Gently, lad, gently," said Natty; "I'll spear the creater up in half the time, and no risk to anybody."

The form of Benjamin was lying, about halfway to the bottom, grasping with both hands some broken rushes. The blood of Elizabeth curdled to her heart, as she saw the figure of a fellow creature thus extended under an immense sheet of water, apparently in motion, by the undulations of the dying waves, with its face and hands, viewed by that light, and through the medium of the fluid, already colored with hues like death.

At the same instant, she saw the shining tines of Natty's spear approaching the head of the sufferer, and entwining themselves rapidly and dexterously in the hairs of his queue and the cape of his coat. The body was now raised slowly, looking ghastly and grim, as its features turned upwards to the light, and approached the surface. The arrival of the nostrils of Benjamin into their own atmosphere was announced by a breathing that would have done credit to a porpoise. For a moment, Natty held the steward suspended, with his head just above the water, while his eyes slowly opened, and stared about him, as if he thought that he had reached a new and unexplored country.

As all the parties acted and spoke together, much less time was consumed in the occurrence of these events than in their narration. To bring the bateau to the end of the spear, and to raise the form of Benjamin into the boat, and for the whole party to gain the shore, required but a minute. Kirby, aided by Richard, whose anxiety induced him to run into the water to meet his favorite assistant, carried the motionless steward up the bank and seated him before the fire, while the Sheriff proceeded to order the most approved measures then in use, for the resuscitation of the drowned.

"Run, Billy," he cried, "to the village, and bring up the rum hogshead that lies before the door, in which I am making vinegar, and be quick, boy, don't stay to empty the vinegar; and stop at Mr. Le Quoi's, and buy a paper of tobacco and half a dozen pipes; and ask Remarkable for some salt, and one of her flannel petticoats; and ask Dr.

Todd to send his lancet, and to come himself; and——ha!
Duke, what are you about? Would you strangle a man who
is full of water, by giving him rum! Help me to open his
hand, that I may pat it."

All this time Benjamin sat, with his muscles fixed, his
mouth shut, and his hands clenching the rushes, which he
had seized in the confusion of the moment, and which, as
he held fast, like a true seaman, had been the means of
preventing his body from rising again to the surface. His
eyes, however, were open, and stared wildly on the group
about the fire, while his lungs were playing like a blacksmith's bellows, as if to compensate themselves for the minute
of inaction to which they had been subjected. As he kept
his lips compressed, with a most inveterate determination,
the air was compelled to pass through his nostrils, and he
rather snorted than breathed, and in such a manner that
nothing but the excessive agitation of the Sheriff could at
all justify his precipitous orders.

The bottle, applied to the steward's lips by Marmaduke,
acted like a charm. His mouth opened instinctively; his
hands dropped the rushes and seized the glass; his eyes
raised from their horizontal stare to the heavens; and the
whole man was lost, for a moment, in a new sensation. Un-
happily for the propensity of the steward, breath was as
necessary after one of these draughts as after his submersion,
and the time at length arrived when he was compelled to
let go the bottle.

"Why, Benjamin!" roared the Sheriff; "you amaze me!
For a man of your experience in drownings to act so fool-
ishly! Just now, you were half-full of water, and now you
are——"

"Full of grog," interrupted the steward, his features settling down, with amazing flexibility, into their natural economy. "But, d'ye see, Squire, I kept my hatches close, and it
is but little water that ever gets into my scuttle butt. Harkee,
Master Kirby! I've followed the salt water for the better
part of a man's life, and have seen some navigation on the
fresh; but this here matter I will say in your favor, and that
is, that you're the awk'ardest green'un that ever straddled a
boat's thwart. Them that likes you for a shipmate may sail
with you and no thanks; but dam'me if I even walk on the
lake shore in your company. For why? You'd as lief drown a

man as one of them there fish; not to throw a Christian creature so much as a rope's end, when he was adrift, and no
life buoy in sight!— Natty Bumppo, give us your fist. There's
them that says you're an Indian, and a scalper, but you've
served me a good turn, and you may set me down for a
friend; tho'f it would have been more shipshape to lower the
bight of a rope, or running bowline, below me, than to seize
an old seaman by his head lanyard; but I suppose you are
used to taking men by the hair, and seeing you did me good
instead of harm thereby, why, it's the same thing, d'ye see."

Marmaduke prevented any reply, and assumimg the direction of matters with a dignity and discretion that at once
silenced all opposition from his cousin, Benjamin was dispatched to the village by land, and the net was hauled to
shore in such a manner that the fish for once escaped its
meshes with impunity.

The division of the spoils was made in the ordinary manner, by placing one of the party with his back to the game,
who named the owner of each pile. Billy Kirby stretched his
large frame on the grass by the side of the fire, as sentinel
until morning, over net and fish; and the remainder of the
party embarked in the bateau, to return to the village.

The wood chopper was seen broiling his supper on the
coals as they lost sight of the fire; and when the boat approached the shore, the torch of Mohegan's canoe was shining again under the gloom of the eastern mountain. Its
motion ceased suddenly; a scattering of brands was in the
air, and then all remained dark as the conjunction of night,
forest, and mountain could render the scene.

The thoughts of Elizabeth wandered from the youth,
who was holding a canopy of shawls over herself and Louisa,
hunter and the Indian warrior; and she felt an awaken-
ing curiosity to visit a hut, where men of such different
habits and temperament were drawn together as by common
impulse.

CHAPTER XXV

Cease all this parlance about hills and dales;
None listen to thy scenes of boyish frolic,
Fond dotard! with such tickled ears as thou dost;
Comel to thy tale.   Duo

MR. JONES arose on the following morning with the sun, and ordering his own and Marmaduke's steeds to be saddled, he proceeded, with a countenance big with some business of unusual moment, to the apartment of the Judge. The door was unfastened, and Richard entered with the freedom that characterized not only the intercourse between the cousins, but the ordinary manners of the Sheriff.

"Well, 'duke, to horse," he cried, "and I will explain to you my meaning in the allusions I made last night. David says, in the Psalms—no, it was Solomon, but it was all in the family —Solomon said there was a time for all things; and in my humble opinion, a fishing party is not the moment for discussing important subjects. Ha! why, what the devil ails you, Marmaduke? An't you well? Let me feel your pulse: my grandfather, you know——"

"Quite well in the body, Richard," interrupted the Judge, repulsing his cousin, who was about to assume the functions that properly belonged to Dr. Todd; "but ill at heart. I received letters by the post of last night, after we returned from the point, and this among the number."

The Sheriff took the letter, but without turning his eyes on the writing, for he was examining the appearance of the other with astonishment. From the face of his cousin the gaze of Richard wandered to the table, which was covered with letters, packets and newspapers; then to the apartment and all that it contained. On the bed there was the impression that had been made by a human form, but the coverings were unmoved, and everything indicated that the occupant of the room had passed a sleepless night. The candles had burned to the sockets and had evidently extinguished themselves in their own fragments. Marmaduke had drawn his curtains and opened both the shutters and the sashes to

263

admit the balmy air of a spring morning; but his pale cheek, his quivering lip, and his sunken eye presented altogether so very different an appearance from the usual calm, manly, and cheerful aspect of the Judge, that the Sheriff grew each moment more and more bewildered with astonishment. At length Richard found time to cast his eyes on the direction of the letter, which he still held unopened, crumbling it in his hand.

"What! a ship letter!" he exclaimed: "and from England! Ha! 'duke, there must be news of importance indeed!"

"Read it," said Marmaduke, pacing the floor in excessive agitation.

Richard, who commonly thought aloud, was unable to read a letter without suffering part of its contents to escape him in audible sounds. So much of the epistle as was divulged in that manner, we shall lay before the reader, accompanied by the passing remarks of the Sheriff:

" 'London, February 12th, 1793.' What a devil of a passage she had! But the wind has been northwest for six weeks, until within the last fortnight.

" 'Sir, your favors of August 10th, September 23d, and of December 1st, were received in due season, and the first answered by return of packet. Since the receipt of the last, I' "—Here a long passage was rendered indistinct, by a kind of humming noise made by the Sheriff. " 'I grieve to say that' —hum, hum, bad enough to be sure—'but trust that a merciful Providence has seen fit'—hum, hum, hum; seems to be a good pious sort of a man, 'duke; belongs to the established church, I dare say; hum, hum—'vessel sailed from Falmouth on or about the 1st September of last year, and'— hum, hum, hum. 'If anything should transpire on this afflicting subject shall not fail'—hum, hum; really a good-hearted man, for a lawyer—'but can communicate nothing further at present'—hum, hum—'The national convention' —hum, hum—'unfortunate Louis'—hum, hum—'example of your Washington'—a very sensible man, I declare, and none of your crazy democrats. Hum, hum—'our gallant navy'—hum, hum—'under our most excellent monarch'—ay, a good man enough, that King George, but bad advisers; hum, hum—'I beg to conclude with assurances of my perfect respect'— hum, hum—'ANDREW HOLT.'—Andrew Holt—a very sensible,

feeling man, this Mr. Andrew Holt—but the writer of evil
tidings. What will you do next, cousin Marmaduke?"

"What can I do, Richard, but trust to time, and the will of
Heaven? Here is another letter from Connecticut, but it
only repeats the substance of the last. There is but one
consoling reflection to be gathered from the English news,
which is, that my last letter was received by him before
the ship sailed."

"This is bad enough, indeed! 'duke, bad enough, indeed!
And away go all my plans of putting wings to the house, to
the devil. I had made arrangements for a ride to introduce
you to something of a very important nature. You know
how much you think of mines——"

"Talk not of mines," interrupted the Judge; "there is a
sacred duty to be performed, and that without delay. I must
devote this day to writing; and thou must be my assistant,
Richard; it will not do to employ Oliver in a matter of such
secrecy and interest."

"No, no, 'duke," cried the Sheriff, squeezing his hand; "I
am your man, just now: we are sisters' children, and blood,
after all, is the best cement to make friendship stick together. Well, well, there is no hurry about the silver mine,
just now; another time will do as well. We shall want Dirky
Van, I suppose?"

Marmaduke assented to this indirect question, and the
Sheriff relinquished all his intentions on the subject of the
ride, and repairing to the breakfast parlor, he dispatched a
messenger to require the immediate presence of Dirck
Van der School.

The village of Templeton at that time supported but two
lawyers, one of whom was introduced to our readers in the
barroom of the "Bold Dragoon," and the other was the gentleman of whom Richard spoke by the friendly yet familiar
appellation of Dirck, or Dirky Van. Great good nature, a
very tolerable share of skill in his profession, and considering the circumstances, no contemptible degree of honesty
were the principal ingredients in the character of this man,
who was known to the settlers as Squire Van der School,
and sometimes by the flattering, though anomalous title of
the "Dutch" or "honest lawyer." We would not wish to mis-
lead our readers in their conceptions of any of our characters, and we therefore feel it necessary to add, that the ad-

jective, in the preceding agnomen of Mr. Van der School, was used in direct reference to its substantive. Our orthodox friends need not be told that all merit in this world is comparative; and once for all, we desire to say that where anything which involves qualities or character is asserted, we must be understood to mean, "under the circumstances."

During the remainder of the day, the Judge was closeted with his cousin and his lawyer; and no one else was admitted to his apartment, excepting his daughter. The deep distress that so evidently affected Marmaduke was in some measure communicated to Elizabeth also: for a look of dejection shaded her intelligent features, and the buoyancy of her animated spirits was sensibly softened. Once on that day, young Edwards, who was a wondering and observant spectator of the sudden alteration produced in the heads of the family, detected a tear stealing over the cheek of Elizabeth, and suffusing her bright eyes with a softness that did not always belong to their expression.

"Have any evil tidings been received, Miss Temple?" he inquired, with an interest and voice that caused Louisa Grant to raise her head from her needlework, with a quickness at which she instantly blushed herself. "I would offer my services to your father, if, as I suspect, he needs an agent in some distant place, and I thought it would give you relief."

"We have certainly heard bad news," returned Elizabeth, "and it may be necessary that my father should leave home for a short period; unless I can persuade him to trust my cousin Richard with the business, whose absence from the country, just at this time, too, might be inexpedient."

The youth paused a moment, and the blood gathered slowly to his temples, as he continued:

"If it be of a nature that I could execute——"

"It is such as can only be confided to one we know—one of ourselves."

"Surely, you know me, Miss Temple!" he added, with a warmth that he seldom exhibited, but which did sometimes escape him, in the moments of their frank communications. "Have I lived five months under your roof to be a stranger?"

Elizabeth was engaged with her needle also, and she bent her head to one side, affecting to arrange her muslin; but her hand shook, her color heightened, and her eyes lost their moisture in an expression of ungovernable interest, as she said:

"How much do we know of you, Mr. Edwards?"

"How much!" echoed the youth, gazing from the speaker to the mild countenance of Louisa, that was also illuminated with curiosity; "how much! Have I been so long an inmate with you and not known?"

The head of Elizabeth turned slowly from its affected position, and the look of confusion that had blended so strongly with an expression of interest changed to a smile.

"We know you, sir, indeed: you are called Mr. Oliver Edwards. I understand that you have informed my friend, Miss Grant, that you are a native——"

"Elizabeth!" exclaimed Louisa, blushing to the eyes, and trembling like an aspen, "you misunderstood me, dear Miss Temple; I—I—it was only conjecture. Besides, if Mr. Edwards is related to the natives, why should we reproach him? In what are we better? At least I, who am the child of a poor and unsettled clergyman?"

Elizabeth shook her head doubtingly, and even laughed, but made no reply; until, observing the melancholy which pervaded the countenance of her companion, who was thinking of the poverty and labors of her father, she continued:

"Nay, Louisa, humility carries you too far. The daughter of a minister of the church can have no superiors. Neither I nor Mr. Edwards is quite your equal, unless," she added, again smiling, "he is in secret a king."

"A faithful servant of the King of Kings, Miss Temple, is inferior to none on earth," said Louisa; "but his honors are his own; I am only the child of a poor and friendless man and can claim no other distinction. Why, then, should I feel myself elevated above Mr. Edwards, because—because—perhaps he is only very, very distantly related to John Mohegan?"

Glances of a very comprehensive meaning were exchanged between the heiress and the young man, as Louisa betrayed, while vindicating his lineage, the reluctance with which she admitted his alliance with the old warrior; but not even a smile at the simplicity of their companion was indulged by either.

"On reflection, I must acknowledge that my situation here

is somewhat equivocal," said Edwards, "though I may be said to have purchased it with my blood."

"The blood, too, of one of the native lords of the soil!" cried Elizabeth, who evidently put little faith in his aboriginal descent.

"Do I bear the marks of my lineage so very plainly impressed on my appearance? I am dark, but not very red—not more so than common?"

"Rather more so, just now."

"I am sure, Miss Temple," cried Louisa, "you cannot have taken much notice of Mr. Edwards. His eyes are not so black as Mohegan's, or even your own, nor is his hair!"

"Very possibly, then, I can lay claim to the same descent. It would be a great relief to my mind to think so, for I own that I grieve when I see old Mohegan walking about these lands, like the ghost of one of their ancient possessors, and feel how small is my own right to possess them."

"Do you?" cried the youth, with a vehemence that startled the ladies.

"I do, indeed," returned Elizabeth, after suffering a moment to pass in surprise; "but what can I do? What can my father do? Should we offer the old man a home and a maintenance, his habits would compel him to refuse us. Neither, were we so silly as to wish such a thing, could we convert these clearings and farms again into hunting grounds, as the Leatherstocking would wish to see them."

"You speak the truth, Miss Temple," said Edwards. "What can you do, indeed? But there is one thing that I am certain you can and will do, when you become the mistress of these beautiful valleys—use your wealth with indulgence to the poor and charity to the needy—indeed, you can do no more."

"And that will be doing a good deal," said Louisa, smiling in her turn. "But there will, doubtless, be one to take the direction of such things from her hands."

"I am not about to disclaim matrimony, like a silly girl, who dreams of nothing else from morning till night; but I am a nun here, without the vow of celibacy. Where shall I find a husband in these forests?"

"There is none, Miss Temple," said Edwards, quickly; "there is none who has a right to aspire to you, and I know that you will wait to be sought by your equal; or die, as you live, loved, respected, and admired by all who know you."

The young man seemed to think that he had said all that was required by gallantry, for he arose, and taking his hat, hurried from the apartment. Perhaps Louisa thought that he had said more than was necessary, for she sighed, with an aspiration so low that it was scarcely audible to herself, and bent her head over her work again. And it is possible that Miss Temple wished to hear more, for her eyes continued fixed for a minute on the door through which the young man had passed, then glanced quickly towards her companion, when the long silence that succeeded manifested how much zest may be given to the conversation of two maidens under eighteen, by the presence of a youth of three-and-twenty.

The first person encountered by Mr. Edwards, as he rather rushed than walked from the house, was the little square-built lawyer, with a large bundle of papers under his arm, a pair of green spectacles on his nose, with glasses at the sides, as if to multiply his power of detecting frauds, by additional organs of vision.

Mr. Van der School was a well-educated man, but of slow comprehension, who had imbibed a wariness in his speeches and actions from having suffered by his collisions with his more mercurial and apt brethren who had laid the foundations of their practice in the eastern courts, and who had sucked in shrewdness with their mother's milk. The caution of this gentleman was exhibited in his actions, by the utmost method and punctuality, tinctured with a good deal of timidity; and in his speeches, by a parenthetical style that frequently left to his auditors a long search after his meaning.

"A good morning to you, Mr. Van der School," said Edwards. "It seems to be a busy day with us at the mansion house."

"Good morning, Mr. Edwards (if that is your name (for, being a stranger, we have no other evidence of the fact than your own testimony), as I understand you have given it to Judge Temple), good morning, sir. It is, apparently, a busy day (but a man of your discretion need not be told (having, doubtless, discovered it of your own accord) that appearances are often deceitful) up at the mansion house."

"Have you papers of consequence that will require copying? Can I be of assistance in any way?"

"There are papers (as doubtless you see (for your eyes are young) by the outsides) that require copying."

"Well, then, I will accompany you to your office, and receive such as are most needed, and by night I shall have them done, if there be much haste."

"I shall be always glad to see you, sir, at my office (as in duty bound (not that it is obligatory to receive any man within your dwelling (unless so inclined), which is a castle), according to the forms of politeness), or at any other place; but the papers are most strictly confidential (and as such, cannot be read by anyone), unless so directed (by Judge Temple's solemn injunctions), and are invisible to all eyes; excepting those whose duties (I mean assumed duties) require it of them."

"Well, sir, as I perceive that I can be of no service, I wish you another good morning; but beg you will remember that I am quite idle just now, and I wish you would intimate as much to Judge Temple, and make him a tender of my services in any part of the world, unless—unless—it be far from Templeton."

"I will make the communication, sir, in your name (with your own qualifications), as your agent. Good morning, sir.—But stay proceedings, Mr. Edwards (so-called), for a moment. Do you wish me to state the offer of traveling as a final contract (for which consideration has been received at former dates (by sums advanced), which would be binding), or as a tender of services for which compensation is to be paid (according to future agreement between the parties), on performance of the conditions?"

"Any way, any way," said Edwards. "He seems in distress, and I would assist him."

"The motive is good, sir (according to appearances (which are often deceitful) on first impressions), and does you honor. I will mention your wish, young gentleman (as you now seem), and will not fail to communicate the answer by five o'clock P.M. of this present day (God willing), if you give me an opportunity so to do."

The ambiguous nature of the situation and character of Mr. Edwards had rendered him an object of peculiar suspicion to the lawyer, and the youth was consequently too much accustomed to similar equivocal and guarded speeches to feel any unusual disgust at the present dialogue. He saw at once that it was the intention of the practitioner to conceal the nature of his business, even from the private secretary of Judge Temple; and he knew too well the difficulty of comprehending the meaning of Mr. Van der School, when the gentleman most wished to be luminous in his discourse, not to abandon all thoughts of a discovery, when he perceived that the attorney was endeavoring to avoid anything like an approach to a cross-examination. They parted at the gate, the lawyer walking, with an important and hurried air, towards his office, keeping his right hand firmly clenched on the bundle of papers.

It must have been obvious to all our readers that the youth entertained an unusual and deeply seated prejudice against the character of the Judge; but, owing to some counteracting cause, his sensations were now those of powerful interest in the state of his patron's present feelings, and in the cause of his secret uneasiness.

He remained gazing after the lawyer until the door closed on both the bearer and the mysterious packet, when he returned slowly to the dwelling, and endeavored to forget his curiosity in the usual avocations of his office.

When the Judge made his reappearance in the circles of his family, his cheerfulness was tempered by a shade of melancholy that lingered for many days around his manly brow; but the magical progression of the season aroused him from his temporary apathy, and his smiles returned with the summer.

The heats of the days and the frequent occurrence of balmy showers had completed, in an incredibly short period, the growth of plants, which the lingering spring had so long retarded in the germ; and the woods presented every shade of green that the American forests know. The stumps in the cleared fields were already hidden beneath the wheat that was waving with every breath of the summer air, shining, and changing its hues like velvet.

During the continuance of his cousin's dejection, Mr. Jones forbore, with much consideration, to press on his attention a business that each hour was drawing nearer to the heart of the Sheriff, and which, if any opinion could be formed by his frequent private conferences with the man who was introduced in these pages by the name of Jotham, at the barroom of the Bold Dragoon, was becoming also of great importance.

At length the Sheriff ventured to allude again to the subject; and one evening, in the beginning of July, Marmaduke made him a promise of devoting the following day to the desired excursion.

Chapter XXVI

Speak on, my dearest father!
Thy words are like the breezes of the West.
MILMAN

IT was a mild and soft morning when Marmaduke and Richard mounted their horses to proceed on the expedition that had so long been uppermost in the thoughts of the latter: and Elizabeth and Louisa appeared at the same instant in the hall, attired for an excursion on foot.

The head of Miss Grant was covered by a neat little hat of green silk, and her modest eyes peered from under its shade, with the soft languor that characterized her whole appearance; but Miss Temple trod her father's wide apartments with the step of their mistress, holding in her hand, dangling by one of its ribands, the gypsy that was to conceal the glossy locks that curled around her polished forehead in rich profusion.

"What! are you for a walk, Bess?" cried the Judge, suspending his movements for a moment, to smile, with a father's fondness, at the display of womanly grace and beauty that his child presented. "Remember the heats of July, my daughter; nor venture further than thou canst retrace before the meridian. Where is thy parasol, girl? Thou wilt lose the polish of that brow under this sun and southern breeze unless thou guard it with unusual care."

"I shall then do more honor to my connections," returned the smiling daughter. "Cousin Richard has a bloom that any lady might envy. At present the resemblance between us is so trifling that no stranger would know us to be 'sisters' children.'"

"Grandchildren, you mean, cousin Bess," said the Sheriff.

"But on, Judge Temple; time and tide wait for no man; and if you take my counsel, sir, in twelve months from this day you may make an umbrella for your daughter of her camel's hair shawl, and have its frame of solid silver. I ask nothing for myself, 'duke; you have been a good friend to me already; besides, all that I have will go to Bess there, one of these melancholy days, so it's as long as it's short, whether I or you leave it. But we have a day's ride before us, sir; so move forward, or dismount, and say you won't go at once."

"Patience, patience, Dickon," returned the Judge, checking his horse and turning again to his daughter. "If thou art for the mountains, love, stray not too deep into the forest, I entreat thee; for, though it is done often with impunity, there is sometimes danger."

"Not at this season, I believe, sir," said Elizabeth; "for, I will confess, it is the intention of Louisa and myself to stroll among the hills."

"Less at this season than in the winter, dear; but still there may be danger in venturing too far. But though thou art resolute, Elizabeth, thou art too much like thy mother not to be prudent."

The eyes of the parent turned reluctantly from his child, and the Judge and Sheriff rode slowly through the gateway and disappeared among the buildings of the village.

During this short dialogue, young Edwards stood, an attentive listener, holding in his hand a fishing rod, the day and the season having tempted him also to desert the house for the pleasure of exercise in the air. As the equestrians turned through the gate, he approached the young females, who were already moving towards the street, and was about to address them, as Louisa paused, and said quickly:

"Mr. Edwards would speak to us, Elizabeth."

The other stopped also, and turned to the youth, politely, but with a slight coldness in her air that sensibly checked the freedom with which he had approached them.

"Your father is not pleased that you should walk unattended in the hills, Miss Temple. If I might offer myself as a protector——"

"Does my father select Mr. Oliver Edwards as the organ of his displeasure?" interrupted the lady.

"Good Heaven! you misunderstood my meaning: I should

have said uneasy for not pleased. I am his servant, madam, and in consequence yours. I repeat that, with your consent, I will change my rod for a fowling piece, and keep nigh you on the mountain."

"I thank you, Mr. Edwards; but where there is no danger, no protection is required. We are not yet reduced to wandering among these free hills accompanied by a bodyguard. If such a one is necessary, there he is, however. Here, Brave—Brave—my noble Brave!"

The huge mastiff, that has been already mentioned, appeared from his kennel, gaping and stretching himself with pampered laziness; but as his mistress again called—"Come, dear Brave; once have you served your master well; let us see how you can do your duty by his daughter"—the dog wagged his tail, as if he understood her language, walked with a stately gait to her side, where he seated himself and looked up at her face with an intelligence but little inferior to that which beamed in her own lovely countenance.

She resumed her walk, but again paused, after a few steps, and added, in tones of conciliation:

"You can be serving us equally, and, I presume, more agreeably to yourself, Mr. Edwards, by bringing us a string of your favorite perch, for the dinner table."

When they again began to walk, Miss Temple did not look back to see how the youth bore this repulse; but the head of Louisa was turned several times before they reached the gate on that considerate errand.

"I am afraid, Elizabeth," she said, "that we have mortified Oliver. He is still standing where we left him leaning on his rod. Perhaps he thinks us proud."

"He thinks justly," exclaimed Miss Temple, as if awaking from a deep musing; "he thinks justly, then. We are too proud to admit of such particular attentions from a young man in an equivocal situation. What! make him the companion of our most private walks! It is pride, Louisa, but it is the pride of a woman."

It was several minutes before Oliver aroused himself from the abstracted position in which he was standing when Louisa last saw him; but when he did, he muttered something rapidly and incoherently, and throwing his rod over his shoulder, he strode down the walk, through the gate, and along one of the streets of the village until he reached the lake shore, with the air of an emperor. At this spot boats were kept for the use of Judge Temple and his family. The young man threw himself into a light skiff, and seizing the oars, he sent it across the lake towards the hut of Leatherstocking with a pair of vigorous arms. By the time he had rowed a quarter of a mile, his reflections were less bitter: and when he saw the bushes that lined the shore in front of Natty's habitation gliding by him, as if they possessed the motion which proceeded from his own efforts, he was quite cooled in mind, though somewhat heated in body. It is quite possible that the very same reason which guided the conduct of Miss Temple suggested itself to a man of the breeding and education of the youth; and it is very certain, that if such were the case, Elizabeth rose instead of falling in the estimation of Mr. Edwards.

The oars were now raised from the water, and the boat shot close in to the land, where it lay gently agitated by waves of its own creating, while the young man, first casting a cautious and searching glance around him in every direction, put a small whistle to his mouth and blew a long, shrill note that rang among the echoing rocks behind the hut. At this alarm, the hounds of Natty rushed out of their bark kennel and commenced their long piteous howls, leaping about as if half-frantic, though restrained by the leashes of buckskin by which they were fastened.

"Quiet, Hector, quiet," said Oliver, again applying his whistle to his mouth and drawing out notes still more shrill than before. No reply was made, the dogs having returned to their kennel at the sounds of his voice.

Edwards pulled the bow of the boat on the shore, and landing, ascended the beach and approached the door of the cabin. The fastenings were soon undone, and he entered, closing the door after him, when all was as silent, in that retired spot, as if the foot of man had never trod the wilderness. The sounds of the hammers that were in incessant motion in the village were faintly heard across the water; but the dogs had crouched into their lairs, satisfied that none but the privileged had approached the forbidden ground.

A quarter of an hour elapsed before the youth reappeared, when he fastened the door again and spoke kindly to the hounds. The dogs came out at the well-known tones, and the slut jumped upon his person, whining and barking, as if entreating Oliver to release her from prison. But old Hector raised his nose to the light current of air and opened a long howl that might have been heard for a mile.

"Ha! what do you scent, old veteran of the woods!" cried Edwards. "If a beast, it is a bold one; and if a man, an impudent."

He sprang through the top of a pine that had fallen near the side of the hut and ascended a small hillock that sheltered the cabin to the south, where he caught a glimpse of the formal figure of Hiram Doolittle, as it vanished with unusual rapidity for the architect, amid the bushes.

"What can that fellow be wanting here?" muttered Oliver. "He has no business in this quarter, unless it be curiosity, which is an endemic in these woods. But against that I will effectually guard, though the dogs should take a liking to his ugly visage, and let him pass." The youth returned to the door, while giving vent to this soliloquy, and completed the fastenings, by placing a small chain through a staple and securing it there by a padlock. "He is a pettifogger and surely must know that there is such a thing as feloniously breaking into a man's house."

Apparently well-satisfied with this arrangement, the youth again spoke to the hounds; and, descending to the shore, he launched his boat, and taking up his oars, pulled off into the lake.

There were several places in the Otsego that were celebrated fishing ground for perch. One was nearly opposite to the cabin, and another, still more famous, was near a point, at the distance of a mile and a half above it, under the brow of the mountain, and on the same side of the lake with the hut. Oliver Edwards pulled his little skiff to the first, and sat, for a minute, undecided whether to continue there, with his eyes on the door of the cabin, or to change his ground, with a view to get superior game. While gazing about him, he saw the light-colored bark canoe of his old companions, riding on the water, at the point we have mentioned, and containing two figures that he at once knew to be Mohegan and the Leatherstocking. This decided the matter, and the youth pulled, in a very few minutes, to the place where his friends were fishing, and fastened his boat to the light vessel of the Indian.

The old men received Oliver with welcoming nods, but neither drew his line from the water, nor in the least varied his occupation. When Edwards had secured his own boat, he baited his hook and threw it into the lake without speaking.

"Did you stop at the wigwam, lad, as you rowed past?" asked Natty.

"Yes, and I found all safe; but that carpenter and justice of the peace, Mr., or as they call him, Squire, Doolittle, was prowling through the woods. I made sure of the door before I left the hut, and I think he is too great a coward to approach the hounds."

"There's little to be said in favor of that man," said Natty, while he drew in a perch and baited his hook. "He craves dreadfully to come into the cabin, and has as good as asked me as much to my face; but I put him off with unsartain answers, so that he is no wiser than Solomon. This comes of having so many laws that such a man may be called on to intarpret them."

"I fear he is more knave than fool," cried Edwards; "he makes a tool of that simple man, the Sheriff; and I dread that his impertinent curiosity may yet give us much trouble."

"If he harbors too much about the cabin, lad, I'll shoot the creater," said the Leatherstocking, quite simply.

"No, no, Natty, you must remember the law," said Edwards, "or we shall have you in trouble; and that, old man, would be an evil day and sore tidings to us all."

"Would it, boy!" exclaimed the hunter, raising his eyes with a look of friendly interest towards the youth. "You have the true blood in your veins, Mr. Oliver; and I'll support it to the face of Judge Temple, or in any court in the country. How is it, John? Do I speak the true word? Is the lad staunch, and of the right blood?"

"He is a Delaware," said Mohegan, "and my brother. The Young Eagle is brave, and he will be a chief. No harm can come."

"Well, well," cried the youth, impatiently, "say no more about it, my good friends; if I am not all that your partiality would make me, I am yours through life, in prosperity as in poverty. We will talk of other matters."

The old hunters yielded to his wish, which seemed to be their law. For a short time a profound silence prevailed, during which each man was very busy with his hook and line; but Edwards, probably feeling that it remained with him to renew the discourse, soon observed, with the air of one who knew not what he said:

"How beautifully tranquil and glassy the lake is! Saw you it ever more calm and even than at this moment, Natty?"

"I have known the Otsego water for five and forty years," said Leatherstocking; "and I will say that for it, which is, that a cleaner spring or better fishing is not to be found in the land. Yes, yes; I had the place to myself once, and a cheerful time I had of it. The game was plenty as heart could wish; and there was none to meddle with the ground, unless there might have been a hunting party of the Delawares crossing the hills, or, maybe, a rifling scout of them thieves, the Iroquois. There was one or two Frenchmen that squatted in the flats, further west, and married squaws; and some of the Scotch-Irishers, from the Cherry Valley, would come on to the lake and borrow my canoe to take a mess of parch, or drop a line for salmon trout; but, in the main, it was a cheerful place, and I had but little to disturb me in it. John would come, and John knows."

Mohegan turned his dark face at this appeal; and, moving his hand forward with a graceful motion of assent, he spoke, using the Delaware language:

"The land was owned by my people; we gave it to my brother, in council—to the Fire-eater; and what the Delawares give lasts as long as the waters run. Hawkeye smoked at that council, for we loved him."

"No, no, John," said Natty; "I was no chief, seeing that I know'd nothing of scholarship and had a white skin. But it was a comfortable hunting ground then, lad, and would have been so to this day, but for the money of Marmaduke Temple, and the twisty ways of the law."

"It must have been a sight of melancholy pleasure indeed," said Edwards, while his eye roved along the shores and over the hills, where the clearings, groaning with the golden corn, were cheering the forests with the signs of life, "to have roamed over these mountains, and along this sheet of beautiful water, without a living soul to speak to, or to thwart your humor."

"Haven't I said it was cheerful?" said Leatherstocking. "Yes, yes; when the trees began to be covered with leaves, and the ice was out of the lake, it was a second paradise. I have traveled the woods for fifty-three years and have made them my home for more than forty; and I can say that I have met but one place that was more to my liking; and that was only to eyesight, and not for hunting or fishing."

"And where was that?" asked Edwards.

"Where! Why up on the Catskills. I used often to go up into the mountains after wolves' skins and bears; once they paid me to get them a stuffed painter, and so I often went. There's a place in them hills that I used to climb to when I wanted to see the carryings on of the world, that would well pay any man for a barked shin or a torn moccasin. You know the Catskills, lad; for you must have seen them on your left as you followed the river up from York, looking as blue as a piece of clear sky, and holding the clouds on their tops, as the smoke curls over the head of an Indian chief at the council fire. Well, there's the High Peak and the Round Top, which lay back like a father and mother among their children, seeing they are far above all the other hills. But the place I mean is next to the river, where one of the ridges juts out a little from the rest, and where the rocks fall, for the best part of a thousand feet, so much up and down, that a man standing on their edges is fool enough to think he can jump from top to bottom."

"What see you when you get there?" asked Edwards.

"Creation," said Natty, dropping the end of his rod into the water and sweeping one hand around him in a circle: "all creation, lad. I was on that hill when Vaughan burned 'Sopus in the last war; and I saw the vessels come out of the Highlands as plain as I can see that lime scow rowing into the Susquehanna, though one was twenty times further from me than the other. The river was in sight for seventy miles, looking like a curled shaving under my feet, though it was eight long miles to its banks. I saw the hills in the Hampshire grants, the highlands of the river, and all that God had done, or man could do, far as eye could reach—you know that the Indians named me for my sight, lad; and from the flat on the top of that mountain, I have often found the place where Albany stands. And as for 'Sopus, the day the

royal troops burnt the town, the smoke seemed so nigh, that
I thought I could hear the screeches of the women."

"It must have been worth the toil to meet with such a
glorious view."

"If being the best part of a mile in the air, and having
men's farms and housen at your feet, with rivers looking
like ribbons, and mountains bigger than the 'Vision,' seeming to be haystacks of green grass under you, gives any
satisfaction to a man, I can recommend the spot. When I first
came into the woods to live, I used to have weak spells when
I felt lonesome; and then I would go into the Catskills and
spend a few days on that hill to look at the ways of men;
but it's now many a year since I felt any such longings, and
I am getting too old for rugged rocks. But there's a place, a
short two miles back of that very hill, that in late times I
relished better than the mountain; for it was more covered
with the trees, and nateral."

"And where was that?" inquired Edwards, whose curiosity
was strongly excited by the simple description of the hunter.

"Why, there's a fall in the hills where the water of two
little ponds that lie near each other breaks out of their bounds
and runs over the rocks into the valley. The stream is,
maybe, such a one as would turn a mill, if so useless a thing
was wanted in the wilderness. But the hand that made that
'Leap' never made a mill. There the water comes crooking
and winding among the rocks; first so slow that a trout could
swim in it, and then starting and running like a crater that
wanted to make a far spring, till it gets to where the mountain divides, like the cleft hoof of a deer, leaving a deep
hollow for the brook to tumble into. The first pitch is nigh
two hundred feet, and the water looks like flakes of driven
snow afore it touches the bottom; and there the stream
gathers itself together again for a new start, and maybe
flutters over fifty feet of flat rock before it falls for another
hundred, when it jumps about from shelf to shelf, first turning this-a-way and then turning that-a-way, striving to get
out of the hollow, till it finally comes to the plain."

"I have never heard of this spot before; it is not mentioned in the books."

"I never read a book in my life," said Leatherstocking;
"and how should a man who has lived in towns and schools
know anything about the wonders of the woods? No, no, lad;

there has that little stream of water been playing among the hills since He made the world, and not a dozen white men have ever laid eyes on it. The rock sweeps like masonwork, in a half-round, on both sides of the fall, and shelves over the bottom for fifty feet; so that when I've been sitting at the foot of the first pitch, and my hounds have run into the caverns behind the sheet of water, they've looked no bigger than so many rabbits. To my judgment, lad, it's the best piece of work that I've met with in the woods; and none know how often the hand of God is seen in the wilderness, but them that rove it for a man's life."

"What becomes of the water? In which direction does it run? Is it a tributary of the Delaware?"

"Anan!" said Natty.

"Does the water run into the Delaware?"

"No, no; it's a drop for the old Hudson, and a merry time it has till it gets down off the mountain. I've sat on the shelving rock many a long hour, boy, and watched the bubbles as they shot by me, and thought how long it would be before that very water, which seemed made for the wilderness, would be under the bottom of a vessel and tossing in the salt sea. It is a spot to make a man solemnize. You can see right down into the valley that lies to the east of the High Peak, where, in the fall of the year, thousands of acres of woods are before your eyes, in the deep hollow, and along the side of the mountain, painted like ten thousand rainbows, by no hand of man, though without the ordering of God's providence."

"You are eloquent, Leatherstocking," exclaimed the youth.

"Anan!" repeated Natty.

"The recollection of the sight has warmed your blood, old man. How many years is it since you saw the place?"

The hunter made no reply; but, bending his ear near the water, he sat holding his breath and listening attentively as if to some distant sound. At length he raised his head and said—

"If I hadn't fastened the hounds with my own hands, with a fresh leash of green buckskin, I'd take a Bible oath that I heard old Hector ringing his cry on the mountain."

"It is impossible," said Edwards; "it is not an hour since I saw him in his kennel."

By this time the attention of Mohegan was attracted to the

sounds; but, notwithstanding the youth was both silent and attentive, he could hear nothing but the lowing of some cattle from the western hills. He looked at the old men, Natty sitting with his hand to his ear, like a trumpet, and Mohegan bending forward, with an arm raised to a level with his face, holding the forefinger elevated as a signal for attention, and laughed aloud at what he deemed to be their imaginary sounds.

"Laugh if you will, boy," said Leatherstocking; "the hounds be out, and are hunting a deer. No man can deceive me in such a matter. I wouldn't have had the thing happen for a beaver's skin. Not that I care for the law! But the venison is lean now, and the dumb things run the flesh off their own bones for no good. Now do you hear the hounds?"

Edwards started, as a full cry broke on his ear, changing from the distant sounds that were caused by some intervening hill to confused echoes that rang among the rocks that the dogs were passing, and then directly to a deep and hollow baying that pealed under the forest on the lake shore. These variations in the tones of the hounds passed with amazing rapidity; and while his eyes were glancing along the margin of the water, a tearing of the branches of the alder and dogwood caught his attention, at a spot near them, and at the next moment a noble buck sprang on the shore and buried himself in the lake. A full-mouthed cry followed, when Hector and the slut shot through the opening in the bushes and darted into the lake also, bearing their breasts gallantly against the water.

CHAPTER XXVII

Oft in the full descending flood he tries
To lose the scent, and lave his burning sides.
                                        THOMSON

"I KNOW'D it—I know'd it!" cried Natty, when both deer and hounds were in full view. "The buck has gone by them with the wind, and it has been too much for the poor rogues; but I must break them of these tricks, or they'll give me a deal of trouble. He-ere, he-ere—shore with you, rascals—shore with you—will ye?—Oh! off with you, old Hector, or I'll hatchel your hide with my ramrod when I get ye."

The dogs knew their master's voice, and after swimming in a circle, as if reluctant to give over the chase, and yet afraid to persevere, they finally obeyed and returned to the land, where they filled the air with their cries.

In the meantime the deer, urged by his fears, had swum over half the distance between the shore and the boats before his terror permitted him to see the new danger. But at the sounds of Natty's voice, he turned short in his course, and for a few moments seemed about to rush back again and brave the dogs. His retreat in this direction was, however, effectually cut off, and turning a second time, he urged his course obliquely for the center of the lake, with an intention of landing on the western shore. As the buck swam by the fishermen, raising his nose high into the air, curling the water before his slim neck like the beak of a galley, the Leatherstocking began to sit very uneasy in his canoe.

" 'Tis a noble creater!" he exclaimed. "What a pair of horns! A man might hang up all his garments on the branches. Let me see—July is the last month, and the flesh must be getting good." While he was talking, Natty had instinctively employed himself in fastening the inner end of the bark rope that served him for a cable to a paddle, and rising suddenly on his legs, he cast this buoy away and cried —"Strike out, John! Let her go. The creater's a fool to tempt a man in this way."

Mohegan threw the fastening of the youth's boat from the canoe and with one stroke of his paddle sent the light bark over the water like a meteor.

"Hold!" exclaimed Edwards. "Remember the law, my old friends. You are in plain sight of the village, and I know that Judge Temple is determined to prosecute all indiscriminately, who kill deer out of season."

The remonstrance came too late: the canoe was already far from the skiff, and the two hunters were too much engaged in the pursuit to listen to his voice.

The buck was now within fifty yards of his pursuers, cutting the water gallantly and snorting at each breath with terror and his exertions, while the canoe seemed to dance over the waves, as it rose and fell with the undulations made by its own motion. Leatherstocking raised his rifle and freshened the priming, but stood in suspense whether to slay his victim or not.

"Shall I, John, or no?" he said. "It seems but a poor advantage to take of the dumb thing, too. I won't; it has taken to the water on its own nater, which is the reason that God has given to a deer, and I'll give it the lake play; so, John, lay out your arm and mind the turn of the buck; it's easy to catch them, but they'll turn like a snake."

The Indian laughed at the conceit of his friend, but continued to send the canoe forward with a velocity that proceeded much more from his skill than his strength. Both of the old men now used the language of the Delawares when they spoke.

"Hugh!" exclaimed Mohegan; "the deer turns his head. Hawkeye, lift your spear."

Natty never moved abroad without taking with him every implement that might, by possibility, be of service in his pursuits. From his rifle he never parted; and although intending to fish with the line, the canoe was invariably furnished with all of its utensils, even to its grate. This precaution grew out of the habits of the hunter, who was often led, by his necessities or his sports, far beyond the limits of his original destination. A few years earlier than the date of our tale, the Leatherstocking had left his hut on the shores of the Otsego with his rifle and his hounds for a few days' hunting in the hills; but before he returned he had seen the waters of Ontario. One, two, or even three hundred miles had once been nothing to his sinews, which were now a little stiffened by age. The hunter did as Mohegan advised and prepared to strike a blow with the barbed weapon into the neck of the buck.

"Lay her more to the left, John," he cried, "lay her more to the left; another stroke of the paddle, and I have him."

While speaking, he raised the spear and darted it from him like an arrow. At that instant the buck turned, the long pole glanced by him, the iron striking against his horn, and buried itself harmlessly in the lake.

"Back water," cried Natty, as the canoe glided over the place where the spear had fallen; "hold water, John."

The pole soon reappeared, shooting upwards from the lake, and as the hunter seized it in his hand, the Indian whirled the

light canoe round and renewed the chase. But this evolution
gave the buck a great advantage; and it also allowed time
for Edwards to approach the scene of action.

"Hold your hand, Natty!" cried the youth, "hold your
hand! Remember it is out of season."

This remonstrance was made as the bateau arrived close to
the place where the deer was struggling with the water, his
back now rising to the surface, now sinking beneath it, as the
waves curled from his neck, the animal still sustaining itself
nobly against the odds.

"Hurrah!" shouted Edwards, inflamed beyond prudence at
the sight; "mind him as he doubles—mind him as he doubles;
sheer more to the right, Mohegan, more to the right, and
I'll have him by the horns; I'll throw the rope over his
antlers."

The dark eye of the old warrior was dancing in his head
with a wild animation, and the sluggish repose in which his
aged frame had been resting in the canoe was now changed
to all the rapid inflections of practiced agility. The canoe
whirled with each cunning evolution of the chase, like a bub-
ble floating in a whirlpool; and when the direction of the
pursuit admitted of a straight course, the little bark skimmed
the lake with a velocity that urged the deer to seek its safety
in some new turn.

It was the frequency of these circuitous movements that,
by confining the action to so small a compass, enabled the
youth to keep near his companions. More than twenty times
both the pursued and the pursuers glided by him, just without the reach of his oars, until he thought the best way to
view the sport was to remain stationary and, by watching a
favorable opportunity, assist as much as he could in taking
the victim.

He was not required to wait long, for no sooner had he
adopted this resolution and risen in the boat, than he saw
the deer coming bravely towards him, with an apparent intention of pushing for a point of land at some distance
from the hounds, who were still barking and howling on the
shore. Edwards caught the painter of his skiff and, making a
noose, cast it from him with all his force and luckily succeeded in drawing its knot close around one of the antlers
of the buck.

For one instant, the skiff was drawn through the water,

but in the next, the canoe glided before it, and Natty, bending low, passed his knife across the throat of the animal, whose blood followed the wound, dyeing the waters. The short time that was passed in the last struggles of the animal was spent by the hunters in bringing their boats together and securing them in that position, when Leatherstocking drew the deer from the water and laid its lifeless form in the bottom of the canoe. He placed his hands on the ribs and on different parts of the body of his prize, and then, raising his head, he laughed in his peculiar manner:

"So much for Marmaduke Temple's law!" he said. "This warms a body's blood, old John; I haven't killed a buck in the lake afore this, sin' many a year. I call that good venison, lad; and I know them that will relish the creater's steaks, for all the betterments in the land."

The Indian had long been drooping with his years, and perhaps under the calamities of his race, but this invigorating and exciting sport caused a gleam of sunshine to cross his swarthy face that had long been absent from his features. It was evident the old man enjoyed the chase more as a memorial of his youthful sports and deeds than with any expectation of profiting by the success. He felt the deer, however, lightly, his hand already trembling with the reaction of his unusual exertions, and smiled with a nod of approbation, as he said, in the emphatic and sententious manner of his people:

"Good."

"I am afraid, Natty," said Edwards, when the heat of the moment had passed, and his blood began to cool, "that we have all been equally transgressors of the law. But keep your own counsel, and there are none here to betray us. Yet, how came those dogs at large? I left them securely fastened, I know, for I felt the thongs and examined the knots, when I was at the hut."

"It has been too much for the poor things," said Natty, "to have such a buck take the wind of them. See, lad, the pieces of the buckskin are hanging from their necks yet. Let us paddle up, John, and I will call them in and look a little into the matter."

When the old hunter landed and examined the thongs that were yet fast to the hounds, his countenance sensibly changed, and he shook his head doubtingly.

"Here has been a knife at work," he said. "This skin was

never torn, nor is this the mark of a hound's tooth. No, no—Hector is not in fault, as I feared."

"Has the leather been cut?" cried Edwards.

"No, no—I didn't say it had been cut, lad; but this is a mark that was never made by a jump or a bite."

"Could that rascally carpenter have dared!"

"Ay! he durst to do anything when there is no danger," said Natty. "He is a curious body and loves to be helping other people on with their consarns. But he had best not harbor so much near the wigwam!"

In the meantime, Mohegan had been examining, with an Indian's sagacity, the place where the leather thong had been separated. After scrutinizing it closely, he said, in Delaware:

"It was cut with a knife—a sharp blade and a long handle—the man was afraid of the dogs."

"How is this, Mohegan?" exclaimed Edwards. "You saw it not! How can you know these facts?"

"Listen, son," said the warrior. "The knife was sharp, for the cut is smooth; the handle was long, for a man's arm would not reach from this gash to the cut that did not go through the skin: he was a coward, or he would have cut the thongs around the necks of the hounds."

"On my life," cried Natty, "John is on the scent! It was the carpenter; and he has got on the rock back of the kennel and let the dogs loose by fastening his knife to a stick. It would be an easy matter to do it, where a man is so minded."

"And why should he do so?" asked Edwards. "Who has done him wrong, that he should trouble two old men like you?"

"It's a hard matter, lad, to know men's ways, I find, since the settlers have brought in their new fashions. But is there nothing to be found out in the place? And maybe he is troubled with his longings after other people's business, as he often is."

"Your suspicions are just. Give me the canoe: I am young and strong, and will get down there yet, perhaps, in time to interrupt his plans. Heaven forbid that we should be at the mercy of such a man!"

His proposal was accepted, the deer being placed in the skiff in order to lighten the canoe, and in less than five minutes the little vessel of bark was gliding over the glassy lake and was soon hid by the points of land, as it shot close along the shore.

Mohegan followed slowly with the skiff, while Natty called his hounds to him, bade them keep close, and, shouldering his rifle, he ascended the mountain with an intention of going to the hut by land.

CHAPTER XXVIII

Ask me not what the maiden feels,
  Left in that dreadful hour alone;.
Perchance, her reason stoops, or reels;
  Perchance, a courage not her own,
  Braces her mind to desperate tone.

SCOTT

WHILE the chase was occurring on the lake, Miss Temple and her companion pursued their walk on the mountain. Male attendants on such excursions were thought to be altogether unnecessary, for none were ever known to offer an insult to a female who respected herself. After the embarrassment created by the parting discourse with Edwards had dissipated, the girls maintained a conversation that was as innocent and cheerful as themselves.

The path they took led them but a short distance above the hut of Leatherstocking, and there was a point in the road which commanded a bird's eye view of the sequestered spot.

From a feeling that might have been natural, and must have been powerful, neither of the friends, in their frequent and confidential dialogues, had ever trusted herself to utter one syllable concerning the equivocal situation in which the young man who was now so intimately associated with them had been found. If Judge Temple had deemed it prudent to make any inquiries on the subject, he had also thought it proper to keep the answers to himself; though it was so common an occurrence to find the well-educated youth of the eastern states in every stage of their career to wealth, that the simple circumstances of his intelligence, connected with his poverty, would not, at that day, and in that country, have excited any very powerful curiosity. With his breeding, it might have been different; but the youth himself had so effectually guarded against surprise on this subject, by his cold, and even, in some cases, rude deportment, that when his manners seemed to soften by time, the Judge, if he thought about it at all, would have been most likely to imagine that the improvement was the result of his late association. But women are always more alive to such subjects than men; and what the abstraction of the father had overlooked, the observation of the daughter had easily detected. In the thousand little courtesies of polished life, she had early discovered that Edwards was not wanting, though his gentleness was so often crossed by marks of what she conceived to be fierce and uncontrollable passions. It may, perhaps, be unnecessary to tell the reader that Louisa Grant never reasoned so much after the fashions of the world. The gentle girl, however, had her own thoughts on the subject, and, like others, she drew her own conclusions.

"I would give all my other secrets, Louisa," exclaimed Miss Temple, laughing, and shaking back her dark locks, with a look of childish simplicity that her intelligent face seldom expressed, "to be mistress of all that those rude logs have heard and witnessed."

They were both looking at the secluded hut at the instant, and Miss Grant raised her mild eyes as she answered:

"I am sure they would tell nothing to the disadvantage of Mr. Edwards."

"Perhaps not; but they might, at least, tell who he is."

"Why, dear Miss Temple, we know all that already. I have heard it all very rationally explained by your cousin—"

"The executive chief! He can explain anything. His ingenuity will one day discover the philosopher's stone. But what did he say?"

"Say!" echoed Louisa, with a look of surprise; "why everything that seemed to me to be satisfactory, and I have believed it to be true. He said that Natty Bumppo had lived most of his life in the woods, and among the Indians, by which means he had formed an acquaintance with old John, the Delaware chief."

"Indeed! That was quite a matter-of-fact tale for cousin Dickon. What came next?"

"I believe he accounted for their close intimacy by some

story about the Leatherstocking saving the life of John in a battle."

"Nothing more likely," said Elizabeth, a little impatiently; "but what is all this to the purpose?"

"Nay, Elizabeth, you must bear with my ignorance, and I will repeat all that I remember to have overheard; for the dialogue was between my father and the Sheriff, so lately as the last time they met. He then added that the kings of England used to keep gentlemen as agents among the different tribes of Indians, and sometimes officers in the army, who frequently passed half their lives on the edge of the wilderness."

"Told with wonderful historical accuracy! And did he end there?"

"Oh! no—then he said that these agents seldom married; and—and—they must have been wicked men, Elizabeth! But I assure you he said so."

"Never mind," said Miss Temple, blushing and smiling, though so slightly that both were unheeded by her companion —"skip all that."

"Well, then, he said that they often took great pride in the education of their children, whom they frequently sent to England and even to the colleges; and this is the way that he accounts for the liberal manner in which Mr. Edwards has been taught; for he acknowledges that he knows almost as much as your father—or mine—or even himself."

"Quite a climax in learning! And so he made Mohegan the granduncle, or grandfather of Oliver Edwards."

"You have heard him yourself, then?" said Louisa.

"Often; but not on this subject. Mr. Richard Jones, you know, dear, has a theory for everything; but has he one which will explain the reason why that hut is the only habitation within fifty miles of us, whose door is not open to every person who may choose to lift its latch?"

"I have never heard him say anything on this subject," returned the clergyman's daughter; "but I suppose that, as they are poor, they very naturally are anxious to keep the little that they honestly own. It is sometimes dangerous to be rich, Miss Temple; but you cannot know how hard it is to be very, very poor."

"Nor you, I trust, Louisa; at least I should hope that, in

this land of abundance, no minister of the church could be left to absolute suffering."

"There cannot be actual misery," returned the other in a low and humble tone, "where there is a dependence on our Maker; but there may be such suffering as will cause the heart to ache."

"But not you—not you," said the impetuous Elizabeth—"not you, dear girl: you have never known the misery that is connected with poverty."

"Ah! Miss Temple, you little understand the troubles of this life, I believe. My father has spent many years as a missionary in the new countries, where his people were poor, and frequently we have been without bread; unable to buy, and ashamed to beg, because we would not disgrace his sacred calling. But how often have I seen him leave his home, where the sick and the hungry felt, when he left them, that they had lost their only earthly friend, to ride on a duty which could not be neglected for domestic evils. Oh! how hard it must be to preach consolation to others when your own heart is bursting with anguish!"

"But it is all over now! Your father's income must now be equal to his wants—it must be—it shall be——"

"It is," replied Louisa, dropping her head on her bosom to conceal the tears which flowed in spite of her gentle Christianity—"for there are none left to be supplied but me."

The turn the conversation had taken drove from the minds of the young maidens all other thoughts but those of holy charity; and Elizabeth folded her friend in her arms, when the latter gave vent to her momentary grief in audible sobs. When this burst of emotion had subsided, Louisa raised her mild countenance, and they continued their walk in silence.

By this time they had gained the summit of the mountain, where they left the highway and pursued their course under the shade of the stately trees that crowned the eminence. The day was becoming warm, and the girls plunged more deeply into the forest, as they found its invigorating coolness agreeably contrasted to the excessive heat they had experienced in the ascent. The conversation, as if by mutual consent, was entirely changed to the little incidents and scenes of their walk, and every tall pine, and every shrub or flower, called forth some simple expression of admiration.

In this manner they proceeded along the margin of the

precipice, catching occasional glimpses of the placid Otsego, or pausing to listen to the rattling of wheels and the sounds of hammers that rose from the valley to mingle the signs of men with the scenes of nature, when Elizabeth suddenly started and exclaimed:

"Listen! There are the cries of a child on this mountain! Is there a clearing near us? Or can some little one have strayed from its parents?"

"Such things frequently happen," returned Louisa. "Let us follow the sounds: it may be a wanderer starving on the hill."

Urged by this consideration, the females pursued the low, mournful sounds that proceeded from the forest with quick and impatient steps. More than once, the ardent Elizabeth was on the point of announcing that she saw the sufferer, when Louisa caught her by the arm, and pointing behind them, cried:

"Look at the dog!"

Brave had been their companion, from the time the voice of his young mistress lured him from his kennel, to the present moment. His advanced age had long before deprived him of his activity; and when his companions stopped to view the scenery, or to add to their bouquets, the mastiff would lay his huge frame on the ground and await their movements, with his eyes closed and a listlessness in his air that ill-accorded with the character of a protector. But when, aroused by this cry from Louisa, Miss Temple turned, she saw the dog with his eyes keenly set on some distant object, his head bent near the ground, and his hair actually rising on his body, through fright or anger. It was most probably the latter, for he was growling in a low key and occasionally showing his teeth, in a manner that would have terrified his mistress had she not so well known his good qualities.

"Brave!" she said, "be quiet, Brave! What do you see, fellow?"

At the sounds of her voice, the rage of the mastiff, instead of being at all diminished, was very sensibly increased. He stalked in front of the ladies and seated himself at the feet of his mistress, growling louder than before and occasionally giving vent to his ire by a short, surly barking.

"What does he see?" said Elizabeth. "There must be some animal in sight."

Hearing no answer from her companion, Miss Temple

turned her head and beheld Louisa, standing with her face whitened to the color of death and her finger pointing upwards with a sort of flickering, convulsed motion. The quick eye of Elizabeth glanced in the direction indicated by her friend, where she saw the fierce front and glaring eyes of a female panther fixed on them in horrid malignity, and threatening to leap.

"Let us fly," exclaimed Elizabeth, grasping the arm of Louisa, whose form yielded like melting snow.

There was not a single feeling in the temperament of Elizabeth Temple that could prompt her to desert a companion in such an extremity. She fell on her knees by the side of the inanimate Louisa, tearing from the person of her friend, with instinctive readiness, such parts of her dress as might obstruct her respiration, and encouraging their only safeguard, the dog, at the same time by the sounds of her voice.

"Courage, Brave!" she cried, her own tones beginning to tremble, "courage, courage, good Brave!"

A quarter-grown cub that had hitherto been unseen now appeared, dropping from the branches of a sapling that grew under the shade of the beech which held its dam. This ignorant but vicious creature approached the dog, imitating the actions and sounds of its parent, but exhibiting a strange mixture of the playfulness of a kitten with the ferocity of its race. Standing on its hind legs, it would rend the bark of a tree with its forepaws and play the antics of a cat; and then by lashing itself with its tail, growling, and scratching the earth, it would attempt the manifestations of anger that rendered its parent so terrific.

All this time Brave stood firm and undaunted, his short tail erect, his body drawn backward on its haunches, and his eyes following the movements of both dam and cub. At every gambol played by the latter, it approached nigher to the dog, the growling of the three becoming more horrid at each moment, until the younger beast overleaping its intended bound fell directly before the mastiff. There was a moment of fearful cries and struggles, but they ended almost as soon as commenced, by the cub appearing in the air, hurled from the jaws of Brave with a violence that sent it against a tree so forcibly as to render it completely senseless.

Elizabeth witnessed the short struggle, and her blood was

warming with the triumph of the dog, when she saw the form of the old panther in the air, springing twenty feet from the branch of the beech to the back of the mastiff. No words of ours can describe the fury of the conflict that followed. It was a confused struggle on the dry leaves, accompanied by loud and terrific cries. Miss Temple continued on her knees, bending over the form of Louisa, her eyes fixed on the animals with an interest so horrid and yet so intense that she almost forgot her own stake in the result. So rapid and vigorous were the bounds of the inhabitant of the forest that its active frame seemed constantly in the air, while the dog nobly faced his foe at each successive leap. When the panther lighted on the shoulders of the mastiff, which was its constant aim, old Brave, though torn with her talons and stained with his own blood that already flowed from a dozen wounds, would shake off his furious foe like a feather and, rearing on his hind legs, rush to the fray again, with jaws distended and a dauntless eye. But age and his pampered life greatly disqualified the noble mastiff for such a struggle. In everything but courage he was only the vestige of what he had once been. A higher bound than ever raised the wary and furious beast far beyond the reach of the dog, who was making a desperate but fruitless dash at her, from which she alighted in a favorable position on the back of her aged foe. For a single moment only could the panther remain there, the great strength of the dog returning with a convulsive effort. But Elizabeth saw, as Brave fastened his teeth in the side of his enemy, that the collar of brass around his neck, which had been glittering throughout the fray, was of the color of blood and, directly, that his frame was sinking to the earth, where it soon lay prostrate and helpless. Several mighty efforts of the wildcat to extricate herself from the jaws of the dog followed, but they were fruitless until the mastiff turned on his back, his lips collapsed, and his teeth loosened, when the short convulsions and stillness that succeeded announced the death of poor Brave.

Elizabeth now lay wholly at the mercy of the beast. There is said to be something in the front of the image of the Maker that daunts the hearts of the inferior beings of his creation; and it would seem that some such power in the present instance suspended the threatened blow. The eyes of the monster and the kneeling maiden met for an instant when the former stopped to examine her fallen foe; next, to scent her luckless cub. From the latter examination it turned, however, with its eyes apparently emitting flashes of fire, its tail lashing its sides furiously, and its claws projecting inches from her broad feet.

Miss Temple did not or could not move. Her hands were clasped in the attitude of prayer, but her eyes were still drawn to her terrible enemy—her cheeks were blanched to the whiteness of marble, and her lips were slightly separated with horror.

The moment seemed now to have arrived for the fatal termination, and the beautiful figure of Elizabeth was bowing meekly to the stroke when a rustling of leaves behind seemed rather to mock the organs than to meet her ears.

"Hist! hist!" said a low voice. "Steep lower, gal; your bonnet hides the creater's head."

It was rather the yielding of nature than a compliance with this unexpected order that caused the head of our heroine to sink on her bosom when she heard the report of the rifle, the whizzing of the bullet, and the enraged cries of the beast, who was rolling over on the earth biting its own flesh and tearing the twigs and branches within its reach. At the next instant the form of the Leatherstocking rushed by her, and he called aloud:

"Come in, Hector, come in, old fool; 'tis a hard-lived animal and may jump ag'in."

Natty fearlessly maintained his position in front of the females, notwithstanding the violent bounds and threatening aspect of the wounded panther, which gave several indications of returning strength and ferocity, until his rifle was again loaded, when he stepped up to the enraged animal, and placing the muzzle close to its head, every spark of life was extinguished by the discharge.

The death of her terrible enemy appeared to Elizabeth like a resurrection from her own grave. There was an elasticity in the mind of our heroine that rose to meet the pressure of instant danger, and the more direct it had been, the more her nature had struggled to overcome them. But still she was a woman. Had she been left to herself in her late extremity, she would probably have used her faculties to the utmost, and with discretion, in protecting her person; but encumbered with her inanimate friend, retreat was a thing not to be attempted. Notwithstanding the fearful aspect of her foe, the eye of Elizabeth had never shrunk from its gaze, and long after the event her thoughts would recur to her passing sensations, and the sweetness of her midnight sleep would be disturbed, as her active fancy conjured, in dreams, the most trifling movements of savage fury that the beast had exhibited in its moment of power.

We shall leave the reader to imagine the restoration of Louisa's senses and the expressions of gratitude which fell from the young women. The former was effected by a little water that was brought from one of the thousand springs of those mountains in the cap of the Leatherstocking; and the latter were uttered with the warmth that might be expected from the character of Elizabeth. Natty received her vehement protestations of gratitude with a simple expression of good will, and with indulgence for her present excitement, but with a carelessness that showed how little he thought of the service he had rendered.

"Well, well," he said, "be it so, gal; let it be so, if you wish it—we'll talk the thing over another time. Come, come—let us get into the road, for you've had terror enough to make you wish yourself in your father's house ag'in."

This was uttered as they were proceeding at a pace that was adapted to the weakness of Louisa towards the highway: on reaching which the ladies separated from their guide, declaring themselves equal to the remainder of the walk without his assistance and feeling encouraged by the sight of the village which lay beneath their feet like a picture, with its limpid lake in front, the winding stream along its margin, and its hundred chimneys of whitened bricks.

The reader need not be told the nature of the emotions which two youthful, ingenuous, and well-educated girls would experience at their escape from a death so horrid as the one which had impended over them, while they pursued their way in silence along the track on the side of the mountain; nor how deep were their mental thanks to that Power which had given them their existence, and which had not deserted them in their extremity; neither how often they pressed each other's arms as the assurance of their present safety came, like a healing balm athwart their troubled spirits, when their thoughts were recurring to the recent moments of horror.

Leatherstocking remained on the hill gazing after their retiring figures until they were hidden by a bend in the road, when he whistled in his dogs, and shouldering his rifle, he returned into the forest.

"Well, it was a skeary thing to the young creaters," said Natty, while he retrod the path towards the plain. "It might frighten an older woman to see a she painter so near her with a dead cub by its side. I wonder if I had aimed at the varmint's eye, if I shouldn't have touched the life sooner than in the forehead; but they are hard-lived animals, and it was a good shot, consid'ring that I could see nothing but the head and the peak of its tail. Hah! who goes there?"

"How goes it, Natty?" said Mr. Doolittle, stepping out of the bushes, with a motion that was a good deal accelerated by the sight of the rifle that was already lowered in his direction. "What! shooting this warm day! Mind, old man, the law don't get hold on you."

"The law, squire! I have shook hands with the law these forty years," returned Natty; "for what has a man who lives in the wilderness to do with the ways of the law?"

"Not much maybe," said Hiram; "but you sometimes trade in venison. I s'pose you know, Leatherstocking, that there is an act passed to lay a fine of five pounds currency, or twelve dollars and fifty cents, by decimals, on every man who kills a deer betwixt January and August. The Judge had a great hand in getting the law through."

"I can believe it," returned the old hunter; "I can believe that or anything of a man who carries on as he does in the country."

"Yes, the law is quite positive, and the Judge is bent on putting it in force—five pounds penalty. I thought I heard your hounds out on the scent of so'thing this morning: I didn't know but they might get you in difficulty."

"They know their manners too well," said Natty, carelessly. "And how much goes to the state's evidence, Squire?"

"How much!" repeated Hiram, quailing under the honest but sharp look of the hunter. "The informer gets half I—I believe—yes, I guess it's half. But there's blood on your sleeve, man—you haven't been shooting anything this morning?"

"I have, though," said the hunter, nodding his head significantly to the other, "and a good shot I made of it."

"H-e-m!" ejaculated the magistrate; "and where is the

game? I s'pose it's of a good nater, for your dogs won't hunt at anything that isn't choice."

"They'll hunt anything I tell them to, Squire," cried Natty, favoring the other with his laugh. "They'll hunt you, if I say so. He-e-e-re, he-e-e-re, Hector—he-e-e-re, slut—come this-a-way, pups—come this-a-way—come hither."

"Oh! I have always heard a good character of the dogs," returned Mr. Doolittle, quickening his pace by raising each leg in rapid succession as the hounds scented around his person. "And where is the game, Leatherstocking?"

During this dialogue, the speakers had been walking at a very fast gait, and Natty swung the end of his rifle round, pointing through the bushes, and replied:

"There lies one. How do you like such meat?"

"This!" exclaimed Hiram. "Why this is Judge Temple's dog Brave. Take care, Leatherstocking, and don't make an enemy of the Judge. I hope you haven't harmed the animal?"

"Look for yourself, Mr. Doolittle," said Natty, drawing his knife from his girdle and wiping it in a knowing manner once or twice across his garment of buckskin. "Does his throat look as if I had cut it with this knife?"

"It is dreadfully torn! It's an awful wound—no knife never did this deed. Who could have done it?"

"The painters behind you, Squire."

"Painters!" echoed Hiram, whirling on his heel with an agility that would have done credit to a dancing master.

"Be easy, man," said Natty; "there's two of the venomous things; but the dog finished one, and I have fastened the other's jaws for her; so don't be frightened, Squire, they won't hurt you."

"And where's the deer?" cried Hiram, staring about him with a bewildered air.

"Anan! deer!" repeated Natty.

"Sartain, an't there venison here, or didn't you kill a buck?"

"What! when the law forbids the thing, Squire!" said the old hunter. "I hope there's no law ag'in killing the painters."

"No; there's a bounty on the scalps—but—will your dogs hunt painters, Natty?"

"Anything; didn't I tell you they'd hunt a man? He-e-re, he-e-re, pups——"

"Yes, yes, I remember. Well, they are strange dogs, I must say—I am quite in a wonderment."

Natty had seated himself on the ground, and having laid the grim head of his late ferocious enemy in his lap, was drawing his knife with a practiced hand around the ears, which he tore from the head of the beast in such a manner as to preserve their connection, when he answered:

"What at, Squire? Did you never see a painter's scalp afore? Come, you are a magistrate, I wish you'd make me out an order for the bounty."

"The bounty!" repeated Hiram, holding the ears on the end of his finger for a moment as if uncertain how to proceed. "Well, let us go down to your hut, where you can take the oath, and I will write out the order. I suppose you have a Bible? All the law wants is the four evangelists and the Lord's Prayer."

"I keep no books," said Natty a little coldly. "Not such a Bible as the law needs."

"Oh! there's but one sort of Bible that's good in law," returned the magistrate; "and yourn will do as well as another's. Come, the carcasses are worth nothing, man; let us go down and take the oath."

"Softly, softly, Squire," said the hunter, lifting his trophies very deliberately from the ground and shouldering his rifle. "Why do you want an oath at all for a thing that your own eyes has seen? Won't you believe yourself, that another man must swear to a fact that you know to be true? You have seen me scalp the creaters, and if I must swear to it, it shall be before Judge Temple, who needs an oath."

"But we have no pen or paper here, Leatherstocking; we must go to the hut for them, or how can I write the order?"

Natty turned his simple features on the cunning magistrate with another of his laughs, as he said:

"And what should I be doing with scholars' tools? I want no pens or paper, not knowing the use of either; and I keep none. No, no, I'll bring the scalps into the village, squire, and you can make out the order on one of your lawbooks, and it will be all the better for it. The deuce take this leather on the neck of the dog, it will strangle the old fool. Can you lend me a knife, Squire?"

Hiram, who seemed particularly anxious to be on good terms with his companion, unhesitatingly complied. Natty cut the thong from the neck of the hound, and, as he returned the knife to its owner, carelessly remarked:

" 'Tis a good bit of steel, and has cut such leather as this very same, before now, I dare say."

"Do you mean to charge me with letting your hounds loose?" exclaimed Hiram, with a consciousness that disarmed his caution.

"Loose!" repeated the hunter—"I let them loose myself. I always let them loose before I leave the hut."

The ungovernable amazement with which Mr. Doolittle listened to this falsehood would have betrayed his agency in the liberation of the dogs had Natty wanted any further confirmation; and the coolness and management of the old man now disappeared in open indignation.

"Look you here, Mr. Doolittle," he said, striking the breech of his rifle violently on the ground; "what there is in the wigwam of a poor man like me, that one like you can crave, I don't know; but this I tell you to your face, that you never shall put foot under the roof of my cabin with my consent, and that if you harbor round the spot as you have done lately, you may meet with treatment that you will little relish."

"And let me tell you, Mr. Bumppo," said Hiram, retreating, however, with a quick step, "that I know you've broke the law, and that I'm a magistrate and will make you feel it, too, before you are a day older."

"That for you and your law, too," cried Natty, snapping his fingers at the justice of the peace. "Away with you, you varmint, before the devil tempts me to give you your desarts. Take care, if I ever catch your prowling face in the woods ag'in, that I don't shoot it for an owl."

There is something at all times commanding in honest indignation, and Hiram did not stay to provoke the wrath of the old hunter to extremities. When the intruder was out of sight, Natty proceeded to the hut, where he found all quiet as the grave. He fastened his dogs, and tapping at the door, which was opened by Edwards, asked:

"Is all safe, lad!"

"Everything," returned the youth. "Someone attempted the lock, but it was too strong for him."

"I know the creatur," said Natty, "but he'll not trust himself within reach of my rifle very soon——" What more was uttered by the Leatherstocking in his vexation was rendered inaudible by the closing of the door of the cabin.

Chapter XXIX

It is noised, he hath a mass of treasure.
TIMON OF ATHENS

WHEN Marmaduke Temple and his cousin rode through the gate of the former, the heart of the father had been too recently touched with the best feelings of our nature to leave inclination for immediate discourse. There was an importance in the air of Richard, which would not have admitted of the ordinary informal conversation of the Sheriff without violating all the rules of consistency; and the equestrians pursued their way with great diligence for more than a mile in profound silence. At length, the soft expression of parental affection was slowly chased from the handsome features of the Judge and was gradually supplanted by the cast of humor and benevolence that was usually seated on his brow.

"Well, Dickon," he said, "since I have yielded myself so far implicitly to your guidance, I think the moment has arrived when I am entitled to further confidence. Why and wherefore are we journeying together in this solemn gait?"

The Sheriff gave a loud hem that rang far in the forest, and keeping his eyes fixed on objects before him, like a man who is looking deep into futurity:

"There has always been one point of difference between us, Judge Temple, I may say, since our nativity," he replied. "Not that I would insinuate that you are at all answerable for the acts of nature; for a man is no more to be condemned for the misfortunes of his birth, than he is to be commended for the natural advantages he may possess; but on one point we may be said to have differed from our births, and they, you know, occurred within two days of each other."

"I really marvel, Richard, what this one point can be;

for, to my eyes, we seem to differ so materially, and so often——"

"Mere consequences, sir," interrupted the Sheriff. "All our minor differences proceed from one cause, and that is our opinions of the universal attainments of genius."

"In what, Dickon?"

"I speak plain English, I believe, Judge Temple; at least I ought; for my father, who taught me, could speak——"

"Greek and Latin," interrupted Marmaduke. "I well know the qualifications of your family in tongues, Dickon. But proceed to the point; why are we traveling over this mountain today?"

"To do justice to any subject, sir, the narrator must be suffered to proceed in his own way," continued the Sheriff. "You are of opinion, Judge Temple, that a man is to be qualified by nature and education to do only one thing well, whereas I know that genius will supply the place of learning and that a certain sort of man can do anything and everything."

"Like yourself, I suppose," said Marmaduke, smiling.

"I scorn personalities, sir, I say nothing of myself; but there are three men on your Patent of the kind that I should term talented by nature for her general purposes, though acting under the influence of different situations."

"We are better off, then, than I had supposed. Who are these triumvirs?"

"Why, sir, one is Hiram Doolittle; a carpenter by trade, as you know—and I need only point to the village to exhibit his merits. Then he is a magistrate and might shame many a man in his distribution of justice who has had better opportunities."

"Well, he is one," said Marmaduke, with the air of a man that was determined not to dispute the point.

"Jotham Riddel is another."

"Who?"

"Jotham Riddel."

"What, that dissatisfied, shiftless, lazy, speculating fellow! He who changes his county every three years, his farm every six months, and his occupation every season! An agriculturist yesterday, a shoemaker today, and a schoolmaster tomorrow? That epitome of all the unsteady and profitless propensities of the settlers without one of their good qualities to counter-

balance the evil! Nay, Richard, this is too bad for even——
but the third?"

"As the third is not used to hearing such comments on his
character, Judge Temple, I shall not name him."

"The amount of all this, then, Dickon, is that the trio, of
which you are one, and the principal, have made some important discovery."

"I have not said that I am one, Judge Temple. As I told
you before, I say nothing egotistical. But a discovery has been
made, and you are deeply interested in it."

"Proceed—I am all ears."

"No, no, 'duke, you are bad enough, I own, but not so bad
as that either: your ears are not quite full grown."

The Sheriff laughed heartily at his own wit and put himself in good humor thereby, when he gratified his patient
cousin with the following explanation:

"You know, 'duke, there is a man living on your estate
that goes by the name of Natty Bumppo. Here has this man
lived, by what I can learn, for more than forty years—by
himself, until lately; and now with strange companions."

"Part very true, and all very probable," said the Judge.

"All true, sir; all true. Well, within these last few months
have appeared as his companions, an old Indian chief, the
last, or one of the last of his tribe that is to be found in
this part of the country, and a young man, who is said to
be the son of some Indian agent by a squaw."

"Who says that?" cried Marmaduke, with an interest that
he had not manifested before.

"Who? Why common sense—common report—the hue and
cry. But listen till you know all. This youth has very pretty
talents—yes, what I call very pretty talents—and has been
well educated, has seen very tolerable company, and knows
how to behave himself when he has a mind to. Now,
Judge Temple, can you tell me what has brought three such
men as Indian John, Natty Bumppo, and Oliver Edwards together?"

Marmaduke turned his countenance, in evident surprise, to
his cousin and replied quickly:

"Thou hast unexpectedly hit on a subject, Richard, that has
often occupied my mind. But knowest thou anything of this
mystery, or are they only the crude conjectures of——"

"Crude nothing, 'duke, crude nothing; but facts, stubborn

facts. You know there are mines in these mountains; I have often heard you say that you believed in their existence."

"Reasoning from analogy, Richard, but not with any certainty of the fact."

"You have heard them mentioned, and have seen specimens of the ore, sir; you will not deny that! And, reasoning from analogy, as you say, if there be mines in South America, ought there not to be mines in North America, too?"

"Nay, nay, I deny nothing, my cousin. I certainly have heard many rumors of the existence of mines in these hills; and I do believe that I have seen specimens of the precious metals that have been found here. It would occasion me no surprise to learn that tin and silver, or what I consider of more consequence, good coal——"

"Damn your coal," cried the Sheriff. "Who wants to find coal in these forests? No, no, silver, 'duke; silver is the one thing needful, and silver is to be found. But listen: you are not to be told that the natives have long known the use of gold and silver; now who so likely to be acquainted where they are to be found, as the ancient inhabitants of a country? I have the best reasons for believing that both Mohegan and the Leatherstocking have been privy to the existence of a mine in this very mountain for many years."

The Sheriff had now touched his cousin in a sensitive spot; and Marmaduke lent a more attentive ear to the speaker, who, after waiting a moment to see the effect of this extraordinary development, proceeded:

"Yes, sir, I have my reasons, and at a proper time you shall know them."

"No time is so good as the present."

"Well, well, be attentive," continued Richard, looking cautiously about him to make certain that no eavesdropper was hid in the forest, though they were in constant motion. "I have seen Mohegan and the Leatherstocking with my own eyes—and my eyes are as good as anybody's eyes—I have seen them, I say, both going up the mountain and coming down it, with spades and picks; and others have seen them carrying things into their hut, in a secret and mysterious manner, after dark. Do you call this a fact of importance?"

The Judge did not reply, but his brow had contracted with a thoughtfulness that he always wore when much interested, and his eyes rested on his cousin in expectation of hearing more. Richard continued:

"It was ore. Now, sir, I ask if you can tell me who this Mr. Oliver Edwards is, that has made a part of your household since Christmas?"

Marmaduke again raised his eyes, but continued silent, shaking his head in the negative.

"That he is a half-breed we know, for Mohegan does not scruple to call him openly his kinsman; that he is well educated we know. But as to his business here—do you remember that about a month before this young man made his appearance among us, Natty was absent from home several days? You do; for you inquired for him, as you wanted some venison to take to your friends when you went for Bess. Well, he was not to be found. Old John was left in the hut alone; and when Natty did appear, although he came on in the night, he was seen drawing one of those jumpers that they carry their grain to mill in, and to take out something with great care, that he had covered up under his bearskins. Now let me ask you, Judge Temple, what motive could induce a man like the Leatherstocking to make a sled and toil with a load over these mountains, if he had nothing but his rifle or his ammunition to carry?"

"They frequently make these jumpers to convey their game home, and you say he had been absent many days."

"How did he kill it? His rifle was in the village to be mended. No, no—that he was gone to some unusual place is certain; that he brought back some secret utensils is more certain; and that he has not allowed a soul to approach his hut since is most certain of all."

"He was never fond of intruders——"

"I know it," interrupted Richard; "but did he drive them from his cabin morosely? Within a fortnight of his return, this Mr. Edwards appears. They spend whole days in the mountains, pretending to be shooting, but in reality exploring; the frosts prevent their digging at that time, and he avails himself of a lucky accident to get into good quarters. But even now, he is quite half of his time in that hut—many hours every night. They are smelting, 'duke, they are smelting, and as they grow rich, you grow poor."

"How much of this is thine own, Richard, and how much comes from others? I would sift the wheat from the chaff."

"Part is my own, for I saw the jumper, though it was broken up and burnt in a day or two. I have told you that I saw the old man with his spades and picks. Hiram met Natty, as he was crossing the mountain, the night of his arrival with the sled, and very good-naturedly offered— Hiram *is* good natured—to carry up part of his load, for the old man had a heavy pull up the back of the mountain, but he wouldn't listen to the thing and repulsed the offer in such a manner that the Squire said he had half a mind to swear the peace against him. Since the snow has been off, more especially after the frosts got out of the ground, we have kept a watchful eye on the gentleman, in which we have found Jotham useful."

Marmaduke did not much like the associates of Richard in this business; still he knew them to be cunning and ready in expedients; and as there was certainly something mysterious not only in the connection between the old hunters and Edwards but in what his cousin had just related, he began to revolve the subject in his own mind with more care. On reflection, he remembered various circumstances that tended to corroborate these suspicions, and, as the whole business favored one of his infirmities, he yielded the more readily to their impression. The mind of Judge Temple, at all times comprehensive, had received from his peculiar occupations a bias to look far into futurity in his speculations on the improvements that posterity were to make in his lands. To his eye, where others saw nothing but a wilderness, towns, manufactories, bridges, canals, mines, and all the other resources of an old country were constantly presenting themselves, though his good sense suppressed in some degree the exhibition of these expectations.

As the Sheriff allowed his cousin full time to reflect on what he had heard, the probability of some pecuniary adventure being the connecting link in the chain that brought Oliver Edwards into the cabin of Leatherstocking appeared to him each moment to be stronger. But Marmaduke was too much in the habit of examining both sides of a subject not to perceive the objections, and he reasoned with himself aloud:

"It cannot be so, or the youth would not be driven so near the verge of poverty."

"What so likely to make a man dig for money, as being poor?" cried the Sheriff.

"Besides, there is an elevation of character about Oliver that proceeds from education which would forbid so clandestine a proceeding."

"Could an ignorant fellow smelt?" continued Richard.

"Bess hints that he was reduced even to his last shilling when we took him into our dwelling."

"He had been buying tools. And would he spend his last sixpence for a shot at a turkey, had he not known where to get more?"

"Can I have possibly been so long a dupe! His manner has been rude to me at times; but I attributed it to his conceiving himself injured, and to his mistaking the forms of the world."

"Haven't you been a dupe all your life, 'duke? And an't what you call ignorance of forms deep cunning, to conceal his real character?"

"If he were bent on deception, he would have concealed his knowledge and passed with us for an inferior man."

"He cannot. I could no more pass for a fool, myself, than I could fly. Knowledge is not to be concealed like a candle under a bushel."

"Richard," said the Judge, turning to his cousin, "there are many reasons against the truth of thy conjectures; but thou hast awakened suspicions which must be satisfied. But why are we traveling here?"

"Jotham, who has been much in the mountain latterly, being kept there by me and Hiram, has made a discovery, which he will not explain, he says, for he is bound by an oath; but the amount is, that he knows where the ore lies, and he has this day begun to dig. I would not consent to the thing, 'duke, without your knowledge, for the land is yours; and now you know the reason of our ride. I call this a countermine, ha!"

"And where is the desirable spot?" asked the Judge, with an air half comical, half serious.

"At hand; and when we have visited that, I will show you one of the places that we have found within a week, where our hunters have been amusing themselves for six months past."

The gentlemen continued to discuss the matter while

their horses picked their way under the branches of trees and over the uneven ground of the mountain. They soon arrived at the end of their journey, where, in truth, they found Jotham already buried to his neck in a hole that he had been digging.

Marmaduke questioned the miner very closely as to his reasons for believing in the existence of the precious metals near that particular spot; but the fellow maintained an obstinate mystery in his answers. He asserted that he had the best of reasons for what he did and inquired of the Judge what portion of the profits would fall to his own share in the event of success, with an earnestness that proved his faith. After spending an hour near the place, examining the stones and searching for the usual indications of the proximity of ore, the Judge remounted, and suffered his cousin to lead the way to the place where the mysterious trio had been making their excavation.

The spot chosen by Jotham was on the back of the mountain that overhung the hut of Leatherstocking, and the place selected by Natty and his companions was on the other side of the same hill, but above the road, and, of course, in an opposite direction to the route taken by the ladies in their walk.

"We shall be safe in approaching the place now," said Richard, while they dismounted and fastened their horses; "for I took a look with the glass and saw John and Leatherstocking in their canoe fishing, before we left home, and Oliver is in the same pursuit; but these may be nothing but shams, to blind our eyes, so we will be expeditious, for it would not be pleasant to be caught here by them."

"Not on my own land!" said Marmaduke sternly. "If it be as you suspect, I will know their reasons for making this excavation."

"Mum," said Richard, laying a finger on his lip and leading the way down a very difficult descent to a sort of natural cavern, which was found in the face of the rock and was not unlike a fireplace in shape. In front of this place lay a pile of earth, which had evidently been taken from the recess, and part of which was yet fresh. An examination of the exterior of the cavern left the Judge in doubt whether it was one of nature's frolics that had thrown it into that shape, or whether it had been wrought by the hands of man, at some earlier period. But there could be no doubt that the whole of the interior was of recent formation, and the marks of the pick were still visible, where the soft, lead-colored rock had opposed itself to the progress of the miners. The whole formed an excavation of about twenty feet in width, and nearly twice that distance in depth. The height was much greater than was required for the ordinary purposes of experiment; but this was evidently the effect of chance, as the roof of the cavern was a natural stratum of rock that projected many feet beyond the base of the pile. Immediately in front of the recess, or cave, was a little terrace, partly formed by nature, and partly by the earth that had been carelessly thrown aside by the laborers. The mountain fell off precipitously in front of the terrace, and the approach by its sides, under the ridge of the rocks, was difficult and a little dangerous. The whole was wild, rude, and apparently incomplete: for, while looking among the bushes, the Sheriff found the very implements that had been used in the work.

When the Sheriff thought that his cousin had examined the spot sufficiently, he asked solemnly:

"Judge Temple, are you satisfied?"

"Perfectly, that there is something mysterious and perplexing in this business. It is a secret spot, and cunningly devised, Richard; yet I see no symptoms of ore."

"Do you expect, sir, to find gold and silver lying like pebbles on the surface of the earth? Dollars and dimes ready coined to your hands! No, no—the treasure must be sought after to be won. But let them mine; I shall countermine."

The Judge took an accurate survey of the place and noted in his memorandum book such marks as were necessary to find it again, in the event of Richard's absence; when the cousins returned to their horses.

On reaching the highway they separated, the Sheriff to summon twenty-four "good men and true" to attend as the inquest of the county, on the succeeding Monday, when Marmaduke held his stated court of "common pleas and general sessions of the peace," and the Judge to return, musing deeply on what he had seen and heard in the course of the morning.

When the horse of the latter reached the spot where the

highway fell towards the valley, the eye of Marmaduke rested, it is true, on the same scene that had, ten minutes before, been so soothing to the feelings of his daughter and her friend as they emerged from the forest; but it rested in vacancy. He threw the reins to his sure-footed beast and suffered the animal to travel at its own gait, while he soliloquized as follows:

"There may be more in this than I at first supposed. I have suffered my feeling to blind my reason, in admitting an unknown youth in this manner to my dwelling; yet this is not the land of suspicion. I will have the Leatherstocking before me, and, by a few direct questions, extract the truth from the simple old man."

At that instant the Judge caught a glimpse of the figures of Elizabeth and Louisa, who were slowly descending the mountain, a short distance before him. He put spurs to his horse, and riding up to them, dismounted, and drove his steed along the narrow path. While the agitated parent was listening to the vivid description that his daughter gave of her recent danger and her unexpected escape, all thoughts of mines, vested rights, and examinations were absorbed in emotion; and when the image of Natty again crossed his recollection, it was not as a lawless and depredating squatter, but as the preserver of his child.

CHAPTER XXX

The court awards it, and the law doth give it.
                                    MERCHANT OF VENICE

REMARKABLE PETTIBONE, who had forgotten the wound received by her pride, in contemplation of the ease and comforts of her situation, and who still retained her station in the family of Judge Temple, was dispatched to the humble dwelling which Richard already styled "The Rectory" in attendance on Louisa, who was soon consigned to the arms of her father.

In the meantime, Marmaduke and his daughter were closeted for more than an hour, nor shall we invade the sanctuary of parental love by relating the conversation. When the curtain rises on the reader, the Judge is seen walking up and down the apartment, with a tender melancholy in his air, and his child reclining on a settee, with a flushed cheek, and her dark eyes seeming to float in crystals.

"It was a timely rescue! It was, indeed, a timely rescue, my child!" cried the Judge. "Then thou didst not desert thy friend, my noble Bess?"

"I believe I may as well take the credit of fortitude," said Elizabeth, "though I much doubt if flight would have availed me anything, had I even courage to execute such an intention. But I thought not of the expedient."

"Of what didst thou think, love? Where did thy thoughts dwell most at that fearful moment?"

"The beast! the beast!" cried Elizabeth, veiling her face with her hand. "Oh! I saw nothing, I thought of nothing but the beast. I tried to think of better things, but the horror was too glaring, the danger too much before my eyes."

"Well, well, thou art safe, and we will converse no more on the unpleasant subject. I did not think such an animal yet remained in our forests; but they will stray far from their haunts when pressed by hunger, and——"

A loud knocking at the door of the apartment interrupted what he was about to utter, and he bid the applicant enter. The door was opened by Benjamin, who came in with a discontented air, as if he felt that he had a communication to make that would be out of season.

"Here is Squire Doolittle below, sir," commenced the major-domo. "He has been standing off and on in the dooryard for the matter of a glass; and he has sum'mat on his mind that he wants to heave up, d'ye see; but I tells him, says I, man, would you be coming aboard with your complaints, said I, when the Judge has gotten his own child, as it were, out of the jaws of a lion? But damn the bit of manners has the fellow, any more than if he was one of them Guineas down in the kitchen there; and so as he was sheering nearer, every stretch he made towards the house, I could do no better than to let your honor know that the chap was in the offing."

"He must have business of importance," said Marmaduke; "something in relation to his office, most probably, as the court sits so shortly."

"Ay, ay, you have it, sir," cried Benjamin. "It's sum'mat about a complaint that he has to make of the old Leatherstocking, who, to my judgment, is the better man of the two. It's a very good sort of a man is this Master Bumppo, and he has a way with a spear, all the same as if he was brought up at the bow oar of the captain's barge, or was born with a boat hook in his hand."

"Against the Leatherstocking!" cried Elizabeth, rising from her reclining posture.

"Rest easy, my child; some trifle, I pledge you; I believe I am already acquainted with its import. Trust me, Bess, your champion shall be safe in my care. Show Mr. Doolittle in, Benjamin."

Miss Temple appeared satisfied with this assurance, but fastened her dark eyes on the person of the architect, who profited by the permission and instantly made his appearance.

All the impatience of Hiram seemed to vanish the instant he entered the apartment. After saluting the Judge and his daughter, he took the chair to which Marmaduke pointed and sat for a minute, composing his straight black hair, with a gravity of demeanor that was intended to do honor to his official station. At length he said:

"It's likely, from what I hear, that Miss Temple had a pretty narrow chance with the painters on the mountain."

Marmaduke made a gentle inclination of his head by way of assent, but continued silent.

"I s'pose the law gives a bounty on the scalps," continued Hiram, "in which case the Leatherstocking will make a good job on't."

"It shall be my care to see that he is rewarded," returned the Judge.

"Yes, yes, I rather guess that nobody hereabouts doubts the Judge's generosity. Does he know whether the Sheriff has fairly made up his mind to have a reading desk or a deacon's pew under the pulpit?"

"I have not heard my cousin speak on that subject lately," replied Marmaduke.

"I think it's likely that we will have a pretty dull court on't, from what I can gather. I hear that Jotham Riddel and the man who bought his betterments have agreed to leave their difference to men, and I don't think there'll be more than two civil cases in the calendar."

"I am glad of it," said the Judge; "nothing gives me more pain than to see my settlers wasting their time and substance in the unprofitable struggles of the law. I hope it may prove true, sir."

"I rather guess 'twill be left out to men," added Hiram, with an air equally balanced between doubt and assurance, but which Judge Temple understood to mean certainty; "I some think that I am appointed a referee in the case myself; Jotham as much as told me that he should take me. The defendant, I guess, means to take Captain Hollister, and we two have partly agreed on Squire Jones for the third man."

"Are there any criminals to be tried?" asked Marmaduke.

"There's the counterfeiters," returned the magistrate; "as they were caught in the fact, I think it likely that they'll be indicted, in which case it's probable they'll be tried."

"Certainly, sir, I had forgotten those men. There are no more, I hope."

"Why, there is a threaten to come forrad with an assault, that happened at the last Independence Day; but I'm not sartain that the law'll take hold on't. There was plaguey hard words passed, but whether they struck or not I haven't heard. There's some folks talk of a deer or two being killed out of season, over on the west side of the Patent, by some of the squatters on the 'Fractions.' "

"Let a complaint be made, by all means," cried the Judge. "I am determined to see the law executed to the letter on all such depredators."

"Why, yes, I thought the Judge was of that mind; I come partly on such a business myself."

"You!" exclaimed Marmaduke, comprehending in an instant how completely he had been caught by the other's cunning. "And what have you to say, sir?"

"I some think that Natty Bumppo has the carcass of a deer in his hut at this moment, and a considerable part of my business was to get a search warrant to examine."

"You think, sir! Do you know that the law exacts an oath before I can issue such a precept? The habitation of a citizen is not to be idly invaded on light suspicion."

"I rather think I can swear to it myself," returned the immovable Hiram; "and Jotham is in the street, and as good as ready to come in and make oath to the same thing."

"Then issue the warrant thyself; thou art a magistrate, Mr. Doolittle. Why trouble me with the matter?"

"Why, seeing it's the first complaint under the law, and knowing the Judge set his heart on the thing, I thought it best that the authority to search should come from himself. Besides, as I'm much in the woods, among the timber, I don't altogether like making an enemy of the Leatherstocking. Now the Judge has a weight in the county that puts him above fear."

Miss Temple turned her face to the callous architect as she said:

"And what has any honest person to dread from so kind a man as Bumppo?"

"Why, it's as easy, Miss, to pull a rifle trigger on a magistrate as on a painter. But if the Judge don't conclude to issue the warrant, I must go home and make it out myself."

"I have not refused your application, sir," said Marmaduke, perceiving at once that his reputation for impartiality was at stake; "go into my office, Mr. Doolittle, where I will join you and sign the warrant."

Judge Temple stopped the remonstrances which Elizabeth was about to utter, after Hiram had withdrawn, by laying his hand on her mouth and saying:

"It is more terrific in sound than frightful in reality, my child. I suppose that the Leatherstocking has shot a deer, for the season is nearly over, and you say that he was hunting with his dogs when he came so timely to your assistance. But it will be only to examine his cabin, and find the animal, when you can pay the penalty out of your own pocket, Bess. Nothing short of the twelve dollars and a half will satisfy this harpy, I perceive; and surely my reputation as a Judge is worth that trifle."

Elizabeth was a good deal pacified with this assurance and suffered her father to leave her to fulfill his promise to Hiram.

When Marmaduke left his office after executing his disagreeable duty, he met Oliver Edwards, walking up the graveled walk in front of the mansion house, with great strides, and with a face agitated by feeling. On seeing Judge Temple, the youth turned aside, and with a warmth in his manner that was not often exhibited to Marmaduke, he cried:

"I congratulate you, sir; from the bottom of my soul I

congratulate you, Judge Temple. Oh! it would have been too horrid to have recollected for a moment! I have just left the hut, where, after showing me his scalps, old Natty told me of the escape of the ladies, as a thing to be mentioned last. Indeed, indeed, sir, no words of mine can express half of what I have felt"—the youth paused a moment, as if suddenly recollecting that he was overstepping prescribed limits, and concluded with a good deal of embarrassment— "what I have felt at this danger to Miss—Grant, and—and your daughter, sir."

But the heart of Marmaduke was too much softened to admit of his caviling at trifles, and without regarding the confusion of the other, he replied:

"I thank thee, thank thee, Oliver; as thou sayest, it is almost too horrid to be remembered. But come, let us hasten to Bess, for Louisa has already gone to the rectory."

The young man sprang forward and, throwing open a door, barely permitted the Judge to precede him, when he was in the presence of Elizabeth in a moment.

The cold distance that often crossed the demeanor of the heiress in her intercourse with Edwards was now entirely banished, and two hours were passed by the party in the free, unembarrassed, and confiding manner of old and esteemed friends. Judge Temple had forgotten the suspicions engendered during his morning's ride, and the youth and maiden conversed, laughed, and were sad by turns, as impulse directed. At length, Edwards, after repeating his intention to do so for the third time, left the mansion house to go to the rectory on a similar errand of friendship.

During this short period, a scene was passing at the hut that completely frustrated the benevolent intentions of Judge Temple in favor of the Leatherstocking, and at once destroyed the short-lived harmony between the youth and Marmaduke.

When Hiram Doolittle had obtained his search warrant, his first business was to procure a proper officer to see it executed. The Sheriff was absent, summoning in person the grand inquest for the county; the deputy, who resided in the village, was riding on the same errand, in a different part of the settlement; and the regular constable of the township had been selected for his station from motives of charity, being lame of a leg. Hiram intended to accompany the officer as a spectator, but he felt no very strong desire to bear the brunt of the battle. It was, however, Saturday, and the sun was already turning the shadows of the pines towards the east; on the morrow the conscientious magistrate could not engage in such an expedition at the peril of his soul; and long before Monday, the venison, and all vestiges of the death of the deer, might be secreted or destroyed. Happily, the lounging form of Billy Kirby met his eye, and Hiram, at all times fruitful in similar expedients, saw his way clear at once. Jotham, who was associated in the whole business, and who had left the mountain in consequence of a summons from his coadjutor, but who failed, equally with Hiram, in the unfortunate particular of nerve, was directed to summon the wood chopper to the dwelling of the magistrate.

When Billy appeared, he was very kindly invited to take the chair in which he had already seated himself, and was treated in all respects as if he were an equal.

"Judge Temple has set his heart on putting the deer law in force," said Hiram, after the preliminary civilities were over, "and a complaint has been laid before him that a deer has been killed. He has issued a search warrant and sent for me to get somebody to execute it."

Kirby, who had no idea of being excluded from the deliberative part of any affair in which he was engaged, drew up his bushy head in a reflecting attitude and, after musing a moment, replied by asking a few questions.

"The Sheriff is gone out of the way?"

"Not to be found."

"And his deputy, too?"

"Both gone on the skirts of the Patent."

"But I saw the constable hobbling about town an hour ago."

"Yes, yes," said Hiram with a coaxing smile and knowing nod, "but this business wants a man—not a cripple."

"Why," said Billy, laughing, "will the chap make fight?"

"He's a little quarrelsome at times, and thinks he's the best man in the country at rough-and-tumble."

"I heard him brag once," said Jotham, "that there wasn't a man 'twixt the Mohawk Flats and the Pennsylvany line that was his match at a close hug."

"Did you?" exclaimed Kirby, raising his huge frame in his seat, like a lion stretching in his lair. "I rather guess he never felt a Varmounter's knuckles on his backbone. But who is the chap?"

"Why," said Jotham, "it's——"

"It's ag'in law to tell," interrupted Hiram, "unless you'll qualify to sarve. You'd be the very man to take him, Bill; and I'll make out a special deputation in a minute, when you will get the fees."

"What's the fees?" said Kirby, laying his large hand on the leaves of a statute book that Hiram had opened in order to give dignity to his office, which he turned over in his rough manner as if he were reflecting on a subject about which he had, in truth, already decided. "Will they pay a man for a broken head?"

"They'll be something handsome," said Hiram.

"Damn the fees," said Billy, again laughing. "Does the fellow think he's the best wrestler in the county, though? What's his inches?"

"He's taller than you be," said Jotham, "and one of the biggest——"

Talkers, he was about to add, but the impatience of Kirby interrupted him. The wood chopper had nothing fierce or even brutal in his appearance; the character of his expression was that of good-natured vanity. It was evident he prided himself on the powers of the physical man, like all who have nothing better to boast of; and, stretching out his broad hand, with the palm downwards, he said, keeping his eyes fastened on his own bones and sinews:

"Come, give us a touch of the book. I'll swear, and you'll see that I'm a man to keep my oath."

Hiram did not give the wood chopper time to change his mind, but the oath was administered without unnecessary delay. So soon as this preliminary was completed, the three worthies left the house and proceeded by the nearest road towards the hut. They had reached the bank of the lake, and were diverging from the route of the highway, before Kirby recollected that he was now entitled to the privilege of the initiated, and repeated his question as to the name of the offender.

"Which way, which way, Squire?" exclaimed the hardy wood chopper. "I thought it was to search a house that you wanted me, not the woods. There is nobody lives on this side of the lake, for six miles, unless you count the Leatherstocking and old John for settlers. Come, tell me the chap's name, and I warrant me that I lead you to his clearing by a straighter path than this, for I know every sapling that grows within two miles of Templetown."

"This is the way," said Hiram, pointing forward and quickening his step, as if apprehensive that Kirby would desert, "and Bumppo is the man."

Kirby stopped short and looked from one of his companions to the other in astonishment. He then burst into a loud laugh, and cried:

"Who? Leatherstocking! He may brag of his aim and his rifle, for he has the best of both, as I will own myself, for sin' he shot the pigeon I knock under to him; but for a wrestle! Why, I would take the creatur' between my finger and thumb and tie him in a bowknot around my neck for a barcelony. The man is seventy and was never anything particular for strength."

"He's a deceiving man," said Hiram, "like all the hunters; he is stronger than he seems; besides, he has his rifle."

"That for his rifle!" cried Billy. "He'd no more hurt me with his rifle than he'd fly. He is a harmless creatur', and I must say that I think he has as good right to kill deer as any man on the Patent. It's his main support, and this is a free country, where a man is privileged to follow any calling he likes."

"According to that doctrine," said Jotham, "anybody may shoot a deer."

"This is the man's calling, I tell you," returned Kirby, "and the law was never made for such as he."

"The law was made for all," observed Hiram, who began to think that the danger was likely to fall to his own share, notwithstanding his management; "and the law is particular in noticing parjury."

"See here, Squire Doolittle," said the reckless wood chopper; "I don't care the valie of a beetle ring for you and your parjury, too. But as I have come so far, I'll go down and have a talk with the old man and maybe we'll fry a steak of the deer together."

"Well, if you can get in peaceably, so much the better," said the magistrate. "To my notion, strife is very unpopular; I prefer, at all times, clever conduct to an ugly temper."

As the whole party moved at a great pace, they soon

reached the hut, where Hiram thought it prudent to halt on the outside of the top of the fallen pine, which formed a chevaux-de-frise, to defend the approach to the fortress, on the side next the village. The delay was little relished by Kirby, who clapped his hands to his mouth and gave a loud halloo that brought the dogs out of their kennel and, almost at the same instant, the scantily covered head of Natty from the door.

"Lie down, old fool," cried the hunter. "Do you think there's more painters about you?"

"Ha! Leatherstocking, I've an arrand with you," cried Kirby; "here's the good people of the state have been writing you a small letter, and they've hired me to ride post."

"What would you have with me, Billy Kirby?" said Natty, stepping across his threshold, and raising his hand over his eyes to screen them from the rays of the setting sun while he took a survey of his visitor. "I've no land to clear; and heaven knows I would set out six trees afore I would cut down one. Down, Hector, I say; into your kennel with ye."

"Would you, old boy?" roared Billy. "Then so much the better for me. But I must do my arrand. Here's a letter for you, Leatherstocking. If you can read it, it's all well, and if you can't, here's Squire Doolittle at hand to let you know what it means. It seems you mistook the twentieth of July for the first of August, that's all."

By this time Natty had discovered the lank person of Hiram, drawn up under the cover of a high stump; and all that was complacent in his manner instantly gave way to marked distrust and dissatisfaction. He placed his head within the door of his hut and said a few words in an undertone, when he again appeared, and continued:

"I've nothing for ye; so away, afore the evil one tempts me to do you harm. I owe you no spite, Billy Kirby, and what for should you trouble an old man, who has done you no harm?"

Kirby advanced through the top of the pine to within a few feet of the hunter, where he seated himself on the end of a log with great composure and began to examine the nose of Hector, with whom he was familiar from their frequently meeting in the woods, where he sometimes fed the dog from his own basket of provisions.

"You've outshot me, and I'm not ashamed to say it," said

the wood chopper; "but I don't owe you a grudge for that,
Natty! Though it seems that you've shot once too often, for
the story goes that you've killed a buck."

"I've fired but twice today, and both times at the painters,"
returned the Leatherstocking. "See, here are the scalps! I
was just going in with them to the Judge's to ask the
bounty."

While Natty was speaking, he tossed the ears to Kirby, who
continued playing with them, with a careless air, holding
them to the dogs and laughing at their movements when
they scented the unusual game.

But Hiram, emboldened by the advance of the deputed
constable, now ventured to approach, also, and took up the
discourse with the air of authority that became his commission. His first measure was to read the warrant aloud,
taking care to give due emphasis to the most material parts,
and concluding with the name of the Judge in very audible
and distinct tones.

"Did Marmaduke Temple put his name to that bit of
paper?" said Natty, shaking his head. "Well, well, that man
loves the new ways, and his betterments, and his lands,
afore his own flesh and blood. But I won't mistrust the gal:
she has an eye like a full-grown buck! Poor thing, she
didn't choose her father and can't help it. I know but little
of the law, Mr. Doolittle; what is to be done, now you've
read your commission?"

"Oh! it's nothing but form, Natty," said Hiram, endeavoring to assume a friendly aspect. "Let's go in, and talk the
thing over in reason; I dare to say that the money can be
easily found, and I partly conclude, from what passed, that
Judge Temple will pay it himself."

The old hunter had kept a keen eye on the movements of
his three visitors from the beginning and had maintained
his position, just without the threshold of his cabin, with a
determined manner that showed he was not to be easily
driven from his post. When Hiram drew nigher, as if expecting his proposition would be accepted, Natty lifted his
hand and motioned for him to retreat.

"Haven't I told you more than once not to tempt me?"
he said. "I trouble no man; why can't the law leave me to
myself? Go back—go back, and tell your Judge that he may

keep his bounty; but I won't have his wasty ways brought into my hut."

This offer, however, instead of appeasing the curiosity of Hiram, seemed to inflame it the more; while Kirby cried:

"Well, that's fair, Squire; he forgives the county his demand, and the county should forgive him the fine; it's what I call an even trade and should be concluded on the spot. I like quick dealings, and what's fair 'twixt man and man."

"I demand entrance into this house," said Hiram, summoning all the dignity he could muster to his assistance, "in the name of the people; and by the virtue of this warrant, and of my office, and with this peace officer."

"Stand back, stand back, Squire, and don't tempt me," said the Leatherstocking, motioning for him to retire, with great earnestness.

"Stop us at your peril," continued Hiram. "Billy! Jotham! Close up—I want testimony."

Hiram had mistaken the mild but determined air of Natty for submission, and had already put his foot on the threshold to enter when he was seized unexpectedly by his shoulders and hurled over the little bank towards the lake, to the distance of twenty feet. The suddenness of the movement and the unexpected display of strength on the part of Natty created a momentary astonishment in his invaders that silenced all noises; but at the next instant Billy Kirby gave vent to his mirth in peals of laughter that he seemed to heave up from his very soul.

"Well done, old stub!" he shouted. "The Squire know'd you better than I did. Come, come, here's a green spot; take it out like men, while Jotham and I see fair play."

"William Kirby, I order you to do your duty," cried Hiram, from under the bank; "seize that man; I order you to seize him in the name of the people."

But the Leatherstocking now assumed a more threatening attitude; his rifle was in his hand, and its muzzle was directed towards the wood chopper.

"Stand off, I bid ye," said Natty; "you know my aim, Billy Kirby; I don't crave your blood, but mine and yourn both shall turn this green grass red, afore you put foot into the hut."

While the affair appeared trifling, the wood chopper seemed disposed to take sides with the weaker party; but when the firearms were introduced, his manner very sensibly changed. He raised his large frame from the log, and facing the hunter with an open front, he replied:

"I didn't come here as your enemy, Leatherstocking; but I don't value the hollow piece of iron in your hand so much as a broken ax helve; so, Squire, say the word, and keep within the law, and we'll soon see who's the best man of the two."

But no magistrate was to be seen! The instant the rifle was produced Hiram and Jotham vanished; and when the wood chopper bent his eyes about him in surprise at receiving no answer, he discovered their retreating figures moving towards the village at a rate that sufficiently indicated that they had not only calculated the velocity of a rifle bullet, but also its probable range.

"You've scared the creaters off," said Kirby, with great contempt expressed on his broad features; "but you are not going to scare me; so, Mr. Bumppo, down with your gun, or there'll be trouble 'twixt us."

Natty dropped his rifle, and replied:

"I wish you no harm, Billy Kirby; but I leave it to your self, whether an old man's hut is to be run down by such varmint. I won't deny the buck to you, Billy, and you may take the skin in, if you please, and show it as testimony. The bounty will pay the fine, and that ought to satisfy any man."

" 'Twill, old boy, 'twill," cried Kirby, every shade of displeasure vanishing from his open brow at the peace offering; "throw out the hide, and that shall satisfy the law."

Natty entered the hut and soon reappeared bringing with him the desired testimonial; and the wood chopper departed, as thoroughly reconciled to the hunter as if nothing had happened. As he paced along the margin of the lake he would burst into frequent fits of laughter while he recollected the somersault of Hiram; and, on the whole, he thought the affair a very capital joke.

Long before Billy reached the village, however, the news of his danger, and of Natty's disrespect of the law, and of Hiram's discomfiture were in circulation. A good deal was said about sending for the Sheriff; some hints were given about calling out the *posse comitatus* to avenge the insulted laws; and many of the citizens were collected, deliberating how to proceed. The arrival of Billy with the skin, by removing all grounds for a search, changed the complexion of things materially. Nothing now remained but to collect the fine and assert the dignity of the people; all of which, it was unanimously agreed, could be done as well on the succeeding Monday as on Saturday night—a time kept sacred by a large portion of the settlers. Accordingly, all further proceedings were suspended for six-and-thirty hours.

Chapter XXXI

And dar'st thou then
To beard the lion in his den,
The Douglass in his hall?

MARMION

THE commotion was just subsiding, and the inhabitants of the village had begun to disperse from the little groups they had formed, each retiring to his own home and closing his door after him with the grave air of a man who consulted public feeling in his exterior deportment, when Oliver Edwards, on his return from the dwelling of Mr. Grant, encountered the young lawyer, who is known to the reader as Mr. Lippet. There was very little similarity in the manners or opinions of the two; but as they both belonged to the more intelligent class of a very small community, they were, of course, known to each other, and as their meeting was at a point where silence would have been rudeness, the following conversation was the result of their interview:

"A fine evening, Mr. Edwards," commenced the lawyer, whose disinclination to the dialogue was, to say the least, very doubtful; "we want rain sadly; that's the worst of this climate of ours, it's either a drought or a deluge. It's likely you've been used to a more equal temperature?"

"I am a native of this state," returned Edwards, coldly.

"Well, I've often heard that point disputed; but it's so easy to get a man naturalized that it's of little consequence where he was born. I wonder what course the Judge means to take in this business of Natty Bumppo!"

"Of Natty Bumppo!" echoed Edwards. "To what do you allude, sir?"

"Haven't you heard!" exclaimed the other with a look of

surprise so naturally assumed as completely to deceive his auditor. "It may turn out an ugly business. It seems that the old man has been out in the hills, and has shot a buck this morning, and that, you know, is a criminal matter in the eyes of Judge Temple."

"O! he has, has he?" said Edwards, averting his face to conceal the color that collected in his sunburned cheek. "Well, if that be all, he must even pay the fine."

"It's five pounds currency," said the lawyer. "Could Natty muster so much money at once?"

"Could he!" cried the youth. "I am not rich, Mr. Lippet; far from it—I am poor, and I have been hoarding my salary for a purpose that lies near my heart; but before that old man should lie one hour in a jail, I would spend the last cent to prevent it. Besides, he has killed two panthers, and the bounty will discharge the fine many times over."

"Yes, yes," said the lawyer, rubbing his hands together, with an expression of pleasure that had no artifice about it; "we shall make it out; I see plainly we shall make it out."

"Make what out, sir? I must beg an explanation."

"Why, killing the buck is but a small matter compared to what took place this afternoon," continued Mr. Lippet, with a confidential and friendly air that insensibly won upon the youth, little as he liked the man. "It seems that a complaint was made of the fact, and a suspicion that there was venison in the hut was sworn to, all which is provided for in the statute, when Judge Temple granted a search warrant——"

"A search warrant!" echoed Edwards, in a voice of horror, and with a face that should have been again averted to conceal its paleness. "And how much did they discover? What did they see?"

"They saw old Bumppo's rifle; and that is a sight which will quiet most men's curiosity in the woods."

"Did they! Did they!" shouted Edwards, bursting into a convulsive laugh. "So the old hero beat them back! He beat them back! Did he?"

The lawyer fastened his eyes in astonishment on the youth, but as his wonder gave way to the thoughts that were commonly uppermost in his mind, he replied:

"It's no laughing matter, let me tell you, sir; the forty dollars of bounty, and your six months of salary, will be much reduced before you can get the matter fairly settled.

Assaulting a magistrate in the execution of his duty and menacing a constable with firearms at the same time is a pretty serious affair, and is punishable with both fine and imprisonment."

"Imprisonment!" repeated Oliver. "Imprison the Leatherstocking! No, no, sir; it would bring the old man to his grave. They shall never imprison the Leatherstocking."

"Well, Mr. Edwards," said Lippet, dropping all reserve from his manner, "you are called a curious man; but if you can tell me how a jury is to be prevented from finding a verdict of guilty, if this case comes fairly before them, and the proof is clear, I shall acknowledge that you know more law than I do, who have had a license in my pocket for three years."

By this time the reason of Edwards was getting the ascendency of his feelings, and as he began to see the real difficulties of the case, he listened more readily to the conversation of the lawyer. The ungovernable emotion that escaped the youth in the first moments of his surprise entirely passed away; and although it was still evident that he continued to be much agitated by what he had heard, he succeeded in yielding forced attention to the advice which the other uttered.

Not withstanding the confused state of his mind, Oliver soon discovered that most of the expedients of the lawyer were grounded in cunning and plans that required a time to execute them that neither suited his disposition nor his necessities. After, however, giving Mr. Lippet to understand that he retained him in the event of a trial, an assurance that at once satisfied the lawyer, they parted, one taking his course, with a deliberate tread, in the direction of the little building that had a wooden sign over its door with "Chester Lippet, Attorney at Law," painted on it; and the other pacing over the ground with enormous strides towards the mansion house. We shall take leave of the attorney for the present, and direct the attention of the reader to his client.

When Edwards entered the hall, whose enormous doors were opened to the passage of the air of a mild evening, he found Benjamin engaged in some of his domestic avocations, and in a hurried voice inquired where Judge Temple was to be found.

"Why, the Judge has stept into his office, with that master

carpenter, Mister Doolittle; but Miss Lizzy is in that there parlor. I say, Master Oliver, we'd like to have had a bad job of that panther, or painter's work—some calls it one, and some calls it t'other—but I know little of the beast, seeing that it is not of British growth. I said as much as that it was in the hills the last winter; for I heard it moaning on the lake shore one evening in the fall, when I was pulling down from the fishing point in the skiff. Had the animal come into open water, where a man could see where and how to work his vessel, I would have engaged the thing myself; but looking aloft among the trees is all the same to me as standing on the deck of one ship and looking at another vessel's tops. I never can tell one rope from another——"

"Well, well," interrupted Edwards; "I must see Miss Temple."

"And you shall see her, sir," said the steward; "she's in this here room. Lord, Master Edwards, what a loss she'd have been to the Judge! Dam'me if I know where he would have gotten such another daughter; that is, full grown, d'ye see. I say, sir, this Master Bumppo is a worthy man, and seems to have a handy way with him, with firearms and boat hooks. I'm his friend, Master Oliver, and he and you may both set me down as the same."

"We may want your friendship, my worthy fellow," cried Edwards, squeezing his hand convulsively. "We may want your friendship, in which case you shall know it."

Without waiting to hear the earnest reply that Benjamin meditated, the youth extricated himself from the vigorous grasp of the steward and entered the parlor.

Elizabeth was alone, and still reclining on the sofa, where we last left her. A hand, which exceeded all that the ingenuity of art could model, in shape and color, veiled her eyes; and the maiden was sitting as if in deep communion with herself. Struck by the attitude and loveliness of the form that met his eye, the young man checked his impatience and approached her with respect and caution.

"Miss Temple—Miss Temple," he said, "I hope I do not intrude; but I am anxious for an interview, if it be only for a moment."

Elizabeth raised her face and exhibited her dark eyes swimming in moisture.

"Is it you, Edwards?" she said, with a sweetness in her

voice, and a softness in her air, that she often used to her father, but which, from its novelty to himself, thrilled on every nerve of the youth. "How left you our poor Louisa?"

"She is with her father, happy and grateful," said Oliver. "I never witnessed more feeling than she manifested when I ventured to express my pleasure at her escape. Miss Temple, when I first heard of your horrid situation, my feelings were too powerful for utterance; and I did not properly find my tongue until the walk to Mr. Grant's had given me time to collect myself. I believe—I do believe, I acquitted myself better there, for Miss Grant even wept at my silly speeches."

For a moment Elizabeth did not reply, but again veiled her eyes with her hand. The feeling that caused the action, however, soon passed away, and, raising her face again to his gaze, she continued, with a smile:

"Your friend, the Leatherstocking, has now become my friend, Edwards; I have been thinking how I can best serve him; perhaps you, who know his habits and his wants so well, can tell me——"

"I can," cried the youth, with an impetuosity that startled his companion—"I can, and may Heaven reward you for the wish. Natty has been so imprudent as to forget the law, and has this day killed a deer. Nay, I believe I must share in the crime and the penalty, for I was an accomplice throughout. A complaint has been made to your father, and he has granted a search——"

"I know it all," interrupted Elizabeth; "I know it all. The forms of the law must be complied with, however; the search must be made, the deer found, and the penalty paid. But I must retort your own question. Have you lived so long in our family not to know us? Look at me, Oliver Edwards. Do I appear like one who would permit the man that has just saved her life to linger in a jail for so small a sum as this fine? No, no, sir; my father is a judge, but he is a man and a Christian. It is all understood, and no harm shall follow."

"What a load of apprehension do your declarations remove!" exclaimed Edwards. "He shall not be disturbed again! Your father will protect him! I have your assurance, Miss Temple, that he will, and I must believe it."

"You may have his own, Mr. Edwards," returned Elizabeth, "for here he comes to make it."

But the appearance of Marmaduke, who entered the apartment, contradicted the flattering anticipations of his daughter. His brow was contracted, and his manner disturbed. Neither Elizabeth nor the youth spoke; but the Judge was allowed to pace once or twice across the room without interruption, when he cried:

"Our plans are defeated, girl; the obstinacy of the Leatherstocking has brought down the indignation of the law on his head, and it is now out of my power to avert it."

"How? In what manner?" cried Elizabeth. "The fine is nothing; surely——"

"I did not—I could not anticipate that an old, a friendless man like him, would dare to oppose the officers of justice," interrupted the Judge. "I supposed that he would submit to the search, when the fine could have been paid, and the law would have been appeased; but now he will have to meet its rigor."

"And what must the punishment be, sir?" asked Edwards, struggling to speak with firmness.

Marmaduke turned quickly to the spot where the youth had withdrawn, and exclaimed:

"You here! I did not observe you. I know not what it will be, sir; it is not usual for a judge to decide until he has heard the testimony, and the jury have convicted. Of one thing, however, you may be assured, Mr. Edwards; it shall be whatever the law demands, notwithstanding any momentary weakness I may have exhibited because the luckless man has been of such eminent service to my daughter."

"No one, I believe, doubts the sense of justice which Judge Temple entertains!" returned Edwards bitterly. "But let us converse calmly, sir. Will not the years, the habits, nay, the ignorance of my old friend, avail him anything against this charge?"

"Ought they? They may extenuate, but can they acquit? Would any society be tolerable, young man, where the ministers of justice are to be opposed by men armed with rifles? Is it for this that I have tamed the wilderness?"

"Had you tamed the beasts that so lately threatened the life of Miss Temple, sir, your arguments would apply better."

"Edwards!" exclaimed Elizabeth.

"Peace, my child," interrupted the father; "the youth is unjust; but I have not given him cause. I overlook thy remark, Oliver, for I know thee to be the friend of Natty, and zeal in his behalf has overcome thy discretion."

"Yes, he is my friend," cried Edwards, "and I glory in the title. He is simple, unlettered, even ignorant; prejudiced, perhaps, though I feel that his opinion of the world is too true; but he has a heart, Judge Temple, that would atone for a thousand faults; he knows his friends, and never deserts them, even if it be his dog."

"This is a good character, Mr. Edwards," returned Marmaduke, mildly; "but I have never been so fortunate as to secure his esteem, for to me he has been uniformly repulsive; yet I have endured it, as an old man's whim. However, when he appears before me, as his judge, he shall find that his former conduct shall not aggravate, any more than his recent services shall extenuate, his crime."

"Crime!" echoed Edwards; "is it a crime to drive a prying miscreant from his door? Crime! Oh, no, sir; if there be a criminal involved in this affair, it is not he."

"And who may it be, sir?" asked Judge Temple, facing the agitated youth, his features settled to their usual composure.

This appeal was more than the young man could bear. Hitherto he had been deeply agitated by his emotions, but now the volcano burst its boundaries.

"Who! and this to me!" he cried. "Ask your own conscience, Judge Temple. Walk to that door, sir, and look out upon the valley, that placid lake, and those dusky mountains, and say to your own heart, if heart you have, Whence came these riches, this vale, those hills, and why am I their owner? I should think, sir, that the appearance of Mohegan and the Leatherstocking, stalking through the country, impoverished and forlorn, would wither your sight."

Marmaduke heard this burst of passion at first with deep amazement: but when the youth had ended, he beckoned to his impatient daughter for silence, and replied:

"Oliver Edwards, thou forgettest in whose presence thou standest. I have heard, young man, that thou claimest descent from the native owners of the soil; but surely thy education has been given thee to no effect, if it has not taught thee the validity of the claims that have transferred the title to the whites. These lands are mine by the very grants of thy ancestry, if thou art so descended; and I appeal to Heaven for a testimony of the uses I have put them to. After this lan-

guage, we must separate. I have too long sheltered thee in
my dwelling; but the time has arrived when thou must quit
it. Come to my office, and I will discharge the debt I owe
thee. Neither shall thy present intemperate language mar thy
future fortunes, if thou wilt hearken to the advice of one
who is by many years thy senior."

The ungovernable feeling that caused the violence of the
youth had passed away, and he stood gazing after the retiring figure of Marmaduke, with a vacancy in his eye that
denoted the absence of his mind. At length he recollected
himself, and, turning his head slowly around the apartment,
he beheld Elizabeth, still seated on the sofa, but with her
head dropped on her bosom, and her face again concealed
by her hands.

"Miss Temple," he said—all violence had left his manner
—"Miss Temple—I have forgotten myself—forgotten you.
You have heard what your father has decreed, and this night
I leave here. With you, at least, I would part in amity."

Elizabeth slowly raised her face, across which a momentary expression of sadness stole; but as she left her seat, her
dark eyes lighted with their usual fire, her cheek flushed to
burning, and her whole air seemed to belong to another
nature.

"I forgive you, Edwards, and my father will forgive you,"
she said, when she reached the door. "You do not know us,
but the time may come when your opinions shall change——"

"Of you! never!" interrupted the youth. "I—"

"I would speak, sir, and not listen. There is something in
this affair that I do not comprehend; but tell the Leatherstocking he has friends as well as judges in us. Do not let
the old man experience unnecessary uneasiness at this rupture. It is impossible that you could increase his claims here;
neither shall they be diminished by anything you have said.
Mr. Edwards, I wish you happiness and warmer friends."

The youth would have spoken, but she vanished from the
door so rapidly that when he reached the hall her form was
nowhere to be seen. He paused a moment, in stupor, and then,
rushing from the house, instead of following Marmaduke to
his "office," he took his way directly for the cabin of the
hunters.

CHAPTER XXXII

Who measured earth, described the starry spheres,
And traced the long records of lunar years. POPE

RICHARD did not return from the exercise of his official duties until late in the evening of the following day. It had been one portion of his business to superintend the arrest of part of a gang of counterfeiters that had, even at that early period, buried themselves in the woods to manufacture their base coin, which they afterwards circulated from one end of the Union to the other. The expedition had been completely successful, and about midnight the Sheriff entered the village at the head of a posse of deputies and constables, in the center of whom rode, pinioned, four of the malefactors. At the gate of the mansion house they separated, Mr. Jones directing his assistants to proceed with their charge to the county jail, while he pursued his own way up the graveled walk, with the kind of self-satisfaction that a man of his organization would feel, who had really, for once, done a very clever thing.

"Holla! Aggy!" shouted the Sheriff when he reached the door. "Where are you, you black dog? Will you keep me here in the dark all night? Holla! Aggy! Brave! Brave! Hoy, hoy —where have you got to, Brave? Off his watch! Everybody is asleep but myself! Poor I must keep my eyes open, that others may sleep in safety. Brave! Brave! Well, I will say this for the dog, lazy as he's grown, that it is the first time I ever knew him let anyone come to the door after dark, without having a smell to know whether it was an honest man or not. He could tell by his nose, almost as well as I could myself by looking at them. Holla! you Agamemnon! Where are you? Oh! here comes the dog at last."

By this time the Sheriff had dismounted and observed a form, which he supposed to be that of Brave, slowly creeping out of the kennel; when, to his astonishment, it reared itself on two legs instead of four, and he was able to distinguish, by the starlight, the curly head and dark visage of the Negro.

"Ha! what the devil are you doing there, you black rascal?" he cried. "Is it not hot enough for your Guinea blood in the house, this warm night, but you must drive out the poor dog and sleep in his straw?"

By this time the boy was quite awake, and, with a blubbering whine, he attempted to reply to his master.

"Oh! Masser Richard! Masser Richard! Such a ting! such a ting! I neber tink a could 'appen! Neber tink he die! Oh, Lor-a-gor! An't bury—keep 'em till masser Richard get back —got a grabe dug——"

Here the feelings of the Negro completely got the mastery, and instead of making any intelligible explanation of the causes of his grief, he blubbered aloud.

"Eh! what! buried! grave! dead!" exclaimed Richard, with a tremor in his voice. "Nothing serious? Nothing has happened to Benjamin, I hope? I know he has been bilious, but I gave him——"

"Oh! worser 'an dat! worser 'an dat!" sobbed the Negro. "Oh! de Lor! Miss 'Lizzy an' Miss Grant—walk—mountain —poor Bravy!—kill a lady—painter—Oh! Lor, Lor!—Natty Bumppo—tare he troat open—come a see, Masser Richard— here he be—here he be."

As all this was perfectly inexplicable to the Sheriff, he was very glad to wait patiently until the black brought a lantern from the kitchen, when he followed Aggy to the kennel, where he beheld poor Brave, indeed, lying in his blood, stiff and cold, but decently covered with the greatcoat of the Negro. He was on the point of demanding an explanation; but the grief of the black, who had fallen asleep on his voluntary watch, having burst out afresh on his waking utterly disqualified the lad from giving one. Luckily, at this moment the principal door of the house opened, and the coarse features of Benjamin were thrust over the threshold, with a candle elevated above them, shedding its dim rays around in such a manner as to exhibit the lights and shadows of his countenance. Richard threw his bridle to the black, and bidding him look to the horse, he entered the hall.

"What is the meaning of the dead dog?" he cried. "Where is Miss Temple?"

Benjamin made one of his square gestures, with the thumb of his left hand pointing over his right shoulder, as he answered:

"Turned in."

"Judge Temple—where is he?"

"In his berth."

"But explain; why is Brave dead? And what is the cause of Aggy's grief?"

"Why, it's all down, Squire," said Benjamin, pointing to a slate that lay on the table by the side of a mug of toddy, a short pipe in which the tobacco was yet burning, and a prayer book.

Among the other pursuits of Richard, he had a passion to keep a register of all passing events; and his diary, which was written in the manner of a journal, or logbook, embraced not only such circumstances as affected himself, but observations on the weather, and all the occurrences of the family, and frequently of the village. Since his appointment to the office of Sheriff, and his consequent absences from home, he had employed Benjamin to make memoranda on a slate of whatever might be thought worth remembering, which, on his return, were regularly transferred to the journal with proper notations of the time, manner, and other little particulars. There was, to be sure, one material objection to the clerkship of Benjamin which the ingenuity of no one but Richard could have overcome. The steward read nothing but his prayer book, and that only in particular parts, and by the aid of a good deal of spelling and some misnomers; but he could not form a single letter with a pen. This would have been an insuperable bar to journalizing, with most men; but Richard invented a kind of hieroglyphical character, which was intended to note all the ordinary occurrences of a day, such as how the wind blew, whether the sun shone, or whether it rained, the hours, etc.; and for the extraordinary, after giving certain elementary lectures on the subject, the Sheriff was obliged to trust to the ingenuity of the major-domo. The reader will at once perceive that it was to this chronicle that Benjamin pointed, instead of directly answering the Sheriff's interrogatory.

When Mr. Jones had drunk a glass of toddy, he brought forth from its secret place his proper journal, and, seating himself by the table, he prepared to transfer the contents of the slate to the paper, at the same time that he appeased his curiosity. Benjamin laid one hand on the back of the Sheriff's chair, in a familiar manner, while he kept the other at liberty to make use of a forefinger, that was bent like some of his own characters, as an index to point out his meaning.

The first thing referred to by the Sheriff was the diagram of a compass, cut in one corner of the slate for permanent use. The cardinal points were plainly marked on it, and all the usual divisions were indicated in such a manner that no man who had ever steered a ship could mistake them.

"Oh!" said the Sheriff, settling himself down comfortably in his chair—"you'd the wind southeast, I see, all last night; I thought it would have blown up rain."

"Devil the drop, sir," said Benjamin; "I believe that the scuttle butt up aloft is emptied, for there hasn't so much water fell in the country for the last three weeks as would float Indian John's canoe, and that draws just one inch nothing, light."

"Well, but didn't the wind change here this morning? There was a change where I was."

"To be sure it did, Squire; and haven't I logged it as a shift of wind."

"I don't see where, Benjamin——"

"Don't see!" interrupted the steward, a little crustily. "An't there a mark ag'in east-and-by-nothe-half-nothe, with sum'mat like a rising sun at the end of it, to show 'twas in the morning watch?"

"Yes, yes, that is very legible; but where is the change noted?"

"Where! why doesn't it see this here teakettle, with a mark run from the spout straight, or mayhap a little crooked or so, into west-and-by-southe-half-southe? Now I call this a shift of wind, Squire. Well, do you see this here boar's head that you made for me, alongside of the compass——"

"Ay, ay—Boreas—I see. Why you've drawn lines from its mouth, extending from one of your marks to the other."

"It's no fault of mine, Squire Dickens; 'tis your d—d climate. The wind has been at all them there marks this very day; and that's all round the compass, except a little matter of an Irishman's hurricane at meridium, which you'll find marked right up and down. Now, I've known a souwester blow for three weeks, in the channel, with a clean drizzle in which you might wash your face and hands without the trouble of hauling in water from alongside."

"Very well, Benjamin," said the Sheriff, writing in his

journal; "I believe I have caught the idea. Oh! here's a cloud over the rising sun—so you had it hazy in the morning?"

"Ay, ay, sir," said Benjamin.

"Ah! it's Sunday, and here are the marks for the length of the sermon—one, two, three, four—what! did Mr. Grant preach forty minutes?"

"Ay, sum'mat like it; it was a good half-hour by my own glass, and then there was the time lost in turning it, and some little allowance for leeway in not being oversmart about it."

"Benjamin, this is as long as a Presbyterian; you never could have been ten minutes in turning the glass!"

"Why, do you see, Squire, the parson was very solemn, and I just closed my eyes in order to think the better with myself, just the same as you'd put in the deadlights to make all snug, and when I opened them ag'in I found the congregation were getting under weigh for home, so I calculated the ten minutes would cover the leeway after the glass was out. It was only some such matter as a cat's nap."

"Oh, ho! master Benjamin, you were asleep, were you! But I'll set down no such slander against an orthodox divine." Richard wrote twenty-nine minutes in his journal, and continued—"Why, what's this you've got opposite ten o'clock A.M.? A full moon! Had you a moon visible by day! I have heard of such portents before now, but—eh! what's this alongside of it? An hourglass?"

"That!" said Benjamin, looking coolly over the Sheriff's shoulder, and rolling the tobacco about in his mouth with a jocular air; "why, that's a small matter of my own. It's no moon, Squire, but only Betty Hollister's face; for, d'ye see, sir, hearing all the same as if she had got up a new cargo of Jamaiky from the river, I called in as I was going to the church this morning—ten A.M. was it?—just the time—and tried a glass; and so I logged it, to put me in mind of calling to pay her like an honest man."

"That was it, was it?" said the Sheriff, with some displeasure at this innovation on his memoranda. "And could you not make a better glass than this? It looks like a death's head and an hourglass."

"Why, as I liked the stuff, Squire," returned the steward, "I turned in, homeward bound, and took t'other glass, which I set down at the bottom of the first, and that gives the thing the shape it has. But as I was there again tonight and paid for the three at once, your honor may as well run the sponge over the whole business."

"I will buy you a slate for your own affairs, Benjamin," said the Sheriff; "I don't like to have the journal marked over in this manner."

"You needn't—you needn't, Squire; for seeing that I was likely to trade often with the woman while this barrel lasted, I've opened a fair account with Betty, and she keeps her marks on the back of her bar door, and I keeps the tally on this here bit of a stick."

As Benjamin concluded he produced a piece of wood on which five very large, honest notches were apparent. The Sheriff cast his eyes on this new ledger for a moment, and continued:

"What have we here! Saturday, two P.M.—why here's a whole family piece! Two wine glasses upside down!"

"That's two women; the one this-a-way is Miss 'Lizzy, and t'other is the parson's young'un."

"Cousin Bess and Miss Grant!" exclaimed the Sheriff in amazement. "What have they to do with my journal?"

"They'd enough to do to get out of the jaws of that there painter, or panther," said the immovable steward.

"This here thingum'y, Squire, that maybe looks sum'mat like a rat, is the beast, d'ye see; and this here t'other thing, keel uppermost, is poor old Brave, who died nobly, all the same as an admiral fighting for his king and country: and that there——"

"Scarecrow," interrupted Richard.

"Ay, mayhap it do look a little wild or so," continued the steward; "but to my judgment, Squire, it's the best image I've made, seeing it's most like the man himself—well, that's Natty Bumppo, who shot this here painter, that killed that there dog, who would have eaten or done worse to them here young ladies."

"And what the devil does all this mean?" cried Richard, impatiently.

"Mean!" echoed Benjamin; "it is as true as the Boadishey's logbook——"

He was interrupted by the Sheriff, who put a few direct questions to him that obtained more intelligible answers, by which means he became possessed of a tolerably correct idea of the truth. When the wonder and, we must do Richard the justice to say, the feelings also that were created by this narrative had in some degree subsided, the Sheriff turned his eyes again on his journal, where more inexplicable hieroglyphics met his view.

"What have we here!" he cried. "Two men boxing! Has there been a breach of the peace? Ah, that's the way, the moment my back is turned——"

"That's the Judge and young Master Edwards," interrupted the steward, very cavalierly.

"How! 'duke fighting with Oliver! What the devil has got into you all? More things have happened within the last thirty-six hours than in the preceding six months."

"Yes, it's so indeed, Squire," returned the steward; "I've known a smart chase, and a fight at the tail of it, where less has been logged than I've got on that there slate. Howsomnever, they didn't come to facers, only passed a little jaw fore and aft."

"Explain! explain!" cried Richard. "It was about the mines, ha!—ay, ay, I see it, I see it; here is a man with a pick on his shoulder. So you heard it all, Benjamin?"

"Why, yes, it was about their minds, I believe, Squire," returned the steward; "and by what I can learn, they spoke them pretty plainly to one another. Indeed, I may say that I overheard a small matter of it myself, seeing that the windows was open, and I hard by. But this here is no pick, but an anchor on a man's shoulder; and here's the other fluke down his back, maybe a little too close, which signifies that the lad has got under weigh and left his moorings."

"Has Edwards left the house?"

"He has."

Richard pursued this advantage; and, after a long and close examination, he succeeded in getting out of Benjamin all that he knew not only concerning the misunderstanding but of the attempt to search the hut and Hiram's discomfiture. The Sheriff was no sooner possessed of these facts, which Benjamin related with all possible tenderness to the Leatherstocking, than, snatching up his hat and bidding the astonished steward secure the doors and go to his bed, he left the house.

For at least five minutes after Richard disappeared, Benjamin stood with his arms akimbo and his eyes fastened on the door; when, having collected his astonished faculties, he prepared to execute the orders he had received.

It has been already said that the "court of common pleas and general sessions of the peace" or, as it is commonly called, the "county court," over which Judge Temple presided, held one of its stated sessions on the following morning. The attendants of Richard were officers who had come to the village, as much to discharge their usual duties at this court as to escort the prisoners; and the Sheriff knew their habits too well not to feel confident he should find most, if not all of them, in the public room of the jail, discussing the qualities of the keeper's liquors. Accordingly, he held his way through the silent streets of the village, directly to the small and insecure building that contained all the unfortunate debtors, and some of the criminals of the county, and where justice was administered to such unwary applicants as were so silly as to throw away two dollars in order to obtain one from their neighbors. The arrival of four malefactors in the custody of a dozen officers was an event, at that day, in Templeton; and when the Sheriff reached the jail, he found every indication that his subordinates intended to make a night of it.

The nod of the Sheriff brought two of his deputies to the door, who in their turn drew off six or seven of the constables. With this force Richard led the way through the village towards the bank of the lake, undisturbed by any noise, except the barking of one or two curs, who were alarmed by the measured tread of the party, and by the low murmurs that ran through their own numbers, as a few cautious questions and answers were exchanged, relative to the object of their expedition. When they had crossed the little bridge of hewn logs that was thrown over the Susquehanna, they left the highway and struck into that field which had been the scene of the victory over the pigeons. From this they followed their leader into the low bushes of pines and chestnuts which had sprung up along the shores of the lake, where the plow had not succeeded the fall of the trees, and soon entered the forest itself. Here Richard paused and collected his troop around him.

"I have required your assistance, my friends," he said, in a low voice, "in order to arrest Nathaniel Bumppo, commonly called the Leatherstocking. He has assaulted a magistrate

and resisted the execution of a search warrant by threatening
the life of a constable with his rifle. In short, my friends, he
has set an example of rebellion to the laws, and has become
a kind of outlaw. He is suspected of other misdemeanors
and offenses against private rights; and I have this night taken
on myself, by the virtue of my office of Sheriff, to arrest the
said Bumppo and bring him to the county jail, that he may
be present and forthcoming to answer to these heavy charges
before the court tomorrow morning. In executing this duty,
friends and fellow citizens, you are to use courage and discretion. Courage, that you may not be daunted by any lawless
attempts that this man may make with his rifle and his dogs
to oppose you; and discretion, which here means caution
and prudence, that he may not escape from this sudden attack—and for other good reasons that I need not mention.
You will form yourselves in a complete circle around his hut,
and at the word 'advance,' called aloud by me, you will rush
forward and, without giving the criminal time for deliberation, enter his dwelling by force and make him your prisoner.
Spread yourselves for this purpose, while I shall descend to
the shore with a deputy to take charge of that point; and all
communications must be made directly to me, under the bank
in front of the hut, where I shall station myself and remain
in order to receive them."

This speech, which Richard had been studying during his
walk, had the effect that all similar performances produce, of
bringing the dangers of the expedition immediately before
the eyes of his forces. The men divided, some plunging
deeper into the forest in order to gain their stations without
giving an alarm, and others continuing to advance at a gait
that would allow the whole party to go in order: but all de-
vising the best plan to repulse the attack of a dog, or to escape a rifle bullet. It was a moment of dread expectation and
interest.

When the Sheriff thought time enough had elapsed for
the different divisions of his force to arrive at their stations,
he raised his voice in the silence of the forest and shouted
the watchword. The sounds played among the arched
branches of the trees in hollow cadences; but when the last
sinking tone was lost on the ear, in place of the expected
howls of the dogs, no other noises were returned but the
crackling of torn branches and dried sticks as they yielded

before the advancing steps of the officers. Even this soon
ceased, as if by a common consent, when the curiosity and
impatience of the Sheriff getting the complete ascendency
over discretion, he rushed up the bank, and in a moment
stood on the little piece of cleared ground in front of the
spot where Natty had so long lived. To his amazement, in
place of the hut he saw only its smoldering ruins.

The party gradually drew together about the heap of ashes
and the ends of smoking logs; while a dim flame in the center of the ruin, which still found fuel to feed its lingering
life, threw its pale light, flickering with the passing currents
of the air, around the circle, now showing a face with eyes
fixed in astonishment, and then glancing to another countenance, leaving the former shaded in the obscurity of night.
Not a voice was raised in inquiry, nor an exclamation made
in astonishment. The transition from excitement to disappointment was too powerful for speech: and even Richard
lost the use of an organ that was seldom known to fail him.

The whole group were yet in the fullness of their surprise
when a tall form stalked from the gloom into the circle,
treading down the hot ashes and dying embers with callous
feet; and standing over the light, lifted his cap, and exposed
the bare head and weather-beaten features of the Leatherstocking. For a moment he gazed at the dusky figures who
surrounded him, more in sorrow than in anger, before he
spoke.

"What would ye with an old and helpless man?" he said.
"You've driven God's creaters from the wilderness, where his
providence had put them for his own pleasure: and you've
brought in the troubles and divilties of the law, where no man
was ever known to disturb another. You have driven me, that
have lived forty long years of my appointed time in this very
spot, from my home and the shelter of my head, lest you
should put your wicked feet and wasty ways in my cabin.
You've driven me to burn these logs under which I've eaten
and drunk—the first of Heaven's gifts, and the other of the
pure springs—for the half of a hundred years; and to mourn
the ashes under my feet, as a man would weep and mourn
for the children of his body. You've rankled the heart of an
old man, that has never harmed you or you'rn, with bitter
feelings towards his kind, at a time when his thoughts should
be on a better world; and you've driven him to wish that the

beasts of the forest, who never feast on the blood of their own families, was his kindred and race: and now, when he has come to see the last brand of his hut, before it is melted into ashes, you follow him up, at midnight, like hungry hounds on the track of a worn-out and dying deer. What more would ye have? For I am here—one too many. I come to mourn, not to fight; and, if it is God's pleasure, work your will on me."

When the old man ended, he stood, with the light glimmering around his thinly covered head, looking earnestly at the group, which receded from the pile with an involuntary movement, without the reach of the quivering rays, leaving a free passage for his retreat into the bushes, where pursuit, in the dark, would have been fruitless. Natty seemed not to regard this advantage; but stood facing each individual in the circle in succession, as if to see who would be the first to arrest him. After a pause of a few moments, Richard began to rally his confused faculties; and, advancing, apologized for his duty and made him his prisoner. The party now collected; and, preceded by the Sheriff, with Natty in their center, they took their way towards the village.

During the walk, divers questions were put to the prisoner concerning his reasons for burning the hut, and whither Mohegan had retreated; but to all of them he observed a profound silence, until, fatigued with their previous duties and the lateness of the hour, the Sheriff and his followers reached the village and dispersed to their several places of rest, after turning the key of a jail on the aged and apparently friendless Leatherstocking.

Chapter XXXIII

Fetch here the stocks, ho!
You stubborn ancient knave, you reverend braggart
We'll teach you.   Lear

The long days and early sun of July allowed time for a gathering of the interested before the little bell of the academy announced that the appointed hour had arrived for ad-

ministering right to the wronged, and punishment to the
guilty. Ever since the dawn of day, the highways and wood-
paths that, issuing from the forests, and winding along the
sides of the mountains, centered in Templeton, had been
thronged with equestrians and footmen bound to the haven
of justice. There was to be seen a well-clad yeoman, mounted
on a sleek, switch-tailed steed, ambling along the highway,
with his red face elevated in a manner that said, "I have
paid for my land, and fear no man," while his bosom was
swelling with the pride of being one of the grand inquest for
the county. At his side rode a companion, his equal in independence of feeling, perhaps, but his inferior in thrift, as
in property and consideration. This was a professed dealer
in lawsuits—a man whose name appeared in every calendar
—whose substance, gained in the multifarious expedients of
a settler's changeable habits, was wasted in feeding the
harpies of the courts. He was endeavoring to impress the
mind of the grand juror with the merits of a cause now at
issue. Along with these was a pedestrian, who, having thrown
a rifle frock over his shirt and placed his best wool hat above
his sunburned visage, had issued from his retreat in the
woods by a footpath and was striving to keep company with
the others, on his way to hear and to decide the disputes of
his neighbors as a petit juror. Fifty similar little knots of
countrymen might have been seen, on that morning, journeying towards the shire town on the same errand.

By ten o'clock the streets of the village were filled with
busy faces; some talking of their private concerns, some listening to a popular expounder of political creeds; and others
gaping in at the open stores, admiring the finery, or examining
scythes, axes, and such other manufactures as attracted their
curiosity or excited their admiration. A few women were in
the crowd, most carrying infants, and followed, at a lounging,
listless gait, by their rustic lords and masters. There was one
young couple, in whom connubial love was yet fresh, walking at a respectful distance from each other; while the swain
directed the timid steps of his bride by a gallant offering of
a thumb!

At the first stroke of the bell, Richard issued from the door
of the "Bold Dragoon," flourishing a sheathed sword that he
was fond of saying his ancestors had carried in one of
Cromwell's victories and crying, in an authoritative tone, to

"clear the way for the court." The order was obeyed promptly, though not servilely, the members of the crowd nodding familiarly to the members of the procession as it passed. A party of constables with their staves followed the Sheriff, preceding Marmaduke and four plain, grave-looking yeomen, who were his associates on the bench. There was nothing to distinguish these subordinate judges from the better part of the spectators except gravity, which they affected a little more than common, and that one of their number was attired in an old-fashioned military coat, with skirts that reached no lower than the middle of his thighs and bearing two little silver epaulets, not half so big as a modern pair of shoulder knots. This gentleman was a colonel of the militia, in attendance on a court-martial, who found leisure to steal a moment from his military to attend to his civil jurisdiction; but this incongruity excited neither notice nor comment. Three or four clean-shaven lawyers followed, as meekly as if they were lambs going to the slaughter. One or two of their number had contrived to obtain an air of scholastic gravity by wearing spectacles. The rear was brought up by another posse of constables, and the mob followed the whole into the room where the court held its sittings.

The edifice was composed of a basement of squared logs, perforated here and there with small grated windows, through which a few wistful faces were gazing at the crowd without. Among the captives were the guilty, downcast countenances of the counterfeiters, and the simple but honest features of the Leatherstocking. The dungeons were to be distinguished, externally, from the debtors' apartments only by the size of the apertures, the thickness of the grates, and by the heads of the spikes that were driven into the logs as a protection against the illegal use of edge tools. The upper story was of framework, regularly covered with boards, and contained one room decently fitted up for the purposes of justice. A bench, raised on a narrow platform to the height of a man above the floor, and protected in front by a light railing, ran along one of its sides. In the center was a seat, furnished with rude arms, that was always filled by the presiding judge. In front, on a level with the floor of the room, was a large table covered with green baize and surrounded by benches; and at either of its ends were rows of seats, rising one over the other, for jury boxes. Each of these divisions was surrounded by a railing. The remainder of the room was an open square, appropriated to the spectators.

When the judges were seated, the lawyers had taken possession of the table, and the noise of moving feet had ceased in the area, the proclamations were made in the usual form, the jurors were sworn, the charge was given, and the court proceeded to hear the business before them.

We shall not detain the reader with a description of the captious discussions that occupied the court for the first two hours. Judge Temple had impressed on the jury, in his charge, the necessity for dispatch on their part, recommending to their notice, from motives of humanity, the prisoners in the jail as the first objects of their attention. Accordingly, after the period we have mentioned had elapsed, the cry of the officer to "clear the way for the grand jury" announced the entrance of that body. The usual forms were observed, when the foreman handed up to the bench two bills, on both of which the Judge observed, at the first glance of his eye, the name of Nathaniel Bumppo. It was a leisure moment with the court; some low whispering passed between the bench and the Sheriff, who gave a signal to his officers, and in a very few minutes the silence that prevailed was interrupted by a general movement in the outer crowd; when presently the Leatherstocking made his appearance, ushered into the criminal's bar under the custody of two constables. The hum ceased, the people closed into the open space again, and the silence soon became so deep that the hard breathing of the prisoner was audible.

Natty was dressed in his buckskin garments, without his coat, in place of which he wore only a shirt of coarse linen check, fastened at his throat by the sinew of a deer, leaving his red neck and weather-beaten face exposed and bare. It was the first time that he had ever crossed the threshold of a court of justice, and curiosity seemed to be strongly blended with his personal feelings. He raised his eyes to the bench, thence to the jury boxes, the bar, and the crowd without, meeting everywhere looks fastened on himself. After surveying his own person, as searching the cause of this unusual attraction, he once more turned his face around the assemblage, and opened his mouth in one of his silent and remarkable laughs.

"Prisoner, remove your cap," said Judge Temple.

The order was either unheard or unheeded.

"Nathaniel Bumppo, be uncovered," repeated the Judge.

Natty started at the sound of his name, and raising his face earnestly towards the bench, he said:

"Anan!"

Mr. Lippet arose from his seat at the table and whispered in the ear of the prisoner; when Natty gave him a nod of assent and took the deerskin covering from his head.

"Mr. District Attorney," said the Judge, "the prisoner is ready; we wait for the indictment."

The duties of public prosecutor were discharged by Dirck Van der School, who adjusted his spectacles, cast a cautious look around him at his brethren of the bar, which he ended by throwing his head aside so as to catch one glance over the glasses, when he proceeded to read the bill aloud. It was the usual charge for an assault and battery on the person of Hiram Doolittle and was couched in the ancient language of such instruments, especial care having been taken by the scribe not to omit the name of a single offensive weapon known to the law. When he had done, Mr. Van der School removed his spectacles, which he closed and placed in his pocket, seemingly for the pleasure of again opening and replacing them on his nose. After this evolution was repeated once or twice, he handed the bill over to Mr. Lippet with a cavalier air that said as much as "Pick a hole in that if you can."

Natty listened to the charge with great attention, leaning forward towards the reader with an earnestness that denoted his interest; and when it was ended, he raised his tall body to the utmost and drew a long sigh. All eyes were turned to the prisoner, whose voice was vainly expected to break the stillness of the room.

"You have heard the presentment that the grand jury have made, Nathaniel Bumppo," said the Judge. "What do you plead to the charge?"

The old man dropped his head for a moment in a reflecting attitude, and then raising it, he laughed before he answered:

"That I handled the man a little rough or so is not to be denied; but that there was occasion to make use of all the things that the gentleman has spoken of, is downright untrue. I am not much of a wrestler, seeing that I'm getting old;

but I was out among the Scotch-Irishers—let me see—it must have been as long ago as the first year of the old war——"

"Mr. Lippet, if you are retained for the prisoner," interrupted Judge Temple, "instruct your client how to plead; if not, the court will assign him counsel."

Aroused from studying the indictment by this appeal, the attorney got up, and after a short dialogue with the hunter in a low voice, he informed the court that they were ready to proceed.

"Do you plead guilty or not guilty?" said the Judge.

"I may say not guilty with a clean conscience," returned Natty; "for there's no guilt in doing what's right; and I'd rather died on the spot, than had him put foot in the hut at that moment."

Richard started at this declaration and bent his eyes significantly on Hiram, who returned the look with a slight movement of his eyebrows.

"Proceed to open the cause, Mr. District Attorney," continued the Judge. "Mr. Clerk, enter the plea of not guilty."

After a short opening address from Mr. Van der School, Hiram was summoned to the bar to give his testimony. It was delivered to the letter, perhaps, but with all that moral coloring which can be conveyed under such expressions as "thinking no harm," "feeling it my bounden duty as a magistrate," and "seeing that the constable was back'ard in the business." When he had done, and the district attorney declined putting any further interrogatories, Mr. Lippet arose, with an air of keen investigation, and asked the following questions:

"Are you a constable of this county, sir?"

"No, sir," said Hiram, "I'm only a justice-peace."

"I ask you, Mr. Doolittle, in the face of this court, putting it to your conscience and your knowledge of the law, whether you had any right to enter that man's dwelling?"

"Hem!" said Hiram, undergoing a violent struggle between his desire for vengeance and his love of legal fame; "I do suppose—that in—that is—strict law—that supposing—maybe I hadn't a real—lawful right;—but as the case was—and Billy was so back'ard—I thought I might come for'ard in the business."

"I ask you again, sir," continued the lawyer, following up

his success, "whether this old, this friendless old man, did or did not repeatedly forbid your entrance?"

"Why, I must say," said Hiram, "that he was considerable cross-grained; not what I call clever, seeing that it was only one neighbor wanting to go into the house of another."

"Oh! then you own it was only meant for a neighborly visit on your part, and without the sanction of law. Remember, gentlemen, the words of the witness, 'one neighbor wanting to enter the house of another.' Now, sir, I ask you if Nathaniel Bumppo did not again and again order you not to enter?"

"There was some words passed between us," said Hiram, "but I read the warrant to him aloud."

"I repeat my question; did he tell you not to enter his habitation?"

"There was a good deal passed betwixt us—but I've the warrant in my pocket; maybe the court would wish to see it?"

"Witness," said Judge Temple, "answer the question directly; did or did not the prisoner forbid your entering his hut?"

"Why, I some think——"

"Answer without equivocation," continued the Judge, sternly.

"He did."

"And did you attempt to enter after this order?"

"I did; but the warrant was in my hand."

"Proceed, Mr. Lippet, with your examination."

But the attorney saw that the impression was in favor of his client, and, waving his hand with a supercilious manner, as if unwilling to insult the understanding of the jury with any further defense, he replied:

"No, sir; I leave it for your honor to charge; I rest my case here."

"Mr. District Attorney," said the Judge, "have you anything to say?"

Mr. Van der School removed his spectacles, folded them, and replacing them once more on his nose, eyed the other bill which he held in his hand, and then said, looking at the bar over the top of his glasses:

"I shall rest the prosecution here, if the court please."

Judge Temple arose and began the charge.

"Gentlemen of the jury," he said, "you have heard the testimony, and I shall detain you but a moment. If an officer meet with resistance in the execution of a process, he has an undoubted right to call any citizen to his assistance; and the acts of such assistant come within the protection of the law. I shall leave you to judge, gentlemen, from the testimony, how far the witness in this prosecution can be so considered, feeling less reluctance to submit the case thus informally to your decision, because there is yet another indictment to be tried, which involves heavier charges against the unfortunate prisoner."

The tone of Marmaduke was mild and insinuating, and as his sentiments were given with such apparent impartiality, they did not fail of carrying due weight with the jury. The grave-looking yeomen who composed this tribunal laid their heads together for a few minutes, without leaving the box, when the foreman arose, and after the forms of the court were duly observed, he pronounced the prisoner to be:

"Not guilty."

"You are acquitted of this charge, Nathaniel Bumppo," said the Judge.

"Anan!" said Natty.

"You are found not guilty of striking and assaulting Mr. Doolittle."

"No, no, I'll not deny but that I took him a little roughly by the shoulders," said Natty, looking about him with great simplicity, "and that I——"

"You are acquitted," interrupted the Judge, "and there is nothing further to be said or done in the matter."

A look of joy lighted up the features of the old man, who now comprehended the case, and placing his cap eagerly on his head again, he threw up the bar of his little prison and said feelingly:

"I must say this for you, Judge Temple, that the law has not been so hard on me as I dreaded. I hope God will bless you for the kind things you've done to me this day."

But the staff of the constable was opposed to his egress, and Mr. Lippet whispered a few words in his ear, when the aged hunter sank back into his place, and, removing his cap, stroked down the remnants of his gray and sandy locks, with an air of mortification mingled with submission.

"Mr. District Attorney," said Judge Temple, affecting to

busy himself with his minutes, "proceed with the second indictment."

Mr. Van der School took great care that no part of the presentment, which he now read, should be lost on his auditors. It accused the prisoner of resisting the execution of a search warrant by force of arms and particularized, in the vague language of the law, among a variety of other weapons, the use of the rifle. This was indeed a more serious charge than an ordinary assault and battery, and a corresponding degree of interest was manifested by the spectators in its result. The prisoner was duly arraigned, and his plea again demanded. Mr. Lippet had anticipated the answers of Natty, and in a whisper advised him how to plead. But the feelings of the old hunter were awakened by some of the expressions of the indictment, and, forgetful of his caution, he exclaimed:

" 'Tis a wicked untruth; I crave no man's blood. Them thieves, the Iroquois, won't say it to my face, that I ever thirsted after man's blood. I have fou't as a soldier that feared his Maker and his officer, but I never pulled trigger on any but a warrior that was up and awake. No man can say that I ever struck even a Mingo in his blanket. I believe there's some who thinks there's no God in a wilderness!"

"Attend to your plea, Bumppo," said the Judge; "you hear that you are accused of using your rifle against an officer of justice? Are you guilty or not guilty?"

By this time the irritated feelings of Natty had found vent; and he rested on the bar for a moment, in a musing posture, when he lifted his face, with his silent laugh, and, pointing to where the wood chopper stood, he said:

"Would Billy Kirby be standing there, d'ye think, if I had used the rifle?"

"Then you deny it," said Mr. Lippet; "you plead not guilty?"

"Sartain," said Natty; "Billy knows that I never fired at all. Billy, do you remember the turkey last winter? Ah! me! That was better than common firing; but I can't shoot as I used to could."

"Enter the plea of not guilty," said Judge Temple, strongly affected by the simplicity of the prisoner.

Hiram was again sworn, and his testimony given on the second charge. He had discovered his former error and proceeded more cautiously than before. He related very distinctly, and for the man, with amazing terseness, the suspicion against the hunter, the complaint, the issuing of the warrant, and the swearing in of Kirby; all of which, he affirmed, were done in due form of law. He then added the manner in which the constable had been received; and stated distinctly that Natty had pointed the rifle at Kirby and threatened his life if he attempted to execute his duty. All this was confirmed by Jotham, who was observed to adhere closely to the story of the magistrate. Mr. Lippet conducted an artful cross-examination of these two witnesses, but after consuming much time, was compelled to relinquish the attempt to obtain any advantage, in despair.

At length the district attorney called the wood chopper to the bar. Billy gave an extremely confused account of the whole affair, although he evidently aimed at the truth, until Mr. Van der School aided him by asking some direct questions:

"It appears from examining the papers that you demanded admission into the hut legally; so you were put in bodily fear by his rifle and threats?"

"I didn't mind them that, man," said Billy, snapping his fingers; "I should be a poor stick to mind old Leatherstocking."

"But I understood you to say (referring to your previous words (as delivered here in court) in the commencement of your testimony) that you thought he meant to shoot you?"

"To be sure I did; and so would you too, Squire, if you had seen the chap dropping a muzzle that never misses, and cocking an eye that has a natural squint by long practice. I thought there would be a dust on't, and my back was up at once; but Leatherstocking gi'n up the skin, and so the matter ended."

"Ah! Billy," said Natty, shaking his head, "'twas a lucky thought in me to throw out the hide, or there might have been blood spilt; and I'm sure, if it had been yourn, I should have mourn'd it sorely the little while I have to stay."

"Well, Leatherstocking," returned Billy, facing the prisoner with a freedom and familiarity that utterly disregarded the presence of the court, "as you are on the subject, it may be that you've no——"

"Go on with your examination, Mr. District Attorney."

That gentleman eyed the familiarity between his witness and the prisoner with manifest disgust, and indicated to the court that he was done.

"Then you didn't feel frightened, Mr. Kirby?" said the counsel for the prisoner.

"Me! no," said Billy, casting his eyes over his own huge frame with evident self-satisfaction; "I'm not to be skeared so easy."

"You look like a hardy man; where were you born, sir?"

"Varmount state; 'tis a mountaynious place, but there's a stiff soil, and it's pretty much wooded with beech and maple."

"I have always heard so," said Mr. Lippet, soothingly. "You have been used to the rifle yourself, in that country?"

"I pull the second-best trigger in this county. I knock under to Natty Bumppo there, sin' he shot the pigeon."

Leatherstocking raised his head and laughed again, when he abruptly thrust out a wrinkled hand and said:

"You're young yet, Billy, and hav'n't seen the matches that I have; but here's my hand; I bear no malice to you, I don't."

Mr. Lippet allowed this conciliatory offering to be accepted, and judiciously paused, while the spirit of peace was exercising its influence over the two; but the Judge interposed his authority.

"This is an improper place for such dialogues," he said. "Proceed with your examination of this witness, Mr. Lippet, or I shall order the next."

The attorney started, as if unconscious of any impropriety, and continued:

"So you settled the matter with Natty amicably on the spot, did you?"

"He gi'n me the skin, and I didn't want to quarrel with an old man; for my part, I see no such mighty matter in shooting a buck!"

"And you parted friends? And you would never have thought of bringing the business up before a court, hadn't you been subpoenaed?"

"I don't think I should; he gi'n the skin, and I didn't feel a hard thought, though Squire Doolittle got some affronted."

"I have done, sir," said Mr. Lippet, probably relying on

the charge of the Judge, as he again seated himself, with the air of a man who felt that his success was certain.

When Mr. Van der School arose to address the jury, he commenced by saying:

"Gentlemen of the jury, I should have interrupted the leading questions put by the prisoner's counsel (by leading questions I mean telling him what to say), did I not feel confident that the law of the land was superior to any advantages (I mean legal advantages) which he might obtain by his art. The counsel for the prisoner, gentlemen, has endeavored to persuade you, in opposition to your own good sense, to believe that pointing a rifle at a constable (elected or deputed) is a very innocent affair; and that society (I mean the commonwealth, gentlemen) shall not be endangered thereby. But let me claim your attention while we look over the particulars of this heinous offense." Here Mr. Van der School favored the jury with an abridgment of the testimony, recounted in such a manner as utterly to confuse the faculties of his worthy listeners. After this exhibition he closed as follows: "And now, gentlemen, having thus made plain to your senses the crime of which this unfortunate man has been guilty (unfortunate both on account of his ignorance and his guilt), I shall leave you to your own consciences; not in the least doubting that you will see the importance (notwithstanding the prisoner's counsel (doubtless relying on your former verdict) wishes to appear so confident of success) of punishing the offender, and asserting the dignity of the laws."

It was now the duty of the Judge to deliver his charge. It consisted of a short, comprehensive summary of the testimony, laying bare the artifice of the prisoner's counsel, and placing the facts in so obvious a light that they could not well be misunderstood. "Living as we do, gentlemen," he concluded, "on the skirts of society, it becomes doubly necessary to protect the ministers of the law. If you believe the witnesses, in their construction of the acts of the prisoner, it is your duty to convict him; but if you believe that the old man, who this day appears before you, meant not to harm the constable, but was acting more under the influence of habit than by the instigations of malice, it will be your duty to judge him, but to do it with lenity."

As before, the jury did not leave their box; but, after a

consultation of some little time, their foreman arose and pronounced the prisoner:

"Guilty."

There was but little surprise manifested in the courtroom at this verdict, as the testimony, the greater part of which we have omitted, was too clear and direct to be passed over. The judges seemed to have anticipated this sentiment, for a consultation was passing among them also, during the deliberation of the jury, and the preparatory movements of the "bench" announced the coming sentence.

"Nathaniel Bumppo," commenced the Judge, making the customary pause.

The old hunter, who had been musing again, with his head on the bar, raised himself and cried, with a prompt, military tone:

"Here."

The Judge waved his hand for silence, and proceeded:

"In forming their sentence, the court have been governed as much by the consideration of your ignorance of the laws as by a strict sense of the importance of punishing such outrages as this of which you have been found guilty. They have therefore passed over the obvious punishment of whipping on the bare back, in mercy to your years; but as the dignity of the law requires an open exhibition of the consequences of your crime, it is ordered that you be conveyed from this room to the public stocks, where you are to be confined for one hour: that you pay a fine to the state of one hundred dollars; and that you be imprisoned in the jail of this county for one calendar month, and, furthermore, that your imprisonment do not cease until the said fine shall be paid. I feel it my duty, Nathaniel Bumppo——"

"And where should I get the money?" interrupted the Leatherstocking, eagerly; "where should I get the money? You'll take away the bounty on the painters because I cut the throat of a deer; and how is an old man to find so much gold or silver in the woods? No, no, Judge: think better of it, and don't talk of shutting me up in a jail for the little time I have to stay."

"If you have anything to urge against the passing of the sentence, the court will yet hear you," said the Judge, mildly.

"I have enough to say ag'in it," cried Natty, grasping the bar on which his fingers were working with a convulsed motion. "Where am I to get the money? Let me out into the woods and hills, where I've been used to breathe the clean air, and though I'm threescore and ten, if you've left game enough in the country, I'll travel night and day but I'll make you up the sum afore the season is over. Yes, yes— you see the reason of the thing, and the wickedness of shutting up an old man that has spent his days, as one may say, where he could always look into the windows of heaven."

"I must be governed by the law——"

"Talk not to me of law, Marmaduke Temple," interrupted the hunter. "Did the beast of the forest mind your laws when it was thirsty and hungering for the blood of your own child! She was kneeling to her God for a greater favor than I ask, and he heard her; and if you now say no to my prayers, do you think he will be deaf?"

"My private feelings must not enter into——"

"Hear me, Marmaduke Temple," interrupted the old man, with melancholy earnestness, "and hear reason. I've traveled these mountains when you was no judge, but an infant in your mother's arms; and I feel as if I had a right and a privilege to travel them ag'in afore I die. Have you forgot the time that you come on to the lake shore, when there wasn't even a jail to lodge in; and didn't I give you my own bearskin to sleep on, and the fat of a noble buck to satisfy the cravings of your hunger? Yes, yes— you thought it no sin then to kill a deer! And this I did, though I had no reason to love you, for you had never done anything but harm to them that loved and sheltered me. And now, will you shut me up in your dungeons to pay me for my kindness? A hundred dollars! Where should I get the money? No, no—there's them that says hard things of you, Marmaduke Temple, but you an't so bad as to wish to see an old man die in a prison because he stood up for the right. Come, friend, let me pass; it's long sin' I've been used to such crowds, and I crave to be in the woods ag'in. Don't fear me, Judge—I bid you not to fear me; for if there's beaver enough left on the streams, or the buckskins will sell for a shilling apiece, you shall have the last penny of the fine. Where are ye, pups! Come away, dogs! come away! We have a grievous toil to do for our years, but it shall be done—yes, yes, I've promised it, and it shall be done!"

It is unnecessary to say that the movement of the Leather-stocking was again intercepted by the constable; but before he had time to speak, a bustling in the crowd, and a loud hem, drew all eyes to another part of the room.

Benjamin had succeeded in edging his way through the people, and was now seen balancing his short body with one foot in a window and the other on a railing of the jury box. To the amazement of the whole court, the steward was evidently preparing to speak. After a good deal of difficulty, he succeeded in drawing from his pocket a small bag, and then found utterance.

"If so be," he said, "that your honor is agreeable to trust the poor fellow out on another cruise among the beasts, here's a small matter that will help to bring down the risk, seeing that there's just thirty-five of your Spaniards in it; and I wish, from the bottom of my heart, that they was raal British guineas, for the sake of the old boy. But 'tis as it is; and if Squire Dickens will just be so good as to overhaul this small bit of an account, and take enough from the bag to settle the same, he's welcome to hold on upon the rest, till such time as the Leatherstocking can grapple with them said beaver, or, for that matter, forever, and no thanks asked."

As Benjamin concluded, he thrust out the wooden register of his arrears to the Bold Dragoon with one hand, while he offered his bag of dollars with the other. Astonishment at this singular interruption produced a profound stillness in the room, which was only interrupted by the Sheriff, who struck his sword on the table, and cried:

"Silence!"

"There must be an end to this," said the Judge, struggling to overcome his feelings. "Constable, lead the prisoner to the stocks. Mr. Clerk, what stands next on the calendar?"

Natty seemed to yield to his destiny, for he sank his head on his chest and followed the officer from the courtroom in silence. The crowd moved back for the passage of the prisoner, and when his tall form was seen descending from the outer door, a rush of the people to the scene of his disgrace followed.

CHAPTER XXXIV

Ha! ha! look! he wears cruel garters! LEAR

THE punishments of the common law were still known, at the time of our tale, to the people of New York; and the whipping post and its companion, the stocks, were not yet supplanted by the more merciful expedients of the public prison. Immediately in front of the jail those relics of the elder times were situated, as a lesson of precautionary justice to the evildoers of the settlement.

Natty followed the constables to this spot, bowing his head with submission to a power that he was unable to oppose, and surrounded by the crowd that formed a circle about his person, exhibiting in their countenances strong curiosity. A constable raised the upper part of the stocks and pointed with his finger to the holes where the old man was to place his feet. Without making the least objection to the punishment, the Leatherstocking quietly seated himself on the ground and suffered his limbs to be laid in the openings, without even a murmur; though he cast one glance about him in quest of that sympathy that human nature always seems to require under suffering. If he met no direct manifestations of pity, neither did he see any unfeeling exultation, or hear a single reproachful epithet. The character of the mob, if it could be called by such a name, was that of attentive subordination.

The constable was in the act of lowering the upper plank when Benjamin, who had pressed close to the side of the prisoner, said, in his hoarse tones, as if seeking for some cause to create a quarrel:

"Where away, master constable, is the use of clapping a man in them here bilboes? It neither stops his grog nor hurts his back; what for is it that you do the thing?"

" 'Tis the sentence of the court, Mr. Penguillan, and there's law for it, I s'pose."

"Ay, ay, I know that there's law for the thing; but where away do you find the use, I say? It does no harm, and it only keeps a man by the heels for the small matter of two glasses."

"Is it no harm, Benny Pump," said Natty, raising his eyes with a piteous look in the face of the steward—"is it no harm to show off a man in his seventy-first year, like a tame bear, for the settlers to look on! Is it no harm to put an old soldier, that has sarved through the war of 'fifty-six and seen the inimy in the 'seventy-six business, into a place like this, where the boys can point at him and say, I have known the time when he was a spectacle for the county! Is it no harm to bring down the pride of an honest man to be the equal of the beasts of the forest!"

Benjamin stared about him fiercely, and could he have found a single face that expressed contumely, he would have been prompt to quarrel with its owner; but meeting everywhere with looks of sobriety, and occasionally of commiseration, he very deliberately seated himself by the side of the hunter, and placing his legs in the two vacant holes of the stocks, he said:

"Now lower away, master constable, lower away, I tell ye! If so be there's such a thing hereabouts as a man that wants to see a bear, let him look and be d—d, and he shall find two of them, and mayhap one of the same that can bite as well as growl."

"But I have no orders to put you in the stocks, Mr. Pump," cried the constable; "you must get up and let me do my duty."

"You've my orders, and what do you need better to meddle with my own feet? So lower away, will ye, and let me see the man that chooses to open his mouth with a grin on it."

"There can't be any harm in locking up a creater that will enter the pound," said the constable, laughing and closing the stocks on them both.

It was fortunate that this act was executed with decision, for the whole of the spectators, when they saw Benjamin assume the position he took, felt an inclination for merriment, which few thought it worth while to suppress. The steward struggled violently for his liberty again, with an evident intention of making battle on those who stood nearest to him; but the key was already turned, and all his efforts were vain.

"Hark ye, master constable," he cried, "just clear away your bilboes for the small matter of a log glass, will ye, and let me show some of them there chaps who it is they are so merry about."

"No, no, you would go in, and you can't come out," returned the officer, "until the time has expired that the Judge directed for the keeping of the prisoner."

Benjamin, finding that his threats and his struggles were useless, had good sense enough to learn patience from the resigned manner of his companion, and soon settled himself down by the side of Natty, with a contemptuousness expressed in his hard features that showed he had substituted disgust for rage. When the violence of the steward's feelings had in some measure subsided, he turned to his fellow-sufferer, and, with a motive that might have vindicated a worse effusion, he attempted the charitable office of consolation.

"Taking it by and large, Master Bump-ho, 'tis but a small matter, after all," he said. "Now, I've known very good sort of men, aboard of the Boadishey, laid by the heels, for nothing, mayhap, but forgetting that they'd drunk their allowance already, when a glass of grog has come in their way. This is nothing more than riding with two anchors ahead, waiting for a turn in the tide, or a shift of wind, d'ye see, with a soft bottom and plenty of room for the sweep of your hawse. Now I've seen many a man, for overshooting his reckoning, as I told ye, moored head and starn, where he couldn't so much as heave his broadside round, and mayhap a stopper clapt on his tongue, too, in the shape of a pump bolt lashed athwartship his jaws, all the same as an outrigger alongside of a taffarel rail."

The hunter appeared to appreciate the kind intentions of the other, though he could not understand his eloquence; and raising his humbled countenance, he attempted a smile, as he said:

"Anan!"

" 'Tis nothing, I say, but a small matter of a squall that will soon blow over," continued Benjamin. "To you that has such a length of keel, it must be all the same as nothing; tho'f, seeing that I'm a little short in my lower timbers, they've triced my heels up in such a way as to give me a bit of a cant. But what cares I, Master Bump-ho, if the ship strains a little at her anchor; it's only for a dogwatch, and dam'me but she'll sail with you then on that cruise after them said beaver. I'm not much used to small arms, seeing that I was stationed at the ammunition boxes, being sum'mat too low-rigged to see over the hammock cloths; but I can carry the game, d'ye see, and mayhap make out to lend a hand with the traps; and if so be you're any way so handy with them as ye be with your boat hook, 'twill be but a short cruise, after all. I've squared the yards with Squire Dickens this morning, and I shall send him word that he needn't bear my name on the books again till such time as the cruise is over."

"You're used to dwell with men, Benny," said Leatherstocking, mournfully, "and the ways of the woods would be hard on you, if——"

"Not a bit—not a bit," cried the steward; "I'm none of your fair-weather chaps, Master Bump-ho, as sails only in smooth water. When I find a friend, I sticks by him, d'ye see. Now, there's no better man agoing than Squire Dickens, and I love him about the same as I loves Mistress Hollister's new keg of Jamaiky." The steward paused, and turning his uncouth visage on the hunter, he surveyed him with a roguish leer of his eye, and gradually suffered the muscles of his hard features to relax, until his face was illuminated by the display of his white teeth, when he dropped his voice, and added,—"I say, Master Leatherstocking, 'tis fresher and livelier than any Hollands you'll get in Garnsey. But we'll send a hand over and ask the woman for a taste, for I'm so jamb'd in these here bilboes that I begin to want sum'mat to lighten my upper works."

Natty sighed, and gazed about him on the crowd, that already began to disperse, and which had now diminished greatly as its members scattered in their various pursuits. He looked wistfully at Benjamin, but did not reply; a deeply seated anxiety seeming to absorb every other sensation, and to throw a melancholy gloom over his wrinkled features, which were working with the movements of his mind.

The steward was about to act on the old principle that silence gives consent, when Hiram Doolittle, attended by Jotham, stalked out of the crowd, across the open space, and approached the stocks. The magistrate passed by the end where Benjamin was seated and posted himself, at a safe distance from the steward, in front of the Leatherstocking. Hiram stood, for a moment, cowering before the keen looks that Natty fastened on him, and suffering under an embarrassment that was quite new; when, having in some degree recovered himself, he looked at the heavens, and then at the smoky atmosphere, as if it were only an ordinary meeting with a friend, and said in his formal hesitating way:

"Quite a scurcity of rain lately; I some think we shall have a long drought on't."

Benjamin was occupied in untying his bag of dollars and did not observe the approach of the magistrate, while Natty turned his face, in which every muscle was working, away from him in disgust, without answering. Rather encouraged than daunted by this exhibition of dislike, Hiram, after a short pause, continued.

"The clouds look as if they'd no water in them, and the earth is dreadfully parched. To my judgment, there'll be short crops this season, if the rain doesn't fall quite speedily."

The air with which Mr. Doolittle delivered this prophetical opinion was peculiar to his species. It was a jesuitical, cold, unfeeling, and selfish manner that seemed to say, "I have kept within the law," to the man he had so cruelly injured. It quite overcame the restraint that the old hunter had been laboring to impose on himself, and he burst out in a warm glow of indignation.

"Why should the rain fall from the clouds," he cried, "when you force the tears from the eyes of the old, the sick, and the poor! Away with ye—away with ye! You may be formed in the image of the Maker, but Satan dwells in your heart. Away with ye, I say! I am mournful, and the sight of ye brings bitter thoughts."

Benjamin ceased thumbing his money, and raised his head at the instant that Hiram, who was thrown off his guard by the invectives of the hunter, unluckily trusted his person within reach of the steward, who grasped one of his legs with a hand that had the grip of a vise and whirled the magistrate from his feet, before he had either time to collect his senses or to exercise the strength he did really possess. Benjamin wanted neither proportions nor manhood in his head, shoulders, and arms, though all the rest of his frame appeared to be originally intended for a very different sort of a man. He exerted his physical powers on the present occasion with much discretion; and as he had taken his antagonist at a great disadvantage, the struggle resulted, very soon, in Benjamin getting the magistrate fixed in a posture somewhat similar to his own, and manfully placed face to face.

"You're a ship's cousin, I tell ye, Master Doo-but-little," roared the steward; "some such matter as a ship's cousin, sir. I know you, I do, with your fair-weather speeches to Squire Dickens, to his face, and then you go and sarve out your grumbling to all the old women in the town, do ye. An't it enough for any Christian, let him harbor never so much malice, to get an honest old fellow laid by the heels in this fashion, without carrying sail so hard on the poor dog, as if you would run him down as he lay at his anchors? But I've logged many a hard thing against your name, master, and now the time's come to foot up the day's work, d'ye see; so square yourself, you lubber, square yourself, and we'll soon know who's the better man."

"Jotham!" cried the frightened magistrate—"Jotham! Call in the constables. Mr. Penguillium, I command the peace—I order you to keep the peace."

"There's been more peace than love atwixt us, master," cried the steward, making some very unequivocal demonstrations towards hostility; "so mind yourself! Square yourself, I say! Do you smell this here bit of a sledge hammer?"

"Lay hands on me if you dare!" exclaimed Hiram, as well as he could under the grasp which the steward held on his throttle—"lay hands on me if you dare!"

"If ye call this laying, master, you are welcome to the eggs," roared the steward.

It becomes our disagreeable duty to record here that the acts of Benjamin now became violent; for he darted his sledge hammer violently on the anvil of Mr. Doolittle's countenance, and the place became, in an instant, a scene of tumult and confusion. The crowd rushed in a dense circle around the spot, while some ran to the courtroom to give the alarm, and one or two of the more juvenile part of the multitude had a desperate trial of speed to see who should be the happy man to communicate the critical situation of the magistrate to his wife.

Benjamin worked away with great industry and a good deal of skill at his occupation, using one hand to raise up his antagonist, while he knocked him over with the other; for he would have been disgraced in his own estimation had he struck a blow on a fallen adversary. By this considerate arrangement he had found means to hammer the visage of Hiram out of all shape by the time Richard succeeded in forcing his way through the throng to the point of combat. The Sheriff afterwards declared that independently of his mortification, as preserver of the peace of the county, at this interruption to its harmony, he was never so grieved in his life as when he saw this breach of unity between his favorites. Hiram had in some degree become necessary to his vanity, and Benjamin, strange as it may appear, he really loved. This attachment was exhibited in the first words that he uttered.

"Squire Doolittle! Squire Doolittle! I am ashamed to see a man of your character and office forget himself so much as to disturb the peace, insult the court, and beat poor Benjamin in this manner!"

At the sound of Mr. Jones's voice, the steward ceased his employment, and Hiram had an opportunity of raising his discomfited visage towards the mediator. Emboldened by the sight of the Sheriff, Mr. Doolittle again had recourse to his lungs.

"I'll have the law on you for this," he cried desperately; "I'll have the law on you for this. I call on you, Mr. Sheriff, to seize this man, and I demand that you take his body into custody."

By this time Richard was master of the true state of the case, and, turning to the steward, he said, reproachfully:

"Benjamin, how came you in the stocks? I always thought you were mild and docile as a lamb. It was for your docility that I most esteemed you. Benjamin! Benjamin! you have not only disgraced yourself, but your friends, by this shameless conduct. Bless me! bless me! Mr. Doolittle, he seems to have knocked your face all of one side."

Hiram by this time had got on his feet again, and without the reach of the steward, when he broke forth in violent appeals for vengeance. The offense was too apparent to be passed over, and the Sheriff, mindful of the impartiality exhibited by his cousin in the recent trial of the Leatherstocking, came to the painful conclusion that it was necessary to commit his major-domo to prison. As the time of Natty's punishment was expired, and Benjamin found that they were to be confined, for that night at least, in the same apartment, he made no very strong objections to the measure, nor spoke of bail, though, as the Sheriff preceded the party of constables

that conducted them to the jail, he uttered the following remonstrance:

"As to being berthed with Master Bump-ho for a night or
so, it's but little I think of it, Squire Dickens, seeing that I
calls him an honest man, and one as has a handy way with
boat hooks and rifles; but as for owning that a man desarves
anything worse than a double allowance, for knocking that
carpenter's face a-one-side, as you call it, I'll maintain it's
ag'in reason and Christianity. If there's a bloodsucker in this
'ere county, it's that very chap. Ay! I know him! And if he
hasn't got all the same as deadwood in his headworks, he
knows sum'mat of me. Where's the mighty harm, Squire,
that you take it so much to heart? It's all the same as any
other battle, d'ye see, sir, being broadside to broadside, only
that it was fout at anchor, which was what we did in Port
Praya roads, when Suff'ring came in among us; and a suff'ring
time he had of it, before he got out again."

Richard thought it unworthy of him to make any reply to
this speech; but when his prisoners were safely lodged in an
outer dungeon, ordering the bolts to be drawn and the key
turned, he withdrew.

Benjamin held frequent and friendly dialogues with different people through the iron gratings during the afternoon;
but his companion paced their narrow limits in his moccasins
with quick, impatient treads, his face hanging on his breast
in dejection, or when lifted, at moments, to the idlers at the
window, lighted, perhaps, for an instant, with the childish
aspect of aged forgetfulness, which would vanish directly in
an expression of deep and obvious anxiety.

At the close of the day, Edwards was seen at the window
in earnest dialogue with his friend; and after he departed, it
was thought that he had communicated words of comfort
to the hunter, who threw himself on his pallet and was soon
in a deep sleep. The curious spectators had exhausted the
conversation of the steward, who had drunk good fellowship
with half of his acquaintance, and as Natty was no longer in
motion, by eight o'clock, Billy Kirby, who was the last lounger
at the window, retired into the "Templetown Coffeehouse,"
when Natty rose and hung a blanket before the opening,
and the prisoners apparently retired for the night.

CHAPTER XXXV

And to avoid the foe's pursuit,
With spurring put their cattle to't;
And till all four were out of wind,
And danger too, ne'er looked behind.

HUDIBRAS

As the shades of evening approached, the jurors, witnesses, and other attendants on the court began to disperse, and before nine o'clock the village was quiet, and its streets nearly deserted. At that hour Judge Temple and his daughter, followed at a short distance by Louisa Grant, walked slowly down the avenue under the slight shadows of the young poplars, holding the following discourse:

"You can best soothe his wounded spirit, my child," said Marmaduke; "but it will be dangerous to touch on the nature of his offense; the sanctity of the laws must be respected."

"Surely, sir," cried the impatient Elizabeth, "those laws that condemn a man like the Leatherstocking to so severe a punishment, for an offense that even I must think very venial, cannot be perfect in themselves."

"Thou talkest of what thou dost not understand, Elizabeth," returned her father. "Society cannot exist without wholesome restraints. Those restraints cannot be inflicted without security and respect to the persons of those who administer them; and it would sound ill indeed to report that a judge had extended favor to a convicted criminal because he had saved the life of his child."

"I see—I see the difficulty of your situation, dear sir," cried the daughter; "but in appreciating the offense of poor Natty, I cannot separate the minister of the law from the man."

"There thou talkest as a woman, child; it is not for an assault on Hiram Doolittle, but for threatening the life of a constable, who was in the performance of——"

"It is immaterial whether it be one or the other," interrupted Miss Temple, with a logic that contained more feeling

364

than reason; "I know Natty to be innocent, and, thinking so, I must think all wrong who oppress him."

"His judge among the number! Thy father, Elizabeth?"

"Nay, nay, nay; do not put such questions to me; give me my commission, father, and let me proceed to execute it."

The Judge paused a moment, smiling fondly on his child, and then dropped his hand affectionately on her shoulder, as he answered:

"Thou hast reason, Bess, and much of it, too, but thy heart lies too near thy head. But listen: in this pocketbook are two hundred dollars. Go to the prison—there are none in this place to harm thee—give this note to the jailor, and when thou seest Bumppo, say what thou wilt to the poor old man; give scope to the feelings of thy warm heart; but try to remember, Elizabeth, that the laws alone remove us from the condition of the savages; that he has been criminal, and that his judge was thy father."

Miss Temple made no reply, but she pressed the hand that held the pocketbook to her bosom, and taking her friend by the arm, they issued together from the enclosure into the principal street of the village.

As they pursued their walk in silence, under the row of houses, where the deeper gloom of the evening effectually concealed their persons, no sound reached them, excepting the slow tread of a yoke of oxen, with the rattling of a cart, that were moving along the street in the same direction with themselves. The figure of the teamster was just discernible by the dim light, lounging by the side of his cattle with a listless air, as if fatigued by the toil of the day. At the corner, where the jail stood, the progress of the ladies was impeded, for a moment, by the oxen, who were turned up to the side of the building and given a lock of hay, which they had carried on their necks as a reward for their patient labor. The whole of this was so natural, and so common, that Elizabeth saw nothing to induce a second glance at the team, until she heard the teamster speaking to his cattle in a low voice:

"Mind yourself, Brindle; will you, sir! will you!"

The language itself was unusual to oxen, with which all who dwell in a new country are familiar; but there was something in the voice, also, that startled Miss Temple. On turning the corner, she necessarily approached the man, and her look was enabled to detect the person of Oliver Edwards, concealed under the coarse garb of a teamster. Their eyes met at the same instant, and, notwithstanding the gloom and the enveloping cloak of Elizabeth, the recognition was mutual.

"Miss Temple!" "Mr. Edwards!" were exclaimed simultaneously, though a feeling that seemed common to both rendered the words nearly inaudible.

"Is it possible!" exclaimed Edwards, after the moment of doubt had passed. "Do I see you so nigh the jail! But you are going to the rectory; I beg pardon, Miss Grant, I believe; I did not recognize you at first."

The sigh which Louisa uttered was so faint that it was only heard by Elizabeth, who replied quickly:

"We are going not only to the jail, Mr. Edwards, but into it. We wish to show the Leatherstocking that we do not forget his services, and that at the same time we must be just, we are also grateful. I suppose you are on a similar errand; but let me beg that you will give us leave to precede you ten minutes. Good night, sir; I—I—am quite sorry, Mr. Edwards, to see you reduced to such labor; I am sure my father would——"

"I shall wait your pleasure, madam," interrupted the youth, coldly. "May I beg that you will not mention my being here?"

"Certainly," said Elizabeth, returning his bow by a slight inclination of her head, and urging the tardy Louisa forward. As they entered the jailor's house, however, Miss Grant found leisure to whisper:

"Would it not be well to offer part of your money to Oliver? Half of it will pay the fine of Bumppo; and he is so unused to hardships! I am sure my father will subscribe much of his little pittance to place him in a station that is more worthy of him."

The involuntary smile that passed over the features of Elizabeth was blended with an expression of deep and heartfelt pity. She did not reply, however, and the appearance of the jailor soon recalled the thoughts of both to the object of their visit.

The rescue of the ladies and their consequent interest in his prisoner, together with the informal manners that prevailed in the country, all united to prevent any surprise, on the part of the jailor, at their request for admission to Bumppo. The note of Judge Temple, however, would have

silenced all objections, if he had felt them, and he led the
way without hesitation to the apartment that held the prisoners. The instant the key was put into the lock, the hoarse
voice of Benjamin was heard, demanding:

"Yo! hoy! Who comes there?"

"Some visitors that you'll be glad to see," returned the
jailor. "What have you done to the lock, that it won't turn?"

"Handsomely, handsomely, master," cried the steward; "I
have just drove a nail into a berth alongside of this here bolt,
as a stopper, d'ye see, so that Master Do-but-little can't be
running in and breezing up another fight atwixt us; for, to
my account, there'll be but a banyan with me soon, seeing
that they'll mulct me of my Spaniards, all the same as if I'd
overflogged the lubber. Throw your ship into the wind, and
lay by for a small matter, will ye? And I'll soon clear a passage."

The sounds of hammering gave an assurance that the
steward was in earnest, and in a short time the lock yielded,
when the door was opened.

Benjamin had evidently been anticipating the seizure of his
money, for he had made frequent demands on the favorite
cask at the "Bold Dragoon," during the afternoon and evening, and was now in that state which by marine imagery is
called "half-seas over." It was no easy thing to destroy the
balance of the old tar by the effects of liquor, for, as he expressed it himself, "he was too low-rigged not to carry sail in
all weathers"; but he was precisely in that condition which
is so expressively termed "muddy." When he perceived who
the visitors were, he retreated to the side of the room where
his pallet lay, and, regardless of the presence of his young
mistress, seated himself on it with an air of great sobriety,
placing his back firmly against the wall.

"If you undertake to spoil my locks in this manner, Mr.
Pump," said the jailor, "I shall put a stopper, as you call it,
on your legs and tie you down to your bed."

"What for should ye, master?" grumbled Benjamin. "I've
rode out one squall today anchored by the heels, and I wants
no more of them. Where's the harm of doing all the same as
yourself? Leave that there door free outboard, and you'll
find no locking inboard, I'll promise ye."

"I must shut up for the night at nine," said the jailor,

"and it's now forty-two minutes past eight." He placed the little candle on a rough pine table and withdrew.

"Leatherstocking!" said Elizabeth when the key of the door was turned on them again, "my good friend Leather-stocking! I have come on a message of gratitude. Had you submitted to the search, worthy old man, the death of the deer would have been a trifle, and all would have been well——"

"Submit to the sarch!" interrupted Natty, raising his face from resting on his knees, without rising from the corner where he had seated himself. "D'ye think, gal, I would let such a varmint into my hut? No, no—I wouldn't have opened the door to your own sweet countenance then. But they are wilcome to sarch among the coals and ashes now; they'll find only some such heap as is to be seen at every pot-ashery in the mountains."

The old man dropped his face again on one hand and seemed to be lost in melancholy.

"The hut can be rebuilt and made better than before," returned Miss Temple; "and it shall be my office to see it done, when your imprisonment is ended."

"Can ye raise the dead, child?" said Natty, in a sorrow-ful voice. "Can ye go into the place where you've laid your fathers, and mothers, and children and gather together their ashes and make the same men and women of them as afore? You do not know what 'tis to lay your head for more than forty years under the cover of the same logs, and to look on the same things for the better part of a man's life. You are young yet, child, but you are one of the most precious of God's creaters. I had a hope for ye that it might come to pass, but it's all over now; this put to that will drive the thing quite out of his mind forever."

Miss Temple must have understood the meaning of the old man better than the other listeners; for, while Louisa stood innocently by her side, commiserating the griefs of the hunter, she bent her head aside, so as to conceal her features. The action and the feeling that caused it lasted but a moment.

"Other logs, and better, though, can be had, and shall be found for you, my old defender," she continued. "Your confinement will soon be over, and, before that time ar-rives, I shall have a house prepared for you, where you may spend the close of your harmless life in ease and plenty."

"Ease and plenty! House!" repeated Natty, slowly. "You mean well, you mean well, and I quite mourn that it cannot be; but he has seen me a sight and a laughingstock for——"

"Damn your stocks," said Benjamin, flourishing his bottle with one hand, from which he had been taking hasty and repeated draughts, while he made gestures of disdain with the other; "who cares for his bilboes? There's a leg that's been stuck up an end like a jib boom for an hour, d'ye see, and what's it the worse for't, ha! Canst tell me, what's it the worser, ha!"

"I believe you forget, Mr. Pump, in whose presence you are," said Elizabeth.

"Forget you, Miss Lizzy," returned the steward; "if I do, dam'me; you are not to be forgot, like Goody Prettybones, up at the big house there. I say, old sharpshooter, she may have pretty bones, but I can't say so much for her flesh, d'ye see, for she looks somewhat like an atomy with another man's jacket on. Now, for the skin of her face, it's all the same as a new topsail with a taut boltrope, being snug at the leaches, but all in a bight about the inner cloths."

"Peace—I command you to be silent, sir!" said Elizabeth.

"Ay, ay, ma'am," returned the steward. "You didn't say I shouldn't drink, though."

"We will not speak of what is to become of others," said Miss Temple, turning again to the hunter—"but of your own fortunes, Natty. It shall be my care to see that you pass the rest of your days in ease and plenty."

"Ease and plenty!" again repeated the Leatherstocking. "What ease can there be to an old man who must walk a mile across the open fields before he can find a shade to hide him from a scorching sun! Or what plenty is there where you may hunt a day, and not start a buck, or see anything bigger than a mink, or maybe a stray fox! Ah! I shall have a hard time after them very beavers, for this fine. I must go low toward the Pennsylvany line in search of the creaters, maybe a hundred mile; for they are not to be got hereaway. No, no,—your betterments and clearings have druv the knowing things out of the country; and instead of beaver dams, which is the nater of the animal, and according to Providence, you turn back the waters over the low grounds with your milldams, as if 'twas in man to stay the drops from going where He wills them to go.—Benny, unless you stop your hand from going so often to your mouth, you won't be ready to start when the time comes."

"Hark'ee, Master Bump-ho," said the steward; "don't you fear for Ben. When the watch is called, set me on my legs and give me the bearings and distance of where you want to steer, and I'll carry sail with the best of you, I will."

"The time has come now," said the hunter, listening; "I hear the horns of the oxen rubbing ag'in the side of the jail."

"Well, say the word, and then heave ahead, shipmate," said Benjamin.

"You won't betray us, gal?" said Natty, looking simply into the face of Elizabeth. "You won't betray an old man, who craves to breathe the clear air of heaven? I mean no harm; and if the law says that I must pay the hundred dollars, I'll take the season through, but it shall be forthcoming; and this good man will help me."

"You catch them," said Benjamin, with a sweeping gesture of his arm, "and if they get away again, call me a slink, that's all."

"But what mean you?" cried the wondering Elizabeth. "Here you must stay for thirty days; but I have the money for your fine in this purse. Take it; pay it in the morning and summon patience for your month. I will come often to see you, with my friend; we will make up your clothes with our own hands; indeed, indeed, you shall be comfortable."

"Would ye, children?" said Natty, advancing across the floor with an air of kindness and taking the hand of Elizabeth. "Would ye be so kearful of an old man, and just for shooting the beast which cost him nothing? Such things doesn't run in the blood, I believe, for you seem not to forget a favor. Your little fingers couldn't do much on a buckskin, nor be you used to such a thread as sinews. But if he hasn't got past hearing, he shall hear it and know it, that he may see, like me, there is some who know how to remember a kindness."

"Tell him nothing," cried Elizabeth, earnestly; "if you love me, if you regard my feelings, tell him nothing. It is of yourself only I would talk, and for yourself only I act. I grieve, Leatherstocking, that the law requires that you should be detained here so long; but, after all, it will be only a short month, and——"

"A month!" exclaimed Natty, opening his mouth with his usual laugh. "Not a day, nor a night, nor an hour, gal. Judge Temple may sintence, but he can't keep, without a better dungeon than this. I was taken once by the French, and they put sixty-two of us in a blockhouse, nigh hand to old Frontinac; but 'twas easy to cut through a pine log to them that was used to timber." The hunter paused and looked cautiously around the room, when, laughing again, he shoved the steward gently from his post, and removing the bedclothes, discovered a hole recently cut in the logs with a mallet and chisel. "It's only a kick, and the outside piece is off, and then——"

"Off! Ay, off!" cried Benjamin, rousing from his stupor. "Well, here's off. Ay! ay! You catch 'em, and I'll hold on to them said beaver hats."

"I fear this lad will trouble me much," said Natty; " 'twill be a hard pull for the mountain, should they take the scent soon, and he is not in a state of mind to run."

"Run!" echoed the steward. "No, sheer alongside, and let's have a fight of it."

"Peace!" ordered Elizabeth.

"Ay, ay, ma'am."

"You will not leave us, surely, Leatherstocking," continued Miss Temple; "I beseech you, reflect that you will be driven to the woods entirely, and that you are fast getting old. Be patient for a little time, when you can go abroad openly and with honor."

"Is there beaver to be catched here, gal?"

"If not, here is money to discharge the fine, and in a month you are free. See, here it is in gold."

"Gold!" said Natty, with a kind of childish curiosity. "It's long sin' I've seen a gold piece. We used to get the broad joes, in the old war, as plenty as the bears be now. I remember there was a man in Dieskau's army, that was killed, who had a dozen of the shining things sewed up in his shirt. I didn't handle them myself, but I seen them cut out with my own eyes; they was bigger and brighter than them be."

"These are English guineas and are yours," said Elizabeth; "an earnest of what shall be done for you."

"Me! Why should you give me this treasure?" said Natty, looking earnestly at the maiden.

"Why! Have you not saved my life? Did you not rescue me from the jaws of the beast?" exclaimed Elizabeth, veiling her eyes, as if to hide some hideous object from her view.

The hunter took the money, and continued turning it in his hand for some time, piece by piece, talking aloud during the operation.

"There's a rifle, they say, out on the Cherry Valley, that will carry a hundred rods and kill. I've seen good guns in my day, but none quite equal to that. A hundred rods with any sartainty is great shooting! Well, well—I'm old, and the gun I have will answer my time. Here, child, take back your gold. But the hour has come; I hear him talking to the cattle, and I must be going. You won't tell of us, gal—you won't tell of us, will ye?"

"Tell of you!" echoed Elizabeth. "But take the money, old man; take the money, even if you go into the mountains."

"No, no," said Natty, shaking his head kindly; "I would not rob you so for twenty rifles. But there's one thing you can do for me, if ye will, that no other is at hand to do."

"Name it—name it."

"Why, it's only to buy a canister of powder—'twill cost two silver dollars. Benny Pump has the money ready, but we daren't come into the town to get it. Nobody has it but the Frenchman. 'Tis of the best, and just suits a rifle. Will you get it for me, gal?—say, will you get it for me?"

"Will I! I will bring it to you, Leatherstocking, though I toil a day in quest of you through the woods. But where shall I find you, and how?"

"Where!" said Natty, musing a moment—"tomorrow, on the Vision; on the very top of the Vision, I'll meet you, child, just as the sun gets over our heads. See that it's the fine grain; you'll know it by the gloss and the price."

"I will do it," said Elizabeth, firmly.

Natty now seated himself, and, placing his feet in the hole, with a slight effort he opened a passage through into the street. The ladies heard the rustling of hay, and well understood the reason why Edward was in the capacity of a teamster.

"Come, Benny," said the hunter; " 'twill be no darker to-night, for the moon will rise in an hour."

"Stay!" exclaimed Elizabeth. "It should not be said that you escaped in the presence of the daughter of Judge Temple. Return, Leatherstocking, and let us retire, before you ex-cute your plan."

Natty was about to reply when the approaching footsteps of the jailor announced the necessity of his immediate re-turn. He had barely time to regain his feet, and to conceal the hole with the bedclothes, across which Benjamin very opportunely fell, before the key was turned, and the door of the apartment opened.

"Isn't Miss Temple ready to go?" said the civil jailor. "It's the usual hour for locking up."

"I follow you, sir," returned Elizabeth, "good night, Leatherstocking."

"It's a fine grain, gal, and I think 'twill carry lead further than common. I am getting old, and can't follow up the game with the step that I used to could."

Miss Temple waved her hand for silence, and preceded Louisa and the keeper from the apartment. The man turned the key once, and observed that he would return and se-cure his prisoners, when he had lighted the ladies to the street. Accordingly, they parted at the door of the building, when the jailor retired to his dungeons, and the ladies walked, with throbbing hearts, towards the corner.

"Now the Leatherstocking refuses the money," whispered Louisa, "it can all be given to Mr. Edwards, and that added to——"

"Listen!" said Elizabeth; "I hear the rustling of the hay; they are escaping at this moment. Oh! they will be detected instantly!"

By this time they were at the corner, where Edwards and Natty were in the act of drawing the almost helpless body of Benjamin through the aperture. The oxen had started back from their hay, and were standing with their heads down the street, leaving room for the party to act in.

"Throw the hay into the cart," said Edwards, "or they will suspect how it has been done. Quick, that they may not see it."

Natty had just returned from executing this order when the light of the keeper's candle shone through the hole, and instantly his voice was heard in the jail, exclaiming for his prisoners.

"What is to be done now?" said Edwards. "This drunken fellow will cause our detection, and we have not a moment to spare."

"Who's drunk, ye lubber!" muttered the steward.

"A break-jail! a break-jail!" shouted five or six voices from within.

"We must leave him," said Edwards.

" 'Twouldn't be kind, lad," returned Natty; "he took half the disgrace of the stocks on himself today, and the creater has feeling."

At this moment two or three men were heard issuing from the door of the "Bold Dragoon," and among them the voice of Billy Kirby.

"There's no moon yet," cried the wood chopper; "but it's a clear night. Come, who's for home! Hark! What a rumpus they're kicking up in the jail—here's go and see what it's about."

"We shall be lost," said Edwards, "if we don't drop this man."

At that instant Elizabeth moved close to him, and said rapidly, in a low voice:

"Lay him in the cart and start the oxen; no one will look there."

"There's a woman's quickness in the thought," said the youth.

The proposition was no sooner made than executed. The steward was seated on the hay, and enjoined to hold his peace, and apply the goad that was placed in his hand, while the oxen were urged on. So soon as this arrangement was completed, Edwards and the hunter stole along the houses for a short distance, when they disappeared through an opening that led into the rear of the buildings. The oxen were in brisk motion, and presently the cries of pursuit were heard in the street. The ladies quickened their pace, with a wish to escape the crowd of constables and idlers that were approaching, some execrating, and some laughing at the exploit of the prisoners. In the confusion, the voice of Kirby was plainly distinguishable above all the others, shouting and swearing that he would have the fugitives, threatening to bring back Natty in one pocket, and Benjamin in the other.

"Spread yourselves, men," he cried, as he passed the ladies, his heavy feet sounding along the street like the tread of a dozen; "spread yourselves; to the mountains; they'll be in the mountain in a quarter of an hour, and then look out for a long rifle."

His cries were echoed from twenty mouths, for not only the jail but the taverns had sent forth their numbers, some earnest in the pursuit, and others joining it as in sport.

As Elizabeth turned in at her father's gate, she saw the wood chopper stop at the cart, when she gave Benjamin up for lost. While they were hurrying up the walk, two figures, stealing cautiously but quickly under the shades of the trees, met the eyes of the ladies, and in a moment Edwards and the hunter crossed their path.

"Miss Temple, I may never see you again," exclaimed the youth; "let me thank you for all your kindness; you do not, cannot know, my motives."

"Fly! fly!" cried Elizabeth. "The village is alarmed. Do not be found conversing with me at such a moment, and in these grounds."

"Nay, I must speak, though detection were certain."

"Your retreat to the bridge is already cut off; before you can gain the wood your pursuers will be there.—If—"

"If what?" cried the youth. "Your advice has saved me once already; I will follow it to death."

"The street is now silent and vacant," said Elizabeth, after a pause; "cross it, and you will find my father's boat in the lake. It would be easy to land from it where you please in the hills."

"But Judge Temple might complain of the trespass."

"His daughter shall be accountable, sir."

The youth uttered something in a low voice that was heard only by Elizabeth and turned to execute what she had suggested. As they were separating, Natty approached the females, and said:

"You'll remember the canister of powder, children. Them beavers must be had, and I and the pups be getting old; we want the best of ammunition."

"Come, Natty," said Edwards, impatiently.

"Coming, lad, coming. God bless you, young ones, both of ye, for ye mean well and kindly to the old man."

The ladies paused until they had lost sight of the retreating figures, when they immediately entered the mansion house.

While this scene was passing in the walk, Kirby had overtaken the cart, which was his own, and had been driven by Edwards without asking the owner, from the place where the patient oxen usually stood at evening, waiting the pleasure of their master.

"Whoa—come hither, Golden," he cried. "Why, how come you off the end of the bridge, where I left you, dummies?"

"Heave ahead," muttered Benjamin, giving a random blow with his lash that alighted on the shoulder of the other.

"Who the devil be you?" cried Billy, turning round in surprise, but unable to distinguish, in the dark, the hard visage that was just peering over the cart rails.

"Who be I? Why I'm helmsman aboard of this here craft, d'ye see, and a straight wake I'm making of it. Ay, ay! I've got the bridge right ahead, and the bilboes dead aft; I calls that good steerage, boy. Heave ahead."

"Lay your lash in the right spot, Mr. Benny Pump," said the wood chopper, "or I'll put you in the palm of my hand and box your ears. Where be you going with my team?"

"Team!"

"Ay, my cart and oxen."

"Why, you must know, Master Kirby, that the Leatherstocking and I—that's Benny Pump—you knows Ben?—well, Benny and I—no, me and Benny; dam'me if I know how 'tis; but some of us are bound after a cargo of beaver skins, d'ye see, and so we've pressed the cart to ship them 'ome in. I say, Master Kirby, what a lubberly oar you pull—you handle an oar, boy, pretty much as a cow would a musket, or a lady would a marlinespike."

Billy had discovered the state of the steward's mind, and he walked for some time alongside of the cart, musing with himself, when he took the goad from Benjamin (who fell back on the hay and was soon asleep) and drove his cattle down the street, over the bridge, and up the mountain, towards a clearing, in which he was to work the next day, without any other interruption than a few hasty questions from parties of the constables.

Elizabeth stood for an hour at the window of her room, and saw the torches of the pursuers gliding along the side of the mountain, and heard their shouts and alarms; but, at the end of that time, the last party returned, wearied and disappointed, and the village became as still as when she issued from the gate on her mission to the jail.

CHAPTER XXXVI

> "And I could weep"—th' Oneida chief
> His descant wildly thus begun—
> "But that I may not stain with grief
> The death song of my father's son."
> GERTRUDE OF WYOMING

IT was yet early on the following morning, when Elizabeth and Louisa met by appointment and proceeded to the store of Monsieur Le Quoi in order to redeem the pledge the former had given to the Leatherstocking. The people were again assembling for the business of the day, but the hour was too soon for a crowd, and the ladies found the place in possession of its polite owner, Billy Kirby, one female customer, and the boy who did the duty of helper or clerk.

Monsieur Le Quoi was perusing a packet of letters with manifest delight, while the wood chopper, with one hand thrust in his bosom, and the other in the folds of his jacket, holding an ax under his right arm, stood sympathizing in the Frenchman's pleasure with good-natured interest. The freedom of manners that prevailed in the new settlements commonly leveled all difference in rank, and with it, frequently, all considerations of education and intelligence. At the time the ladies entered the store, they were unseen by the owner, who was saying to Kirby:

"Ah! ha! Monsieur Beel, dis lettair mak me de most happi of mans. Ah! ma chère France! I vill see you aga'n."

"I rejoice, Monsieur, at anything that contributes to your happiness," said Elizabeth, "but hope we are not going to lose you entirely."

The complaisant shopkeeper changed the language to

French and recounted rapidly to Elizabeth his hopes of being permitted to return to his own country. Habit had, however, so far altered the manners of this pliable personage that he continued to serve the wood chopper, who was in quest of some tobacco, while he related to his more gentle visitor the happy change that had taken place in the dispositions of his own countrymen.

The amount of it all was that Mr. Le Quoi, who had fled from his own country more through terror than because he was offensive to the ruling powers in France, had succeeded at length in getting an assurance that his return to the West Indies would be unnoticed; and the Frenchman, who had sunk into the character of a country shopkeeper with so much grace, was about to emerge again from his obscurity into his proper level in society.

We need not repeat the civil things that passed between the parties on this occasion, nor recount the endless repetitions of sorrow that the delighted Frenchman expressed at being compelled to quit the society of Miss Temple. Elizabeth took an opportunity, during this expenditure of polite expressions, to purchase the powder privately of the boy, who bore the generic appellation of Jonathan. Before they parted, however, Mr. Le Quoi, who seemed to think that he had not said enough, solicited the honor of a private interview with the heiress, with a gravity in his air that announced the importance of the subject. After conceding the favor, and appointing a more favorable time for the meeting, Elizabeth succeeded in getting out of the store, into which the countrymen now began to enter, as usual, where they met with the same attention and *bienséance* as formerly.

Elizabeth and Louisa pursued their walk as far as the bridge in profound silence; but when they reached that place, the latter stopped, and appeared anxious to utter something that her diffidence suppressed.

"Are you ill, Louisa?" exclaimed Miss Temple. "Had we not better return, and seek another opportunity to meet the old man?"

"Not ill, but terrified. Oh! I never, never can go on that hill again with you only. I am not equal to it, indeed I am not."

This was an unexpected declaration to Elizabeth, who, although she experienced no idle apprehension of a danger that no longer existed, felt most sensitively all the delicacy of maiden modesty. She stood for some time, deeply reflecting within herself; but, sensible it was a time for action instead of reflection, she struggled to shake off her hesitation, and replied firmly:

"Well, then it must be done by me alone. There is no other than yourself to be trusted, or poor old Leatherstocking will be discovered. Wait for me in the edge of these woods, that at least I may not be seen strolling in the hills by myself just now. One would not wish to create remarks, Louisa—if —if—. You will wait for me, dear girl?"

"A year, in sight of the village, Miss Temple," returned the agitated Louisa, "but do not, do not ask me to go on that hill."

Elizabeth found that her companion was really unable to proceed, and they completed their arrangement by posting Louisa out of the observation of the people who occasionally passed, but nigh the road, and in plain view of the whole valley. Miss Temple then proceeded alone. She ascended the road which has been so often mentioned in our narrative, with an elastic and firm step, fearful that the delay in the store of Mr. Le Quoi, and the time necessary for reaching the summit, would prevent her being punctual to the appointment. Whenever she passed an opening in the bushes, she would pause for breath, or, perhaps, drawn from her pursuit by the picture at her feet, would linger a moment to gaze at the beauties of the valley. The long drought had, however, changed its coat of verdure to a hue of brown, and, though the same localities were there, the view wanted the lively and cheering aspect of early summer. Even the heavens seemed to share in the dried appearance of the earth, for the sun was concealed by a haziness in the atmosphere, which looked like a thin smoke without a particle of moisture, if such a thing were possible. The blue sky was scarcely to be seen, though now and then there was a faint lighting up in spots, through which masses of rolling vapor could be discerned gathering around the horizon, as if nature were struggling to collect her floods for the relief of man. The very atmosphere that Elizabeth inhaled was hot and dry, and by the time she reached the point where the course led her from the highway, she experienced a sensation like suffocation. But, disregarding her feelings, she hastened to execute her mission, dwelling on nothing but the disappointment, and even the helplessness, the hunter would experience without her aid.

On the summit of the mountain which Judge Temple had named the "Vision," a little spot had been cleared in order that a better view might be obtained of the village and the valley. At this point Elizabeth understood the hunter she was to meet him; and thither she urged her way, as expeditiously as the difficulty of the ascent and the impediments of a forest in a state of nature would admit. Numberless were the fragments of rocks, trunks of fallen trees, and branches, with which she had to contend; but every difficulty vanished before her resolution, and by her own watch, she stood on the desired spot several minutes before the appointed hour.

After resting a moment on the end of a log, Miss Temple cast a glance about her in quest of her old friend, but he was evidently not in the clearing; she arose and walked around its skirts, examining every place where she thought it probable Natty might deem it prudent to conceal himself. Her search was fruitless; and, after exhausting not only herself, but her conjectures, in efforts to discover or imagine his situation, she ventured to trust her voice in that solitary place.

"Natty! Leatherstocking! Old man!" she called aloud, in every direction; but no answer was given, excepting the reverberations of her own clear tones as they were echoed in the parched forest.

Elizabeth approached the brow of the mountain, where a faint cry, like the noise produced by striking the hand against the mouth at the same time that the breath is strongly exhaled, was heard answering to her own voice. Not doubting in the least that it was the Leatherstocking lying in wait for her, and who gave that signal to indicate the place where he was to be found, Elizabeth descended for near a hundred feet, until she gained a little natural terrace, thinly scattered with trees, that grew in the fissures of the rocks, which were covered by a scanty soil. She had advanced to the edge of this platform, and was gazing over the perpendicular precipice that formed its face, when a rustling among the dry leaves near her drew her eyes in another direction. Our heroine certainly was startled by the object that she then saw, but a moment restored her self-possession, and she advanced firmly, and with some interest in her manner, to the spot.

Mohegan was seated on the trunk of a fallen oak, with his tawny visage turned towards her, and his eyes fixed on her face with an expression of wildness and fire that would have terrified a less resolute female. His blanket had fallen from his shoulders, and was lying in folds around him, leaving his breast, arms, and most of his body bare. The medallion of Washington reposed on his chest, a badge of distinction that Elizabeth well knew he only produced on great and solemn occasions. But the whole appearance of the aged chief was more studied than common, and in some particulars it was terrific. The long black hair was plaited on his head, falling away, so as to expose his high forehead and piercing eyes. In the enormous incisions of his ears were entwined ornaments of silver, beads, and porcupines' quills, mingled in a rude taste, and after the Indian fashions. A large drop, composed of similar materials, was suspended from the cartilage of his nose, and, falling below his lips, rested on his chin. Streaks of red paint crossed his wrinkled brow, and were traced down his cheeks with such variations in the lines as caprice or custom suggested. His body was also colored in the same manner; the whole exhibiting an Indian warrior, prepared for some event of more than usual moment.

"John! How fare you, worthy John?" said Elizabeth, as she approached him. "You have long been a stranger in the village. You promised me a willow basket, and I have long had a shirt of calico in readiness for you."

The Indian looked steadily at her for some time without answering, and then, shaking his head, he replied, in his low, guttural tones:

"John's hand can make baskets no more—he wants no shirt."

"But if he should, he will know where to come for it," returned Miss Temple. "Indeed, old John, I feel as if you had a natural right to order what you will from us."

"Daughter," said the Indian, "listen: Six times ten hot summers have passed since John was young; tall like a pine; straight like the bullet of Hawkeye; strong as the buffalo; spry as the cat of the mountain. He was strong, and a warrior like the Young Eagle. If his tribe wanted to track the Maquas for many suns, the eye of Chingachgook found the print of their moccasins. If the people feasted and were glad, as they counted the scalps of their enemies, it was on his pole they hung. If the squaws cried because there was no meat for their children, he was the first in the chase. His bullet was swifter than the deer. Daughter, then Chingachgook struck his tomahawk into the trees; it was to tell the lazy ones where to find him and the Mingoes—but he made no baskets."

"Those times have gone by, old warrior," returned Elizabeth; "since then your people have disappeared, and, in place of chasing your enemies, you have learned to fear God and to live at peace."

"Stand here, daughter, where you can see the great spring, the wigwams of your father, and the land on the crooked river. John was young when his tribe gave away the country, in council, from where the blue mountain stands above the water to where the Susquehanna is hid by the trees. All this, and all that grew in it, and all that walked over it, and all that fed there, they gave to the Fire-eater—for they loved him. He was strong, and they were women, and he helped them. No Delaware would kill a deer that ran in his woods, nor stop a bird that flew over his land; for it was his. Has John lived in peace? Daughter, since John was young, he has seen the white man from Frontinac come down on his white brothers at Albany and fight. Did they fear God? He has seen his English and his American fathers burying their tomahawks in each other's brains, for this very land. Did they fear God, and live in peace? He has seen the land pass away from the Fire-eater, and his children, and the child of his child, and a new chief set over the country. Did they live in peace who did this? Did they fear God?"

"Such is the custom of the whites, John. Do not the Delawares fight, and exchange their lands for powder, and blankets, and merchandise?"

The Indian turned his dark eyes on his companion and kept them there with a scrutiny that alarmed her a little.

"Where are the blankets and merchandise that bought the right of the Fire-eater?" he replied, in a more animated voice. "Are they with him in his wigwam? Did they say to him, Brother, sell us your land, and take this gold, this silver, these blankets, these rifles, or even this rum? No; they tore it from him, as a scalp is torn from an enemy; and they that did it looked not behind them to see whether he lived or died.

Do such men live in peace, and fear the Great Spirit?"

"But you hardly understand the circumstances," said Elizabeth, more embarrassed than she would own, even to herself. "If you knew our laws and customs better, you would judge differently of our acts. Do not believe evil of my father, old Mohegan, for he is just and good."

"The brother of Miquon is good, and he will do right. I have said it to Hawkeye—I have said it to the Young Eagle, that the brother of Miquon would do justice."

"Whom call you the Young Eagle?" said Elizabeth, averting her face from the gaze of the Indian, as she asked the question. "Whence comes he, and what are his rights?"

"Has my daughter lived so long with him to ask this question?" returned the Indian warily. "Old age freezes up the blood, as the frosts cover the great spring in winter; but youth keeps the streams of the blood open like a sun in the time of blossoms. The Young Eagle has eyes; had he no tongue?"

The loveliness to which the old warrior alluded was in no degree diminished by his allegorical speech; for the blushes of the maiden who listened covered her burning cheeks, till her dark eyes seemed to glow with their reflection; but, after struggling a moment with shame, she laughed, as if unwilling to understand him seriously, and replied in pleasantry:

"Not to make me the mistress of his secret. He is too much of a Delaware to tell his secret thoughts to a woman."

"Daughter, the Great Spirit made your father with a white skin, and he made mine with a red; but he colored both their hearts with blood. When young, it is swift and warm; but when old, it is still and cold. Is there difference below the skin? No. Once John had a woman. She was the mother of so many sons"—he raised his hand with three fingers elevated—"and she had daughters that would have made the young Delawares happy. She was kind, daughter, and what I said she did. You have different fashions; but do you think John did not love the wife of his youth—the mother of his children?"

"And what has become of your family, John, your wife and your children?" asked Elizabeth, touched by the Indian's manner.

"Where is the ice that covered the great spring? It is melted and gone with the waters. John has lived till all his people have left him for the land of spirits; his time has come, and he is ready."

Mohegan dropped his head in his blanket and sat in silence. Miss Temple knew not what to say. She wished to draw the thoughts of the old warrior from his gloomy recollections, but there was a dignity in his sorrow, and in his fortitude, that repressed her efforts to speak. After a long pause, however, she renewed the discourse, by asking:

"Where is the Leatherstocking, John? I have brought this canister of powder at his request; but he is nowhere to be seen. Will you take charge of it, and see it delivered?"

The Indian raised his head slowly, and looked earnestly at the gift, which she put into his hand.

"This is the great enemy of my nation. Without this, when could the white men drive the Delawares? Daughter, the Great Spirit gave your fathers to know how to make guns and powder, that they might sweep the Indians from the land. There will soon be no redskin in the country. When John has gone, the last will leave these hills, and his family will be dead." The aged warrior stretched his body forward, leaning an elbow on his knee, and appeared to be taking a parting look at the objects of the vale, which were still visible through the misty atmosphere, though the air seemed to thicken at each moment around Miss Temple, who became conscious of an increased difficulty of respiration. The eye of Mohegan changed gradually from its sorrowful expression to a look of wildness that might be supposed to border on the inspiration of a prophet, as he continued—"But he will go to the country where his fathers have met. The game shall be plenty as the fish in the lakes. No woman shall cry for meat; no Mingo can ever come. The chase shall be for children; and all just red men shall live together as brothers."

"John! This is not the heaven of a Christian!" cried Miss Temple. "You deal now in the superstition of your forefathers."

"Fathers! sons!" said Mohegan with firmness—"all gone—all gone!—I have no son but the Young Eagle, and he has the blood of a white man."

"Tell me, John," said Elizabeth, willing to draw his thoughts to other subjects, and at the same time yielding to her own powerful interest in the youth; "who is this Mr. Edwards? Why are you so fond of him, and whence does he come?"

The Indian started at the question, which evidently re-called his recollection to earth. Taking her hand, he drew Miss Temple to a seat beside him and pointed to the country beneath them:

"See, daughter," he said, directing her looks towards the north; "as far as your young eyes can see, it was the land of his——"

But immense volumes of smoke at that moment rolled over their heads, and, whirling in the eddies formed by the mountains, interposed a barrier to their sight, while he was speaking. Startled by this circumstance, Miss Temple sprang on her feet, and turning her eyes towards the summit of the mountain, she beheld it covered by a similar canopy, while a roaring sound was heard in the forest above her like the rushing of winds.

"What means it, John!" she exclaimed. "We are enveloped in smoke, and I feel a heat like the glow of a furnace."

Before the Indian could reply, a voice was heard crying in the woods:

"John! Where are you, old Mohegan! The woods are on fire, and you have but a minute for escape."

The chief put his hand before his mouth, and making it play on his lips, produced the kind of noise that had attracted Elizabeth to the place, when a quick and hurried step was heard dashing through the dried underbrush and bushes, and presently Edwards rushed to his side, with horror in every feature.

CHAPTER XXXVII

Love rules the court, the camp, the grove.
LAY OF THE LAST MINSTREL

"IT would have been sad, indeed, to lose you in such a manner, my old friend," said Oliver, catching his breath for utterance. "Up and away! Even now we may be too late; the flames are circling round the point of the rock below, and, unless we can pass there, our only chance must be over the precipice. Away! away! Shake off your apathy, John; now is the time of need."

Mohegan pointed towards Elizabeth, who, forgetting her danger, had shrunk back to a projection of the rock as soon as she recognized the sounds of Edwards's voice, and said with something like awakened animation:

"Save her—leave John to die."

"Her! Whom mean you?" cried the youth, turning quickly to the place the other indicated; but when he saw the figure of Elizabeth bending towards him in an attitude that powerfully spoke terror, blended with reluctance to meet him in such a place, the shock deprived him of speech.

"Miss Temple!" he cried, when he found words. "You here! Is such a death reserved for you!"

"No, no, no—no death, I hope, for any of us, Mr. Edwards," she replied, endeavoring to speak calmly. "There is smoke, but no fire to harm us. Let us endeavor to retire."

"Take my arm," said Edwards; "there must be an opening in some direction for your retreat. Are you equal to the effort?"

"Certainly. You surely magnify the danger, Mr. Edwards. Lead me out the way you came."

"I will—I will," cried the youth with a kind of hysterical utterance. "No, no—there is no danger—I have alarmed you unnecessarily."

"But shall we leave the Indian—can we leave him, as he says, to die?"

An expression of painful emotion crossed the face of the young man; he stopped, and cast a longing look at Mohegan; but, dragging his companion after him, even against her will, he pursued his way with enormous strides towards the pass by which he had just entered the circle of flame.

"Do not regard him," he said, in those tones that denote a desperate calmness; "he is used to the woods, and such scenes; and he will escape up the mountain—over the rock— or he can remain where he is in safety."

"You thought not so this moment, Edwards! Do not leave him there to meet with such a death," cried Elizabeth, fixing a look on the countenance of her conductor that seemed to distrust his sanity.

"An Indian burn! Who ever heard of an Indian dying by

fire? An Indian cannot burn; the idea is ridiculous. Hasten, hasten, Miss Temple, or the smoke may incommode you."

"Edwards! Your look, your eye, terrifies me! Tell me the danger; is it greater than it seems? I am equal to any trial?"

"If we reach the point of yon rock before that sheet of fire, we are safe, Miss Temple!" exclaimed the young man, in a voice that burst without the bounds of his forced composure. "Fly! The struggle is for life!"

The place of the interview between Miss Temple and the Indian has already been described as one of those platforms of rock, which form a sort of terrace in the mountains of that country, and the face of it, we have said, was both high and perpendicular. Its shape was nearly a natural arc, the ends of which blended with the mountain, at points where its sides were less abrupt in their descent. It was round one of these terminations of the sweep of the rock that Edwards had ascended, and it was towards the same place that he urged Elizabeth to a desperate exertion of speed.

Immense clouds of white smoke had been pouring over the summit of the mountain, and had concealed the approach and ravages of the element; but a crackling sound drew the eyes of Miss Temple, as she flew over the ground, supported by the young man, towards the outline of smoke, where she already perceived the waving flames shooting forward from the vapor, now flaring high in the air, and then bending to the earth, seeming to light into combustion every stick and shrub on which they breathed. The sight aroused them to re-doubled efforts; but, unfortunately, a collection of the tops of trees, old and dried, lay directly across their course; and, at the very moment when both had thought their safety ensured, the warm currents of the air swept a forked tongue of flame across the pile, which lighted at the touch; and when they reached the spot, the flying pair were opposed by the surly roaring of a body of fire, as if a furnace were glowing in their path. They recoiled from the heat and stood on a point of the rock, gazing in a stupor at the flames, which were spreading rapidly down the mountain, whose side soon became a sheet of living fire. It was dangerous for one clad in the light and airy dress of Elizabeth to approach even the vicinity of the raging element; and those flowing robes that gave such softness and grace to her form seemed now to be formed for the instruments of her destruction.

The villagers were accustomed to resort to that hill in quest of timber and fuel; in procuring which, it was their usage to take only the bodies of the trees, leaving the tops and branches to decay under the operations of the weather. Much of the hill was, consequently, covered with such light fuel, which, having been scorched under the sun for the last two months, was ignited with a touch. Indeed, in some cases, there did not appear to be any contact between the fire and these piles, but the flames seemed to dart from heap to heap, as the fabulous fire of the temple is represented to reillume its neglected lamp.

There was beauty as well as terror in the sight, and Edwards and Elizabeth stood viewing the progress of the desolation, with a strange mixture of horror and interest. The former, however, shortly roused himself to new exertions, and drawing his companion after him, they skirted the edge of the smoke, the young man penetrating frequently into its dense volumes in search of a passage, but in every instance without success. In this manner they proceeded in a semicircle around the upper part of the terrace, until, arriving at the verge of the precipice, opposite to the point where Edwards had ascended, the horrid conviction burst on both at the same instant that they were completely encircled by the fire. So long as a single pass up or down the mountain was unexplored, there was hope; but when retreat seemed to be absolutely impracticable, the horror of their situation broke upon Elizabeth as powerfully as if she had hitherto considered the danger light.

"This mountain is doomed to be fatal to me!" she whispered. "We shall find our graves on it!"

"Say not so, Miss Temple; there is yet hope," returned the youth, in the same tone, while the vacant expression of his eye contradicted his words. "Let us return to the point of the rock; there is—there must be—some place about it where we can descend."

"Lead me there," exclaimed Elizabeth; "let us leave no effort untried." She did not wait for his compliance, but, turning, retraced her steps to the brow of the precipice, murmuring to herself, in suppressed, hysterical sobs, "My father! My poor, my distracted father!"

Edwards was by her side in an instant, and with aching eyes he examined every fissure in the crags, in quest of some opening that might offer facilities for flight. But the smooth, even surface of the rocks afforded hardly a resting place for a foot, much less those continued projections which would have been necessary for a descent of nearly a hundred feet. Edwards was not slow in feeling the conviction that this hope was also futile, and, with a kind of feverish despair that still urged him to action, he turned to some new expedient.

"There is nothing left, Miss Temple," he said, "but to lower you from this place to the rock beneath. If Natty were here, or even that Indian could be roused, their ingenuity and long practice would easily devise methods to do it; but I am a child at this moment in everything but daring. Where shall I find means? This dress of mine is so light, and there is so little of it—then the blanket of Mohegan;—we must try—we must try—anything is better than to see you a victim to such a death!"

"And what will become of you?" said Elizabeth. "Indeed, indeed, neither you nor John must be sacrificed to my safety."

He heard her not, for he was already by the side of Mohegan, who yielded his blanket without a question, retaining his seat with Indian dignity and composure, though his own situation was even more critical than that of the others. The blanket was cut into shreds, and the fragments fastened together; the loose linen jacket of the youth and the light muslin shawl of Elizabeth were attached to them, and the whole thrown over the rocks, with the rapidity of lightning; but the united pieces did not reach halfway to the bottom.

"It will not do—it will not do!" cried Elizabeth. "For me there is no hope! The fire comes slowly, but certainly. See, it destroys the very earth before it!"

Had the flames spread on that rock with half the quickness with which they leaped from bush to tree, in other parts of the mountain, our painful task would have soon ended; for they would have consumed already the captives they enclosed. But the peculiarity of their situation afforded Elizabeth and her companion the respite of which they had availed themselves to make the efforts we have recorded.

The thin covering of earth on the rock supported but a scanty and faded herbage, and most of the trees that had found root in the fissures had already died during the intense heats of preceding summers. Those which still retained the appearance of life bore a few dry and withered leaves, while the others were merely the wrecks of pines, oaks, and maples. No better materials to feed the fire could be found had there been a communication with the flames; but the ground was destitute of the brush that led the destructive element, like a torrent, over the remainder of the hill. As auxiliary to this scarcity of fuel, one of the large springs which abound in that country gushed out of the side of the ascent above, and, after creeping sluggishly along the level land, saturating the mossy covering of the rock with moisture, it swept round the base of the little cone that formed the pinnacle of the mountain, and, entering the canopy of smoke near one of the terminations of the terrace, found its way to the lake, not by dashing from rock to rock, but by the secret channels of the earth. It would rise to the surface, here and there, in the wet seasons, but in the droughts of summer it was to be traced only by the bogs and moss that announced the proximity of water. When the fire reached this barrier, it was compelled to pause until a concentration of its heat could overcome the moisture, like an army waiting the operations of a battering train, to open its way to desolation.

That fatal moment seemed now to have arrived, for the hissing steams of the spring appeared to be nearly exhausted, and the moss of the rocks was already curling under the intense heat, while fragments of bark that yet clung to the dead trees began to separate from their trunks and fall to the ground in crumbling masses. The air seemed quivering with rays of heat, which might be seen playing along the parched stems of the trees. There were moments when dark clouds of smoke would sweep along the little terrace; and, as the eye lost its power, the other senses contributed to give effect to the fearful horror of the scene. At such moments, the roaring of the flames, the crackling of the furious element, with the tearing of falling branches, and, occasionally, the thundering echoes of some falling tree, united to alarm the victims. Of the three, however, the youth appeared much the most agitated. Elizabeth, having relinquished entirely the idea of escape, was fast obtaining that resigned composure with which the most delicate of her sex are sometimes known to meet unavoidable evils; while Mohegan, who was much nearer to the danger, maintained his seat with the invincible resignation of an Indian warrior. Once or twice the eye of the aged chief, which was ordinarily fixed in the direction of the distant hills, turned towards the young pair, who seemed doomed to so early a death, with a slight indication of pity crossing his composed features, but it would immediately revert again to its former gaze, as if already looking into the womb of futurity. Much of the time he was chanting a kind of low dirge, in the Delaware tongue, using the deep and remarkably guttural tones of his people.

"At such a moment, Mr. Edwards, all earthly distinctions end," whispered Elizabeth; "persuade John to move nearer to us—let us die together."

"I cannot—he will not stir," returned the youth, in the same horridly still tones. "He considers this as the happiest moment of his life. He is past seventy, and has been decaying rapidly for some time: he received some injury in chasing that unlucky deer, too, on the lake. Oh! Miss Temple that was an unlucky chase indeed! It has led, I fear, to this awful scene."

The smile of Elizabeth was celestial. "Why name such a trifle now—at this moment the heart is dead to all earthly emotions!"

"If anything could reconcile a man to this death," cried the youth, "it would be to meet it in such company!"

"Talk not so, Edwards, talk not so," interrupted Miss Temple. "I am unworthy of it; and it is unjust to yourself. We must die; yes—yes—we must die—it is the will of God, and let us endeavor to submit like his own children."

"Die!" the youth rather shrieked than exclaimed, "No—no—no—there must yet be hope—you at least must not, shall not die."

"In what way can we escape?" asked Elizabeth, pointing with a look of heavenly composure towards the fire. "Observe! The flame is crossing the barrier of wet ground—it comes slowly Edwards, but surely.—Ah! see! The tree! the tree is already lighted!"

Her words were too true. The heat of the conflagration had at length overcome the resistance of the spring, and the fire was slowly stealing along the half-dried moss; while a dead pine kindled with the touch of a forked flame that, for a moment, wreathed around the stem of the tree, as it

whirled, in one of its evolutions, under the influence of the
air. The effect was instantaneous. The flames danced along
the parched trunk of the pine like lightning quivering on a
chain, and immediately a column of living fire was raging
on the terrace. It soon spread from tree to tree: and the
scene was evidently drawing to a close. The log on which
Mohegan was seated lighted at its further end, and the Indian
appeared to be surrounded by fire. Still he was unmoved.
As his body was unprotected, his sufferings must have been
great; but his fortitude was superior to all. His voice could
yet be heard even in the midst of these horrors. Elizabeth
turned her head from the sight, and faced the valley. Furious
eddies of wind were created by the heat, and just at the moment, the canopy of fiery smoke that overhung the valley
was cleared away, leaving a distinct view of the peaceful
village beneath them.

"My father! My father!" shrieked Elizabeth. "Oh! this
—this surely might have been spared me—but I submit."

The distance was not so great but the figure of Judge
Temple could be seen, standing in his own grounds, and apparently contemplating, in perfect unconsciousness of the
danger of his child, the mountain in flames. This sight was
still more painful than the approaching danger, and Elizabeth
again faced the hill.

"My intemperate warmth has done this!" cried Edwards,
in the accents of despair. "If I had possessed but a moiety
of your heavenly resignation, Miss Temple, all might yet have
been well."

"Name it not—name it not," she said. "It is now of no
avail. We must die, Edwards, we must die—let us do so
as Christians. But—no—you may yet escape, perhaps.
Your dress is not so fatal as mine. Fly! Leave me. An
opening may yet be found for you, possibly—certainly it
is worth the effort. Fly! Leave me—but stay! You will see
my father; my poor, my bereaved father! Say to him, then,
Edwards, say to him all that can appease his anguish. Tell
him that I died happy and collected; that I have gone to
my beloved mother; that the hours of this life are as nothing when balanced in the scales of eternity. Say how we
shall meet again. And say," she continued, dropping her
voice, that had risen with her feelings, as if conscious of
her worldly weaknesses, "how dear, how very dear, was my

love for him; that it was near, too near, to my love for God."

The youth listened to her touching accents, but moved not. In a moment he found utterance, and replied:

"And is it me that you command to leave you! To leave you on the edge of the grave! Oh! Miss Temple, how little have you known me!" he cried, dropping on his knees at her feet, and gathering her flowing robe in his arms as if to shield her from the flames. "I have been driven to the woods in despair; but your society has tamed the lion within me. If I have wasted my time in degradation, 'twas you that charmed me to it. If I have forgotten my name and family, your form supplied the place of memory. If I have forgotten my wrongs, 'twas you that taught me charity. No— no—dearest Elizabeth, I may die with you, but I can never leave you!"

Elizabeth moved not, nor answered. It was plain that her thoughts had been raised from the earth. The recollection of her father and her regrets at their separation had been mellowed by a holy sentiment that lifted her above the level of earthly things, and she was fast losing the weakness of her sex in the near view of eternity. But as she listened to these words she became once more woman. She struggled against these feelings, and smiled, as she thought she was shaking off the last lingering feeling of nature, when the world, and all its seductions, rushed again to her heart, with the sounds of a human voice, crying in piercing tones:

"Gal! Where be ye, gal! Gladden the heart of an old man, if ye yet belong to 'arth!"

"List!" said Elizabeth. " 'Tis the Leatherstocking; he seeks me!"

" 'Tis Natty!" shouted Edwards, "and we may yet be saved!"

A wide and circling flame glared on their eyes for a moment, even above the fire of the woods, and a loud report followed.

" 'Tis the canister! 'Tis the powder," cried the same voice, evidently approaching them. " 'Tis the canister, and the precious child is lost!"

At the next instant Natty rushed through the steams of the spring, and appeared on the terrace, without his deerskin cap, his hair burnt to his head, his shirt, of country check, black and filled with holes, and his red features of a deeper color than ever by the heat he had encountered.

Chapter XXXVIII

Even from the land of shadows, now,
My father's awful ghost appears.
                    GERTRUDE OF WYOMING

FOR an hour after Louisa Grant was left by Miss Temple, in the situation already mentioned, she continued in feverish anxiety, awaiting the return of her friend. But as the time passed by without the reappearance of Elizabeth, the terror of Louisa gradually increased until her alarmed fancy had conjured every species of danger that appertained to the woods, excepting the one that really existed. The heavens had become obscured by degrees, and vast volumes of smoke were pouring over the valley; but the thoughts of Louisa were still recurring to beasts, without dreaming of the real cause for apprehension. She was stationed in the edge of the low pines and chestnuts that succeed the first or large growth of the forest, and directly above the angle where the highway turned from the straight course to the village and ascended the mountain laterally. Consequently, she commanded a view not only of the valley, but of the road beneath her. The few travelers that passed, she observed, were engaged in earnest conversation and frequently raised their eyes to the hill, and at length she saw the people leaving the courthouse, and gazing upwards also. While under the influence of the alarm excited by such unusual movements, reluctant to go, and yet fearful to remain, Louisa was startled by the low, cracking, but cautious treads of someone approaching through the bushes. She was on the eve of flight when Natty emerged from the cover and stood at her side. The old man laughed as he shook her kindly by a hand that was passive with fear.

"I am glad to meet you here, child," he said; "for the back of the mountain is afire, and it would be dangerous to go up it now, till it has been burnt over once, and the dead-wood is gone. There's a foolish man, the comrade of that varmint who has given me all this trouble, digging for ore on the east side. I told him that the kearless fellows, who thought to catch a practys'd hunter in the woods after dark, had thrown the lighted pine knots in the brush, and that 'twould kindle like tow, and warned him to leave the hill. But he was set upon his business, and nothing short of Providence could move him. If he isn't burnt and buried in a grave of his own digging, he's made of salamanders. Why, what ails the child! You look as skeary as if you see'd more painters! I wish there were more to be found; they'd count up faster than the beaver. But where's the good child of a bad father? Did she forget her promise to the old man?"

"The hill! the hill!" shrieked Louisa. "She seeks you on the hill with the powder!"

Natty recoiled several feet at this unexpected intelligence.

"The Lord of Heaven have mercy on her! She's on the Vision, and that's a sheet of fire ag'in this. Child, if ye love the dear one, and hope to find a friend when ye need it most, to the village, and give the alarm. The men are used to fighting fire, and there may be a chance left. Fly! I bid ye fly! Nor stop even for breath."

The Leatherstocking had no sooner uttered this injunction, than he disappeared in the bushes, and when last seen by Louisa, was rushing up the mountain with a speed that none but those who were accustomed to the toil could attain.

"Have I found ye!" the old man exclaimed, when he burst out of the smoke. "God be praised that I've found ye; but follow—there's no time for talking."

"My dress!" said Elizabeth. "It would be fatal to trust myself nearer to the flames in it."

"I bethought me of your flimsy things," cried Natty, throwing loose the folds of a covering of buckskin that he carried on his arm, and wrapping her form in it, in such a manner as to envelope her whole person; "now follow, for it's a matter of life and death to us all."

"But John! What will become of John?" cried Edwards. "Can we leave the old warrior here to perish?"

The eyes of Natty followed the direction of Edwards's finger, when he beheld the Indian still seated as before,

with the very earth under his feet consuming with fire.
Without delay the hunter approached the spot, and spoke
in Delaware:

"Up and away, Chingachgook! Will ye stay here to burn,
like a Mingo at the stake? The Moravians have teached ye
better, I hope; the Lord preserve me if the powder hasn't
flashed atween his legs, and the skin of his back is roasting.
Will ye come, I say; will ye follow?"

"Why should Mohegan go?" returned the Indian gloomily.
"He has seen the days of an eagle, and his eye grows dim.
He looks on the valley; he looks on the water; he looks in the
hunting grounds—but he sees no Delawares. Everyone has
a white skin. My fathers say, from the far-off land, come.
My woman, my young warriors, my tribe, say, come. The
Great Spirit says, come. Let Mohegan die."

"But you forget your friend," cried Edwards.

" 'Tis useless to talk to an Indian with the death fit on
him, lad," interrupted Natty, who seized the strips of the
blanket, and with wonderful dexterity strapped the passive
chieftain to his own back; when he turned, and with a
strength that seemed to bid defiance not only to his years
but to his load, he led the way to the point whence he had
issued. As they crossed the little terrace of rock, one of the
dead trees that had been tottering for several minutes fell
on the spot where they had stood, and filled the air with
its cinders.

Such an event quickened the steps of the party, who followed the Leatherstocking with the urgency required by the
occasion.

"Tread on the soft ground," he cried, when they were in a
gloom where sight availed them but little, "and keep in the
white smoke; keep the skin close on her, lad; she's a precious
one, another will be hard to be found."

Obedient to the hunter's directions, they followed his steps
and advice implicitly; and although the narrow passage along
the winding of the spring led amid burning logs and falling branches, they happily achieved it in safety. No one but
a man long accustomed to the woods could have traced his
route through a smoke in which respiration was difficult and
sight nearly useless; but the experience of Natty conducted
them to an opening through the rocks, where, with a little

difficulty, they soon descended to another terrace and emerged at once into a tolerably clear atmosphere.

The feelings of Edwards and Elizabeth at reaching this spot may be imagined, though not easily described. No one seemed to exult more than their guide, who turned, with Mohegan still lashed to his back, and laughing in his own manner, said:

"I know'd 'twas the Frenchman's powder, gal; it went so altogether; your coarse grain will squib for a minute. The Iroquois had none of the best powder when I went ag'in the Canada tribes, under Sir William. Did I ever tell you the story, lad, consarning the scrimmage with——"

"For God's sake, tell me nothing now, Natty, until we are entirely safe. Where shall we go next?"

"Why, on the platform of rock over the cave, to be sure; you will be safe enough there, or we'll go into it, if you be so minded."

The young man started, and appeared agitated; but looking around him with an anxious eye, said quickly:

"Shall we be safe on the rock? Cannot the fire reach us there, too?"

"Can't the boy see?" said Natty, with the coolness of one accustomed to the kind of danger he had just encountered. "Had ye stayed in the place above ten minutes longer, you would both have been in ashes, but here you may stay forever, and no fire can touch you, until they burn the rocks as well as the woods."

With this assurance, which was obviously true, they proceeded to the spot, and Natty deposited his load, placing the Indian on the ground with his back against a fragment of the rocks. Elizabeth sank on the ground and buried her face in her hands, while her heart was swelling with a variety of conflicting emotions.

"Let me urge you to take a restorative, Miss Temple," said Edwards respectfully; "your frame will sink else."

"Leave me, leave me," she said, raising her beaming eyes for a moment to his; "I feel too much for words! I am grateful, Oliver, for this miraculous escape; and next to my God to you."

Edwards withdrew to the edge of the rock, and shouted— "Benjamin! Where are you, Benjamin?"

A hoarse voice replied, as if from the bowels of the earth,

"Hereaway, master; stowed in this here bit of a hole, which is all the same as hot as the cook's coppers. I'm tired of my berth, d'ye see, and if so be that Leatherstocking has got much overhauling to do before he sails after them said beaver, I'll go into dock again, and ride out my quarantine till I can get prottick from the law, and so hold on upon the rest of my 'spaniolas."

"Bring up a glass of water from the spring," continued Edwards, "and throw a little wine in it; hasten, I entreat you?"

"I knows but little of your small drink, master Oliver," returned the steward, his voice issuing out of the cave into the open air, "and the Jamaiky held out no longer than to take a parting kiss with Billy Kirby, when he anchored me alongside the highway last night, where you run me down in the chase. But here's sum'mat of a red color that may suit a weak stomach, mayhap. That Master Kirby is no first-rate in a boat; but he'll tack a cart among the stumps, all the same as a Lon'on pilot will back and fill through the colliers in the Pool."

As the steward ascended while talking, by the time he had ended his speech, he appeared on the rock with the desired restoratives, exhibiting the worn-out and bloated features of a man who had run deep in a debauch, and that lately.

Elizabeth took from the hands of Edwards the liquor which he offered, and then motioned to be left again to herself.

The youth turned at her bidding, and observed Natty kindly assiduous around the person of Mohegan. When their eyes met, the hunter said sorrowfully:

"His time has come, lad; I see it in his eyes. When an Indian fixes his eye, he means to go but to one place; and what the willful creaters put their minds on, they're sure to do."

A quick tread prevented the reply, and in a few moments, to the amazement of the whole party, Mr. Grant was seen clinging to the side of the mountain and striving to reach the place where they stood. Oliver sprang to his assistance, and by their united efforts the worthy divine was soon placed safely among them.

"How came you added to our number?" cried Edwards. "Is the hill alive with people at a time like this?"

The hasty but pious thanksgivings of the clergyman were soon ejaculated; and when he succeeded in collecting his bewildered senses, he replied:

"I heard that my child was seen coming to the mountain; and when the fire broke over its summit, my uneasiness drew me up the road, where I found Louisa, in terror for Miss Temple. It was to seek her that I came into this dangerous place; and I think, but for God's mercy, through the dogs of Natty, I should have perished in the flames myself."

"Ay! follow the hounds, and if there's an opening they'll scent it out," said Natty; "their noses be given them the same as man's reason."

"I did so, and they led me to this place; but, praise be to God, that I see you all safe and well."

"No, no," returned the hunter; "safe we be, but as for well, John can't be called in a good way, unless you'll say that for a man that's taking his last look at 'arth."

"He speaks the truth!" said the divine, with the holy awe with which he ever approached the dying. "I have been by too many deathbeds not to see that the hand of the tyrant is laid on this old warrior. Oh! how consoling it is to know that he has not rejected the offered mercy in the hour of his strength and of worldly temptations! The offspring of a race of heathens, he has in truth been 'as a brand plucked from the burning.' "

"No, no," returned Natty, who alone stood with him by the side of the dying warrior, "it's no burning that ails him, though his Indian feelings made him scorn to move, unless it be the burning of man's wicked thoughts for near fourscore years; but it's nater giving out in a chase that's run too long. Down with ye, Hector! Down, I say!—Flesh isn't iron, that a man can live forever, and see his kith and kin driven to a far country, and he left to mourn, with none to keep him company."

"John," said the divine, tenderly, "do you hear me? Do you wish the prayers appointed by the church, at this trying moment?"

The Indian turned his ghastly face towards the speaker and fastened his dark eyes on him, steadily, but vacantly. No sign of recognition was made; and in a moment he moved his head again slowly towards the vale and began to sing, using his own language, in those low, guttural tones that have been so often mentioned, his notes rising with his theme till they swelled so loud as to be distinct.

"I will come! I will come! To the land of the just I will come! The Maquas I have slain!—I have slain the Maquas! and the Great Spirit calls to his son. I will come! I will come! To the land of the just I will come!"

"What says he, Leatherstocking?" inquired the priest, with tender interest. "Sings he the Redeemer's praise?"

"No, no—'tis his own praise that he speaks now," said Natty, turning in a melancholy manner from the sight of his dying friend; "and a good right he has to say it all, for I know every word to be true."

"May Heaven avert such self-righteousness from his heart! Humility and penitence are the seals of Christianity; and without feeling them deeply seated in the soul, all hope is delusive, and leads to vain expectations. Praise himself! When his whole soul and body should unite to praise his Maker! John! You have enjoyed the blessings of a gospel ministry, and have been called from out a multitude of sinners and pagans, and I trust, for a wise and gracious purpose. Do you now feel what it is to be justified by our Saviour's death, and reject all weak and idle dependence on good works, that spring from man's pride and vainglory?"

The Indian did not regard his interrogator, but he raised his head again, and said in a low, distinct voice:

"Who can say that the Maquas know the back of Mohegan? What enemy that trusted in him did not see the morning? What Mingo that he chased ever sang the song of triumph? Did Mohegan ever lie? No; the truth lived in him, and none else could come out of him. In his youth he was a warrior, and his moccasins left the stain of blood. In his age, he was wise; his words at the council fire did not blow away with the winds."

"Ah! he has abandoned that vain relic of paganism, his songs," cried the divine. "What says he now? Is he sensible of his lost state?"

"Lord! man," said Natty, "he knows his end is at hand as well as you or I; but, so far from thinking it a loss, he believes it to be a great gain. He is old and stiff, and you have made the game so scarce and shy that better shots than him find it hard to get a livelihood. Now he thinks he shall travel where it will always be good hunting; where no wicked or unjust Indians can go; and where he shall meet all his tribe together ag'in. There's not much loss in that to a man whose hands are hardly fit for basketmaking. Loss! If there be any loss, 'twill be to me. I'm sure, after he's gone, there will be but little left for me but to follow."

"His example and end, which, I humbly trust, shall yet be made glorious," returned Mr. Grant, "should lead your mind to dwell on the things of another life. But I feel it to be my duty to smooth the way for the parting spirit. This is the moment, John, when the reflection that you did not reject the mediation of the Redeemer will bring balm to your soul. Trust not to any act of former days, but lay the burden of your sins at His feet, and you have His own blessed assurance that He will not desert you."

"Though all you say be true, and you have scripter gospels for it, too," said Natty, "you will make nothing of the Indian. He hasn't seen a Moravian priest sin' the war; and it's hard to keep them from going back to their native ways. I should think 'twould be as well to let the old man pass in peace. He's happy now; I know it by his eye; and that's more than I would say for the chief, sin' the time the Delawares broke up from the headwaters of their river and went west. Ah's me! 'Tis a grievous long time that, and many dark days have we seen together sin' it."

"Hawkeye!" said Mohegan, rousing with the last glimmering of life. "Hawkeye! Listen to the words of your brother."

"Yes, John," said the hunter, in English, strongly affected by the appeal, and drawing to his side; "we have been brothers; and more so than it means in the Indian tongue. What would ye have with me, Chingachgook?"

"Hawkeye! My fathers call me to the happy hunting grounds. The path is clear, and the eyes of Mohegan grow young. I look—but I see no white skins; there are none to be seen but just and brave Indians. Farewell, Hawkeye—you shall go with the Fire-eater and the Young Eagle to the white man's heaven; but I go after my fathers. Let the bow, and tomahawk, and pipe, and the wampum of Mohegan be laid in his grave; for when he starts 'twill be in the night, like a warrior on a war party, and he cannot stop to seek them."

"What says he, Nathaniel?" cried Mr. Grant, earnestly, and with obvious anxiety. "Does he recall the promises of the mediation? And trust his salvation to the Rock of Ages?"

Although the faith of the hunter was by no means clear, yet the fruits of early instruction had not entirely fallen in the wilderness. He believed in one God and one heaven; and when the strong feeling excited by the leave-taking of his old companion, which was exhibited by the powerful working of every muscle in his weather-beaten face, suffered him to speak, he replied:

"No—no—he trusts only to the Great Spirit of the savages, and to his own good deeds. He thinks, like all his people, that he is to be young ag'in, and to hunt, and be happy to the end of eternity. It's pretty much the same with all colors, parson. I could never bring myself to think that I shall meet with these hounds, or my piece, in another world; though the thoughts of leaving them forever sometimes brings hard feelings over me, and makes me cling to life with a greater craving than beseems three-score-and-ten."

"The Lord in his mercy avert such a death from one who has been sealed with the sign of the cross!" cried the minister, in holy fervor. "John—"

He paused for the elements. During the period occupied by the events which we have related, the dark clouds in the horizon had continued to increase in numbers and magnitude; and the awful stillness that now pervaded the air announced a crisis in the state of the atmosphere. The flames, which yet continued to rage along the sides of the mountain, no longer whirled in uncertain currents of their own eddies, but blazed high and steadily towards the heavens. There was even a quietude in the ravages of the destructive element, as if it foresaw that a hand, greater than even its own desolating power, was about to stay its progress. The piles of smoke which lay above the valley began to rise, and were dispelling rapidly; and streaks of vivid lightning were dancing through the masses of clouds that impended over the western hills. While Mr. Grant was speaking, a flash, which sent its quivering light through the gloom, laying bare the whole opposite horizon, was followed by a loud crash of thunder that rolled away among the hills, seeming to shake the foundations of the earth to their center. Mohegan raised himself, as if in obedience to a signal for his departure, and stretched his wasted arm towards the west. His dark face lighted with a look of joy; which, with all other expression, gradually disappeared; the muscles stiffening as they retreated to a state of rest; a slight convulsion played for a single instant about his lips; and his arm slowly dropped by his side; leaving the frame of the dead warrior reposing against the rock, with its glassy eyes open, and fixed on the distant hills, as if the deserted shell were tracing the flight of the spirit to its new abode.

All this Mr. Grant witnessed in silent awe; but when the last echoes of the thunder died away, he clasped his hands together with pious energy and repeated, in the full, rich tones of assured faith:

"O Lord! How unsearchable are thy judgments: and thy ways past finding out! 'I know that my Redeemer liveth, and that he shall stand at the latter day upon the earth: and though after my skin, worms destroy this body, yet in my flesh shall I see God: whom I shall see for myself, and mine eyes shall behold, and not another.' "

As the divine closed this burst of devotion, he bowed his head meekly to his bosom, and looked all the dependence and humility that the inspired language expressed.

When Mr. Grant retired from the body, the hunter approached, and taking the rigid hand of his friend, looked him wistfully in the face for some time without speaking, when he gave vent to his feelings by saying, in the mournful voice of one who felt deeply:

"Red skin or white, it's all over now! He's to be judged by a righteous Judge, and by no laws that's made to suit times, and new ways. Well, there's only one more death, and the world will be left to me and the hounds. Ah's me! A man must wait the time of God's pleasure, but I begin to weary of life. There is scarcely a tree standing that I know, and it's hard to find a face that I was acquainted with in my younger days."

Large drops of rain began now to fall and diffuse themselves over the dry rock, while the approach of the thundershower was rapid and certain. The body of the Indian was hastily removed into the cave beneath, followed by the whining hounds, who missed, and moaned for the look of intelligence that had always met their salutations to the chief.

Edwards made some hasty and confused excuse for not taking Elizabeth into the same place, which was now completely closed in front with logs and bark, saying something that she hardly understood about its darkness, and the unpleasantness of being with the dead body. Miss Temple, however, found a sufficient shelter against the torrent of rain that fell, under the projection of a rock which overhung them. But long before the shower was over, the sounds of voices were heard below them crying aloud for Elizabeth, and men soon appeared, beating the dying embers of the bushes, as they worked their way cautiously among the unextinguished brands.

At the first short cessation in the rain, Oliver conducted Elizabeth to the road, where he left her. Before parting, however, he found time to say, in a fervent manner that his companion was now at no loss to interpret:

"The moment of concealment is over, Miss Temple. By this time tomorrow, I shall remove a veil that perhaps it has been weakness to keep around me and my affairs so long. But I have had romantic and foolish wishes and weaknesses: and who has not, that is young and torn by conflicting passions? God bless you! I hear your father's voice; he is coming up the road, and I would not, just now, subject myself to detention. Thank Heaven, you are safe again; that alone removes the weight of a world from my spirit!"

He waited for no answer, but sprang into the woods. Elizabeth, notwithstanding she heard the cries of her father as he called upon her name, paused until he was concealed among the smoking trees, when she turned, and in a moment rushed into the arms of her half-distracted parent.

A carriage had been provided, into which Miss Temple hastily entered; when the cry was passed along the hill that the lost one was found, and the people returned to the village, wet and dirty, but elated with the thought that the daughter of their landlord had escaped from so horrid and untimely an end.*

* The probability of a fire in the woods, similar to that here described, has been questioned. The writer can only say that he once witnessed a fire in another part of New York that compelled a man to desert his wagon and horses in the highway, and in which the latter were destroyed. In order to estimate the probability of such an event, it is necessary to remember the effects of a long drought in that climate, and the abundance of deadwood which is found in a forest like that described. The fires in the American forests frequently rage to such an extent as to produce a sensible effect on the atmosphere at the distance of fifty miles. Houses, barns, and fences are quite commonly swept away in their course.

Chapter XXXIX

Selictar! unsheathe then our chief's scimitar;
Tambourgi! thy 'larum gives promise of war;
Ye mountains! that see us descend to the shore,
Shall view us as victors, or view us no more.   Byron

The heavy showers that prevailed during the remainder of the day completely stopped the progress of the flames; though glimmering fires were observed during the night, on different parts of the hill, wherever there was a collection of fuel to feed the element. The next day the woods, for many miles, were black and smoking, and were stripped of every vestige of brush and deadwood; but the pines and hemlocks still reared their heads proudly among the hills, and even the smaller trees of the forest retained a feeble appearance of life and vegetation.

The many tongues of rumor were busy in exaggerating the miraculous escape of Elizabeth; and a report was generally credited that Mohegan had actually perished in the flames. This belief became confirmed, and was indeed rendered probable, when the direful intelligence reached the village that Jotham Riddell, the miner, was found in his hole, nearly dead with suffocation and burnt to such a degree that no hopes were entertained of his life.

The public attention became much alive to the events of the last few days; and just at this crisis, the convicted counterfeiters took the hint from Natty, and, on the night succeeding the fire, found means to cut through their log prison also, and to escape unpunished. When this news began to circulate through the village, blended with the fate of Jotham, and the exaggerated and tortured reports of the events on the hill, the popular opinion was freely expressed as to the propriety of seizing such of the fugitives as remained within reach. Men talked of the cave as a secret receptacle of guilt; and as the rumor of ores and metals found its way into the confused medley of conjectures, counterfeiting and everything else that was wicked and dangerous to the peace of society suggested themselves to the busy fancies of the populace.

While the public mind was in this feverish state, it was hinted that the wood had been set on fire by Edwards and the Leatherstocking and that, consequently, they alone were responsible for the damages. This opinion soon gained ground, being most circulated by those who, by their own heedlessness, had caused the evil; and there was one irresistible burst of the common sentiment that an attempt should be made to punish the offenders. Richard was by no means deaf to this appeal, and by noon he set about in earnest to see the laws executed.

Several stout young men were selected, and taken apart with an appearance of secrecy, where they received some important charge from the Sheriff, immediately under the eyes, but far removed from the ears, of all in the village. Possessed of a knowledge of their duty, these youths hurried into the hills, with a bustling manner, as if the fate of the world depended on their diligence, and, at the same time, with an air of mystery, as great as if they were engaged on secret matters of the state.

At twelve precisely, a drum beat the "long roll" before the "Bold Dragoon," and Richard appeared, accompanied by Captain Hollister, who was clad in his vestments as commander of the "Templeton Light Infantry," when the former demanded of the latter the aid of the *posse comitatus*, in enforcing the laws of the country. We have not room to record the speeches of the two gentlemen on this occasion, but they are preserved in the columns of the little blue newspaper, which is yet to be found on the file, and are said to be highly creditable to the legal formula of one of the parties, and to the military precision of the other. Everything had been previously arranged, and as the red-coated drummer continued to roll out his clattering notes, some five-and-twenty privates appeared in the ranks, and arranged themselves in order of battle.

As this corps was composed of volunteers, and was commanded by a man who had passed the first five-and-thirty years of his life in camps and garrisons, it was the nonpareil of military science in that country, and was confidently pronounced by the judicious part of the Templeton community to be equal in skill and appearance to any troops in the known world; in physical endowments they were, certainly, much superior! To this assertion there were but three dissenting voices, and one dissenting opinion. The opinion belonged to Marmaduke, who, however, saw no necessity for its promulgation. Of the voices, one, and that a pretty loud one, came from the spouse of the commander himself, who frequently reproached her husband for condescending to lead such an irregular band of warriors after he had filled the honorable station of sergeant major to a dashing corps of Virginian cavalry through much of the recent war.

Another of these skeptical sentiments was invariably expressed by Mr. Pump whenever the company paraded, generally in some such terms as these, which were uttered with that sort of meekness that a native of the island of our forefathers is apt to assume when he condescends to praise the customs or character of her truant progeny:

"It's mayhap that they knows sum'mat about loading and firing, d'ye see; but as for working ship! Why a corporal's guard of the Boadishey's marines would back and fill on their quarters in such a manner as to surround and captivate them all in half a glass." As there was no one to deny this assertion, the marines of the Boadicea were held in a corresponding degree of estimation.

The third unbeliever was Monsieur Le Quoi, who merely whispered to the Sheriff that the corps was one of the finest he had ever seen, second only to the Mousquetaires of Le Bon Louis! However, as Mrs. Hollister thought there was something like actual service in the present appearances, and was, in consequence, too busily engaged with certain preparations of her own to make her comments; as Benjamin was absent, and Monsieur Le Quoi too happy to find fault with anything, the corps escaped criticism and comparison altogether on this momentous day, when they certainly had greater need of self-confidence than on any other previous occasion. Marmaduke was said to be again closeted with Mr. Van der School, and no interruption was offered to the movements of the troops. At two o'clock precisely the corps shouldered arms, beginning on the right wing, next to the veteran, and carrying the motion through to the left with great regularity. When each musket was quietly fixed in its proper situation, the order was given to wheel to

the left, and march. As this was bringing raw troops, at
once, to face their enemy, it is not to be supposed that
the maneuver was executed with their usual accuracy; but
as the music struck up the inspiring air of Yankee-Doodle,
and Richard, accompanied by Mr. Doolittle, preceded the
troops boldly down the street, Captain Hollister led on, with
his head elevated to forty-five degrees, with a little, low-
cocked hat perched on his crown, carrying a tremendous
dragoon saber at a poise, and trailing at his heels a huge
steel scabbard that had war in its very clattering. There was a
good deal of difficulty in getting all the platoons (there
were six) to look the same way; but, by the time they
reached the defile of the bridge, the troops were in sufficiently compact order. In this manner they marched up the
hill to the summit of the mountain, no other alteration taking place in the disposition of the forces, excepting that a
mutual complaint was made by the Sheriff and the magistrate, of a failure in wind, which gradually brought these
gentlemen to the rear. It will be unnecessary to detail the
minute movements that succeeded. We shall briefly say that
the scouts came in and reported that, so far from retreating,
as had been anticipated, the fugitives had evidently gained a
knowledge of the attack and were fortifying for a desperate
resistance. This intelligence certainly made a material
change not only in the plans of the leaders but in the
countenances of the soldiery also. The men looked at one
another with serious faces, and Hiram and Richard began
to consult together, apart.

At this conjuncture, they were joined by Billy Kirby, who
came along the highway, with his ax under his arm, as
much in advance of his team as Captain Hollister had been
of his troops in the ascent. The wood chopper was amazed
at the military array, but the Sheriff eagerly availed himself
of this powerful reinforcement and commanded his assistance in putting the laws in force. Billy held Mr.
Jones in too much deference to object; and it was finally
arranged that he should be the bearer of a summons to the
garrison to surrender, before they proceeded to extremities.
The troops now divided, one party being led by the captain,
over the Vision, and were brought in on the left of the
cave, while the remainder advanced upon its right, under
the orders of the lieutenant. Mr. Jones and Dr. Todd—for

the surgeon was in attendance also—appeared on the platform of rock, immediately over the heads of the garrison, though out of their sight. Hiram thought this approaching too near, and he therefore accompanied Kirby along the side of the hill to within a safe distance of the fortifications, where he took shelter behind a tree. Most of the men discovered great accuracy of eye in bringing some object in range between them and their enemy, and the only two of the besiegers who were left in plain sight of the besieged were Captain Hollister on one side, and the wood chopper on the other. The veteran stood up boldly to the front, supporting his heavy sword in one undeviating position, with his eye fixed firmly on his enemy, while the huge form of Billy was placed in that kind of quiet repose, with either hand thrust into his bosom, bearing his ax under his right arm, which permitted him, like his own oxen, to rest standing. So far, not a word had been exchanged between the belligerents. The besieged had drawn together a pile of black logs and branches of trees, which they had formed into a chevaux-de-frise, making a little circular abatis in front of the entrance to the cave. As the ground was steep and slippery in every direction around the place, and Benjamin appeared behind the works on one side, and Natty on the other, the arrangement was by no means contemptible, especially as the front was sufficiently guarded by the difficulty of the approach. By this time, Kirby had received his orders, and he advanced coolly along the mountain, picking his way with the same indifference as if he were pursuing his ordinary business. When he was within a hundred feet of the works, the long and much dreaded rifle of the Leatherstocking was seen issuing from the parapet, and his voice cried aloud:

"Keep off! Billy Kirby, keep off! I wish ye no harm; but if a man of ye all comes a step nigher, there'll be blood spilt atwixt us. God forgive the one that draws it first, but so it must be."

"Come, old chap," said Billy, good-naturedly, "don't be crabb'd, but hear what a man has got to say. I've no consarn in the business, only to see right 'twixt man and man; and I don't kear the valie of a beetle ring which gets the better; but there's Squire Doolittle, yonder behind the beech sap-

ling, he has invited me to come in and ask you to give up
to the law—that's all."

"I see the varmint! I see his clothes!" cried the indignant
Natty. "And if he'll only show so much flesh as will bury a
rifle bullet, thirty to the pound, I'll make him feel me. Go
away, Billy, I bid ye: you know my aim, and I bear you
no malice."

"You overcalculate your aim, Natty," said the other, as he
stepped behind a pine that stood near him; "if you think to
shoot a man through a tree with a three-foot butt. I can lay
this tree right across you in ten minutes, by any man's
watch, and in less time, too; so be civil—I want no more
than what's right."

There was a simple seriousness in the countenance of
Natty that showed he was much in earnest; but it was also
evident that he was reluctant to shed human blood. He answered the vaunt of the wood chopper, by saying:

"I know you drop a tree where you will, Billy Kirby;
but if you show a hand, or an arm, in doing it, there'll be
bones to be set, and blood to stanch. If it's only to get into
the cave that ye want, wait till a two hours' sun, and you
may enter it in welcome; but come in now you shall not.
There's one dead body already, lying on the cold rocks,
and there's another in which the life can hardly be said to
stay. If you will come in, there'll be dead without as well as
within."

The wood chopper stepped out fearlessly from his cover,
and cried:

"That's fair; and what's fair is right. He wants you to
stop till it's two hours to sundown; and I see reason in the
thing. A man can give up when he's wrong, if you don't
crowd him too hard; but you crowd a man, and he gets
to be like a stubborn ox—the more you beat, the worse he
kicks."

The sturdy notions of independence maintained by Billy
neither suited the emergency nor the impatience of Mr.
Jones, who was burning with a desire to examine the hidden mysteries of the cave. He therefore interrupted this
amicable dialogue with his own voice.

"I command you, Nathaniel Bumppo, by my authority, to
surrender your person to the law," he cried. "And I command you, gentlemen, to aid me in performing my duty.

Benjamin Penguillan, I arrest you, and order you to follow me to the jail of the county, by virtue of this warrant."

"I'd follow ye, Squire Dickens," said Benjamin, removing the pipe from his mouth (for during the whole scene the ex-major-domo had been very composedly smoking); "ay! I'd sail in your wake, to the end of the world, if so be that there was such a place, where there isn't seeing that it's round. Now, mayhap, Master Hollister, having lived all your life on shore, you isn't acquainted that the world, d'ye see——"

"Surrender!" interrupted the veteran, in a voice that startled his hearers, and which actually caused his own forces to recoil several paces. "Surrender, Benjamin Penguillan, or expect no quarter."

"Damn your quarter!" said Benjamin, rising from the log on which he was seated, and taking a squint along the barrel of the swivel, which had been brought on the hill during the night and now formed the means of defense on his side of the works. "Look you, Master, or Captain, tho'f I questions if ye know the name of a rope, except the one that's to hang ye, there's no need of singing out, as if ye was hailing a deaf man on a topgallant yard. Mayhap you think you've got my true name in your sheepskin; but what British sailor finds it worth while to sail in these seas, without a sham on his stern, in case of need, d'ye see. If you call me Penguillan, you calls me by the name of the man on whose land, d'ye see, I hove into daylight; and he was a gentleman; and that's more than my worst enemy will say of any of the family of Benjamin Stubbs."

"Send the warrant round to me, and I'll put in an alias," cried Hiram, from behind his cover.

"Put in a jackass, and you'll put in yourself, Mister Doobut-little," shouted Benjamin, who kept squinting along his little iron tube, with great steadiness.

"I give you but one moment to yield," cried Richard. "Benjamin! Benjamin! This is not the gratitude I expected from you."

"I tell you, Richard Jones," said Natty, who dreaded the Sheriff's influence over his comrade; "though the canister the gal brought be lost, there's powder enough in the cave to lift the rock you stand on. I'll take off my roof if you don't hold your peace."

"I think it beneath the dignity of my office to parley

further with the prisoners," the Sheriff observed to his
companion, while they both retired with a precipitancy that
Captain Hollister mistook for the signal to advance.

"Charge baggonet!" shouted the veteran. "March!"

Although this signal was certainly expected, it took the
assailed a little by surprise, and the veteran approached the
works, crying, "Courage, my brave lads! Give them no quarter unless they surrender"; and struck a furious blow upwards with his saber that would have divided the steward
into moieties, by subjecting him to the process of decapita-
tion, but for the fortunate interference of the muzzle of the
swivel. As it was, the gun was dismounted at the critical moment that Benjamin was applying his pipe to the priming,
and, in consequence, some five or six dozen of rifle bullets
were projected into the air, in nearly a perpendicular line.
Philosophy teaches us that the atmosphere will not retain
lead; and two pounds of the metal, molded into bullets of
thirty to the pound, after describing an ellipsis in their journey, returned to the earth rattling among the branches of
the trees directly over the heads of the troops stationed in
the rear of their captain. Much of the success of an attack made by irregular soldiers depends on the direction in
which they are first got in motion. In the present instance,
it was retrograde, and in less than a minute after the bellow-
ing report of the swivel among the rocks and caverns, the
whole weight of the attack from the left rested on the prowess of the single arm of the veteran. Benjamin received a
severe contusion from the recoil of his gun, which produced
a short stupor, during which period the ex-steward was
prostrate on the ground. Captain Hollister availed himself
of this circumstance to scramble over the breastwork and obtain a footing in the bastion—for such was the nature of the
fortress, as connected with the cave. The moment the veteran found himself within the works of his enemy, he
rushed to the edge of the fortification, and waving his saber
over his head, shouted:

"Victory! Come on, my brave boys, the work's our own!"

All this was perfectly military, and was such an example
as a gallant officer was in some measure bound to exhibit to
his men; but the outcry was the unlucky cause of turning the
tide of success. Natty, who had been keeping a vigilant eye on
the wood chopper, and the enemy immediately before him,

wheeled at this alarm and was appalled at beholding his comrade on the ground and the veteran standing on his own bulwark, giving forth the cry of victory! The muzzle of the long rifle was turned instantly towards the captain. There was a moment when the life of the old soldier was in great jeopardy; but the object to shoot at was both too large and too near for the Leatherstocking, who, instead of pulling his trigger, applied the gun to the rear of his enemy, and by a powerful shove sent him outside of the works with much greater rapidity than he had entered them. The spot on which Captain Hollister alighted was directly in front, where, as his feet touched the ground, so steep and slippery was the side of the mountain, it seemed to recede from under them. His motion was swift, and so irregular as utterly to confuse the faculties of the old soldier. During its continuance, he supposed himself to be mounted, and charging through the ranks of his enemy. At every tree he made a blow, of course, as at a foot soldier; and just as he was making the cut "St. George" at a half-burnt sapling, he landed in the highway, and, to his utter amazement, at the feet of his own spouse. When Mrs. Hollister, who was toiling up the hill followed by at least twenty curious boys, leaning with one hand on the staff with which she ordinarily walked and bearing in the other an empty bag, witnessed this exploit of her husband, indignation immediately got the better, not only of her religion, but of her philosophy.

"Why, sargeant! Is it flying ye are?" she cried—"That I should live to see a husband of mine turn his back to the inimy! And sich a one! Here have I been telling the b'ys, as we come along, all about the saige of Yorrektown, and how ye was hurted; and how ye'd be acting the same ag'in the day; and I mate ye retraiting jist as the first gun is. fired. Och! I may trow away the bag! For if there's plunder, 'twill not be the wife of sich as yeerself that will be privileged to be getting the same. They do say, too, there is a power of goold and silver in the place—the Lord forgive me for setting my heart on worreldly things; but what falls in the battle, there's scripter for believing, is the just property of the victor."

"Retreating!" exclaimed the amazed veteran. "Where's my horse? He has been shot under me—I——"

"Is the man mad?" interrupted his wife—"Divil the horse

do ye own, sargeant, and ye're nothing but a shabby captain
of malaishy. Oh! If the ra'al captain was here, 'tis the other
way ye'd be riding, dear, or you would not follow your
laider!"

While this worthy couple were thus discussing events, the
battle began to rage more violently than ever above them.
When the Leatherstocking saw his enemy fairly under
headway, as Benjamin would express it, he gave his attention again to the right wing of the assailants. It would have
been easy for Kirby, with his powerful frame, to have seized
the moment to scale the bastion, and, with his great strength,
to have sent both its defenders in pursuit of the veteran; but
hostility appeared to be the passion that the wood chopper
indulged the least in at that moment, for, in a voice that was
heard by the retreating left wing, he shouted:

"Hurra! Well done, captain! Keep it up! How he handles
his bush hook! He makes nothing of a sapling!" and such
other encouraging exclamations to the flying veteran, until,
overcome by mirth, the good-natured fellow seated himself
on the ground, kicking the earth with delight, and giving
vent to peal after peal of laughter.

Natty stood all this time in a menacing attitude, with his
rifle pointed over the breastwork, watching with a quick and
cautious eye the least movement of the assailants. The outcry unfortunately tempted the ungovernable curiosity of
Hiram to take a peep from behind his cover at the state
of the battle. Though this evolution was performed with
great caution, in protecting his front, he left, like many a
better commander, his rear exposed to the attacks of his
enemy. Mr. Doolittle belonged physically to a class of his
countrymen, to whom nature has denied, in their formation,
the use of curved lines. Everything about him was either
straight or angular. But his tailor was a woman who worked,
like a regimental contractor, by a set of rules that gave the
same configuration to the whole human species. Consequently when Mr. Doolittle leaned forward in the manner described, a loose drapery appeared behind the tree, at which
the rifle of Natty was pointed with the quickness of lightning.
A less experienced man would have aimed at the flowing
robe, which hung like a festoon halfway to the earth; but the
Leatherstocking knew both the man and his female tailor
better; and when the smart report of the rifle was heard,

Kirby, who watched the whole maneuver in breathless expectation, saw the bark fly from the beech, and the cloth, at some distance above the loose folds, wave at the same instant. No battery was ever unmasked with more promptitude than Hiram advanced from behind the tree at this summons.

He made two or three steps, with great precision, to the front, and placing one hand on the afflicted part, stretched forth the other, with a menacing air towards Natty, and cried aloud:

"Gawl darn ye! This shan't be settled so easy; I'll follow it up from the 'common pleas' to the 'court of errors.' "

Such a shocking imprecation, from the mouth of so orderly a man as Squire Doolittle, with the fearless manner in which he exposed himself, together with, perhaps, the knowledge that Natty's rifle was unloaded, encouraged the troops in the rear, who gave a loud shout, and fired a volley into the treetops, after the contents of the swivel. Animated by their own noise, the men now rushed on in earnest; and Billy Kirby, who thought the joke, good as it was, had gone far enough was in the act of scaling the works when Judge Temple appeared on the opposite side, exclaiming:

"Silence and peace! Why do I see murder and bloodshed attempted? Is not the law sufficient to protect itself, that armed bands must be gathered, as in rebellion and war, to see justice performed?"

" 'Tis the *posse comitatus*," shouted the Sheriff, from a distant rock, "who——"

"Say rather a posse of demons. I command the peace."

"Hold! Shed not blood!" cried a voice from the top of the Vision. "Hold, for the sake of Heaven, fire no more! All shall be yielded! You shall enter the cave!"

Amazement produced the desired effect. Natty, who had reloaded his piece, quietly seated himself on the logs, and rested his head on his hand, while the "Light Infantry" ceased their military movements and waited the issue in suspense.

In less than a minute, Edwards came rushing down the hill, followed by Major Hartmann with a velocity that was surprising for his years. They reached the terrace in an instant, from which the youth led the way, by the hollow in the rock, to the mouth of the cave, into which they both entered; leaving all without silent and gazing after them with astonishment.

CHAPTER XL

I am dumb.
Were you the Doctor, and I knew you not?
SHAKESPEARE

DURING the five or six minutes that elapsed before the youth and Major reappeared, Judge Temple and the Sheriff, together with most of the volunteers, ascended to the terrace, where the latter began to express their conjectures of the result and to recount their individual services in the conflict. But the sight of the peacemakers ascending the ravine shut every mouth.

On a rude chair, covered with undressed deerskins, they supported a human being, whom they seated carefully and respectfully in the midst of the assembly. His head was covered by long smooth locks of the color of snow. His dress, which was studiously neat and clean, was composed of such fabrics as none but the wealthiest classes wear, but was threadbare and patched; and on his feet were placed a pair of moccasins, ornamented in the best manner of Indian ingenuity. The outlines of his face were grave and dignified, though his vacant eye, which opened and turned slowly to the faces of those around him in unmeaning looks, too surely announced that the period had arrived when age brings the mental imbecility of childhood.

Natty had followed the supporters of this unexpected object to the top of the cave and took his station at a little distance behind him, leaning on his rifle, in the midst of his pursuers, with a fearlessness that showed that heavier interests than those which affected himself were to be decided. Major Hartmann placed himself beside the aged man, uncovered, with his whole soul beaming through those eyes which so commonly danced with frolic and humor. Edwards rested with one hand familiarly, but affectionately, on the chair, though his heart was swelling with emotions that denied him utterance.

All eyes were gazing intently, but each tongue continued mute. At length the decrepit stranger, turning his vacant looks from face to face, made a feeble attempt to rise, while a faint smile crossed his wasted face, like an habitual effort at courtesy, as he said, in a hollow, tremulous voice:

"Be pleased to be seated, gentlemen. The council will open immediately. Each one who loves a good and virtuous king will wish to see these colonies continue loyal. Be seated—I pray you, be seated, gentlemen. The troops shall halt for the night."

"This is the wandering of insanity!" said Marmaduke. "Who will explain this scene?"

"No, sir," said Edwards, firmly, " 'tis only the decay of nature; who is answerable for its pitiful condition remains to be shown."

"Will the gentlemen dine with us, my son?" said the old stranger, turning to a voice that he both knew and loved. "Order a repast suitable for his Majesty's officers. You know we have the best of game always at command."

"Who is this man?" asked Marmaduke, in a hurried voice, in which the dawnings of conjecture united with interest to put the question.

"This man!" returned Edwards calmly, his voice, however, gradually rising as he proceeded. "This man, sir, whom you behold hid in caverns, and deprived of everything that can make life desirable, was once the companion and counselor of those who ruled your country. This man, whom you see helpless and feeble, was once a warrior so brave and fearless that even the intrepid natives gave him the name of the Fire-eater. This man, whom you now see destitute of even the ordinary comfort of a cabin, in which to shelter his head, was once the owner of great riches; and, Judge Temple, he was the rightful proprietor of this very soil on which we stand. This man was the father of—"

"This then," cried Marmaduke, with a powerful emotion, "this, then, is the lost Major Effingham!"

"Lost indeed," said the youth, fixing a piercing eye on the other.

"And you! And you!" continued the Judge, articulating with difficulty.

"I am his grandson."

A minute passed in profound silence. All eyes were fixed on the speakers, and even the old German appeared to wait the issue in deep anxiety. But the moment of agitation soon passed. Marmaduke raised his head from his bosom, where it had sunk, not in shame, but in devout mental thanksgivings, and, as large tears fell over his fine manly face, he grasped the hand of the youth warmly and said:

"Oliver, I forgive all thy harshness—all thy suspicions. I now see it all. I forgive thee everything but suffering this aged man to dwell in such a place when not only my habitation but my fortune were at his and thy command."

"He's true as ter steel!" shouted Major Hartmann. "Titn't I tell you, lat, dat Marmatuke Temple vast a frient dat woult never fail in ter dime as of neet?"

"It is true, Judge Temple, that my opinions of your conduct have been staggered by what this worthy gentleman has told me. When I found it impossible to convey my grandfather back whence the enduring love of this old man brought him, without detection and exposure, I went to the Mohawk in quest of one of his former comrades, in whose justice I had dependence. He is your friend, Judge Temple, but if what he says be true, both my father and myself may have judged you harshly."

"You name your father!" said Marmaduke, tenderly. "Was he, indeed, lost in the packet?"

"He was. He had left me, after several years of fruitless application and comparative poverty, in Nova Scotia, to obtain the compensation for his losses which the British Commissioners had at length awarded. After spending a year in England, he was returning to Halifax on his way to a government to which he had been appointed in the West Indies, intending to go to the place where my grandfather had sojourned during and since the war and take him with us."

"But thou!" said Marmaduke, with powerful interest. "I had thought that thou hadst perished with him."

A flush passed over the cheeks of the young man, who gazed about him at the wondering faces of the volunteers and continued silent. Marmaduke turned to the veteran captain, who just then rejoined his command, and said:

"March thy soldiers back again and dismiss them; the zeal of the Sheriff has much mistaken his duty. Dr. Todd, I will thank you to attend to the injury which Hiram Doolittle has received in this untoward affair. Richard, you will oblige me by sending up the carriage to the top of the hill. Benjamin, return to your duty in my family."

Unwelcome as these orders were to most of the auditors, the suspicion that they had somewhat exceeded the wholesome restraints of the law, and the habitual respect with which all the commands of the Judge were received, induced a prompt compliance.

When they were gone, and the rock was left to the parties most interested in an explanation, Marmaduke, pointing to the aged Major Effingham, said to his grandson:

"Had we not better remove thy parent from this open place until my carriage can arrive?"

"Pardon me, sir, the air does him good, and he has taken it whenever there was no dread of a discovery. I know not how to act, Judge Temple; ought I, can I, suffer Major Effingham to become an inmate of your family?"

"Thou shall be thyself the judge," said Marmaduke. "Thy father was my early friend. He entrusted his fortune to my care. When we separated, he had such confidence in me that he wished no security, no evidence of the trust, even had there been time or convenience for exacting it. This thou hast heard?"

"Most truly, sir," said Edwards, or rather Effingham, as we must now call him.

"We differed in politics. If the cause of this country was successful, the trust was sacred with me, for none knew of thy father's interest. If the crown still held its sway, it would be easy to restore the property of so loyal a subject as Colonel Effingham. Is not this plain?"

"The premises are good, sir," continued the youth, with the same incredulous look as before.

"Listen—listen, poy," said the German. "Dere is not a hair as of ter rogue in ter het of her Tchooge."

"We all know the issue of the struggle," continued Marmaduke, disregarding both. "Thy grandfather was left in Connecticut, regularly supplied by thy father with the means of such a subsistence as suited his wants. This I well knew, though I never had intercourse with him, even in our happiest days. Thy father retired with the troops to prosecute his claims on England. At all events, his losses must be great, for his real estates were sold, and I became the lawful purchaser. It was not unnatural to wish that he might have no bar to its just recovery."

"There was none but the difficulty of providing for so many claimants."

"But there would have been one, and an insuperable one, had I announced to the world that I held these estates, multiplied, by the times and my industry, a hundredfold in value, only as his trustee. Thou knowest that I supplied him with considerable sums immediately after the war."

"You did, until——"

"My letters were returned unopened. Thy father had much of thy own spirit, Oliver; he was sometimes hasty and rash." The Judge continued, in a self-condemning manner—"Perhaps my fault lies the other way; I may possibly look too far ahead and calculate too deeply. It certainly was a severe trial to allow the man whom I most loved to think ill of me for seven years in order that he might honestly apply for his just remunerations. But had he opened my last letters, thou wouldst have learned the whole truth. Those I sent him to England, by what my agent writes me, he did read. He died, Oliver, knowing all. He died, my friend, and I thought thou hadst died with him."

"Our poverty would not permit us to pay for two passages," said the youth, with the extraordinary emotion with which he ever alluded to the degraded state of his family; "I was left in the Province to wait for his return, and when the sad news of his loss reached me, I was nearly penniless."

"And what didst thou, boy?" asked Marmaduke in a faltering voice.

"I took my passage here in search of my grandfather; for I well knew that his resources were gone, with the half pay of my father. On reaching his abode, I learnt that he had left it in secret; though the reluctant hireling, who had deserted him in his poverty, owned to my urgent entreaties that he believed he had been carried away by an old man who had formerly been his servant. I knew at once it was Natty, for my father often——"

"Was Natty a servant of thy grandfather?" exclaimed the Judge.

"Of that, too, were you ignorant?" said the youth, in evident surprise.

"How should I know it? I never met the Major, nor was the name of Bumppo ever mentioned to me. I knew him only as a man of the woods, and one who lived by hunting. Such men are too common to excite surprise."

"He was reared in the family of my grandfather; served him for many years during their campaigns at the west, where he became attached to the woods; and he was left here as a kind of locum tenens on the lands that old Mohegan (whose life my grandfather once saved) induced the Delawares to grant to him, when they admitted him as an honorary member of their tribe."

"This, then, is thy Indian blood?"

"I have no other," said Edwards, smiling;—"Major Effingham was adopted as the son of Mohegan, who at that time was the greatest man in his nation; and my father, who visited those people when a boy, received the name of the Eagle from them on account of the shape of his face, as I understand. They have extended his title to me. I have no other Indian blood or breeding; though I have seen the hour, Judge Temple, when I could wish that such had been my lineage and education."

"Proceed with thy tale," said Marmaduke.

"I have but little more to say, sir. I followed to the lake where I had so often been told that Natty dwelt, and found him maintaining his old master in secret; for even he could not bear to exhibit to the world, in his poverty and dotage, a man whom a whole people once looked up to with respect."

"And what did you?"

"What did I! I spent my last money in purchasing a rifle, clad myself in a coarse garb, and learned to be a hunter by the side of Leatherstocking. You know the rest, Judge Temple."

"Ant vere vast olt Fritz Hartmann?" said the German reproachfully. "Didst never hear a name as of olt Fritz Hartmann from ter mout of ter fader, lat?"

"I may have been mistaken, gentlemen," returned the youth; "but I had pride and could not submit to such an exposure as this day even has reluctantly brought to light. I had plans that might have been visionary; but, should my parent survive till autumn, I purposed taking him with me to the city, where we have distant relatives who must have learnt to forget the Tory by this time. He decays rapidly," he continued, mournfully, "and must soon lie by the side of old Mohegan."

The air being pure and the day fine, the party continued conversing on the rock, until the wheels of Judge Temple's carriage were heard clattering up the side of the mountain, during which time the conversation was maintained with deep interest, each moment clearing up some doubtful action and lessening the antipathy of the youth to Marmaduke. He no longer objected to the removal of his grandfather, who displayed a childish pleasure when he found himself seated once more in a carriage. When placed in the ample hall of the mansion house, the eyes of the aged veteran turned slowly to the objects in the apartment, and a look like the dawn of intellect would, for moments, flit across his features when he invariably offered some useless courtesies to those near him, wandering painfully in his subjects. The exercise and the change soon produced an exhaustion that caused them to remove him to his bed, where he lay for hours, evidently sensible of the change in his comforts and exhibiting that mortifying picture of human nature which too plainly shows that the propensities of the animal continue even after the nobler part of the creature appears to have vanished.

Until his parent was placed comfortably in bed, with Natty seated at his side, Effingham did not quit him. He then obeyed a summons to the library of the Judge, where he found the latter, with Major Hartmann, waiting for him.

"Read this paper, Oliver," said Marmaduke to him, as he entered, "and thou wilt find that, so far from intending thy family wrong during life, it has been my care to see that justice should be done at even a later day."

The youth took the paper, which his first glance told him was the will of the Judge. Hurried and agitated as he was, he discovered that the date corresponded with the time of the unusual depression of Marmaduke. As he proceeded, his eyes began to moisten, and the hand which held the instrument shook violently.

The will commenced with the usual forms, spun out by the ingenuity of Mr. Van der School; but after this subject was fairly exhausted, the pen of Marmaduke became plainly visible. In clear, distinct, manly, and even eloquent language, he recounted his obligations to Colonel Effingham, the nature of their connection, and the circumstances in

which they separated. He then proceeded to relate the motives of his long silence, mentioning, however, large sums
that he had forwarded to his friend, which had been returned with the letters unopened. After this, he spoke of
his search for the grandfather, who had unaccountably disappeared, and his fears that the direct heir of the trust was
buried in the ocean with his father.

After, in short, recounting in a clear narrative the events
which our readers must now be able to connect, he proceeded
to make a fair and exact statement of the sums left in his
care by Colonel Effingham. A devise of his whole estate to
certain responsible trustees followed; to hold the same for
the benefit, in equal moieties, of his daughter, on one part,
and of Oliver Effingham, formerly a major in the army of
Great Britain, and of his son, Edward Effingham, and of
his son, Edward Oliver Effingham, or to the survivor of them,
and the descendants of such survivor, forever, on the other
part. The trust was to endure until 1810, when, if no person appeared or could be found after sufficient notice to
claim the moiety so devised, then a certain sum, calculating
the principal and interest of his debt to Colonel Effingham, was to be paid to the heirs at law of the Effingham
family, and the bulk of his estate was to be conveyed
in fee to his daughter, or her heirs.

The tears fell from the eyes of the young man, as he
read this undeniable testimony of the good faith of Marmaduke, and his bewildered gaze was still fastened on the
paper when a voice that thrilled on every nerve spoke near
him, saying:

"Do you yet doubt us, Oliver?"

"I have never doubted *you!*" cried the youth, recovering
his recollection and his voice, as he sprang to seize the hand
of Elizabeth. "No, not one moment has my faith in you
wavered."

"And my father——"

"God bless him!"

"I thank thee, my son," said the Judge, exchanging a warm
pressure of the hand with the youth; "but we have both
erred; thou hast been too hasty, and I have been too slow.
One half of my estates shall be thine as soon as they can be
conveyed to thee; and if what my suspicions tell me be true,
I suppose the other must follow speedily." He took the hand

which he held, and united it with that of his daughter, and motioned towards the door to the Major.

"I telt you vat, gal?" said the old German, good-humoredly. "If I vast as I vast ven I servit mit his grandfader on ter lakes, ter lazy tog shouldn't vin ter prize as for nottin."

"Come, come, old Fritz," said the Judge; "you are seventy, not seventeen; Richard waits for you with a bowl of eggnog, in the hall."

"Richart! Ter duyvel!" exclaimed the other, hastening out of the room. "He makes ter nog ast for ter horse. I vilt show ter Sheriff mit my own hants! Ter duyvel! I pelieve he sweetens mit ter yankee melasses!"

Marmaduke smiled and nodded affectionately at the young couple and closed the door after them. If any of our readers expect that we are going to open it again, for their gratification, they are mistaken.

The tête-à-tête continued for a very unreasonable time; how long we shall not say; but it was ended by six o'clock in the evening, for at that hour Monsieur Le Quoi made his appearance agreeably to the appointment of the preceding day and claimed the ear of Miss Temple. He was admitted, when he made an offer of his hand, with much suavity, together with his "amis beeg and leet', his père, his mère, and his sucreboosh." Elizabeth might possibly have previously entered into some embarrassing and binding engagements with Oliver, for she declined the tender of all, in terms as polite, though perhaps a little more decided, than those in which they were made.

The Frenchman soon joined the German and the Sheriff in the hall, who compelled him to take a seat with them at the table, where, by the aid of punch, wine, and eggnog, they soon extracted from the complaisant Monsieur Le Quoi the nature of his visit. It was evident that he had made the offer as a duty which a well-bred man owed to a lady in such a retired place, before he left the country, and that his feelings were but very little, if at all, interested in the matter. After a few potations, the waggish pair persuaded the exhilarated Frenchman that there was an inexcusable partiality in offering to one lady and not extending a similar courtesy to another. Consequently, about nine, Monsieur Le Quoi sallied forth to the rectory on a similar mission to

Miss Grant, which proved as successful as his first effort in love.

When he returned to the mansion house, at ten, Richard and the Major were still seated at the table. They attempted to persuade the Gaul, as the Sheriff called him, that he should next try Remarkable Pettibone. But, though stimulated by mental excitement and wine, two hours of abstruse logic were thrown away on this subject; for he declined their advice, with a pertinacity truly astonishing in so polite a man.

When Benjamin lighted Monsieur Le Quoi from the door, he said, at parting:

"If so be, Mounsheer, you'd run alongside Mistress Prettybones, as the Squire Dickens was bidding ye, 'tis my notion you'd have been grappled; in which case, d'ye see, you mought have been troubled in swinging clear again in a handsome manner; for tho'f Miss 'Lizzy and the parson's young'un be tidy little vessels, that shoot by a body on a wind, Mistress Remarkable is sum'mat of a galiot fashion; when you once takes 'em in tow, they doesn't like to be cast off again."

CHAPTER XLI

Yes, sweep ye on!—We will not leave,
For them who triumph those who grieve.
With that armada gay
Be laughter loud, and jocund shout—
—But with that skiff
Abides the minstrel tale.

LORD OF THE ISLES

THE events of our tale carry us through the summer; and after making nearly the circle of the year, we must conclude our labors in the delightful month of October. Many important incidents had, however, occurred in the intervening period; a few of which it may be necessary to recount.

The two principal were the marriage of Oliver and Elizabeth and the death of Major Effingham. They both took place early in September, and the former preceded the latter only a few days. The old man passed away like the last glimmering of a taper; and though his death cast a melancholy over the family, grief could not follow such an end.

One of the chief concerns of Marmaduke was to reconcile the even conduct of a magistrate with the course that his feelings dictated to the criminals. The day succeeding the discovery at the cave, however, Natty and Benjamin re-entered the jail peaceably, where they continued, well fed and comfortable, until the return of an express to Albany, who brought the Governor's pardon to the Leatherstocking. In the meantime, proper means were employed to satisfy Hiram for the assaults on his person; and on the same day, the two comrades issued together into society again, with their characters not at all affected by the imprisonment.

Mr. Doolittle began to discover that neither architecture nor his law was quite suitable to the growing wealth and intelligence of the settlement; and after exacting the last cent that was attainable in his compromises, to use the language of the country, he "pulled up stakes," and proceeded further west, scattering his professional science and legal learning through the land; vestiges of both of which are to be discovered there even to the present hour.

Poor Jotham, whose life paid the forfeiture of his folly, acknowledged before he died that his reasons for believing in a mine were extracted from the lips of a sibyl, who, by looking in a magic glass, was enabled to discover the hidden treasures of the earth. Such superstition was frequent in the new settlements; and after the first surprise was over, the better part of the community forgot the subject. But, at the same time that it removed from the breast of Richard a lingering suspicion of the acts of the three hunters, it conveyed a mortifying lesson to him which brought many quiet hours, in future, to his cousin Marmaduke. It may be remembered that the Sheriff confidently pronounced this to be no "visionary" scheme, and that word was enough to shut his lips at any time within the next ten years.

Monsieur Le Quoi, who has been introduced to our readers, because no picture of that country would be faithful without some such character, found the island of Martinique, and his "sucreboosh," in possession of the English; but Marmaduke and his family were much gratified in soon hearing that he had returned to his bureau, in Paris; where he afterwards issued yearly bulletins of his happiness and of his gratitude to his friends in America.

With this brief explanation, we must return to our narrative. Let the American reader imagine one of our mildest October mornings, when the sun seems a ball of silvery fire, and the elasticity of the air is felt while it is inhaled, imparting vigor and life to the whole system—the weather, neither too warm nor too cold, but of that happy temperature which stirs the blood, without bringing the lassitude of spring. It was on such a morning, about the middle of the month, that Oliver entered the hall where Elizabeth was issuing her usual orders for the day, and requested her to join him in a short excursion to the lake side. The tender melancholy in the manner of her husband caught the attention of Elizabeth, who instantly abandoned her concerns, threw a light shawl across her shoulders, and concealing her raven hair under a gypsy, she took his arm and submitted herself, without a question, to his guidance. They crossed the bridge and had turned from the highway, along the margin of the lake, before a word was exchanged. Elizabeth well knew, by the direction, the object of the walk and respected the feelings of her companion too much to indulge in untimely conversation. But when they gained the open fields, and her eye roamed over the placid lake, covered with wild fowl already journeying from the great northern waters to seek a warmer sun, but lingering to play in the limpid sheet of the Otsego, and to the sides of the mountain, which were gay with the thousand dyes of autumn, as if to grace their bridal, the swelling heart of the young wife burst out in speech.

"This is not a time for silence, Oliver!" she said, clinging more fondly to his arm. "Everything in nature seems to speak the praises of the Creator; why should we, who have so much to be grateful for, be silent?"

"Speak on!" said her husband, smiling. "I love the sounds of your voice. You must anticipate our errand hither. I have told you my plans: how do you like them?"

"I must first see them," returned his wife. "But I have had my plans, too; it is time I should begin to divulge them."

"You! It is something for the comfort of my old friend Natty, I know."

"Certainly of Natty; but we have other friends besides the

Leatherstocking to serve. Do you forget Louisa and her father?"

"No, surely; have I not given one of the best farms in the county to the good divine. As for Louisa, I should wish you to keep her always near us."

"You do!" said Elizabeth, slightly compressing her lips; "but poor Louisa may have other views for herself; she may wish to follow my example and marry."

"I don't think it," said Effingham, musing a moment; "I really don't know any one hereabouts good enough for her."

"Perhaps not here; but there are other places besides Templeton and other churches besides 'New St. Paul's.' "

"Churches, Elizabeth! You would not wish to lose Mr. Grant, surely! Though simple, he is an excellent man. I shall never find another who has half the veneration for my orthodoxy. You would humble me from a saint to a very common sinner."

"It must be done, sir," returned the lady, with a half-concealed smile, "though it degrades you from an angel to a man."

"But you forget the farm."

"He can lease it, as others do. Besides, would you have a clergyman toil in the fields?"

"Where can he go? You forget Louisa."

"No, I do not forget Louisa," said Elizabeth, again compressing her beautiful lips. "You know, Effingham, that my father has told you that I ruled him and that I should rule you. I am now about to exert my power."

"Anything, anything, dear Elizabeth, but not at the expense of us all; not at the expense of your friend."

"How do you know, sir, that it will be so much at the expense of my friend?" said the lady, fixing her eyes with a searching look on his countenance, where they met only the unsuspecting expression of manly regret.

"How do I know it? Why, it is natural that she should regret us."

"It is our duty to struggle with our natural feelings," returned the lady; "and there is but little cause to fear that such a spirit as Louisa's will not effect it."

"But what is your plan?"

"Listen, and you shall know. My father has procured a call for Mr. Grant to one of the towns on the Hudson, where he can live more at his ease than in journeying through these woods; where he can spend the evening of his life in comfort and quiet; and where his daughter may meet with such society, and form such a connection, as may be proper for one of her years and character."

"Bess! You amaze me! I did not think you had been such a manager!"

"Oh! I manage more deeply than you imagine, sir," said the wife, archly smiling again; "but it is my will, and it is your duty to submit—for a time at least."

Effingham laughed; but as they approached the end of their walk, the subject was changed by common consent.

The place at which they arrived was the little spot of level ground, where the cabin of the Leatherstocking had so long stood. Elizabeth found it entirely cleared of rubbish and beautifully laid down in turf, by the removal of sods which, in common with the surrounding country, had grown gay under the influence of profuse showers, as if a second spring had passed over the land. This little place was surrounded by a circle of masonwork, and they entered by a small gate, near which, to the surprise of both, the rifle of Natty was leaning against the wall. Hector and the slut reposed on the grass by its side, as if conscious that, however altered, they were lying on the ground and were surrounded by objects with which they were familiar. The hunter himself was stretched on the earth before a headstone of white marble, pushing aside with his fingers the long grass that had already sprung up from the luxuriant soil around its base, apparently to lay bare the inscription. By the side of this stone, which was a simple slab at the head of a grave, stood a rich monument, decorated with an urn and ornamented with the chisel.

Oliver and Elizabeth approached the graves with a light tread, unheard by the old hunter, whose sunburned face was working, and whose eyes twinkled as if something impeded their vision. After some little time, Natty raised himself slowly from the ground and said aloud:

"Well, well—I'm bold to say it's all right! There's something that I suppose is reading; but I can't make anything of it; though the pipe and the tomahawk, and the moccasins, be pretty well—pretty well for a man that, I dares to say, never seed 'ither of the things. Ah's me! There they lie, side by side, happy enough! Who will there be to put me in the 'arth when my time comes?"

"When that unfortunate hour arrives, Natty, friends shall not be wanting to perform the last offices for you," said Oliver, a little touched at the hunter's soliloquy.

The old man turned without manifesting surprise, for he had got the Indian habits in this particular, and running his hand under the bottom of his nose, seemed to wipe away his sorrow with the action.

"You've come out to see the graves, children, have ye?" he said. "Well, well, they're wholesome sights to young as well as old."

"I hope they are fitted to your liking," said Effingham; "no one has a better right than yourself to be consulted in the matter."

"Why, seeing that I an't used to fine graves," returned the old man, "it is but little matter consarning my taste. Ye laid the Major's head to the west, and Mohegan's to the east, did ye, lad?"

"At your request it was done."

"It's so best," said the hunter. "They thought they had to journey different ways, children; though there is One greater than all, who'll bring the just together, at his own time, and who'll whiten the skin of a blackamoor and place him on a footing with princes."

"There is but little reason to doubt that," said Elizabeth, whose decided tones were changed to a soft, melancholy voice; "I trust we shall all meet again and be happy together."

"Shall we, child, shall we?" exclaimed the hunter, with unusual fervor. "There's comfort in that thought too. But before I go, I should like to know what 'tis you tell these people that be flocking into the country like pigeons in the spring of the old Delaware, and of the bravest white man that ever trod the hills."

Effingham and Elizabeth were surprised at the manner of the Leatherstocking, which was unusually impressive and solemn; but, attributing it to the scene, the young man turned to the monument, and read aloud:

" 'Sacred to the memory of Oliver Effingham, Esquire, formerly a Major in his B. Majesty's 60th Foot; a soldier of tried valor; a subject of chivalrous loyalty; and a man of honesty. To these virtues, he added the graces of a Christian. The morning of his life was spent in honor, wealth, and power; but its evening was obscured by poverty, neglect, and disease, which were alleviated only by the tender care of his old, faithful, and upright friend and attendant, Nathaniel Bumppo. His descendants rear this stone to the virtues of the master, and to the enduring gratitude of the servant.' "

The Leatherstocking stared at the sound of his own name, and a smile of joy illumined his wrinkled features, as he said:

"And did ye say it, lad? Have you then got the old man's name cut in the stone, by the side of his master's? God bless ye, children! 'Twas a kind thought, and kindness goes to the heart as life shortens."

Elizabeth turned her back to the speakers. Effingham made a fruitless effort before he succeeded in saying:

"It is there cut in plain marble; but it should have been written in letters of gold!"

"Show me the name, boy," said Natty, with simple eagerness; "let me see my own name placed in such honor. 'Tis a gin'rous gift to a man who leaves none of his name and family behind him in a country where he has tarried so long."

Effingham guided his finger to the spot, and Natty followed the windings of the letters to the end with deep interest, when he raised himself from the tomb, and said:

"I suppose it's all right; and it's kindly thought, and kindly done! But what have ye put over the Redskin?"

"You shall hear—

" 'This stone is raised to the memory of an Indian Chief, of the Delaware tribe, who was known by the several names of John Mohegan; Mohican——' "

"Mo-hee-can, lad, they call theirselves! 'he-can."

" 'Mohican; and Chingagook——' "

" 'Gach, boy;—'gach-gook; Chingachgook, which, intarpreted, means Big-sarpent. The name should be set down right, for an Indian's name has always some meaning in it."

"I will see it altered. 'He was the last of his people who continued to inhabit this country; and it may be said of him that his faults were those of an Indian and his virtues those of a man.' "

"You never said truer word, Mr. Oliver; ah's me! If you had know'd him as I did, in his prime, in that very battle where the old gentleman who sleeps by his side saved his life, when them thieves, the Iroquois, had him at the stake, you'd have said all that, and more too. I cut the thongs with this very hand and gave him my own tomahawk and knife, seeing that the rifle was always my fav'rite weapon. He did lay about him like a man! I met him as I was coming home from the trail, with eleven Mingo scalps on his pole. You needn't shudder, Madam Effingham, for they was all from shaved heads and warriors. When I look about me at these hills, where I used to could count sometimes twenty smokes, curling over the treetops from the Delaware camps, it raises mournful thoughts to think that not a redskin is left of them all; unless it be a drunkard vagabond from the Oneidas, or them Yankee Indians, who, they say, be moving up from the seashore; and who belong to none of God's creaters, to my seeming, being, as it were, neither fish nor flesh—neither white man nor savage. Well, well! The time has come at last, and I must go—"

"Go!" echoed Edwards. "Whither do you go?"

The Leatherstocking, who had imbibed, unconsciously, many of the Indian qualities, though he always thought of himself as of a civilized being, compared with even the Delawares, averted his face to conceal the workings of his muscles, as he stooped to lift a large pack from behind the tomb, which he placed deliberately on his shoulders.

"Go!" exclaimed Elizabeth, approaching him with a hurried step. "You should not venture so far in the woods alone at your time of life, Natty; indeed, it is imprudent. He is bent, Effingham, on some distant hunting."

"What Mrs. Effingham tells you is true, Leatherstocking," said Edwards; "there can be no necessity for your submitting to such hardships now! So throw aside your pack and confine your hunt to the mountains near us, if you will go."

"Hardship! 'Tis a pleasure, children, and the greatest that is left me on this side the grave."

"No, no; you shall not go to such a distance," cried Elizabeth, laying her white hand on his deerskin pack. "I am right! I feel his camp kettle and a canister of powder! He must not be suffered to wander so far from us, Oliver; remember how suddenly Mohegan dropped away."

"I know'd the parting would come hard, children; I know'd it would!" said Natty. "And so I got aside to look at the graves by myself, and thought if I left ye the keepsake which the Major gave me, when we first parted in the woods, ye wouldn't take it unkind, but would know that, let the old man's body go where it might, his feelings stayed behind him."

"This means something more than common!" exclaimed the youth. "Where is it, Natty, that you purpose going?"

The hunter drew nigh him with a confident, reasoning air, as if what he had to say would silence all objections, and replied:

"Why, lad, they tell me that on the Big-lakes there's the best of hunting, and a great range, without a white man on it, unless it may be one like myself. I'm weary of living in clearings and where the hammer is sounding in my ears from sunrise to sundown. And though I'm much bound to ye both, children—I wouldn't say it if it was not true—I crave to go into the woods ag'in, I do."

"Woods!" echoed Elizabeth, trembling with her feelings; "Do you not call these endless forests woods?"

"Ah! Child, these be nothing to a man that's used to the wilderness. I have took but little comfort sin' your father come on with his settlers; but I wouldn't go far, while the life was in the body that lies under the sod there. But now he's gone, and Chingachgook is gone; and you be both young and happy. Yes! The big house has rung with merriment this month past! And now, I thought, was the time to try to get a little comfort in the close of my days. Woods! Indeed! I doesn't call these woods, Madam Effingham, where I lose myself every day of my life in the clearings."

"If there be anything wanting to your comfort, name it, Leatherstocking; if it be attainable it is yours."

"You mean all for the best, lad; I know it; and so does Madam, too: but your ways isn't my ways. 'Tis like the dead there, who thought, when the breath was in them, that one went east, and one went west, to find their heavens; but they'll meet at last; and so shall we, children. Yes, end as you've begun, and we shall meet in the land of the just at last."

"This is so new! So unexpected!" said Elizabeth, in almost breathless excitement. "I had thought you meant to live with us and die with us, Natty."

"Words are of no avail," exclaimed her husband; "the habits of forty years are not to be dispossessed by the ties of a day. I know you too well to urge you further, Natty; unless you will let me build you a hut on one of the distant hills, where we can sometimes see you and know that you are comfortable."

"Don't fear for the Leatherstocking, children; God will see that his days be provided for, and his end happy. I know you mean all for the best, but our ways doesn't agree. I love the woods, and ye relish the face of man; I eat when hungry, and drink when adry; and ye keep stated hours and rules: nay, nay, you even overfeed the dogs, lad, from pure kindness; and hounds should be gaunty to run well. The meanest of God's creaters be made for some use, and I'm formed for the wilderness; if ye love me, let me go where my soul craves to be ag'in!"

The appeal was decisive; and not another word of entreaty for him to remain was then uttered; but Elizabeth bent her head to her bosom and wept, while her husband dashed away the tears from his eyes; and, with hands that almost refused to perform their office, he produced his pocketbook and extended a parcel of bank notes to the hunter.

"Take these," he said, "at least take these; secure them about your person, and in the hour of need, they will do you good service."

The old man took the notes and examined them with a curious eye.

"This, then, is some of the new-fashioned money that they've been making at Albany, out of paper! It can't be worth much to they that hasn't larning! No, no, lad—take back the stuff; it will do me no sarvice. I took kear to get all the Frenchman's powder afore he broke up, and they say lead grows where I'm going. It isn't even fit for wads, seeing that I use none but leather!—Madam Effingham, let an old man kiss your hand, and wish God's choicest blessings on you and your'n."

"Once more let me beseech you, stay!" cried Elizabeth. "Do not, Leatherstocking, leave me to grieve for the man who has twice rescued me from death, and who has served those I love so faithfully. For my sake, if not for your own, stay. I shall see you in those frightful dreams that still haunt my nights, dying in poverty and age, by the side of those terrific beasts you slew. There will be no evil, that sickness, want, and solitude can inflict, that my fancy will not conjure as your fate. Stay with us, old man, if not for your own sake, at least for ours."

"Such thoughts and bitter dreams, Madam Effingham," returned the hunter, solemnly, "will never haunt an innocent parson long. They'll pass away with God's pleasure. And if the catamounts be yet brought to your eyes in sleep, 'tis not for my sake, but to show you the power of Him that led me there to save you. Trust in God, Madam, and your honorable husband, and the thoughts for an old man like me can never be long nor bitter. I pray that the Lord will keep you in mind —the Lord that lives in clearings as well as in the wilderness —and bless you, and all that belong to you, from this time till the great day when the whites shall meet the redskins in judgment, and justice shall be the law, and not power."

Elizabeth raised her head and offered her colorless cheek to his salute, when he lifted his cap and touched it respectfully. His hand was grasped with convulsive fervor by the youth, who continued silent. The hunter prepared himself for his journey, drawing his belt tighter, and wasting his moments in the little reluctant movements of a sorrowful departure. Once or twice he essayed to speak, but a rising in his throat prevented it. At length he shouldered his rifle and cried with a clear huntsman's call that echoed through the woods:

"He-e-e-re, he-e-e-re, pups—away, dogs, away; ye'll be footsore afore ye see the ind of the journey!"

The hounds leaped from the earth at this cry, and scenting around the graves and the silent pair, as if conscious of their own destination, they followed humbly at the heels of their master. A short pause succeeded, during which even the youth concealed his face on his grandfather's tomb. When the pride of manhood, however, had suppressed the feelings of nature, he turned to renew his entreaties, but saw that the cemetery was occupied only by himself and his wife.

"He is gone!" cried Effingham.

Elizabeth raised her face and saw the old hunter standing, looking back for a moment, on the verge of the wood. As he caught their glances, he drew his hard hand hastily across his eyes again, waved it on high for an adieu, and uttering a forced cry to his dogs, who were crouching at his feet, he entered the forest.

This was the last that they ever saw of the Leatherstocking, whose rapid movements preceded the pursuit which Judge Temple both ordered and conducted. He had gone far towards the setting sun—the foremost in that band of pioneers who are opening the way for the march of the nation across the continent.

AFTERWORD

The Pioneers is the fourth novel in the famous Leatherstocking series if we arrange the five in the chronological order of the life of their central character, Natty Bumppo, the wilderness hunter who was variously known as Leatherstocking, Hawkeye, or (by the French) La Longue Carabine. In it, Natty is almost seventy, and he is presented as a somewhat irritable old man who not only boasts of his youthful adventures and the sureness of his aim, but can still prove his skill when challenged to a turkey shoot or his own defense.

Taken in this context, the novel does not have the appeal of *The Deerslayer*, in which Natty is presented in all his youthful vigor; *The Last of the Mohicans* or *The Pathfinder*, in which he is still in his full strength; or *The Prairie*, in which he strikes out once more for the Garden of the West and is at last fully portrayed by his creator as one of the really great characters of fiction.

But *The Pioneers* is also the first novel in which Natty appears, and he is obviously not the principal reason why the novel was written. The reader who picks it up, therefore, as just one of the romantic tales of the wilderness scout is in for a disappointment. Adventures are few, action is restricted, description is plentiful and vivid, and characters—even that of the hero—are not altogether sympathetically drawn. No wonder it has been, down through the years, perhaps the least popular of the popular series. Understanding, and therefore enjoyment, of any work of art is determined as much by what we ask of it as by anything it has in itself to offer. How then should we read *The Pioneers*?

Cooper has himself supplied an answer in his Introduction. ". . . This work," he says, "professes, in its title page, to be a descriptive tale. . . . The author was brought an infant into this valley, and all his first impressions were here obtained. He has inhabited it ever since, at intervals; and he thinks he can answer for the faithfulness of the picture he has drawn." But a ". . . rigid adhesion to truth, an indispensable requisite in history and travels, destroys the charm of fiction; for all that is necessary to be conveyed to the mind by the latter had better be done by delineations of principles, and of characters in their classes, than by a too fastidious attention to originals." In short, we are to have a picture of life on the American frontier in the 1790's, so presented that we may appreciate the underlying, rather than the literal, truth of the scenes and events to be recounted. Cooper's primary purpose in this—even though perhaps not to the same extent in the later Leatherstocking tales—was realism rather than romance, description rather than action, moral and social significance rather than adventure.

Read in this spirit, *The Pioneers* fits better with such novels as *Home as Found, Afloat and Ashore,* and the Antirent series, *Satanstoe, The Chainbearer,* and *The Redskins,* than with the other tales of Indians and settlers for which their author was famous. *The Pioneers* is one of the first, and still one of the best, novels of life on the American frontier in its second stage of establishing a settled way of life on the fringe of the wilderness, with enough of the romantic elements of character and action to bring it to life as a story. Let us forget Natty, therefore, for a moment, and start where Cooper does: in the year 1793, in the primitive town of Cooperstown at the foot of Lake Otsego, one of the smaller finger lakes of central New York and a source for the Susquehanna. What are the facts on which the novel as social commentary is based?

James Cooper (the "Fenimore" was taken from his mother's family later) was four years and three months old on the frosty Christmas Eve with which *The Pioneers* opens. He was probably at home in bed when his father, Judge William Cooper (or Temple), encountered Natty and his friends, Indian John and young Oliver Edwards, and the latter suffered the accident that sets the tone and theme of the novel. In the story (which, of course, we have been told, does not hew too close to the line of literal truth), we are to learn nothing of the mother, who did not share her husband's love of the frontier, or of the five brothers who were either at home or away at college at the time. Of the beloved sister who was early injured fatally by a fall from a horse like the near accident of the beautiful and stately Elizabeth Temple, we learn little if we are to believe Cooper's denial of any similarity. But of the volatile cousin, Richard Jones, and of the many other citizens of the village and lake shore, we are to learn a great deal, much of it wholly literal and accurate even though perhaps a bit shuffled about. The French *émigré* storekeeper Monsieur Le Quoi, the German Major Hartmann, the Reverend Mr. Grant, Dr. Todd, the remarkable Remarkable Pettibone, the voluble ex-seaman Benjamin Penguillan (or Ben Pump), the wood chopper Billy Kirby—even Natty himself—presumably were modeled on originals known personally to the author a few years later if not precisely on that day. Father Nash and the eccentric Dr. Nathaniel Gott are two that can be easily identified, even though there are two Nathaniel Shipmans who contend for the honor of being the original of Natty Bumppo; and equivalents of many of the events and places of the novel are recorded in *The Chronicles of Cooperstown*, which Cooper wrote and his neighbors the Phinneys published in 1838.

By this time, the real wilderness had been tamed and divided among the wealthy Dutch and English landowners, who had long since driven the Indians westward to the central plains and had parceled out small holdings to tenant farmers for clearing and planting. Settlements were, however, still few, and most of the land was still in the first-growth forests that Cooper so vividly describes, even though danger had been reduced to an occasional bear or "painter" (mountain lion) and fire fed by dry brush left behind by woodcutters who had begun to ravage the forests for timber and fuel. Cooperstown already had a main street, a general store, a building that served as both church and school, and a cluster of houses. The lone Indian Chingachgook, or Mohegan as he is called in this novel, was a creature of Cooper's imagination, based probably on his reading of the accounts of missionaries rather than on firsthand experience; but such untamed hunters and trappers as Natty were not uncommon.

The rapid growth and prosperity of Cooperstown even then owed its vitality to the unique land theory of its founder. William Cooper has described in his *Guide in the Wilderness* just how and why he sold rather than rented his small tracts to the settlers. Other holders of patents had wrested their property rights from the Indians by seizure or barter and had held them by royal patent from the King of England. For the Van Rensselaers, the Schuylers, or the Clintons, society depended upon property, and family status upon primogeniture, as rigidly as in England or Holland. This was an aristocratic civilization, as Dixon Ryan Fox has pointed out, inhospitable to the Yankees to the east or the Quakers to the south, who nurtured radical and dangerous ideas that might today be regarded as socialistic. Jefferson and his fellows had substituted the words "pursuit of happiness" for the Lockian "property" in the Declaration of Independence, and the Federalist Judge Cooper brought this concept with him as the founding principle of his colony. The three theories of the relationship of property rights to social stability—the Tory view held by young Oliver, the democratic view held by Judge Temple, and the view of primitive rights held by Indian John—supply the ideological background for this novel and are directly drawn by Cooper from his earliest experience. They were also to remain with him as an unsolved social and political problem and as the theme of all his serious writing. The central conflict in this novel between Judge Temple and Leatherstocking is based on this difference in social theory, and the reconciliation of the Judge with young Oliver is testimony to Cooper's fundamentally conservative leanings, which he carried—albeit as a Democrat rather than as a Federalist like his father —right through the equalitarian era of Jackson and down almost to the eve of the Civil War. This is what he means when he tells us that *The Pioneers* is a study of the principles rather than the facts of the frontier. And the stereotyped plot of the lost heir and the carefully guarded secret, which many critics have thought to be merely a melodramatic device to hold a loosely descriptive tale together, is an integral part of the basic thematic structure of the novel, however creaky it may seem at some points in its development. This is Cooper's first and far from his last exploration of the conflict between the principles of vested family rights, individual democratic initiative, and a moral imperative; between the laws of Man, the laws of Nature, and the laws of the Deity.

At the time of writing *The Pioneers*, however, such general ideas were still largely undefined in the author's mind, and he was primarily concerned with the more immediate and practical problem of how to make literature out of American life. He had always been a great reader of current fiction and poetry and a gentleman-connoisseur of the fine arts; but he came to the profession of writing himself somewhat late, and then only by being prodded by what he considered to be the inadequacies of what he was reading. His first novel, *Precaution,* was the result of his disgust with an English novel of country life, an effort to "do better myself." Realizing at once the fallacy of trying to write about scenes and people he knew only at second hand, he made a resolve with *The Spy* that he never again violated— to use only material from his own experience buttressed by careful study of its historical background. This meant first an attempt to put American life—and only the part of it that he knew—into fiction. A novel drawn from his memory of his own boyhood was the logical next step; *The Pioneers* resulted.

For this kind of thing there was no model, as there had been for a story of English village life in Jane Austen, Amelia Opie, and other novelists of domestic manners, or of historical events in Sir Walter Scott. It would perhaps be possible to find in the mock-heroic realism of Fielding, the homely whimsey of the village pastoral of Thomson or Crabbe, or the moral probings of Richardson, some of the elements that went into Cooper's brew, were there not more immediate and likely sources. James Beard has discovered and recently reprinted two reviews from a short-lived magazine with which Cooper was closely associated at this time, *The Literary and Scientific Repository, and Critical Review,* and has proved conclusively that they were written by Cooper. They are a laudatory review of *A New England Tale,* by Catherine Maria Sedgwick, and an unfavorable review of *Bracebridge Hall,* by Washington Irving. In the former, he points out that "our domestic manners, the social and moral influences, which operate in retirement, and in common intercourse . . . have very seldom been happily exhibited in our literature," and he dismisses Irving as treating only "ludicrous subjects," a charge to which he adds in his review of *Bracebridge Hall* those of "elaborate trifling," lack of narrative unity, caricature, and bad taste. Knowing Cooper's propensity to set things right by redoing them himself, it is a short step to the suggestion of Thomas Philbrick that the Bracebridge episodes of *The Sketch Book* and its sequel were the immediate inspiration, by contraries, for *The Pioneers.* Many elements are parallel in the two books: the setting in comfortable and somewhat remote country houses (the one in England, the other corrected to America); the cast of characters from the squire and his household down through the villagers (the one heavy with nostalgic sentiment, the other corrected to friendly and common-sense realism); the basic pattern of the cycle of the seasons with the opening episode on Christmas Eve (the one warm and traditional, the other corrected to the realities of harsh weather and jangling human nerves); and the burlesque humor (the one broad, the other toned down to a mock realism that echoed Fielding and anticipated Dickens). Cooper was again using his critical reading to sharpen his own creative tools. A fellow citizen for many years of the same small provincial town of New York with Irving, he did not meet his rival until late in life, and even though there was never any overt animosity between them, it was at this point that their divergent paths became evident. In the common task of creating a national American literature, they had nothing in common. The path that Cooper set for himself in *The Pioneers* was to remain his for life, whereas the volatile Irving wandered in Europe and sought exotic and colorful materials for fiction in England, Germany, and Spain. Basing his work firmly in traditional romantic plot structure, Cooper was to try again and again to produce works in which the facts and the principles of an emerging democratic society adapted themselves to a wondrous and apparently limitless new continent. If he was never wholly successful in any single novel, his total accomplishment was in some ways an even greater triumph than any one artistic success could possibly have been.

We come to *The Pioneers*, then, with the realization that it was conceived and planned as a work of art, but as an experimental one in that to its author the problem of giving expression to the proposed subject was more important than the perfection and effect of the result. It is an aesthetically motivated product of a compelling literary imagination rather than a finished work of art. Its excellences are great even though its technical shortcomings are all too obvious, as Mark Twain once maliciously noted. Rewards to the reader come through patient acceptance of long and unrealistic dialogues that, as Cooper himself confesses, are often merely his means of presenting actions or discussing ideas; acceptance of coincidences and stupidities that are useful only to prevent the premature disclosure of the plot; and acceptance of characters who are too much idealized or burlesqued to be convincing. Once these defects are admitted and forgotten, however, the reader moves back in time to an era in our history that only an imagination like Cooper's could re-create. Characters come to life in their responses to nature in both her savage and her grander moments: for example, the icy morning after the winter storm when Elizabeth looks out on a glistening and vibrant world; and the moment of crisis when the smoke and flames of a blazing forest are closing in about her. The complex qualities of a character like Billy Kirby are revealed in the singleness of his devotion to his ax and his boasting courage tempered abruptly by his generosity and his fellow feeling. Only clearness of observation and an appreciation of human nature could produce on paper such an authentic mixture as Billy Kirby, or the impetuous and versatile Dickon Jones, or the morose and loyal Natty, or even the gentlemanly and resentful Oliver. Setting—character—theme: in these the author of *The Pioneers*, inexperienced as he was, knew what he was doing at every point.

The thematic structure of the novel comes to a focus in the conflict, both personal and ideological, between Judge Temple and Natty Bumppo. These two idealized prototypes of real characters, both of whom Cooper admires and at the same time critically understands, admire and are critical of each other. In the opening episode of the accidental shooting of young Edwards-Effingham, both men reveal their strength, which is based on unbending principles, and their generosity, which is based on depth of experience and warmth of human feeling. The issue between them is first that of conflicting temperaments, the Judge being essentially civilized and social in his instincts; and Natty, natural and individual in his. These basic characteristics are closely related to the ideological issue that divides the two men. In perfect agreement that it is sinful to destroy living things wantonly, but that it is justifiable to do so when food is necessary to sustain human life, they disagree on the kind of sanctions that should be applied to make these principles effective. The Judge would rely on law and social organization, Natty solely on innate moral rectitude. This is the same conflict between the laws of Man and the laws of Nature that Huck Finn debated on his raft and that has occupied American fiction from Captain Ahab to Frank Cowperwood and beyond. Natty's philosophy is suited to the earlier frontier days, but those days passed with the establishment of villages in the wilderness. The Judge's one-man principality would now seem better suited to the needs of the times; and Natty survives only on tolerance, even though the value system that he represents must always in some way remain an essential part of the American national character. But the day of personal government is also passing, and the Judge's triumph over his respected opponent in the closing scene is tempered by the realization that his way of life is also a phase of frontier development, and that there are larger political and social structures, derived from tradition and moral law, to which he, too, must give way without sacrificing either his own values or his moral integrity. We may not agree that the restoration of the inherited rights of the Effinghams is a step in this direction, but this is obviously Cooper's conclusion, and with it he closes his novel by resolving the conflicts of character, plot, and theme in a final revelation. Even though we may not at the end be wholly satisfied, we should not forget that it was this same thematic conflict that gave us the scenes in the tavern, the shooting of the pigeons, the night fishing on the lake, the confrontation of the Judge and Natty in the court, and many another vivid reconstruction of early American life. For these we can be grateful, as well as for Cooper's total sense of the stuff of which the American people are made and his power of expression—roughhewn though it may be —which has preserved so much of our "usable past" for our present use.

ROBERT E. SPILLER

University of Pennsylvania

SELECTED BIBLIOGRAPHY

WORKS BY JAMES FENIMORE COOPER

The Spy, 1821   Novel
The Pioneers, 1823   Novel (Signet Classic 0-451-51621-4)
The Pilot, 1824   Novel
The Last of the Mohicans, 1826   Novel (Signet Classic 0-451-51495-5)
The Prairie, 1827   Novel (Signet Classic 0-451-51780-6)
The Red Rover, 1827   Novel
Notions of the Americans, 1828   Social Criticism
The Bravo, 1831   Novel
The Monikins, 1835   Satire
Sketches of Switzerland, Parts I and II, 1836   Travel
Gleanings in Europe (England, France, Italy), 1837-38   Travel
The American Democrat, 1838   Social Criticism
Homeward Bound, 1838   Novel
Home as Found, 1838   Novel
The History of the Navy of the United States of America, 1839
The Pathfinder, 1840   Novel (Signet Classic 0-451-51708-3)
The Deerslayer, 1841   Novel (Signet Classic 0-451-51645-1)
The Wing-and-Wing, 1842   Novel
Wyandotte, 1843   Novel
Afloat and Ashore, 1844   Novel
Satanstoe, 1845   Novel
The Chainbearer, 1845   Novel

The Redskins, 1846   Novel
The Crater, 1847   Novel
The Oak Openings, 1848   Novel
The Sea Lions, 1849   Novel
The Ways of the Hour, 1850   Novel

SELECTED BIOGRAPHY AND CRITICISM

Beard, James Franklin, ed. *The Letters and Journals of James Fenimore Cooper.* 6 vols. Cambridge, Mass.: Harvard University Press, 1960-68.

Bewley, Marius. *The Eccentric Design: Form in the Classic American Novel.* New York: Columbia University Press, 1959.

Collins, Frank M. "Cooper and the American Dream." *PMLA,* 81 (1966), 79-94.

Cunningham, Mary E., ed. *James Fenimore Cooper: A Reappraisal.* Cooperstown, N.Y.: New York State Historical Association, 1954.

Dekker, George, *James Fenimore Cooper: The American Scott.* New York: Barnes & Noble, 1967.

Fiedler, Leslie. *Love and Death in the American Novel.* New York: Criterion, 1960.

Grossman, James. *James Fenimore Cooper.* New York: Sloane, 1949.

House, Kay Seymour. *Cooper's Americans.* Columbus: Ohio State University Press, 1965.

Lawrence, D. H. *Studies in Classic American Literature.* New York: Doubleday, 1961.

Lewis, R. W. B. *The American Adam: Innocence, Tragedy and Tradition in the Nineteenth Century.* Chicago: University of Chicago Press, 1955.

Lounsbury, Thomas R. *James Fenimore Cooper* (American Men of Letters Series). Boston: Houghton Mifflin, 1882.

Pearce, Roy H. "The Leatherstocking Tales Re-Examined." *South Atlantic Quarterly,* 46 (1947), 524-36.

Peck, H. Daniel. *A World By Itself: The Pastoral Moment in Cooper's Fiction.* New Haven: Yale University Press, 1977.

Philbrick, Thomas. *James Fenimore Cooper and the Development of American Sea Fiction.* Cambridge, Mass.: Harvard University Press, 1961.

Ringe, Donald A. *James Fenimore Cooper.* New York: Twayne Publishers, 1961.

Smith, Henry Nash. *Virgin Land.* New York: Knopf, 1957.

Spiller, Robert E. *Fenimore Cooper: Critic of His Time.* New York: Minton, Balch, 1931.

Twain, Mark. "Fenimore Cooper's Literary Offenses." In *How to Tell a Story, and Other Essays.* New York: Harper, 1897.

Walker, Warren S. *James Fenimore Cooper.* New York: Barnes & Noble, 1962.

Waples, Dorothy. *The Whig Myth of James Fenimore Cooper.* New Haven: Yale University Press, 1938.

Winters, Yvor. *Maule's Curse: Seven Studies in the History of American Obscurantism.* New York: New Directions, 1938.

A NOTE ON THE TEXT

The text of this edition is based on the W. A. Townsend and Company edition published in 1859 and reprinted by the Riverside Press in their collected edition of Cooper's works in 1872. The spelling and punctuation have been brought into conformity with modern American usage.